Steal the North

Steal the North

Heather Brittain Bergstrom

VIKING

VIKING
Published by the Penguin Group
Penguin Group (USA) LLC
375 Hudson Street
New York, New York 10014

USA | Canada | UK | Ireland | Australia | New Zealand | India | South Africa | China
penguin.com
A Penguin Random House Company

First published by Viking Penguin, a member of Penguin Group (USA) LLC, 2014

LIBRARY OF CONGRESS CATALOGING-IN-PUBLICATION DATA
Bergstrom, Heather Brittain.
Steal the north : a novel / Heather Brittain Bergstrom.
pages cm
ISBN 978-0-670-78618-3
1. Young women—Fiction. I. Title.
PS3602.E7564S74 2014
813'.6—dc23
2013036976

Printed in the United States of America
10 9 8 7 6 5 4 3 2 1

Set in Agfa Wile Std
Designed by Carla Bolte

For my sisters,

Angie and Jenny,

remember when it was just us?

I have not told you half of what I want to.

—Narcissa Whitman, one of the first two pioneer women to cross the Rockies,

in a letter to her sister, 1836

My parents gave birth to me here, and I fancy this is my country.

—Chief Moses to an Indian agent, Okanogan River, 1870

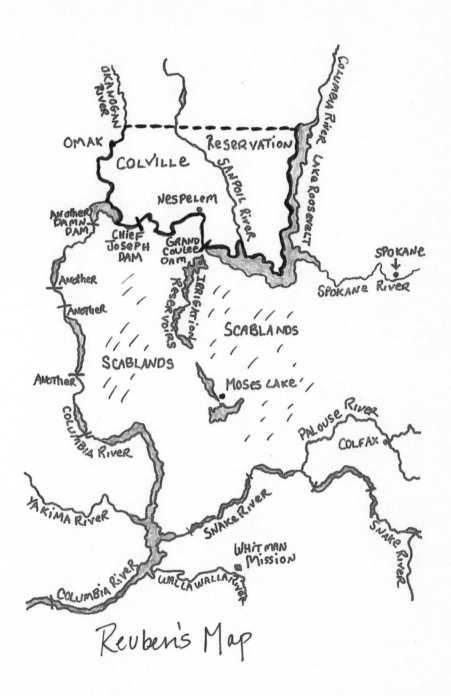

Reuben's Map

Part One

1

Emmy

Until the summer I was sixteen and my mom sent me away, I lived with her in a Sacramento apartment located above a shop that sold seaweed powders, mood mists, Buddha statues, even menstruation journals. According to Mom, the women who frequented the shop were either rich and bored or neurotic. I loved everything about the shop, from the chanting monk music to the smell of sandalwood, and I regularly spent my allowance on tarot cards, amulets, and wishing pots. Mom taught English at three different junior colleges, and because her hours were sporadic and the colleges far apart, I was often alone, though never overnight. We had no family in the Sacramento Valley, or anywhere in California. Our only relatives in the whole world, supposedly, were a few distant cousins up north in Washington, and Mom had left them in the dust when she boarded a southbound bus with me, a baby on her hip. Los Angeles was her original destination, but I kept throwing up, and Mom liked the sycamore trees that shaded the city streets in Sacramento.

As for my dad, I was told he died the day I was born.

Mom didn't mean he literally died. I learned this the hard way after a fellow second grader teased that he too would've keeled over at the sight of my ugly face pushing out of my mom's vagina. "I meant the most important part of your dad died the day you were born and he didn't claim you," Mom explained. "And you have a beautiful face."

"So, he's still alive?" I almost levitated.

She hesitated before replying, which was rare. "No, Emmy." She said my dad, raised on a wheat farm in eastern Washington, was killed in a tractor accident. He'd always been reckless. "I'm sorry, honey."

"Did you love him?"

"Too much." I didn't understand then how you can love someone *too* much. Now I recognize it's the only way I know how to love.

After I finished crying, she made me swear I'd never again have a sad thought for that man. But it was my dad, I soon realized, she thought about when we drove mostly in somber silence around the rice fields north of Sacramento. It cheered Mom to drive east on weekends, through quaint foothill towns or even high into the Sierras, which seemed to me as a little girl the loneliest place, haunted by starving Donner Party ghosts. If Mom were to fall apart, I had no one, so I pretended to forget about my dad. Mom had left her past at the California border and never glanced back. I often consulted my tarot decks about her mysterious past and my future. Not even my favorite pack, *Healing with the Fairies*, warned me about the phone call that came near the end of my junior year.

Actually my life had already been changing behind my mom's back with a boy named Connor, which was why I was late getting home from school the day she got the phone call. I attended a private "artsy-smartsy" school, which Mom mocked, even though she chose it. The high cost of my tuition—despite my almost full-ride scholarship—in addition to Mom's own student loan payments, kept us stuck in the same small apartment we'd always rented. Not that she or I really minded. Mom preferred living in "midtown" among community theaters, ethnic restaurants, and used bookstores. She said it was far better than renting a larger apartment in a gated complex across from a shopping mall. It was Tuesday, and Mom usually taught class until eight. Three days a week I waited in my school library until five for Mom to pick me up, or at least I was supposed to. The other two days, like today, I was supposed to take public transit home. Connor had dropped me off at the corner.

"The service club held an emergency meeting after school," I lied. "About the end-of-the-year food drive." I was on the academic decathlon team and vice president of three clubs on campus. In order to retain my scholarship at Valley Art Academy—the largest secular private high school in northern California, outside the Bay Area—I had to stay involved, and Mom wanted no blanks on my college applications. Connor had written me a list of excuses to use if I ever got busted. At the top, he'd written, "Busy fucking my beautiful boyfriend."

"Sit down," she said. "We need to talk."

"I took the later bus with Harpreet." Another lie. Connor said to keep it simple, but I lacked confidence. "We stopped—" She waved her hand. I was going to say that we'd stopped for samosas at Harpreet's parents' restaurant. I wished. Harpreet had a large family and wasn't really allowed to hang out with anyone except her cousins. Still, she was the closest thing I had to a friend. We both loved Leonardo DiCaprio (she for *Titanic,* which she saw at the theater three times over Christmas break, I for *What's Eating Gilbert Grape* and *Romeo & Juliet*). We ate lunch together every day at school.

Mom seemed distracted and had yet to make eye contact with me.

"What is it, Mom?" I asked, taking off my heavy backpack and leaning my art portfolio against the wall. I sat down obediently on the couch. She continued to stand. I no longer felt worried about getting busted. Something else was wrong. Something bigger. Nonetheless, if Mom had any idea about Connor, especially what he'd just had me do in his bedroom, she would be dumbfounded and probably repulsed. She thought I was still a virgin and encouraged me to remain so until college. I needed to clean myself in the bathroom.

"Fuck," Mom said, and began to pace. She didn't often cuss. "Fuck."

"Did something happen to Spencer?" My heart pounded. He and Mom had been dating since I was twelve. I adored him. She tried to act as if she didn't.

"Spencer?" She almost looked at me, and I wished she would. "This has *nothing* to do with him."

I knew Mom loved Spencer, but sometimes it seemed she didn't want him to be part of anything. She'd had other, far-shorter-term boyfriends in the past, but those men she'd kept completely out of my life as if afraid she'd psychologically scar me. When I was younger, I used to occasionally hear her on the phone late at night with men. Once I found a guy's sock in her room. She insisted the cat must've dragged it in. What cat?

"Sorry," I said now about Spencer. Jeez.

She waved her hand again, then sat down in the European-looking chair we'd bought years ago at a flea market. It had crushed velvet cushions, but one of its legs was too short. She seemed to forget this and jumped when the chair tilted. "Shit chair." She stood back up.

"But so much character," I reminded her, which was why we wouldn't let Spencer fix it. Mom called the chair Isabel, after her favorite Henry James character. Beautiful but flawed.

"You're going to hate me, Emmy." Finally she looked straight at me but remained standing. "I mean *really* hate me before tonight is over with."

"That's stupid." We both had a flair for the dramatic, as Spencer once made the mistake of pointing out to Mom. "I could never hate you." Though I already did sometimes, or almost, and not just for big things like making me switch schools (in her endless pursuit of the best one to get me into U.C. Berkeley). Lately she could just be sitting across the table and I would hate her, just for a second, but it scared me. I'd have to go into my bedroom and light a detoxification candle or make an origami peace crane. Plenty of kids at school despised their parents, or pretended to. I didn't want to despise my mom. She was smart, funny, and hardworking. And yes, she was controlling, as Connor always said. But again, she was all I had.

Mom sat down in the wicker chair over which a paisley throw hid the out-of-style southwestern design. She took a deep breath, paused, and said, "I have a sister—in Washington."

"No, you don't," I protested. She was an only child, like me. Right around the age I quit playing with dolls, I begged her to have another baby. I wanted a relative. What if she were to die? Did she want me all alone on the earth?

"My little sister found me."

"*Found?*" That made no sense. "You've been *hiding* from her?" I figured Mom's childhood hadn't been easy or she would've talked to me more about it, but to have never told me she had a sister and I had an aunt, that was mental.

"Not necessarily hiding." She crossed her legs, then uncrossed them.

Men stared at her legs. Spencer rubbed them when they sat close on the couch. "It's more like I've been keeping some distance between me and the place she is a part of."

"What?" I was even more confused. And keeping "some distance"? She meant a chasm. The walls of our apartment started to close in on me for the first time. "Why would you do that, Mom?" I demanded.

"Hold on. It gets worse." She took another deep breath. "Your aunt isn't the only person I've kept secret from you." She asked me if I was ready for the bomb. "Your dad, Emmy—he isn't dead."

It was all too much. I went to bed for three days, sick like an Austen or a Brontë character who'd foolishly wandered the moors in a storm, with a strong will but weak ankles. Only the moors were my mom's past, and I couldn't find my way. No man on a steed came to rescue me. Connor didn't even call to inquire why I wasn't at school. No doctor, fetched at a great price, came to bleed me, and I was too chicken to cut myself like some girls at school did. Certainly no faithful sister wept at my bedside. As for my "grief-stricken" mom, I didn't want her near me. Whenever she came into my room to bring me food or to plead with me to please get up, I'd hide under the covers. Either she felt terribly guilty for all her monstrous lies or my willfulness shocked and disorientated her because she'd retreat without pulling rank. I spent hours going over everything she'd told me, all the way up to why her sister had called, which was most frightening of all. If I thought of Mom's past like a novel, it was easier.

There once was a girl named Kate, who had a younger sister named Bethany. Their mother died of cancer when the girls were young. The mother might have lived longer, but the family attended a fundamentalist Baptist church that didn't believe in doctors. The church practiced faith healings, and Kate remembered her mother being dipped into one stagnant desert lake after another, even a mineral lake the Indians believed held special powers and was therefore considered pagan and off-limits. This all took place in Washington State, the dry eastern half that not many people know about. Kate and Bethany's father was a stern man of God. In accordance with the church's absurd policies on female modesty and femininity, he didn't permit his daughters to wear pants or to cut their hair or, when they got older, to wear makeup. Their family didn't own a TV, so as children they saw no images of the war raging in Vietnam. And because they weren't allowed to listen to the radio or own rock records, they hadn't the slightest idea who Bob Dylan was, let alone Zeppelin or Springsteen. The county library, with its rows of pornographic novels and atheist manifestos, was as forbidden as the movie theater. The girls attended school in the church basement and were taught by deacons' wives, some of whom hadn't graduated from high school themselves. It would've been a miserable childhood, but the two sisters had each other.

They slept in the same bed, braided each other's hair, and memorized Bible verses together for school. Bethany, a rather frail girl, could sew beautifully and play the piano. Kate preferred to collect rocks, which she kept in her mother's old mason jars, and to study maps when she could get her hands on them. This angered their father, who said Kate should keep her eyes above, not on earthly things, and set a better feminine example for her little sister by learning to cook. Kate insisted she studied the maps so God would direct her where to go as a missionary. One day in a rage her father took Kate's rock collection and threw it into the river.

I forced myself not to feel sympathy for Mom at this point in the story. She had a sister to sleep with as a girl, which was far better than jars of rocks or tarot cards.

The sisters grew into young ladies. At church, they took sacred vows of virginity, promising God and the congregation that they wouldn't so much as hold hands with a boy until they became brides. Most of the males in the church youth group were rawboned farm boys, so this wasn't hard. Boys in town paid them no mind because of their long dresses and nonfeathered hair. Then one week a handsome boy named Matthew Miller came to youth Bible study with his cousin. Matthew's parents weren't religious, but he kept attending because of Bethany. Kate watched with jealousy at first, but Bethany and Matt were made for each other. Even the girls' stern father could see that, although he tried to act as if Matt weren't good enough. Matt and Bethany could sit beside each other at church, but that was all. It was enough for Matt. He was saved, baptized, and even spoke of becoming a preacher one day.

The summer Kate was seventeen and Bethany fifteen, their youth group got sponsored to attend a Bible camp in western Washington. At first their father refused, but Matt promised to watch over the sisters. The campgrounds were green with ferns, and pine trees scraped the sky. The sisters had never been west of the Cascades, though Kate clearly remembered the wistful way their mother talked about the moss-covered rocks of her Puget Sound childhood. Even the air smelled different from that in eastern Washington: dampness instead of dust, ferns and bark instead of hay and fertilizer. Mountains, instead of clumps of algae from farm runoff, were reflected on the lake's surface.

Their small youth group was the only one where the girls always wore dresses, even for physical activities, and all had hair that fell below their waists. Most of the campers from western Washington dressed in expensive sweaters, college sweatshirts, turtlenecks, Windbreakers, name-brand jeans. There was also one decently wealthy group from eastern Washington. They were well-fed wheat farmers' kids from the Palouse region below Spokane. Within this group, a particularly cocky boy named Jamie Kagen wore a cowboy hat and didn't give a crap what the Puget Sound boys thought. Even the Seattle girls with their tennis rackets were impressed. But he wasn't interested in them for long. He liked the girl he found down by the lake filling the pockets of her ridiculously long dress with rocks. "Don't they have rocks where you come from?" Those were his first words to her. They could've been his last and Kate still would've been head over heels.

"Not rocks with moss," she said. "They're soft."

"Slimy, you mean." He stepped nearer. "That's some dress. You just get off the Oregon Trail?"

"That's some hat," she managed to reply, despite trembling. "You about to rustle cattle?"

Grinning, he took his hat off and put it on her.

"Sorry, but you can't have my dress."

I had to pause every time at this point in the story because there'd been something in my mom's voice—or something missing, her usual edginess—when she'd told it to me. She didn't sound that way when she talked about Spencer, or her beloved Bill Clinton, or when she read me her favorite passages from books. She kept touching the ends of her bobbed hair. The image of my parents standing together at the edge of a lake was blurry, at best, but it was more than I'd ever had.

Somehow Jamie managed to sneak Kate away for long, unchaperoned canoe rides on the lake. Time, it seemed to Kate, hung back on the shore with the counselors and other campers. She and Jamie sat close during morning worship service, all three meals, and around the camp bonfire in the evenings. At Bethany's bidding, Matt had a talk with Jamie about his intentions toward Kate. By the end of the conversation, Jamie had convinced Matt that if he really loved Bethany, he would prove it to her by holding her hand, not listening to the church fathers, who were just horny old men. People who love each other hold hands and hug, Jamie claimed. It didn't have to go further, he said, but it *had* to go that far.

Kate had never felt happier. Jamie loved God—not that it mattered to Kate—but he talked of other things also: his dad's wheat farm, which would one day be his; the rolling hills of the Palouse region, like no other place on earth; Washington State University in Pullman, where he planned to enroll in the agricultural science program; and his love for Kate. He'd had other girlfriends. He knew what he was talking about when he said there was something definite between them. Kate didn't need to run off to Africa to get away from her father or to do her Christian duty. She could be his wife. He was serious. He'd prove it to her.

At the last bonfire, there were more testimonials of faith than all the other nights combined. Jamie Kagen took a stand, in his cowboy hat. His confidence and energy had made him a camp favorite with the rich Seattle kids, as well as with the handful of not-so-rich kids from western Washington whose dads worked in the lumber mills. The entire crowd hooted for him. "I want to testify before you guys and before God," he said, "that I love this girl." He pulled Kate to her feet and again put his hat on her head. "I'm going to marry her some-day." The crowd cheered. "In honor, I propose a group hug. Find the babe you love and give her a hug. Right now. A long hug in front of God. Go ahead." The adults in charge swiftly made their way to him, as if he'd just proposed an orgy.

After camp, Jamie and Kate did their best to stay together, though they lived more than two hours apart and Jamie had harvest and planting duties. They were both seniors in high school. Jamie went to public school in Colfax. They met as often as they could before the heavy snows started. He had a pickup truck, and Kate had her moth-er's old car that barely ran. They'd meet midway in tiny farm towns with Indian names, like Washtucna, parking in the shade of enor-mous silos. Or they'd meet at Army Corps of Engineers parks along the Snake River. Kate's father didn't like Jamie, but she didn't care. Her father threatened for a while to take the car, but Bethany relied on Kate for rides, and he knew Kate would walk if she had to or run away.

Jamie's parents weren't enthused to learn their son had found the girl he wanted to marry at age seventeen. They agreed to meet Kate but weren't impressed with her junk car, long dress, and supposedly old-fashioned ways. They wanted their son to meet his future wife at the university, and they wanted this wife's family to have either money or land. Although Kate felt guilty doing so, she hocked her mother's ring for cash to buy gas to meet Jamie. Before long she wound up pregnant. They might not have had premarital sex, hooking up the first time at the Appaloosa Inn, if they could've seen each other more often and if Kate hadn't felt Jamie's resolve faltering as his dad threat-ened to take everything from him unless he dumped Kate.

Jamie loved the land and felt tied to it in a way Kate didn't under-stand. He took her to Palouse Falls to show her the muddy water spill-ing two hundred feet over the canyon edge. The water was so muddy, he told her, because of soil erosion. If farmers didn't find a way to slow the erosion, the Palouse region was doomed. He started to flunk his high school classes, even drink. But once he made his decision, choos-ing the farm over Kate, he didn't waver. Kate's belly, in the meantime, grew round as one of Jamie's beloved Palouse hills. When her father noticed, he let the preacher condemn his daughter from the pulpit, call her a whore. She had to drop out of school. Kate swore to her father that the baby wasn't Jamie's. She said she'd committed adultery with a bunch of public school boys she barely knew.

Why had Mom protected Jamie like that? Was it love? Too much love? Was it pride? The same pride that kept us alone all these years in this apartment? Had Jamie really chosen the endangered land over Mom? Or was it actually his youth that felt eroded?

Every day Kate's father yelled at her, spitting Bible verses in her face about harlots. Bethany swore the baby in her sister's belly was a gift from God, and her father had better accept it as such. He would not, so meek Bethany took charge. She and Matt got married. His parents weren't thrilled, but they conceded and even lent Matt the money to buy a trailer and give those two girls a home. Matt got a job at the potato factory. After Kate gave birth, she too got a job, waitressing at a truck stop café outside town by the interstate. By that time, she heard, Jamie Kagen had started college at WSU. Still, she expected any day for him to show up at the café, even after the first snowstorm had obliterated the highway.

When he didn't, she began living hard, which at first just meant wearing jeans and mascara. Then drinking. Bethany took care of the baby—sewed little dresses and blankets. Kate sank further. She had to get out of the area come spring. It would devastate Bethany to lose the baby, but Kate reasoned her sister could have her own babies soon. Kate couldn't take another day at the café, staring out the windows at the plowed highway, dropping ketchup bottles or spilling coffee when she spotted a pickup similar to Jamie's. Bethany went to their father and demanded the money their mother's family had left for the girls when they turned eighteen. It wasn't a lot, but Bethany gave both halves to her older sister. Kate owed her life and the life of her daughter to Bethany and Matt.

Now, sixteen years later, Kate had just found out that Bethany never had any babies of her own. In those long years, Kate's little sister hadn't once been able to carry a baby to term. She'd lost them all. Kate couldn't even imagine how Bethany had suffered. If only she'd known. So how could Kate possibly tell her sister no, that she wouldn't allow her daughter to fly north to spend the summer and to participate in a faith healing for Bethany, who was pregnant for what she feared was the last time? How could Kate say no, even though she didn't believe in faith healings, even though she found them, in fact, total bullshit? Even though she'd hoped after all these years that her sister would've left that backward church? There was a new young preacher at the church, and he suggested a virgin lay hands on Bethany's belly to help heal her womb. A virgin who was also a relative would be ideal. How excited Bethany was when Matt found Kate's number at the library on the World Wide Web and then again when she learned from Kate that her precious niece was, in fact, still a virgin. How could Kate possibly say no to this request even if it went against everything she believed in, or didn't believe in? Everything she'd worked so hard to get the hell away from?

"I owe Beth," Kate said to her daughter. "And the only gift I can give her is you."

"You're shitting me, right?" asked Connor. "The whole summer? What am I supposed to do?" We were in his bedroom. It was Monday after school.

"Isn't your family going to Hawaii?"

"Hawaii's boring. How fucking suburban." Connor hated the suburbs, found them stifling and unimaginative. I found his house mammoth and beautiful, even if it *did* look just like the other houses on the street with palm trees and Spanish tile and a multiple-car garage. "Besides," he said, "I mean the rest of the summer."

"You can study for the SATs," I suggested. His scores were mediocre, unlike his art. My scores were good, but Mom wanted me to take them again to try for even better. I sat on his bed. It was made up for him every morning by a maid. Other than his art and art supplies all over, and the words PARTY LIKE YOU'RE THE CLASS OF 1999 spray painted on his ceiling, his room looked like one from a Pottery Barn catalog, with solid matching furniture. "Unless you *actually* think you can get into college with your scores."

"Wow. Kitty's got claws today."

I stood up. "I've had a lot to think about," I reminded him. So much I hadn't been sleeping well.

He pulled me to him. "Sorry about your dad not being dead. That's heavy."

"I don't want to go to Washington." It seemed so unreal, all of it. Connor kissed my neck. His tongue was pierced, which he'd done to shock his parents and their country club friends. Occasionally Connor dressed preppy in khaki pants or in vests over white T-shirts, but only when trying to get something from his parents or to get off restriction. Most days he dressed like the members of Green Day, in skinny ties and lots of black. He spiked his hair and dyed the tips bright colors. I incorporated a little punk, a little Goth, a little grunge, a little preppy, and even a little hippie—depending on my mood—into my otherwise basic and clearance rack wardrobe. I feared looking too plain in a student body of expressive dressers, but I just couldn't pick a single style. I liked elements from each.

"I don't want to leave you, Connor."

"Take off your shirt." He liked me to undress myself.

I unbuttoned the first few buttons on my blouse. "Why didn't you call?" I'd never missed three days of school in a row before.

"I'm not allowed to call your apartment, remember?" He sat down on his bed, then scooted back on his elbows.

Actually Mom had never said boys weren't allowed to call me, but I preferred her knowing nothing about Connor. That way she couldn't question me about him or forbid me from seeing him.

"And besides," Connor said, "I *did* call. Ask your master. I mean your mom."

"What?" I stopped unbuttoning my blouse. "You talked to her?"

"Sure. She and I, we had a little chat. I told her she was heartless for never having taken you to Disneyland." He liked the fact that I'd never been there. He also liked that I lived in a small apartment and didn't wear expensive brand names (though he did). "She didn't tell you? Shit, that hurts."

"You're lying. I asked her if anyone called for me."

"She's the liar, Emmy," he said smugly.

"Don't call her that." Not that I really cared. She *was* a liar. She'd been lying to me my whole life. I suspected she was *still* lying to me, that she'd left something out. There was more to deserting her beloved sister and never being in touch than my dad, her dad, and that oppressive church, even combined. I planned to find out the whole story this summer. I also planned, without her help or approval, to locate my dad. He'd probably been searching for me for years.

In the meantime, I was barely talking to Mom. After only allowing me to a few slumber parties in my life (not that I'd had a lot of invitations), she was now forcing me to fly far away and live for three months with religious fanatics. On top of that she was trying to make it seem as if I'd *agreed* to go—as if I'd been given a *choice* and weren't being coerced.

"Just tell your mom you're not a virgin," Connor said. "It's simple. Then you won't have to spend your summer with Bible-thumpers." I finished unbuttoning my blouse. Connor sat up at the sight of my bra.

"It's not that simple."

First, I couldn't tell Mom I wasn't a virgin. According to her, intelligent girls waited until college. Second, Mom already said, in regard to the faith healing, that it didn't matter at all whether I was a virgin or not (though she was proud I was) because the ceremony was bogus. What Mom did believe in, however, and she made this very clear, was in her sister's being so cheered and comforted by my company this summer that she might finally carry a baby past the slippery first trimester. In other words: "Would you actually deny your dear aunt who loved and cared for you as an infant the chance to have a baby of her own?"

"My old man was euphoric the first time I asked him to buy me condoms," Connor said. "It proved his 'artistic' thirteen-year-old son wasn't gay after all."

"The condoms were for you and Alyssa, no doubt." I threw my blouse at him. I despised the way his ex-girlfriend looked at him. He said she offered almost every day at school (backstage in drama class) to show him her thong. I wasn't allowed to wear thongs.

"Oh, fuck. Don't start that again. Take off your pants. No, slower."

I took off my pants quickly and threw them at him, as I had my shirt. He threw them both back at me a little too hard. Screw him. I walked to his window. I peeked out the curtains at the glittering water in his pool and tried not to cry. What if Mom's sister had a miscarriage while I was there? Would my aunt blame me, especially if she found out I wasn't a Christian, let alone a virgin? The closest I'd come to attending church had been last November, when I went to the giant Sikh parade in Yuba City with Harpreet's family and saw the elaborate float with their holy book. I heard Connor sigh on his bed. Would Bethany be able to tell I wasn't a virgin upon first glance? Connor bragged he knew I was a virgin when he first saw me. When he sighed again, I turned around. "I'd still be a virgin, you know," I said, my voice shaking stupidly, "if it weren't for you."

"If you want, Emmy, I can stop touching you."

"How could I go on?" I asked sarcastically. "Besides, you *don't* touch me at school. You don't even hold my hand."

"I thought you were different from all the spoiled bitches at school. No? Maybe you just dress differently. Or your mommy dresses you differently."

"Oh, I'm different. Not only have I never been to Disneyland, but I would *never* cut myself for you, like Alyssa."

"Fuck you."

"Don't say that. I hate it when you say that to me." I crawled onto his bed. "I'm sorry, Connor. Don't get mean. Not today. I'm sorry."

He told me to take off my bra and my "good girl panties," and then we had sex. He was a little cruel, refusing to take my hand, then covering my eyes as he entered me. But he held me longer afterward. I loved to watch TV in his bed after sex. We didn't have cable at our apartment. We had a TV on which I'd watched PBS as a kid. On the other channels Mom and I watched Bill Clinton be elected, then reelected. We watched images of the Gulf War, the L.A. riots, the Oklahoma City bombing, Bosnia—but never silly sitcoms. We watched movies on our VCR, mostly heavy or artsy dramas, but occasionally Mom let me rent popular movies.

"I'm going to miss you," he said, but he sounded as if it were for good and he'd already resigned himself to it. "I'm going to miss how excited you get to watch the stupid fucking Disney Channel."

"We'll stay together, right?" The panic I'd been trying to keep at bay about leaving him, leaving Sacramento, even leaving my mom rushed over me, and I began to sob. It irritated Connor worse than soccer moms and golfing dads when chicks cried after sex. I only cried the first time we did it, but it was more out of anger at myself and embarrassment at the blood on his high-thread-count sheets. "You'll wait for me, Connor, won't you? Please, Connor." Mom had said never to beg and never to tell a guy you love him first. I didn't love Connor, but I could have—it was right there—if only he loved me the tiniest. "You'll wait?" He held me closer, which I hoped meant yes. When I still couldn't quit sobbing, he reached into his bedside table, where he kept his flavored and textured condoms and his collection of souvenir scrunchies and headbands (only two of which were mine).

"Here, take this." It was one of his mom's Vicodin pills. "It'll help you chill."

I stopped crying and sat up. "I don't take drugs." His mom probably did to put up with his unfaithful dad. Connor had told me stories. I got out of his bed. "I hate you."

I expected him to remark, "How original." Instead he said, "That's too bad, Emmy. I could never hate you." He rolled onto his stomach and buried his head under his numerous pillows.

Probably not, but that didn't mean he loved me any more than he'd wait for me.

"Will you wait for me?" I had to ask one more time.

He didn't reply, but at school the final week he held my hand every lunch recess in front of his friends, who smirked. We exchanged gifts in his bedroom our last afternoon. I gave him an amulet key chain with a Tibetan symbol—the umbrella, for protection from desire. I told him it was to protect him from suffering. He gave me two gifts. The first was a bottle of Vicodin. He said I'd need the pills up north living with Jesus freaks.

The second gift was a necklace with a diamond heart-shaped pendant (pretty suburban) that I put on immediately. I already knew what I would say to Mom when she asked who had given it to me. I would hesitate for effect and then stutter while telling her that Hedda, my only other lunchtime friend, bought it for me. I wanted Mom to wonder if a boy at school had really given the necklace to me and what I'd done with the boy (*everything, Mom*) to deserve diamonds. I promised Connor I'd wear the necklace the entire summer—not that he asked me to—but instead I wound up hocking it at the same dusty pawnshop surrounded by sagebrush where my mom had hocked her mother's ring years ago. And so I entered their story.

2

Bethany

I used to park my car at the Greyhound station and wait for the buses. More people got on, I finally realized, than off. My sister wasn't coming back, despite my prayers. Before Kate left, she'd let a truck driver at the highway café where she was working cut off her long hair, which I used to braid. She said he'd offered her "extra" for the souvenir. I understood what she meant, but after all these years I still can't bear to think of it. In the direct sun, Kate's brown hair glowed red underneath. My blond hair also catches the sun, Matt says. But he must see it doesn't hold the rays as Kate's did. Matt claims I've never gotten over the loss of my sister. He says it might've been easier on me if Kate had died like our mother because then I wouldn't feel more betrayed every year that passes without her making contact. But Kate didn't betray me. There's more to her leaving than Matt knows. My husband always has an excuse for my behavior: to his parents, co-workers, the other deacons at church whose wives, especially recently, have complained that I take up too much of the new preacher's time. Probably even in supplication does my husband offer up excuses for me.

I imagine Kate's hair is what first attracted Jamie Kagen to her that summer at camp. There's not a lot of sunshine west of the Cascades, but there's a certain light, the kind right before a storm or right after, that also set Kate's hair ablaze. Matt thinks Kate lost her faith after camp when Jamie shunned her, but faith was never easy for my sister. It kept her awake at night when we were kids. During the day she dragged it around, as she did the awful memories surrounding our mother's death. Without my faith I couldn't get out of bed after each miscarriage. I quit teaching Sunday school years ago. Not out of bitterness—I refuse to drink from that cup—but because of the deep longing the small hands of the children brought out in me. Not just longing for a child of my own but for my niece, Emmy, whom Matt and I cared for every day for seven months before Kate left town with her.

Kate *had* to leave Washington. In truth, I knew that before she did. But sisters can share a baby in such a way. It's not that Emmy loved me more than her mom, but almost as much. After all, it was my voice that lulled her to sleep most nights and Matt or I who brought her warm bottles of milk. Poor Kate would see Jamie in Emmy. I tried to convince her that Emmy got her fair-colored hair from me. We'd nap sometimes, the three of us girls, all on one bed, the baby between. It hurt Kate's feelings when Emmy reached for me first after opening her sleepy little eyes.

I suffered my first miscarriage soon after Kate and Emmy left.

Not wanting to replace Emmy so soon, I was almost relieved. She had this way of looking at me, of pausing in the middle of cooing or crying, and staring intently at me. Perhaps she sensed our time to-gether would be cut bluntly short, like her mother's hair, and she wanted to suspend it. My breath still catches when I remember those moments.

My second miscarriage was probably the hardest. It signaled the first wasn't a fluke and that God had a different plan for me. I wasn't to rush to the church nursery after service with the other young moms to collect my bundle and then show it off to the older ladies. I was to serve refreshments, straighten hymnals, rinse drops of grape juice from communion glasses as I rinsed the drops of blood from my sheets and the carpet. For a few years, at the special Mother's Day service, having neither mother nor child, I handed out the corsages, until Matt put a stop to that, saying it broke his heart. He pleaded with me to see a doctor behind the church's back. He'd take a day off work and drive me to Wenatchee or Spokane. He's probably the only deacon who finds some of the church's rules archaic, even barbaric. But we're to put our trust in God, not man. Matt wasn't raised in a Christian home. "God helps those who help themselves," he persisted.

"I won't go against the church."

"You did before, Beth. We did. For Kate. For us. We did the right thing."

I've never regretted what we did for Kate. And certainly I've never regretted marrying Matt, even if I was only sixteen and he only a year older. We were both ready. My father didn't give his blessing, but neither did he try to prevent the marriage. The church chastised me for helping Kate, but my father never did. He continued to shun Kate until she left. He never met his only grandchild. For years he refused to talk about Kate. As time passed, however, he started to inquire, casually, then with concern, then desperation, if I'd heard from my sister and if I knew how the baby was doing. He died of a massive heart attack. One day he was alive—I phoned to tell him I'd finished his mending and that Matt had some venison for him—and the next day he was dead.

After my third miscarriage, Matt and I fought for weeks over his setting up a doctor's appointment to get a vasectomy. It's the only time we've truly quarreled. He even stayed home from church two Sundays in a row: the first to tie flies at the table, an activity he usually saves for winter evenings, and the second to fish with his new "backslidden flies." That's when I took up herbs to help myself. I make natural remedies from plants I grow in my own garden. For the most part, I do so without the church's knowing the extent. I've been likened to a witch with potions. The new preacher, Brother Mathias—he likes us to call him brother, though he's our shepherd—was so taken with my garden the first time he saw it that he entreated me to plant him a small herb garden between the church and the parsonage. As a single man who cooks his own meals, except when the church widows bring him casseroles, he can use the added flavor. "You're no more a witch, Sister Bethany," he declared when I disclosed to him the rumors, "than I am the devil."

The first time Kate called our father the devil, she and I were alone in the backseat of the car. I was seven and scared. My memories of that evening are like a grainy snapshot. I remember it was Sunday and summertime. I remember foolishly thinking our family was going on a picnic, even though Mother hadn't left the house for months. Women from church had been coming to feed her broth and to read her passages from the Bible. Suddenly the whole family was getting into the car. Father had to carry Mother because her feet curled inward. She moaned. It was hot, but he covered her with a quilt. Father said we were going to a lake, and he wouldn't answer Kate when she asked which one.

He drove us north toward Grand Coulee Dam and its reservoirs. The highway followed the base of a giant basalt cliff. Terrified of large bodies of water as a kid, I knew the farther north we traveled, the deeper and colder the lakes got. Even when instructed to stay dry, Kate waded into any lake or stream. I was almost asleep when I felt the car slow and heard the crunch of gravel under the tires. I didn't immediately recognize the lake. Then I saw the suds along the shoreline and the almost black mud. It was the Indian lake. The church forbade its members to swim in this mineral lake because Indians had supposedly cured their horses and warriors in it years ago. An Indian legend claimed that Coyote, the pagan animal chief and "creator," had defecated in the lake—where had I heard that?—giving it restorative powers. Now white people came from across the state to soak in the soapy water or to smear the mud on their naked bodies and pray to the devil. I feared the worse.

Shutting off the engine, Father said, "We'll wait in the car until the beach clears out." There were about a dozen people around. One fat man in just a pair of shorts had mud smeared all over him. He smiled in our direction. "Unroll the windows back there," Father instructed. But if I did, evil spirits would surely enter the car.

"I'm afraid," I said.

"Of what?" Kate asked. She told me to unroll my window before I suffocated.

"The lake is evil."

"A lake can't be evil," she said. "I'm getting out." She started to open her door.

"Sit back, child," Father said sternly. Then Mother, who'd been asleep, or just in a stupor, tried to say something but choked. She coughed violently, and Kate slipped out of the car, heading toward the swings and the twisty slide. Mother kept coughing and moaning and, I think, unless I remember wrong, begging for it all to be over. How I wanted to get out of the car and join Kate on the playground, not be so near Mother, whose face drooped and whose breath was stale. But terror pinned me in place. Kate swung high in the air, so high no evil spirit could snatch her. I remember a wooden sign hanging between two posts that read HEALING WATERS, swaying as the wind picked up and the ripples on the lake's surface turned white. The spirits were churning it.

"I want to go home, Daddy," I pleaded.

He spoke more gently to me when Kate wasn't around. "Lie down and take a nap."

Something about the inside of a car made me sleepy. So I did as he said, hoping when I woke back up, we'd be home. The sky was tinged pink when I sat bolt upright. Kate was beside me, but our parents were gone from the front seat. "Where are they?" I asked. Kate pointed to the beach, which was now deserted. The wind pushed the empty swings, and the sign squeaked. "Where'd they go?" I started to panic. I may have even screamed.

Kate explained that Father had taken Mother to soak in the lake, to try to heal her without the church elders. "We're supposed to be praying," she said.

"Dear Heavenly Father—"

"You pray. I'm going to go check on Mom."

She started to get out of the car.

"No, Kate. No, Kate. Don't leave me, Kate!"

I remember her pausing, as if trying to decide between Mother and me, and I remember feeling the whole of my life depended on her decision, and maybe it did in some ways. She shut the door behind her. I rolled up all the windows and locked the doors.

If only I'd been brave enough to follow her.

Whatever my sister saw, and she never told me, left her shaking with rage and revulsion when she got back into the car, hair dripping wet, mud smeared on her face and arms. "He's the devil—the devil!"

Mother died a week later with traces of the black mud still under her fingernails.

I keep my fingernails clipped short and soak my hands in herbal tonic water. I tried to wear gloves when I first began gardening, but herbs are delicate, and I like to feel the different textures of the stems and leaves. My touch helps the plants grow. I started with just a few potted herbs I found in Kmart's gardening section: lavender for calm and balance and rosemary for stimulation. Even the mighty King David pleaded, "Purge me with hyssop, and I shall be clean." I soon added chives, sage, mint, basil, oregano, thyme. Driving to out-of-town nurseries made me feel a little like the virtuous woman in Proverbs 31 who "bringeth her food from afar." Chamomile for heart palpitations. Ginger for tiredness. Black cohosh. I ordered seed catalogs. Hyssop as a blood purifier. Sweet marjoram to ease menstruation. Nettles. Calendula. The list goes on. Afternoon sunlight is best for herbs this far north, but because eastern Washington gets so warm, I rotate my pots daily in the summer. There's not a lot of space for a garden between lots in Quail Run Mobile Home Park. I have two raised beds and shelves of pots, plastic buckets, coffee cans. Matt built me a pea gravel walkway and bought me a small stone bench. Sometimes I pretend Kate, her hair glowing, sits on the bench and watches me garden. I think she'd be proud of my handiwork. Instead of Kate, the neighbor lady, an Indian from the Colville Reservation, stares at me through her curtainless kitchen window.

As a member of the church I'm not permitted to buy secular books or to check them out from the library, so my knowledge about herbs remains limited. I have to rely on intuition, which may not be a bad thing. Over the years I've managed to read a few pamphlet-size books while standing in grocery store checkout lanes: *The Power of Healing Herbs* and *Aromatherapy for Housewives*. I used to simply dry my herbs, hang them in bundles. I made lots of teas. Now I also make essential oils, which take a lot of time but are well worth it. Matt drove me to Spokane to buy a distiller and dozens of miniature glass bottles in amber and cobalt blue. Sunlight dispels the oil if it is stored in clear bottles. Our pantry is halfway full of my oils and apparatuses. Besides medicines, I make bath salts, face creams, hand lotions, massage oils, as well as teas and cooking spice packets. I sometimes give them as gifts to the ladies at church.

I haven't yet been able to stop my miscarriages. The last time I conceived—it's been awhile now—I didn't tell Matt. When I lost the baby, I think he suspected. But he didn't ask. I've never lied outright to my husband.

I hope I'm not being deceitful by meeting in confidence with Brother Mathias today in his office at church. I help at the church half a day on Tuesdays and all day on Fridays: cleaning, typing the weekly bulletins, organizing the missionary supply closet, gardening, running errands, anything that needs to be done. I fellowship plenty with Brother Mathias on these days. He even has me help choose hymns for services. Sometimes he asks me to play the hymns for him on the church piano. I prefer the Sunday school piano in the basement because it used to be my mother's. After Father died, I loaned it to the church since there's no room for a piano in our singlewide trailer. Brother Mathias insists I'm a better player than Sister Dorothy, who has slowed with age, and her unmarried daughter, who pounds the keys.

I knock on his office. "Come in, Sister Bethany." I open the door. "I recognized your knock." He gets up from his desk. "Please, come in. Shut the door." We usually leave it open, but this is a confidential meeting.

He seems as nervous as I do, offering me a seat. Matt has teased before that Brother Mathias seems smitten with me. But that's ridiculous. He has a deep respect for Matt and me as a couple. He's mentioned more than once that Matt and I remind him of Priscilla and Aquila, a childless couple in the Bible who befriended and aided the apostle Paul with his ministry. Matt and I are close to Mathias's age. I'm thirty-three and Matt is thirty-four. Brother Mathias is twenty-nine and from the South. He grew up with lots of sisters and is friendly and gentlemanly. Different from men in the West. Not as reserved or stone-faced. "Or masculine," Matt commented once. More than once.

I notice the lavender sprigs on his desk.

"From your garden," he says. He means the garden I started for him. "Freshly cut."

After he prays, I confess that over the course of sixteen years, I've had numerous miscarriages. I tell him I'm embarrassed to say how many, but I do. He looks pained and rubs his forehead. I tell him there isn't a single example in the Bible of a barren woman of prayer who doesn't finally become a mother. For the first time I confess to anyone that my longing for a baby consumes me. In part, because I *haven't* lost faith that my Redeemer will hear my cries. There's a box of tissues on his desk, but he offers me his hankie. I tell him I'm pregnant again. It's been nearly two years. "It's my last chance. A woman knows."

He walks around his desk and sits in the chair next to me. "Bethany," he practically whispers, "I knew you were burdened."

"Who told you?" Maybe my husband already set up a special appointment with Brother Mathias. It doesn't seem like Matt. But he is weary of my pining for a baby. He wants to adopt. He wants to buy land. He wants us to move on, maybe move away.

"'For I have heard a voice as of a woman in travail,'" Brother Mathias quotes. "'The voice of a daughter of Zion.'"

He doesn't try to hide his tears, as Matt always does.

"I heard your voice," he says. "It summoned me west." His countenance is still troubled, but relief flickers in his eyes. "My father, a minister himself, didn't understand why I was moving so far away from him. I told him I heard a voice."

I am speechless and feel more enraptured than during his most passionate sermons.

He continues. "My father feared the voice I heard was just the restlessness of my own spirit. But it wasn't." He pauses, then says with the deep conviction and humility, "Some are called by thousands, others by just one. You are my one, Sister Bethany."

"Sister Bethany," Matt says when I wake him up with a kiss. He calls me that only when joking around in bed or when he feels disgruntled toward the church. He's a field mechanic for Basin Irrigation. He had a long day yesterday with a cranky farmer and a thrice-broken pump, so I insisted he sleep in a bit. I kiss him again. "Rise and shine. You're taking me on a picnic."

"I am?"

"I made chicken, potato salad, and your favorite, apple cake." I plan to tell him the good news that I'm pregnant.

"So, in other words, *you're* taking me." He sits up. "Can I bring a fishing pole?"

"If you bring one for me too."

I used to go fishing with Matt more than I do now. In fact, we even took baby Emmy fishing a few times. Those were the best trips. I still ride along when he goes pheasant hunting. I embroider in the cab of his truck, waiting for him to return across the open fields with a bird or two in his bag. When he hunts deer or elk with his brother, they dress the animals at his brother's because we don't have room. They soak the meat there, and Matt stores our portion in one of his brother's game freezers. He smokes his fish at his parents' place. Sometimes I go over there with him. He keeps his boat at his parents', in one of the large sheds, where he also stores his waders, float tubes, most of his poles, his old dirt bike and snowmobile, along with countless tools, old and new. Soon we'll buy a larger place of our own with a shop and property. We've saved for years, just waiting for the first baby. We planned to have a big family by now.

"Children," the book of Psalms says, "are an heritage of the Lord."

Brother Mathias, after taking time to pray and fast, agreed to perform a public faith healing for me. I'm usually a private person, but sometimes I think I'd do anything for a baby that didn't involve disobeying or denying God. Brother Mathias tried to say all he can do is bless my womb because he doesn't have the gift of healing that the Lord bestows on just a chosen few. I assured him I sensed it in him, and I do. Still, he said we should call it a laying on of hands. He'll ask the congregation to participate. For years the church elders have opted for small, closed-door healings and anointings, so Mathias has to convince them, and I have to persuade Matt. I feel guilty having told another person I'm pregnant before telling my husband. He'll surely be hurt by this, and the longer I wait, the worse.

"What's up, Beth?" Matt asks before we make it halfway to our picnic destination, which is Steamboat Rock State Park. I let him pick the place before we left. He's been unusually quiet on the drive thus far. I sit close to him in the cab of his truck. Steamboat Rock is a mammoth basalt rock with layers that look like steamboat decks. Whenever I come across the verse "As the shadow of a great rock in a weary land," I think about Steamboat Rock before Grand Coulee Dam, and how it used to tower over nothing but endless sage. I've seen photos. Now it towers over the edge of Banks Lake, an enormous reservoir stocked with fish. The park has a green lawn, picnic and camping areas, a sandy beach, boat docks, a few shade trees, and rows of poplars to help block the wind. It's a pretty place as long as I don't think about the rattlesnakes in the sagebrush. I am trying to pretend I didn't hear Matt's question.

"I was excited," he says, "getting the fishing poles ready. Then it dawned on me. The reason for your good mood lately."

"We'll talk at the lake. Let's just enjoy the drive."

"Damn it, Beth." He pulls the truck off the road and shuts off the engine. I hate it when he cusses. "How long have you known?"

"I can't discuss this here."

"How long?" I don't reply. He raises his voice. "How far along?"

"Please. I made rosemary chicken."

He waits minutes, staring first at me, then out the window. His hands are more nicked up than usual from work yesterday. Finally he restarts his truck. I don't scoot away from him, though he probably wishes I would. I wish he were a little excited. God has been merciful to us yet again. We drive in silence. Despite Matt's anger and the knot in my throat, I rest my head on his shoulder. He tenses at first, a reaction I'm not used to, but then he relaxes.

Once we're seated on a blanket under a shade tree—the fishing poles remain in the truck—I tell him how I know this is the last time I'll conceive. When I tell him about the previous pregnancy and miscarriage, he flinches, and then again as I describe to him the two meetings with Brother Mathias and the proposed faith healing. He stands up, but we haven't yet eaten. When he turns to wipe his eyes, guilt tugs my conscience. The wind lifts the corner of the blanket where he sat. Clearing his throat, he says, "I'm going for a walk."

"I'll come too."

He shakes his head. "I'm going to climb the rock."

It's a four-mile hike, vertical in places, with loose sand and rocks and rattlesnakes. He scales rocky embankments while fishing, but this is different. When I try to protest, he reminds me that he and his brother climbed Steamboat Rock more than once as kids. "I used to be kind of adventurous," he says. No, he isn't hungry. I can wait here, he offers, or go home and call his brother to come pick him up. He hands me his truck keys.

"I'll wait," I say. "We need to talk more."

"Go home, Beth." He's never told me to leave before.

Years ago he told me that *I* was his adventure.

Now I watch him walk to the trailhead without me. A younger couple in hiking clothes follows not far behind. I'll wait right here for Matt. I should've packed some calendula oil in the picnic basket, for patience. I look around at the different families in the park: the children with plastic buckets and shovels digging in the sand near the water, probably wishing it was warm enough to swim, the moms filling plates with food, the dads barbecuing or tossing balls. Some of the older kids look bored, and one dad seems angry. But most families appear cheerful. It's spring. Summer is coming. It was a long winter, with half a dozen storms from Canada. There are plenty of boats on the water, people fishing.

Suddenly I feel very alone.

But I'm not alone. There is a baby inside me. And Jesus is always near. And Matt, he would never leave me for good. As Kate did. I never thought she'd stay away, as all my babies have left me so far. But not this one. I sense something different.

Did Brother Mathias really hear my cry clear across the country? He said a voice can travel far in a dry place. Does the older woman looking at me now think she hears my cry? Is my grief that obvious? It's become a barrier between the other women at church and me. This woman picnics with a large group, so why does she keep glancing fretfully in my direction? She looks the age Mother would be if she were still alive. I barely remember her. Kate could recall all kinds of things about Mother: her favorite soap, her thick and chewy homemade noodles, how she'd occasionally play western saloon songs on the piano when our father wasn't home. Kate liked to claim Father ruined Mother. I'm not convinced. When they met, they both worked at a logging camp across the mountains. Her father was in charge. Every morning the men left in trucks to fell trees in remote reaches of forest. They returned each evening. Mother waitressed in the mess hall. Her family had saved money and planned to send her to secretarial school in Tacoma. After my parents ran off and got married, he moved her to eastern Washington, where he was from. Kate alleged that Mother was never the same: that Father, the dust, and the lack of trees almost dried up her spirit. But I think my sister, in her memories, imposed some of her own spunk onto Mother. The ladies at church remember her as quiet. The way this woman now stares unabashedly at me reminds me of the way my neighbor, the Indian lady named Teresa, much younger, watches me. She often has a trailer full of relatives from the reservation, mostly kids whom Matt talks to occasionally. I feel sleepy and lean back against the trunk of the tree to wait for my husband.

I wake up when someone touches my shoulder. "You shouldn't skip meals, ma'am, in your condition." It's Matt. He's forgiven me, I can tell. I sit up. He's dusty, and his hair is tousled and his shirt untucked. He looks like a rowdy boy. I smile. We've both stayed slim despite having no little ones to chase after. The sun has dropped lower in the sky. The shadow of the rock has nearly reached us. His voice cracks as he says, "How about that potato salad?" It may just be that his throat is parched.

"I'm sorry, Matt." He sits down, and I dish up our plates. "I should've told *you* first."

He takes a long drink of water, then says, "You can tell me how *he* plans to heal you."

I explain to him in more detail the ceremony Brother Mathias is proposing. "He thinks a virgin should lay her hands on my belly to purify it."

"Is that a southern thing? Sounds a bit pagan. Or at least Catholic. Isn't Bro Mathias a virgin?"

"Matthew Miller." But I have to admit, I wondered the same thing.

He chuckles as he wolfs down the potato salad and chicken. "Who then?" he asks, trying to be a good sport. "A girl from church—the youth group?"

"Emmy," I say. "That's who first came to my mind."

He stops chewing.

"Ridiculous, I know. We'd never find her."

He swallows hard. "Well, we've never looked for her."

Sometimes I seek so fervently in my dreams for Kate and Emmy that I wake up exhausted in the morning.

Their bus tickets were for California. My sister wouldn't tell me which city. And whether they even made it to California or not, Matt and I never heard. For years I waited for the phone to ring. I still wait. And I still add their names to the prayer chain each week.

"Do you mean drive to California and search?" I ask.

"No. I mean drive downtown to the forbidden library." I see a nasty scratch on his arm and get the chamomile oil and cotton balls from the basket, but he won't let me tend to him. "There are computers at the library," he explains, "that have the new World Wide Web." He says he knows the church views the Web as satanic and a sure sign of the apocalypse, but lately at work he's heard stories on the radio about relatives being reunited through the Web.

"Really, Matt?" He drinks more water. "Do you think?"

"It's worth a shot. But keep in mind, Emmy's almost seventeen. She may not be a virgin. You and I were married at her age."

"Oh, we can worry about that after we find her and Kate." My heart starts to race, as if I too had climbed that rock. "I just want to find them." Could my time in the wilderness be almost over? "Will you go to the library with me on Monday? Will you meet me there on your lunch break?" I wonder if I should ask Brother Mathias first or if maybe we should go to an out-of-town library. "Will you?"

He nods. "But you have to promise me, Beth, that *this* is it. You look ill. My family thinks so." His family thinks I'm crazy. They always have. They are good people, despite not attending church or even saying grace before meals. "You don't realize," he continues. "You're pale. Your hands shake." My hands do shake, but so what, and not always. Not when I play the piano or garden. "You're still a beautiful woman. Don't get me wrong. That's why Bro Mathias—never mind." He stares hard at me. "Do you promise, Beth?"

"I promise." Oh, to see my sister and niece again.

"Understand that I'm getting that surgery, no matter."

"Kate and Emmy." I ignore his comment about surgery. "Do you really think we can find them?" I need to get my garden in order. "Oh, Lord willing."

"He is willing. *We* have to be."

I don't always understand his comments. And Brother Mathias is attracted to my faith, not my face. I almost tell Matt about Mathias hearing my cries, but it's not the right time. It may never be.

"Cake?" I offer, ashamed of my deceit. The list of things I keep from my husband is short, but regrettably, there is starting to be a list.

"Let's save it for at home." He winks. "In bed." He doesn't mean sex. He never wants that when I'm pregnant or when he thinks I look tired. But he likes to hang out in bed with me and do things like eat pie or read me stories from *Outdoor Life*, which isn't a Christian magazine, but we read it anyway. When we were younger and I still taught Sunday school, he liked me to tell him biblical stories in bed with my flannel board and felt characters. I agreed to do it in just my slip, but not naked. It seemed too sacrilegious.

"I could see the Cascades from up there," he says on the drive home. Again I sit close. "Just the outline to the west." He motions. "But what a spectacular view. I'd forgotten." He looks flushed with the same earthly joy that I feel at moments in my garden and that he expresses when he lands a fish. Only now his joy, which I don't think has anything to do with my pregnancy news, seems on such a grand scale that it frightens me: not for his soul, not in the Christian way, but because I can't partake.

"The Lord is manifest," I manage to say.

He reaches for my hand, which shakes. "Darling, if only I could've shown you the view."

It is a Christian wife's most important and rewarding duty to bind her husband to Christ, but for the first time I wonder what Matt's life, rather than his afterlife, would've been like if he'd never met me.

3

Reuben

This is the second time I've seen the girl out watering her aunt's garden by herself. She's from California. My sister told me. She looks lost. Not confident. I assumed California girls were pretty sure of themselves. Pretty damn full of themselves, actually. But what do I know? Up north on the Colville Reservation, where I've lived on and off my whole life, most of the television screens are blurry. I dated a rodeo queen last summer with blonder hair and a better ass than this skinny California girl has. She's not bad, though, and probably pretty up close. The aunt, now: she's crazy. My sister disagrees—thinks the aunt is a healer, or could be. The lady wears a prairie dress and has hair longer than the oldest Indian. Her husband sometimes pauses a moment in his truck after work before getting out and going in to her. He's a nice guy, always nods, waves, or whatever. We've shot the shit more than a couple times about fishing and elk hunting, and once, when I was working on my truck all goddamn afternoon, he came over and gave me a hand. He replaced a vacuum hose and got my truck running right in half an hour, which made me feel like a complete dumb-ass. The girl takes twice as long as her aunt to water the garden and shift the pots, which is perfectly fine with me. Next time she's out by herself, I'll go over and say hey. I've never been shy with girls, even white girls. Right now she sits on the garden bench and looks up at the sky, then over at the row of tall poplar trees that keep the trailer houses in this park from blowing away in the wind. When she looks over at me, I step back from the window. My sister has two sets of chimes hanging on the eaves outside the kitchen window and twice as many kids inside fighting over the remote control and the bag of Doritos I bought for them at the gas station. I hope the girl didn't see me staring at her. She probably looked over because of the racket. I should've waved.

"No fucking way," my cousin Ray says when I show him the girl the next day. She's helping her aunt carry groceries from the car. "Get the fuck out of here." He adjusts his Seattle Mariners ball cap—his prized possession. "And you thought your summer was going to suck." We're smoking cigarettes outside. It's all I smoke, even when Ray offers more. "So, you get down her pants, bro?"

"She's been here less than a week," I say. "And shut up."

"Losing your touch. Me and Benji, man, we're just glad you're away from the rez. Gives us a chance with the ladies this summer."

"Maybe you'll finally get laid." He'd get laid if he'd quit stuffing his face all the time. He weighed two hundred pounds by sixth grade. Kids called him Sasquatch because he barely had a neck. He needs to set his sights a few dozen notches lower if he'll ever get a girlfriend.

"I told you, bro," he says, "your sister took my virginity years ago."

He's kidding. He's the only one I let joke about my sister Teresa because he'd do anything for her—if he could, which he can't without a job. I had two jobs last summer: one with the tribe's Fish and Wildlife Department, which didn't pay but was great experience and will look good on a college application, or so the school counselor said, and another shoveling hot asphalt from the bed of a dump truck, which I got paid for, but under the table because of my age. I'd planned to work again this summer, maybe thinning apple trees or picking cherries on one of the ranches near Chief Joe Dam. Mom and I could really use the cash right now—always—but Teresa begged me to come stay here with her in Moses Lake and help out with her kids since her latest man recently split. What could I say? She practically raised me.

"Can I crash here tonight?" Ray asks. He laughs and adds, "In your sister's bed."

They aren't cousins. Teresa and I have different dads.

"Don't have the gas money to get back to the rez? You fucking loser."

"I'm meeting a guy later."

"Fuck, Ray." He's dealing again. His stint in tribal jail didn't work, obviously, and neither did his forced sweats and drummings with the elders.

I give him the couch and take the floor. He tries to protest, but only halfheartedly, which could be one of his Indian names: Halfheart. The fat fucker looks like my old man sleeping on the couch. I remember how safe it made me feel when I was real young to have my dad sleeping on the couch—night or day, sober or drunk. He'd wake up so easily for me. I just had to touch his shoulder. When Mom tried to wake him to take out the trash, or to go to his job at the mill, or later, when things got real bad, to please go hunting or fishing and put some damn food on the table, he'd keep his eyes shut tight until she walked away cursing him and Teresa's no-good dad in one breath and two languages. Then he'd sit up with a grin and go to work, or not. He'd go hunting, or not. More often he'd go to the casinos, win Mom a couple twenties to get us by, then disappear.

My goal: to not be like my dad. Not dead by the age of thirty-one. Not washed out by the age of twenty-one. People on the rez, even some elders, excuse too much of my dad's bad behavior by thinking of him as a troubled trickster, means well, sometimes awesome Coyote type. Dad was funny as hell, sure, like the real Coyote, whom the Creator—way back—charged with readying the earth for humankind. Dad could also do great impersonations, like Coyote, especially of Mom's boyfriends after my parents split for good. My old man had power, no denying. It came out during stick games and while he was fishing. My best memories are of fishing with my dad, despite his cooler of beer, but there were always root beers floating in the melted ice for me. I loved the stories he'd tell me of things that had happened on the rez before he was born, the pranks he'd pull on the priests at St. Mary's, his dad's Vietnam stories. But above all this, my dad was a drunk. His unquenchable thirst didn't create the Columbia, as Coyote's did. I don't drink alcohol. The stuff scares the shit out of me. Nor do I go out with girls who drink. Ray and Benji wouldn't hang around me, or so they claim, if I weren't related to Ray.

I go to high school in Omak. The Okanogan River divides the town

of Omak in two. The eastern half is on the rez. The high school is on
the west side, the nonrez half. At Omak High, I'm in a program for
kids whose parents didn't go to college (95 percent of the student
body) but who show promise (50 percent) and ambition (5 percent).
The head counselor, who grew up in Seattle, claims no one is too
young to set goals, and we Omak kids, Indian and white, need something to reach for beyond the yearly rodeo and the lumber mills that
keep the area afloat. I want to go to college. Teresa didn't finish high
school, but now she has her LPN certificate. She's my inspiration. I
want a degree in fish biology. I want to help bring the salmon back to
the rivers on the rez, and I want to do more than pray for it. But who
knows? The Colville is five hundred miles upstream from the Pacific.
Nine dams. White and native fishermen on the lower and mid-
Columbia. As I learned working with Tribal Fish and Wildlife last
summer, we're at the end of the food chain so far north. Mom says
Dad dreamed of going to college. She always says shit like that. Sometimes I think she wants me to be my dad, even though she hates him.
The truth is my old man dropped out of high school as soon as he was
old enough to drive. He rodeoed for a bit, even did the Suicide Race a
few years. He never won but always made it to the final night. He also
traveled around for a time in a drum circle. Benji dropped out of high
school. Ray attends school on and off. Sometimes he homeschools,
which a lot of rez kids have to do because of distance. I try to encourage Ray and help him with math.

I play football at Omak High: wingback on offense and strong
safety on defense. As an Indian I'm supposed to like basketball better.
But I love knocking white guys on their asses, and even getting leveled
by them, the yells from the crowd to get back up, and when I catch
that ball, I run like hell—eighty yards for a touchdown last season.
I'm not a big buff guy, even though I weight lift at school. I'm five foot
ten and fast. Coach Wade would start me every game, he said, if I
didn't miss so many practices. I take care of my little sister, Lena, give
her rides and stuff. I also give other relatives rides to wait in line for
food distributions, health services, per capita and settlement checks.
Seems we Indians are always waiting in lines. I wish Coach Wade

yelled at me as much as he does the white boys when they're late for practice. He knows the names of all their parents.

Mom is trying hard for me. We moved back to Omak my freshman year of high school. It's not easy on her or my little sister. Both would rather live deeper on the rez, even though my sister's half white, and we lived here in Moses Lake for one year of my childhood. When we first moved back to Omak, Mom stocked shelves at Walmart and then blended ice cream at Dairy Queen, where teenagers hang out, which was embarrassing. Now she works at a bar, serving whiskey to men who remind her too much of my dad. Next door to the bar is a Laundromat, where Mom goes on her breaks—my little sister and I meet her there sometimes—because bleach smells better than sour beer and stale smoke. We make the rent each month, but barely.

Ray begins to snore on the couch, so I head outside for a cigarette. Everyone else is sleeping. It's eleven. If it were daytime, I'd instantly look west for an outline of the Cascades before remembering I'm a little too far south and east to see the mountains. But on superclear days, you can see Mount Rainier from here. The sprinklers click all day in the potato field across the road from the trailer park, which is a good five miles from downtown and bordered on two sides by poplar trees. It's dustier here than in Omak, and the wind's constant. Up north the wind gusts more, but at least there are reprieves. The lake, around which this town is built, is located at the tail end of a giant irrigation project that begins at Grand Coulee Dam. It reeks with farm runoff, and there's so much algae on the lake's surface I could walk across like Christ Jesus.

I wonder if the girl is up next door. Her aunt's trailer and my sister's trailer sit exactly parallel to each other, and they both face north, toward the rez. I smoke on the front porch. The back steps face the front porch of the aunt's trailer. Singlewides have two bedrooms, one on each end. The girl is no doubt staying in the nonmaster bedroom located on the end by the gravel driveway. A strip of burned grass used to separate our driveways, but the aunt planted lavender bushes there. Teresa takes clippings when she's in an especially good mood.

I pretend to be grabbing something out of my truck to get a better view of the girl's window. The main light is off, but some smaller light glows in there. I wonder if she's bored. I wonder what she's doing here. The aunt—I forget her name or never knew it—doesn't have a TV or a radio. Teresa said the aunt attends a Baptist church that forbids watching TV and prohibits pants for women. The girl wears pants, even shorts that I wish were shorter. And I noticed she doesn't go to church with her aunt and uncle, who go all the time. Why doesn't she? Maybe she's an atheist. Not that I know what an atheist looks like, but I picture glasses and a lab coat. Maybe she's a rebel. In Omak, rebel white girls either dye strips of their already bleached hair pink and wear barely any clothes, or they go Goth by piercing their lips and brows, wearing tons of eyeliner and layers of black clothes. I stay away from both. Their pissed-off, often laid-off dads scare the crap out of me. They blame Indians—the close proximity of the Colville Reservation, just across the Okanogan River—for their woes. And their hoes, as Benji says. We blame whites for the dams that keep the salmon from returning to the rez. It's still fucking cowboys versus Indians up there in Omak and the other towns around the Colville.

I hear a couple coyotes yipyapping. The girl must've heard them also because she flips on the main light for a few minutes. She doesn't peek through the blinds after shutting the light back off. I wonder what she sleeps in? God, what am I—thirteen? Getting hard just thinking about a girl in bed. I go inside, take a shower. Another goal: not to get a girl pregnant. Both Mom and Teresa had babies before eighteen. I won't do that to a girl. Or me. It's simple, really, or it should be. Wear a damn condom even if a chick says she's on the pill. I went through boxes of condoms with Danielle, the rodeo queen, not that I'm complaining. She had a lot of responsibilities that her parents never let her shirk, mostly riding her horse in parades and roundups and speaking at camps and youth meetings and every 4-H and FFA club in Washington State, it seemed. She liked "to let her hair down" with me, or so she said. I think she meant "take her shirt off." Maybe Danielle was just slumming it with me to mess with her parents, as Benji insisted, the asshole.

Tomorrow is my sister's day off. I told her I'd go to the Laundromat because her washer is broken and her back sore from lifting patients. She can veg in front of the TV, watch Home Shopping Network or reruns of her favorite mystery shows. Besides, I barely have any clean clothes myself. I couldn't get her washer to spin. If Ray could fix it, Teresa might actually let him kiss her on the cheek or at least hang out with her at the Fourth of July Pow Wow next month. Instead, before he fell asleep, he offered to move the washer outside. She told him we weren't on the rez. The manager doesn't allow appliances on the front porch, even if it is only a trailer park. He then offered to haul it to the rez and dump it. "Jesus," she said.

Sunday morning. I've been waiting. The aunt and uncle leave for church. The girl immediately opens the blinds that the aunt keeps closed all day. Next time I check, she's outside. I have to at least go introduce myself and find out her name. She must be so bored. I am. And I have a TV and a truck. Tomorrow I'm going to start running three miles a day—and stop smoking—to get in shape for football. I've been doing push-ups, sit-ups, squats, but I need a field for sprints and monkey bars for pull-ups. The girl wears a hippie-looking sun hat, Hollywood shades, and she reads a book on the little stone bench in her aunt's garden. Precious. Ray would splooge his pants. Maybe I shouldn't disturb her. She's not really concentrating—keeps looking at the poplars, whose leaves rustle in the wind, and playing with her necklace. I go out the back door, or attempt to. It sticks, since it's totally off-limits for the kids and never used. The girl looks up. I jump off the last two steps and go over to her.

"Hey," I say. She stands up with the book in her hands, then turns and puts it cover down on the bench, as if to hide the title. She takes off her hat before turning back around. "How's it going? I'm Reuben." She blushes deep red. Wow. I haven't seen a girl blush like that since sixth grade. "You didn't have to get up."

"It's not very good—the book, I mean." She's prettier up close than I expected. "I'm Emmy."

"You from California?"

"Yeah." She touches her ponytail, which is low and off to one side. "And you?"

"Here. I'm from here."

"Of course." She smiles. "Sorry." Definitely pretty. Those teeth. What do they put in the milk down there?

"Sorry for what?" Now I feel nervous. Keep it cool. "You from L.A.?"

"Never even been there," she admits. "Lame, huh?"

"I've never been there either."

"I'm from Sacramento."

"The capital, right?" She nods. "Palm trees?"

"And sycamores."

The diamonds in her heart necklace look real. Cheap imitations can be bought at Walmart for under ten bucks or on HSN for under twenty plus shipping. A cowboy at the bar bought one for Mom. She exchanged it for a new toilet brush, a can of Folgers, and three two liters of Coca-Cola. A married white man once bought my sister a cross necklace with a real diamond in it. Are this girl's teeth real? They're distracting.

"Visiting your aunt and uncle?" I ask. "How long's it been?"

"I don't remember."

"That long, huh?"

"I mean, I don't remember them at all." Her voice gets shaky, or it's been that way. "My aunt thought I would, but I was just a baby. They're so nice to me. I wish I did."

"You okay?" She's scared shitless so far from home.

"Sure." She takes a moment to get control. I give it to her. She's way more fragile than I expected, except those teeth. I want to run my tongue over them. "I was born here."

"No shit."

"That's the first swearword I've heard all week."

"My apologies."

"No. It's refreshing." She takes off her sunglasses. Her eyes are blue. No, gray. She squints them in the sun. I can't tell. I like brown-eyed, dark-haired Indian girls, obviously, but white chicks—give them to me straight: blond hair, blue eyes.

"What book are you reading?" I ask. "It looks pretty thick."

"Um—" She looks back at the book on the bench. "It's boring."

"Can I see it?" She hands it to me. Her fingernails are painted a funky turquoise, but she doesn't wear a lot of makeup. I read the title. *"Sister Carrie.* Is it about a nun?"

"No." She smiles.

"What's it about?"

"It's boring."

"You said that already." I can hear the kids thumping around in the trailer. They were entranced in cartoons when I snuck out.

"My mom's a college English teacher. She makes me read old literature."

"Ouch. So, what's the book about?"

"A girl."

"Named Carrie."

We both laugh.

"She moves to Chicago during the Industrial Revolution. She compromises herself."

"That part's not boring, I'm sure."

She blushes again and puts her sunglasses back on. I almost fucking blush. I'm standing in a garden discussing literature with a professor's kid. What the fuck?

"It's about railroad strikes and stuff," she says. "Carrie becomes an actress."

"And lives happily ever after?"

The thumping gets louder in my sister's trailer. The kids must be hungry.

"Not at all. Dreiser is no Jane Austen."

"Who?"

"No one," she backtracks. "Never mind. Sorry."

"Sounds like you've read the book already." I examine its bulk. "Can I borrow it?"

"For real?"

"Indians read books, on occasion." Hell, some even memorize the Bible.

"I didn't know you were Indian." She sounds excited. "I thought Hispanic. I have a friend, Harpreet. She's Punjabi."

I start laughing. *She's* refreshing. "I'm American Indian."

"Oh, my God. I feel like an idiot."

"I'll call you Columbus." My nephews and nieces start appearing at the windows, pointing and giggling.

"Please, don't."

"So, can I borrow Mr. Dreiser's"—I flip to the back cover— "'great American novel of insight into appetite and innocence'?"

"Sure."

"You want to hang out sometime?"

"I have a boyfriend—in California." She touches her necklace.

Of course she does. "I said hang out, not make out."

I hope the third blush is a charm. It takes her a moment to respond. "It will have to be when my aunt and uncle are at church."

"This evening then?" I suggest. "Same place? I'll bring a lawn chair."

"Yeah. The bench is kind of small—pathetic."

"Solid, though."

"A solitary stone."

She's—what do you call it?—witty. Or maybe just goofy. She's cool.

"It looks lonely," I observe.

"But not *too* homely."

"In need of a friend," I say.

"I *am*." She smiles wide.

Damn. What was that?

I'm out of breath by the time I make it back inside my sister's trailer, and not just because the kids locked the back door and then the front door and then the back door again. Little shits. Even the older boy, Kevin, who usually sides with me because I call him bro. That girl, Emmy, her name should be Emily. She reads books in gardens, for Christ's sake, but, then again, not romances or books about prairie girls, but a revolution and a compromised girl. Has she been compromised? California girls. They do take your breath away. But no, she was born here. She blushes but tells me my cuss words are refreshing.

I need a sweat lodge. Virgil built one in his garage in Omak. He's an elder but doesn't preach or ask questions or try to talk to me about my dad. As soon as my sister comes home for lunch, I'll go for a hard run, but she'll probably bring cheap tacos from the taco van, which are almost as good as "Indian tacos" made with fry bread. Hispanic? That's what most white people around here think, with my short hair, or prefer to think. It's easier for them to dislike immigrants than *be* the immigrants. An Indian from India? Oh, shit, that would bust my dad's gut.

It's the first time in a long time I've wanted to tell him something.

Most of the time I'm glad he's not around anymore. He died when I was thirteen. I spent my whole childhood waiting for that man to come home or to sober up. Sometimes I see my dad's ghost sitting next to me when I'm driving alone in his old truck: only on the rez, those long miles between towns and usually where the land opens up, and most often at dusk when everything's gray. Of course that's also the time of day most people in the area see Sasquatch. Dad used to claim, when he'd come home smelling, that he had a Sasquatch lover. My dad's ghost likes to rummage through the glove box. *Sorry, old man, no whiskey.* I put my football picture in the glove box once, nothing else, so he'd have to look at it. He did. He even put it in his shirt pocket. The next day it was back in the glove box. If there's a girl with me in his—my—truck, he doesn't appear. "Give the boy some space," he used to tell Mom.

"I picked up your dad the other day," an elder said to me a year ago, when I was staying far out on the rez for a few nights with my aunt. "By Coulee Dam."

"You don't say?" How did he want me to respond? My dad's restlessness had caused enough pain. And he wasn't the first elder—and certainly not the first Indian—to have seen my dad's ghost and stopped to tell me. I almost suggested he and the other elders start a column in the tribal newspaper for sightings of my old man, put it right next to the column for neighborhood bear sightings.

"You're a good kid, Reuben. He would've been proud."

"Sure thing."

"You coming to the meeting tonight at the longhouse?"

It had been the first weekend of summer break, but I said, "I got homework."

He asked after my mom and sisters, then warned me not to get too caught up in the world of the white man.

"You want me to go my dad's route instead?"

I didn't mean to sound rude. He had known my grandfather. I should've just let him put his old hand on my shoulder, invite me to drum or to go pray by the creek with him and his wife for the salmon to return.

I'm back from my run and sweaty as hell. "Hit the shower, kid," Teresa says, meeting me on the front porch. "I've got to leave in five."

"Go," I tell her. "I need to cool down first."

"You're supposed to jump into a cold river right away."

"What river around here?" The reservation is bordered on three sides by rivers, and the Sanpoil flows just east of the center. "You must mean an irrigation canal. And no, thanks. I'm no farm kid." Not only do the farm kids here swim in the ditches all summer, but they fish the spillways and canals in the fall for trout. My sister, for some reason, likes how both this town and the lake are named after Chief Moses. Or at least she's not bothered by it. I think it's a kind of insult. But Teresa can be surprisingly chill about certain things, like giving enemas to old dudes at work or feeding fruit cocktail to crazies or the fact that none of her kids' dads pays child support. Sure, the dad of my older niece, Grace, leaves a cooler of salmon on Teresa's porch a few times a year, but that's not quite enough. Teresa is the complete opposite of chill with me about girls. She's nosy and bossy as shit. She and I are both part Moses-Columbia on Mom's side. Dad's a mix of Sanpoil and Okanogan—hence our last name, Tonasket, who was a famous Okanogan chief. I'm a Colville Confederated Tribes mutt, and proud of it.

"There's tacos on the counter," she says. "Kevin insisted we leave you three."

"He's my bro."

She lights a cigarette and offers me one, which I take. She wears scrubs with cartoon character prints. Not very attractive. But maybe a good thing. Teresa used to be kind of pretty, and still is, I guess, though she's chubbier now than ever—but hell, she's had four kids. I think guys like her, and they do, for two reasons, one of which a brother shouldn't mention, but to quote Ray, "*Sesame Street* is brought to you today by the letters *Double D*." The other reason is she's kind of fun and open and cool, though far from hip in her Minnie Mouse scrubs.

"The kids claim you have a new girlfriend next door."

"We exchanged a few words is all."

"Be careful."

Of what? I hand her my cig so I can take off my shirt and wipe my face. "You'll be home by six, at the latest?"

"Got a date with the California girl?"

"She has a boyfriend." If it's any of her business.

"You stink, quarterback. Hit the shower."

"I'm not the quarterback."

"You are in my playbook." She chants in a mocking tone, "Go, Omak Pioneers!"

"Go, make money!" I chant back.

I know she's proud of me. Prouder than Mom is. I'm superproud of her. This full-time LPN job she landed here at the county hospital, and not despite her being Indian but because, is the most secure job she or Mom has ever had. Teresa deserves a break, and she has the perfect personality for a health care worker. She's not a bitch, and like I said, she can be chill, but also she's tough enough to ignore the snide comments by the other female LPNs and RNs. And no dude, be he patient, orderly, nurse, or even doctor, is going to pinch her ass and get away with it, unless he's decent looking and available, of course, and she's feeling lonely. She can come off as abrasive at times—especially to white people, who probably deserve it—but deep down she's a softy. And she's proficient, despite her cluttered trailer and bad track record with men. Half of our relatives, and most of the Indian girls Teresa went to school with, judge her for living off the rez, but she claims she had to get away from the high drama and drugging. It's far less upsetting for her to work at a hospital filled mostly with white patients than sick Indians who've lost their will. She worries, though, about her kids not learning traditions from the elders.

"Go to work," I tell her. "I'll watch your bratty kids."

She drives away in her clunky Toyota van, which I've tried to fix, but can't without money. My truck is easier to work on because it's a Chevy and Dad took great care of it. I don't have time for classes like auto shop at school with all the college prep work. I smoke another cigarette before showering. I'm starving. While the two younger kids nap in the bedroom they all four share, the older two and I watch a *Cosby Show* rerun marathon on TV. I give them the couch so they can stretch out and I hope fall asleep too. My sister's latest man took the La-Z-Boy recliner with him, and she can't get credit at the local furniture store for two more months, so that leaves the floor. The whole time I'm thinking of Emmy's teeth and her brightly colored fingernails and her shaky voice when she talked about not remembering her aunt and uncle.

I doze off to the sound of Theo Huxtable, the only son on *The Cosby Show*, being his usual dumb-ass self, but I don't dream. When I wake up, Dad's sitting on the couch between Kevin and Grace. What the hell? They aren't even really his grandkids. But he loved Teresa as if she were his daughter. Mom always gives him credit for that. Still, my first reaction is to tell him to get the fuck out. The last thing Teresa's kids need is to fall for another man who won't, or can't, be there for them. My old man has never appeared to me off the rez, and I don't like it one bit. Truth is, he shouldn't be appearing at all. He should've moved completely into the spirit world by now. He watches Theo on TV, still being a dumb-ass. He's smiling. Then he looks at me—full on, which certainly isn't a good thing—and his smile fades. He does some gesture with his hand, a traditional gesture of warning that I didn't know I knew until now.

Then he too fades.

4

Emmy

The night before my flight to Washington, I woke to find Mom soaking in a bathtub of water gone cold. She wasn't a bath person like me. She preferred showers. "Mom," I said, opening the pinstriped curtain slowly to give her time to cover her private parts, which she didn't, "what are you doing?"

She said she was thinking about the last time her mother was dipped into a lake for healing. "She was in such pain, Emmy, that even the wind hurt her." Mom claimed the lake water was so salty that people could easily float or bob away. Had her mother bobbed away? She said no more, and I cruelly didn't ask her to. When she refused to get out of the bathtub after I leaned over her and drained the water, I called Spencer.

"Don't worry about your mom," Spencer said to me on the way to the airport the next morning. Mom asked him to take me. She rarely asked him for favors. We were in his work truck with a canvas bag of tools between us on the seat and rolls of blueprints on the dash. He designed and built houses. "I'll take care of her."

I wasn't worried about Mom, not really.

His beeper went off, but he silenced it. Clearing his throat, he said, "I want you to know that I don't agree with her sending you away like this." I knew he'd been wanting to say that to me, and more. We crossed the American River. "Or with her forcing you to take part in that bizarre ceremony." He took a drink of coffee from his travel mug before continuing. "And I don't know *why* she lied to you for all these years about your dad." My eyes got watery. "Parents do strange things, I guess, trying to protect their kids." Why couldn't there be more traffic this morning? Or tule fog like in winter to stall travel? Spencer had never talked to me quite so bluntly about Mom. Usually he just intimated when he thought Mom was being unfair. Connor, on the other hand, often asked me what my mom's fucking problem was. Spencer and I were almost at the turnoff for I-5 North and the airport. I prayed his truck would break down or we'd get in a minor accident. "I wish to hell I had a say in the matter," he continued. I wished to hell he was my dad so I could tell him how much I loved him.

I hoped he would propose to Mom while I was away. I suspected he'd proposed to her once before, but she'd shot him down and I didn't see him for a month. If Mom shot him down a second time, I might never see him again. I stared over at him, then out the window at the rice fields that surrounded the airport. Maybe Mom had shot Spencer down because she still loved Jamie—and not *just* because she was stubborn and independent. Maybe if my farmer father had really died in a tractor accident, she would've married Spencer and we would've already been a family.

"Hey, kiddo," he said, smiling. "Can you keep a secret?" I nodded. "I bought your mom and me tickets to Europe."

I couldn't help but smile too. "That's awesome." *He* was awesome.

Mom had always wanted to travel to England to see the birthplaces of her favorite writers. And to France to tour the Louvre. But she hardly ever let Spencer spend his money on us: a few trips to the Bay Area, once to Tahoe. I felt sick as the airport came into full view. Before getting out of his truck, Spencer gave me an envelope with a dozen prepaid calling cards and more than enough cash for an early ticket home, if need be, or in case of an emergency, or just for fun.

"I'm really scared," I admitted to him at the departure gate. My hands shook. "I don't want to go. I can't do this."

"You'll be okay. You're strong like her." I wasn't strong in the least, but I hugged him a long time for saying so and because I'd given Mom such a short hug. "I love you," he said to me for the first time. I'd felt his love from the beginning.

The card he'd given me last year for Christmas (I didn't show it to Mom), along with the paid receipt for driving lessons, had read, "To make up for not being there when you took your first steps or when you learned to ride a bike." Mom had gotten upset at the prepaid driving lessons, claiming it wasn't her boyfriend's place to decide when I learned to drive a car. She thought it was too dangerous in a big city, despite the fact that she hated my having to take public transit home from school two days a week. The dangerous city excuse was also the one she used for never teaching me to ride a bicycle.

I didn't hide my tears now as I had at Christmas. Panicking, I asked him, "What if you and Mom break up while I'm gone?"

He knew what I was getting at. "You'll always be part of my life, kiddo." I wanted to believe him. "I've known you too long to walk away." His voice strained. "Okay?"

I handed him the origami bird I'd made for him last night when I couldn't sleep. I'd also made one for my aunt and placed both carefully in my backpack.

He took the paper bird but seemed unsure how to hold it. Then he hugged me again. "Call me if you need anything," he said. "Try to think of this summer as an adventure. *Your* adventure, Emmy. Not your mom's. Not from a book. *Yours.*"

WELCOME TO SPOKANE, the airport sign read. Some adventure. I wished the sign read, WELCOME TO PARIS or WELCOME TO NEW DELHI (and I were older and braver).

The inside of the Spokane airport made the Sacramento one look spacious and almost sophisticated, like airports in movies. Then again everything was still a bit blurry from Connor's Vicodin pill, which I'd taken early in the flight to calm myself down after the aromatherapy smelling salts (bought in the shop below our apartment) had quit working and I nearly hyperventilated. For about thirty glorious minutes the drug had calmed me down. It had also made me feel overly tender toward the old couple sitting beside me with their creased pants and spotted hands. When the plane hit some turbulence, I almost asked them if I could call them Grandma and Grandpa, but then I passed out cold. I now had an hour layover in Spokane and then a twenty-minute "hop, skip, and jump," the stewardess said, to the airport in Moses Lake.

Home felt so far away. I needed the courage of a Brontë heroine to complete this journey alone. My stomach fell when I noticed two college-age girls wearing maroon WSU T-shirts. That was the university my dad had gone to instead of taking care of my mom. I'd looked up WSU in the counseling office at school during finals and copied down the phone number for the records office—in case I actually got up the nerve to search for my dad. Instead of finding him, I'd rather be back in my bedroom with the purple felt SACRAMENTO KINGS pennant that Spencer bought for me. If only I could rewind time, a few days even. I wasn't strong. I was wimpy. I could never board a bus as Mom had and leave everything behind. One day I hoped to travel overseas, but for now even the thought of moving away to college at the end of next summer terrified me. I loved my bedroom too much, our apartment, the shop downstairs, Connor, his TV, the way he'd often watch me instead of the screen, my mom.

Mom should've been here with me, despite her busy work schedule and our lack of funds for an additional plane ticket. The fact that she wasn't seemed more unimaginable than my cruelty toward her in the last week or so. Not only had I started referring to her sister as "that born-again lady," which I could tell hurt Mom's feelings, but I also told her bluntly that Jamie was related to me, not her, and I'd look for him over the summer if I wanted to. Swearing to help, she begged me to wait until next summer, after I graduated from high school. I didn't need her help or consent. I did, however, wish she were here to introduce me to my aunt and uncle and then to stick around for a few days, at least, to make sure I behaved correctly. I'd never been around a relative. Mom was better with people than I was. She was reserved, even with her wit, but not shy. She didn't blush. She could be blunt as heck but was always polite to service workers and clerks. With her students, for the most part, she had a great rapport. I'd seen her in action. Even with her least favorite types—snotty rich girls, potheads, young boys who wanted mothering, and flirty male students of all ages—she handled herself in a professional manner.

To give Mom even more credit (why?), she'd been trying desperately to provide me instructional information—"travel tips for my

summer vacation"—and with the umph of her wit. I hadn't been impressed. After twice warning, "It's a whole other world up there,
honey," she went off: "The high school color is camouflage; cars,
trucks, and cheese are American; county fairs and rodeos are considered highly cultural events; crockpots full of wild game and cream of
mushroom soup is as culinary as it gets; Grand Coulee Dam is their
mecca." She claimed men up north went to the slopes and the coulees
(what was a coulee? who cared?) hunting and fishing on the weekends
while their wives stayed home slowly going insane trying to keep the
dust from settling on their assembled furniture. I rolled my eyes. She
said she wanted my stay with her sister to be as comfortable as possible. "Survivable." All I had to do was survive the summer, and then
everything would be back to normal. But what about Connor? She
couldn't control him. On the phone with her sister, Mom laid down
some conditions. She tried to assure me that she wasn't just throwing
me to the wolves (Christians). First and foremost, other than for the
healing ceremony, I wasn't allowed to attend Bethany's fundamentalist church, where I'd be judged as harshly for wearing mascara as for
tattooing "the mark of the beast" (I didn't even ask) on my forehead. If
curiosity got the best of me, I was to look up a nondenominational-
type church in the phone book and go to services there. But she hoped
I wouldn't. I could take as many world religion classes as I wanted to
in college—"at Berkeley." I laughed at *that*. She didn't ask what I found
so amusing, and I'm not sure I knew myself. I knew she'd always been
down on spirituality and tried to make me that way. It wasn't fair. I
was "allowed" religion only in an academic setting? Something changed
between us in that moment: in my laugh and her silence.

I refused to think about that change in this nowhere airport, where
I felt sleepy and alone. Mom said when I was very young, she'd wake
to find me wandering around the apartment, looking for someone, a
woman whose name I didn't know but whose absence I felt so heavily
I couldn't go back to sleep or fully wake up. Was that true? I wish I
could say that I recognized my aunt right away as the woman I used
to look for, but I didn't.

Mom promised I'd have no problem finding Bethany at the airport in Moses Lake because she'd probably be the only person in the tiny lobby. She claimed the airport was used more as a parking lot for crop dusters than a real port of transportation. But just in case, I should expect long, straight hair pulled back tightly in a ponytail or bun, no earrings, a simple homemade dress, hemmed far below the knees, with a stretched-out, dull-colored cardigan overtop. Mom and I bought most of our clothes used at consignment stores or occasionally new at Target or on clearance at the malls. We were fashion conscious, not obsessed.

But I recognized my aunt immediately because she looked like Mom, so much so, in fact, that at first I couldn't register what was happening, and when she took me into her arms, I began to cry. Which wasn't at all how I'd pictured the scene.

"Oh, Emmy. Don't cry." But she too was crying. "Let's sit a minute." She said she wanted to get a better look at me (to make sure I was a virgin?) before we drove home. There were only a dozen seats in the entire lobby. All empty. We sat down, and I tried to stop crying, but her smell was familiar. "I never meant for you to journey alone," she said. "I've been praying all day for you." She hadn't let go of my hand. "You must be so scared."

I wondered where my luggage was—it was all I had of home.

Gaining composure, I said, "I'm okay."

"Your mom kept saying on the phone how brave you were."

Mom wished I were brave. There's a difference. "I'm not."

"You *are*—and so pretty." She squeezed my hand before letting go. "I've never flown." She whispered as if the lobby were full of people who would be surprised by her confession. "Can you believe it?"

"It doesn't matter." Nothing mattered in survival mode. *Right, Mom?* A man in coveralls started carrying in the luggage for the handful of passengers. He placed it in the corner.

"You must miss your mom and the fellowship of your friends."

"I'm fine." *Fellowship?* Her dress was baggy and looked homemade, but the dainty flowered print was pretty. Her hair, blond and straight like mine, was pulled back firmly in a ponytail, but I could tell she'd curled the ends. Mom had wavy auburn hair that she didn't have to curl. I'd always been jealous.

Beth reached into her purse and pulled out a small amber-colored bottle with a handmade label, "peppermint." "I made this for you. In case the flight gave you a headache."

I did have a slight headache and cotton mouth—aftereffects, I assumed, from Connor's Vicodin pill.

"Rub a little on your temples every few hours," she instructed, "until your headache is gone."

In the shop below our apartment there was an entire section devoted to essential oils and another to herbs. Mom didn't really believe in the healing abilities of either, especially after she had sent me down there once in desperation to check for a toothache remedy and I spent seven dollars on ground cloves, which we already had in our spice rack. I wondered if Mom knew Bethany believed in alternative medicine and not just in "bogus" faith healings. Mom hadn't said anything, so probably not. I liked knowing something about her sister that she didn't. "Thank you." I opened the bottle to smell. I figured I'd wait to apply the oil to my temples until we got to Beth's house and I could clip back my bangs.

"Here, let me." She took the bottle. I looked over at the few other people in the lobby. They were busy getting their suitcases. "Hold your bangs up." I was embarrassed, but at least we weren't at the Spokane airport. She rubbed gently in a circular motion. I loved the feel of her touch as much as I did her smell. The oil cooled my temples, then warmed them. Her massaging me was a little too intimate too soon, but no different from the time Mom and I went to a day spa (courtesy of Spencer's secretary). Mom had felt uncomfortable at the spa, which made me uncomfortable, having Korean women rub "our big white feet" for minimum wage.

My whole face felt warm now. Flushed. Beth's face was extremely pale, but probably because she wore absolutely no makeup. "You look like your mom," she commented.

I wasn't told that very often. "So do you." She touched her hair. I told her I had a gift for her also. I pulled from my backpack the origami bird I'd made. It was a little crumpled.

"Oh, Emmy! You *made* it?" I nodded. "I've never—from paper?" I nodded again. "I know right where I'll hang it." She admired it some more. "Thank you so much." Mom had no patience when it came to doing origami. She said she found paper folding about as fun as embroidery. "Now let's get your luggage."

Mom had to buy me suitcases for this trip. We didn't own anything larger than a weekender, which Mom said was pathetic, given how much we talked about traveling and how we hung up postcards depicting faraway places. I wondered if Spencer told Mom yet about the tickets to Europe.

"I'll get the big suitcase." I hurried over to it, a little ashamed now of its bulk.

"Your throat sounds dry," she said with worry. "There's a pop machine out front."

I told her I was fine. I thought Mom was the only person who called soda pop.

"It's dry and dusty here," Beth remarked, as if it were she who'd just stepped off the plane. "Your mom reminded me of that." She quickened her pace. "She asked me to keep you hydrated."

Was I five? And it was certainly dry in Sacramento. The whole valley baked in summer and early fall. Our apartment didn't have air conditioning, so for a third of each year Mom and I went practically naked around the apartment (when Spencer wasn't there), especially in late afternoon and evening. Had Mom been bossy to her sister on the phone? Maybe older sisters were always bossy, but I felt strangely defensive of my aunt, whom, until a month ago, I hadn't even known existed. "I thought of you every day," she said as we wheeled the suitcases outside. It *was* drier here than in Sacramento, but not quite as hot. Had she really thought of me every day? "God finally answered my prayers. He brought you back to me."

Mom would contend, "More like technology and pilots."

But the truth was—though I wouldn't realize this until later—I *had* felt summoned: by my aunt and her prayers; by the lake in which my grandmother had bobbed in pain; by my dad's conscience, or lack thereof, and his hills; by the wind; by a neighbor boy who would tell me only the second time I ever talked to him that the color of my eyes (a drab gray, I'd always thought) reminded him of the sky up north on the reservation, right before nightfall, when Sasquatch warned hunters to get out of the woods and coyotes roamed along the roads and fences white men built over ancient paths.

The ride from the airport to my aunt's house took about twenty minutes, but she drove more slowly than the senior citizen drivers who irritated Mom as she sped between junior college campuses, drinking gas station coffee and trying to make it to her staggered classes and faculty meetings on time. At first I could only see the lake (Moses Lake, which was also the name of the town) down a desert cliff, but then suddenly we were beside it. It was better from a distance, though I admired the two weeping willows I saw by the shore. Mom said eastern Washington was treeless, and she was right as far as oak, sycamore, and palm trees go, but there were rows of poplars everywhere and occasional strands of dusty, sage-colored trees called Russian olives (I asked later), which I found pretty, despite their muted hue. We didn't drive through town. My aunt said we'd go tomorrow or the next day. For a while the landscape was nothing but field after field of sagebrush, then canals, irrigation sprinklers, row crops, horses, and stacks of hay bales as large as the singlewide trailers we'd pass here and there. We turned off the paved road and onto a gravel one at the sign QUAIL RUN MOBILE HOME PARK.

Before touring the rest of the trailer, I was shown the room where I'd be staying. "The bed was your mom's," Beth said. "And the crib was yours." She touched her belly. She didn't look pregnant. Was I supposed to tell her congratulations? Should I call her Aunt right away? I had a card for her and gifts from Mom in my luggage. I'd never seen Mom spend more time picking out items in stores, and she refused to buy her sister anything on sale or clearance. I put my small suitcase and backpack on the floor by the bed. We left the big suitcase in the trunk for Matt to bring in when he got home from work, though

I said I could easily get it. Besides the crib and bed, there was a dresser in the room. All our furniture in Sacramento was also secondhand, but Mom liked to repaint. My dresser in Sac was a cheery French blue. On top of this unassuming dresser sat a vase of freshly cut lavender (how nice) and a pair of glowing ceramic hands held together in prayer (strange). There was also a desk that looked brand new. Beth noticed me eyeing it. "Matt just built that for you." She said Mom told her I'd need a place to study for my college entrance exams. "You're really smart, I hear. That doesn't surprise me."

Jeez, Mom. "I do tons of homework, is all." I'd brought my SAT study guides and flash card packs, but I didn't need a desk. At home Mom and I used the dining table as our communal desk, despite the desks sitting unused in our separate bedrooms.

"The dresser is empty, and half the closet—for your clothes." I apologized for having so many. "No, I'm glad you do. Your mom has taken good care of you." Her eyes got watery. "Thanks for coming, Emmy. I know you probably didn't want to."

"I wanted to meet you."

"I bet Kate has told you all kinds of stories about her and me growing up."

Mom hadn't wanted to tell Beth on the phone that I never knew of her existence. She said it would crush her little sister. And no doubt. It nearly crushed me. "I'd love to hear more," I said, trying to sound genuine. At eight, eleven, or even fifteen, Beth's stories would've been a Disney Channel dream come true, and I still planned to find out whatever I could about Mom's leaving Moses Lake with an infant and a single suitcase—but at that moment, I just wasn't interested in anything that involved my mom.

"Your uncle is so excited to see you. I'm glad we had time first."

On the wall above the crib hung faded pink wooden letters that spelled my name. I noticed them when I first walked into the bedroom but tried not to look at them. The fact that my aunt had kept them up all these years tugged at my heart and made me feel guilty for lying about my virginity. On the phone, Connor would say it was eerie, like in a horror movie, the way Beth had kept the letters on the wall. I disagreed. The glowing hands night-light, kept on day and night, creeped me out a bit at first, but I'd come to love its warm glow.

"Do you remember those?" she asked now, pointing to the letters. I didn't have to lie and say I did because she took my hand. "Matt told me not to overwhelm you right away with all your old baby stuff." She smiled. "Come on then. I'll show you the rest of the house."

Mom had cautioned that Beth's trailer might seem suffocating to me, even with the air conditioning, which she said would run 24/7 (it did, but on low) because of cheap electricity from Grand Coulee Dam. Mom couldn't believe, after all these years, that Beth and Matt still lived in the same singlewide trailer. Didn't we live in the same apartment? She said the trailer wasn't cluttered when she'd lived there with them because they barely had furniture or money to buy stuff, but by now, she warned, it might be. Most mobile homes were cluttered with junk, she said, as if she knew, which she didn't because her sister's trailer wasn't cluttered—at least not with junk. The kitchen was crowded with oil-making tools and bundles of drying herbs, which excited me. The master bedroom held Beth's sewing machine and fabric supplies, as well as Matt's fly-tying station, both of which were probably moved in there from the extra bedroom to make room for me. Beth's living room was actually a little bare for my taste: no stacks of books, no paisley throws, no wooden crate of old *National Geographic* magazines bought at the library for a dime each, no basket full of rolled and folded maps.

Matt was great. I liked him instantly, and I'd been worried, having never before lived in a house with a man. My lunch buddy Hedda hated her dad and was glad he worked in the Bay Area during the week, and Harpreet seemed afraid of her father. Mom hadn't given me any precautions concerning Matt, which I didn't realize was a positive thing. "You've grown," he teased upon first seeing me. "A few feet at least." He lightened the mood, which was what Spencer tried to do with Mom. But Mom's comebacks, which were usually funnier than his, could also be harsh. For the most part, I don't think Spencer minded being trumped by Mom. Matt, pretending to be out of breath as he carried in my big suitcase, asked me, "You smuggle a few movie stars in here? Brad Pitt?"

"Oh, Matt. Emmy probably brought as much of her home as possible."

I'd panicked the last few days before leaving Sacramento and packed random things into my suitcase: my yearbooks, packages of origami paper, a set of Tibetan prayer flags, my collection of tiny Asian bowls, which I wrapped in scarves. I shoved in two decks of tarot cards last minute, despite how Mom said Christians thought evil spirits resided in tarot and they'd frighten my aunt. I think they frightened Mom also. But she would never admit to being afraid of anything other than ignorance, which, she'd warned, was in no short supply in eastern Washington.

My first few days in Washington were easier than the nights. I was used to long summer afternoons without television or other kids. But Beth and Matt both went to bed early, as Mom said they would. Having a bedroom and my own bathroom at the opposite end of the trailer from their bedroom helped with awkwardness but also left me feeling more lonely at night. And a little cold with the air conditioning always on. I hadn't had a bedtime in the summer since I was ten, when I started staying home by myself during the day instead of going to child care centers or day camps on various college campuses. Mom let me stay up as late as I wanted to in the summer—she was great about that—reading, sketching, doing origami, painting, watching movies, and baking (as long as there was a delta breeze). She taught as many classes as she could over the summer for the money, and she stayed up late most nights grading papers and preparing lessons. For a while we called ourselves the Owl Society. I made us feathered hats out of paper grocery bags that I painted, and I secretly logged our literary activities by flashlight (thanks to an obsession with *Dead Poets Society*).

The night noises were different at my aunt's house, and muted because the windows stayed shut. No roaring highways, sirens, car alarms, or rumbling light rail. No scuffling street people. Every once in a while I heard a car horn or the far, far-off sound of a train. I heard wind. I heard coyotes. More wind. More coyotes. Matt said in the summer that juvenile coyotes were trying out their voices. I heard the crunch of gravel when someone returned home late to the trailer park, like the neighbor boy who looked my age and drove an old pickup truck. Where did he go so late? Had he noticed me? When the wind rattled the thin-paned windows, I buried my head under the covers. There were also lapses without any sound, and I'd have to put on my headphones and listen to music to stay asleep.

"One of the guys at work has an old TV," Uncle Matt said to me the third evening at the dinner table. So far I loved Aunt Beth's cooking. "What do you think? We could put it in the bedroom, and get you cable." I looked at Aunt Beth. She didn't say anything, but she put down her fork. "It'll give you something to do at night," he reasoned, "and while we're at church."

"Thanks," I said. "But I'm okay." Beth looked relieved. "We don't have cable at home."

"I'm going to teach Emmy to sew," she said. "And to garden and make oils."

I was thrilled to learn oils, and I'd always wanted to know how to sew—not to make curtains and aprons (well, maybe) but to alter my clothes like the most artistic girls at school did. Mom laughed the time I asked her if I could take sewing lessons. She said at strict Christian schools, the girls took sewing instead of science and they didn't learn math beyond fractions for doubling recipes. She'd have laughed on the phone now if I'd told her I'd just enjoyed meat loaf with a helping of green bean casserole. Mom hated plain food, and she loathed ground beef, which she had been forced to eat almost daily as a child. She bragged she hadn't eaten a canned veggie since crossing the California state line. We ate a lot of salads, rice, chicken stir-fry, couscous, eggplant, fruit, homemade hummus. Shrimp when we had the money. Steak or carne asada when we ate at Spencer's house. Mom and I also ate a lot of grilled cheese sandwiches on sourdough, though every now and then, when she was in a funk, she'd buy cheap white bread and American cheese slices. Once a year Mom tried to make thick, chewy noodles from scratch, but she was never satisfied with how they turned out or with the kitchen and her face covered in flour.

"Let me know if you change your mind about the TV," Matt said.

A few days later, on Saturday, while Aunt Beth napped, Matt and I went into town for briquettes for the barbecue. He offered to let me drive, but I declined. On the way, he said his brother had an extra car that he'd gladly loan me over the summer. It was kind of ugly, but it ran well. I was taken aback, then embarrassed to admit, "I don't have my license." I explained how Mom didn't think high school kids should drive in a big city.

"I'll teach you to drive over the summer. You're plenty old enough." We passed a rodeo arena, more trailers, a few churches, and gas stations where families with trucks and boats and all kinds of fishing gear were filling up gas cans and ice chests.

"Mom won't give permission," I said. "Actually what I mean is—I'm scared."

"We'll stick to county roads at first. You can't get hurt on those, unless you drive into a canal." He smiled.

Mom had sounded strange on the phone both times I'd talked to her—distant, for starters. She'd always been a little remote. Maybe it had made it easier to hide her past? But now she also sounded defeated, which unsettled me. The one time I'd talked on the phone to Connor he'd sounded the opposite of defeated. His parents, despite his deplorable grades, had just bought him a brand-new Acura. He'd been driving his cousin's old one. So much for his stance against suburbia. I waited to call Mom until the next morning, Sunday, after Aunt Beth and Uncle Matt left for church, and I could take a Vicodin pill (my third ever). I asked Mom right away about driving lessons with Matt, almost hoping she'd forbid them.

"I don't see why not," she replied, to my amazement. "Hold on." She put her hand over the receiver. Long pause. "Spencer said it sounds like a great plan."

She'd actually asked his opinion? That was a rarity. "He's there? That's cool."

"Why's that *cool*?"

"I don't like the thought of you all alone."

She laughed but didn't sound amused. "I'm a big girl, Emmy."

Changing the subject, she asked about my morning plans. I told her I was going out to tend Beth's herb garden.

"*Tend*," Mom said. "You're starting to talk like her."

Beth occasionally used old-fashioned words—biblical, though they also sounded like Shakespeare. Or even the Brontës. I liked them.

"I wish you could see how nice her garden is." I bragged how I was learning the names of the different plants. There was a bench where I planned to sit and read *Sister Carrie*. I didn't tell her I hoped to catch another glance of the handsome neighbor boy whom I'd caught staring my way the other day. Connor had stared at me intently for a month—just long enough for me to think maybe he despised me or found me ridiculous—before slipping a naughty note in my locker.

"You okay, Mom?" Shouldn't she be asking me this? "I miss you."

"You've only been gone a week." I felt stupid. She probably didn't even miss me yet. I didn't really miss her. It was the pill making me sentimental. "It seems longer," she said. Then, with a hint of sorrow, she added, "So much longer."

So, she *did* miss me, and she was right that it seemed longer. She was also right about the trailer seeming suffocating, or at least the carpeting. We had hardwood floors in our apartment. I'd been staring at the carpeting while talking to her. Its dingy blah threatened to erase time. Aunt Beth kept the kitchen blinds closed all day because the jars of essential oils needed shade. But she said I could open the living room blinds (I wished I could open the windows) whenever I wanted to, which I had that morning as soon as they'd left for church. Beth usually kept the living room blinds closed too, she admitted, so the carpet stains (probably from previous miscarriages, I later realized with anguish) wouldn't show up as badly. She'd tried to scrub them clean over the years, she told me, but they only got worse, and there was no need to replace the carpeting since she and Uncle Matt were going to buy a new house as soon as they had a baby. Grabbing my sun hat, I walked carefully around the stains, which resembled undefined continents on a map, and then out the door.

5

Kate

🖋 My daughter's been gone now a week and a half.

Unable to sleep, I brood on the couch at 2:00 A.M. I can't focus to grade papers or to read a novel, not even my favorite scenes from Hardy's *Tess*. I keep trying to picture Emmy in eastern Washington: standing in sagebrush, the wind blowing her hair, or sitting inside Beth and Matt's trailer, maybe eating dinner with them at the table, or walking down the same dusty sidewalks in town that I walked down at her age. Because I can't visualize Emmy in the setting of my childhood, it feels as if she's gone someplace farther away than Moses Lake. Or conversely, further back in time but also very much in the present, only completely out of reach. It's hard to articulate. But I'm afraid, and I miss my little girl terribly. I drink a third glass of wine that I'll regret come sunrise. It's one of those cool valley nights, when the heat is broken by the delta breeze. The curtains blow lazily. I'm naked under my short robe, and a naked man sleeps in my bed. The atmosphere doesn't fit my mood. And my teeth hurt.

I didn't realize it at the time, but the day I boarded a bus bound for California, I followed in the footsteps of the Donners and the Joads and the millions of others who have left their pasts behind to seek and, in my case, find redemption in the Golden State. It wasn't easy. When I stepped off that Greyhound in Sacramento at nineteen years old, I was poor, brokenhearted, uneducated, tired, and Emmy had been crying inconsolably for hours for her aunt. I had tickets for L.A., but I couldn't put another mile between Bethany and me.

The gold I dredged in California was education. I had to start at the bottom: adult education classes to get my GED. But the state helped every step of the way. I received grants to attend junior college. I struggled, having never taken a single science class, math beyond decimals and fractions, or much grammar. I'd cry in frustration. I'd cry for Jamie, but more often for Beth. I studied harder and read more books, trying to fill the emptiness. I sinfully went to the movie theater for the first time in my life and watched *E.T.* while Emmy slept in my arms. I bought my first rock-and-roll album, Bruce Springsteen, and an old TV so I could start following the news and Emmy could watch *Sesame Street*. I became a regular at the tutoring center. Even at two years old, Emmy knew how to be quiet in a library with crayons or a stack of picture books. The state allocated more aid when I transferred to Sacramento State University for my BA and eventually my MA. I took out student loans to help pay tuition, child care, and other expenses, but after a decade, I was finally graduated. I've been teaching at three junior colleges now for five years, which is a lot of commuting, but I hope I'll get on full time at one soon. Then I can finally get my wisdom teeth pulled out. They've been impacted since I was pregnant. The top ones shift every six to twelve months, trying to emerge. The throbbing lasts for about a week, with the most intense pain coming in waves. Then they settle back down.

Emmy gave me direction and focus, but also determination. And now I want to help her get into a U.C., I hope U.C. Berkeley, which is the top public university in the country, and it blows her dad's WSU out of the water. Does Emmy *really* plan on looking for her dad? For her sake, I hope not. I know how devastating it is to be rejected by the likes of Jamie Kagen. But if Jamie were to meet Emmy this summer, how could he turn his back? I used to think the same thing after first giving birth to Emmy: if only Jamie would come and actually see his baby girl and hold her and smell her. During my first year in California, the only way I could fall asleep at night was to imagine myself back on that lake at camp. I'd hold Emmy close and pretend my bed was the canoe and Jamie was rowing us. By morning he'd always left us adrift. I made it through college without the help of a man, including my dad, and so will Emmy.

Well, okay, one man helped me, two actually, but both early on, and for relatively short periods of time. The first was a married professor at American River College. He helped me financially for a while. That is to say, three times he bought me groceries, and once he paid the rent. He was intrigued by my "profound" biblical knowledge yet total lack of Christian beliefs. Also, he liked my young ass. He stimulated my love of literature, which, in the end, was about all he stimulated. But *what* a gift. Next there was Hector, an airman stationed at Mather Air Force Base. He was every bit as poor as I was. For months he visited nightly after Emmy had fallen asleep. He'd play me his favorite Hendrix songs, but mostly we listened to Journey while he cooked us homemade beans and rice and sometimes tamales on payday. He brought me 800 mg Motrin, which the military handed out like candy, for my teeth. He also helped me with math. We were more than compatible in bed. If it hadn't been for my daughter, I could've stayed under the covers with Hector's hands on me all weekend. Amen.

I almost called Beth after Hector got restationed. If he'd asked me to marry him and move with him to his new base in San Antonio, I probably would have. But alas, he didn't. I felt so alone at night, my bed so cold. I worried the God of my childhood and of Abraham, Isaac, and Jacob was punishing me for my moral laxity, to say nothing of my disbelief. The Hebrews wandering in the desert had nothing on me as far as lack of faith. I didn't call Beth after Hector flew away on a C-5 because I didn't want to break the promise I'd made to myself: to never look back. I was stronger than Lot's wife—right? No more crusty tears. If my Baptist upbringing taught me anything, it's the notion of "all or nothing." God spews the lukewarm from his mouth.

After Hector, I occasionally dated fellow Sac State students. But I never invited them to the apartment when Emmy was there. I dated mostly ethnic men. I didn't need a white man to remind me of Jamie or of all the boring church boys I'd grown up with. I had an intense two-month affair with a state lobbyist who swore he wasn't married. I had a much longer but less intense affair with a U.C. Davis medical student. Finally he admitted there was no way his family in India or in San Jose would accept a woman who'd had a child out of wedlock. My litany of men ends with Spencer Hensley, who is in my bed now.

We've been dating for four years, with one significant breakup. He's white, and though he doesn't have a degree, he's skilled and works hard at more than sounding smart. He owns a small but reputable custom home-building business with his brother. They do beautiful work, especially in kitchens, which they don't contract out. In my apartment, the kitchen is the least charming room. Emmy and I compensate by hanging postcards of places we'd like to visit, art, and vintage scenes on the cupboards, walls, and fridge.

Emmy took to Spencer instantly. I think it was the way he relaxed around her from the beginning. He didn't push her to interact with him, but he also didn't ignore her. At times their comradery gets under my skin. The first Sunday Spencer took Emmy to a Sacramento Kings basketball game, I cried after they left. I wasn't jealous. That would be ridiculous, and he'd offered to buy me a ticket. No, thanks. I was just moved deeply by his appreciation of Emmy, and scared by it. Until Spencer, I'd managed to keep Emmy off the emotional roller coaster of a single mom's boyfriends.

"Kate."

He's slept over every night since Emmy's been gone, despite the fact I invited him to stay only the first three, and despite my lack of an air conditioner, which Spencer always claims, half-jokingly, makes my landlady a slumlord. He invited me to stay at his place, but all my books and Emmy's things are here.

"I think I'll take off," he says, "if it will help you sleep."

"What do you mean?" I put down my glass of wine next to a stack of student composition papers: two on cloning, two on gays in the military, three on health care reform, four on the death penalty, and, even though it's almost a new century and I teach in the capital of California, sixteen on abortion. I know exactly what Spencer means. I've begun to feel agitated by his constant presence in the apartment— not that I want to be alone and certainly I don't want him sleeping naked in another woman's bed. But he can't replace Emmy. The thought unnerves me. I tried to let him at first. I tried to be a better helpmeet: to cook for him, seek his advice, bring him cold ones, snuggle. But it's not that simple. Or if it is, it's not enough. What is wrong with me? Other single moms—single women, period—would bend over backward for Spencer. Maybe that's just it. If only he were a little chubby or balding, or if he weren't such a fine craftsman and lover. What can a woman do, really, when a man like Spencer walks into her life? She has to play hard to get. And keep on playing it. Or so I've convinced myself.

He heads to the table for his rolled blueprints. "Emmy's okay, you know," he says.

"How do *you* know?"

"Well, I've been thinking. You swear your sister and brother-in-law are good people, right?" I nod. "So maybe other than that absurd healing ceremony, this summer will turn out to be just what Emmy needs."

Ten days ago Spencer was mad as hell at me, and he doesn't get mad that often, for making Emmy go. Why the about-face? And what does he mean: "just what Emmy needs"? I ask him to elaborate, please.

He stops gathering up his prints. "Maybe being away from you this summer will force Emmy to grow up a little—a lot."

"She's pretty mature for her age." I press on the back part of my cheek and jaw to ease the tooth pain. "You've said so many times."

"In some ways, yes, Emmy's *too* mature." He moseys over and sits beside me on the couch as if I'd just popped in a VHS. "And she certainly has direction." He pauses. "But it's your direction, Kate. Not hers."

I take a deep breath. "This comes from a thirty-five-year-old bachelor. Don't presume—"

"I'm not presuming. I *know* Emmy."

"You really don't." I laugh. "You know her good side. Her cheery, I-want-a-daddy, please-take-me-to-a-ball-game side." That was cruel, even for me.

He stands up. "See you later."

I didn't mean to be an ogress. I don't know *how* to accept advice on Emmy. I search on the coffee table for my tube of Anbesol. It's been just my kid and me for so long—for always, except for Emmy's first seven months.

Spencer takes a few steps, then turns back, as I was hoping. "I know Emmy's scared-out-of-her-wits side. Her how-can-I-make-it-without-my-mommy side. I saw it at the airport." He bends and grabs the Anbesol off the floor, where it must've fallen, and tosses it at me. "I love your daughter, Kate. She's going to surprise us both one day."

"Us?"

"Yes, *us*. Fucking *us*. Christ. Did you push away Emmy's real dad this hard?"

"Fuck you." I get to my feet. He's never dared mention Emmy's dad, except once, early in our relationship and not in the same context. My bathrobe falls open, and I let it. My body, for whatever reason, seems to hold some power over Spencer. Just as his body does over me. The first time he touched me, I knew there would be no holding back between the sheets with this man. "Fuck you," I repeat, throwing the tube of Anbesol back on the floor like a child.

"Not to be crude, Kate, but you've been fucking me for four years." He pulls my bathrobe together and starts to tie the belt. "I need more."

I push his hands away and triple knot the belt. "You have no idea about that man, or my past."

"You've made damn sure of that."

He's right. I have. Spencer knows my body more intimately than I do, which is stirring. But my past, I don't want to dump that crap on anyone, especially not on someone as seemingly unscathed as Spencer. His hands are calloused from years of hard work, sure, which I greatly admire, even if he is the boss. But his heart has never been blistered, let alone calloused. His life, and he'd be the first to admit, has been pretty cushy. He's made smart decisions, but also his parents gave him a huge leg up. He's never been part of the great unwashed. He's never been a single parent using WIC coupons at a grocery store while couples in line behind him flutter or huff. He's never worried if a box of generic laundry soap will last until payday. He's probably never spent a single Valentine's Day alone—let alone ten in a row—pining for a first love, a blinking Appaloosa Inn sign, a shoddy motel room surrounded by a sea of wheat.

I try to move away from Spencer. "I don't need you," I say. I've been struggling to convince myself of that since the day we met.

He grabs my arm. "You need me, Kate. Feminist or not." Now it's his turn to laugh. "That's what scares you. It's always scared you."

I pull free. "Oh, but I don't." I gesture toward my books and furniture.

"All I see is mismatched thrift store furniture," he says. "It looks like a damn garage sale in here. I can provide better."

That is the first mean thing he's ever said to me. I try to keep my voice steady as I reply, "Emmy and I do just fine."

"Emmy's not here. *You* sent her away."

That hits me, hard. "She'll—she'll be back."

"It won't be the same. I hope you realize that."

"Please leave."

"As soon as you tell me one thing about your childhood. One day. One moment. Let me in, Kate." I don't respond. I'm tired and afraid what I might confess. "One detail about Emmy's dad then," he says. "At least his name, so I can despise all men with that dickhead's name."

"Fine," I say. "I'll let you in a bit. But remember *you* asked for it." I hesitate because I am about to tell him everything, not just one thing, and it will probably be the end of us. I should shut the windows for privacy, but the cool breeze from the delta will help me not pass out. I press on my jaw once more to stall and to call forth my courage. I begin. "After Emmy's dad—name of Jamie Kagen—took my virginity, then knocked me up, he dumped me. I was shunned, condemned as a *whore* from the church pulpit and by my father at home." Spencer reaches for me. "Wait." I put up my hand. I'm sweating despite the breeze on the back of my knees. "After I gave birth to Emmy, I waitressed at a truck stop café, where I also slept around for money." His face flinches. "With nasty old men in their stinky truck cabs." I've never told anyone other than Beth my secret. "It turns out I *was* a whore after all." He closes his eyes. When he opens them, I continue. "I was only a few years older than Emmy. I let one bastard cut off my hair." I tug at the ends of my bobbed hair. "And I've never grown it back out. I hocked my mother's wedding ring to buy gas. I left my sister, who had turned her life upside down for us, and I wasn't there when she lost baby after baby." Spencer makes a noise in his throat. "Now leave," I whisper. He doesn't, so I turn away. "Please, Spencer. I want to be alone. Please go."

He seems unable to move or speak.

Just as I have been unable to clear from my head, no matter how much literature I read, a certain Bible verse damning a harlot: ". . . days of your youth, when you were naked and bare, struggling in your blood." There are plenty such verses. Biblical prophets blame harlots— not overzealous men, corrupt kings, jealous family members, or warring tribes—for the downfall of Israel.

Finally Spencer speaks. "I love you more," he says, then turns to leave.

What does he mean, "more"? More than he did before I told him about being a hooker?

More than I love him? Maybe I don't love Spencer. Maybe it's all been a game and I'm just trying to overcompensate for my father's and Jamie's rejections. Yeah, right. I've loved Spencer from the start, even if it took a long time to admit it to myself and longer to admit it to him. He would be too hard to get over, harder even than Jamie, because of the way he loves Emmy. And let's face it, the way he loves me. This I have also known from the start: another reason I've kept myself back, except in bed. Airman Hector and I had fun in bed, we were young, he made me laugh, I'd wear his fatigues. But Spencer and I have grown-up fun and we have serious sex and we have pissed-off sex and we have slow, slow lovemaking, during which I dissolve for moments into him. An aware woman should probably never fully render herself, but I can't help it when it comes to Spencer. I'd let that man do anything he wanted to me in bed. It is he who draws the lines we don't cross, and I suppose I love him for that as well. I think all along Spencer has sensed my dark secret in the way my body sometimes responds oddly during sex, and it's kept him intrigued or at least off-kilter. It's kept him coming back.

He doesn't slam the apartment door behind him, but for some reason the gentle click sends a shiver through me as if he had.

"Emmy," I say into the phone, "I'm sorry I made you go there." It's Sunday morning. I usually call when I know Beth and Matt will be gone at church so we can talk openly. "I'm sorry that I sent you away." I know better than to add, "Please don't look for your dad."

As for *my* dad, I was almost relieved to hear from Beth that he'd passed away. It would've been too confusing for Emmy if her grandfather still didn't want to meet her.

"It's okay." Emmy sounds cheery. "I sort of like it here."

"What?"

"I like it here."

She's been there two weeks. Two long weeks. I thought, or rather hoped by now that she'd be phoning every time Beth and Matt left for church and asking to come home. At least then I'd be sure she didn't hate me. Albeit Emmy does have more of a knack than I do for making the best of things. I want her to come home early—after the healing, obviously, but before the physical distance between us turns into an emotional abyss. For now, I ask, "Are you bored, honey? Is Beth always witnessing to you?"

"She is, but I don't really mind. She gave me your old Bible."

I used to record stuff in my Bible about Jamie, which is probably why I didn't toss it, but, luckily, only in the margins of books like Zephaniah and Nahum that even the most faithful, or, as I see it, deluded, don't read. "I wish she hadn't."

"She also gave me an old cassette tape of yours—Emmylou Harris." My daughter's voice gets less cheery as she asks, "Why didn't you tell me I was named after a singer?"

"You're not. Not really. I just liked the name. I still do. I miss you."

"But Aunt Beth said you listened to the tape all the time while you were pregnant."

I rebought that exact tape, and I still listen to Emmylou in the car, but only when I'm driving alone and feeling particularly down and in need of sympathy, which Emmylou's aching voice gives me. The religious nature of her lyrics also comforts me, which I would be ashamed to admit to my daughter. She thinks Bruce Springsteen and Chopin are my favorites. I'd also be embarrassed to admit to Emmy how when I used to take her on drives through the rice fields north of Sac, it was because they reminded me of her dad's wheat fields and I liked to pretend, for an hour or so, that he'd summoned us at last.

Eager to change the subject, I ask when and where the faith healing is to take place. Her tone turns somber real quickly. She says at a lake in ten days at Dry Falls State Park. Beth showed her on a map.

I'm thankful the ceremony isn't being held at the mineral lake. I returned there once when I was about five months pregnant. Dad hadn't noticed my belly yet because of my baggy dresses. But he soon would. Jamie had already dumped me, but I still had hope he'd come around after I gave birth. I didn't swim. I took off my dress—no one was there—and rubbed the black mud on my cantaloupe belly. I believed in the healing powers of that lake. I knew Dad had waited too long to take Mom there. What he should've done was driven her to the fucking hospital, where a doctor could've given her some morphine and thus some dignity and reprieve her last week on earth. Amen. Mom had been impressed, as had her logger father, with Dad's skill and fearlessness as a feller. Even on the steepest incline, Dad could get a tree to fall onto the face of the hill instead of rolling down it. Mom's family wasn't as impressed with the fearless way Dad stole their daughter away. But to be perfectly honest, it was Mom, the mess hall waitress and foreman's daughter, who started the flirtation by putting extra apples into Dad's lunch pail before the crews left in the morning. I inherited some of my dad's tenacity, which scared him, I've come to realize. Why couldn't he have driven Mom boldly to the hospital? She bobbed away from him that day in the lake. I cheered silently from the shore. He almost drowned trying to reach her. Then he made me help drag her, moaning in agony, from the water.

"I'm really scared, Mom," Emmy says now. "What if the ceremony doesn't work because I'm not a Christian?"

"Did you tell Beth you *were*?"

"Sort of."

Just as my inherited tenacity scared my dad, Emmy's spiritual long-ing has always worried me, and reminded me painfully of my little sister. I don't know how many times I've found my daughter in the religious and New Age sections of used bookstores. Because I want her firmly rooted in this world, I never offer to buy her spiritual guide-books. And Emmy, being Emmy, under my scowl, has never asked. She faithfully spends her allowance in the snake oil shop below our apartment.

"Beth wasn't supposed to ask you."

"She couldn't help it. So much depends"—she lowers her voice as if someone might hear her—"on this healing."

"Well, at least you're a virgin. Not that it matters. Don't be scared."

"Yeah, but—"

"But what, honey?"

She doesn't respond.

"Maybe you can come home early," I suggest. "Right after the cere-mony." I'd promised myself for Beth's sake that I wouldn't suggest this, that I'd wait for Emmy to ask.

"Hold on, Mom." She puts her hand over the receiver, and it sounds like she's talking to someone. I don't think she heard my suggestion. I swear I hear a muffled male voice.

"Is someone there?" I ask.

"Who? Aunt Beth and Uncle Matt are at church." Emmy suddenly tries to stifle a giggle. What the heck is going on? "I have to go," she says. I don't want to hang up yet, but Emmy says she's making a cake for Beth and doesn't want it to burn. "Today's her birthday, remem-ber?"

I swallow. Actually I'd forgotten. How alarming. I mean, if Emmy had asked me Beth's birth date, I could've named the month, day, and year, but I'd long ago quit associating the calendar date with Beth. It was too upsetting. "That's why I called," I lie, "to remind you."

"Will you be calling back later, then, to talk to her?"

I've talked to Beth on the phone six or seven times since that initial phone call that shook me to my core. Seven times: that's not even once for every two years we went without speaking. I'm scared of the number of miscarriages she's suffered. I didn't ask specifics after she told me she has never seen a doctor, and won't. Although it made my knees weak, I had to change the subject so I wouldn't inadvertently belittle her beliefs. I also didn't ask specifics about Dad's death. I'd sensed it years ago. Why hadn't I sensed Beth's losses? Maybe I had. Maybe my wisdom teeth shifted and tried to emerge each time she was pregnant, as they had shifted for the very first time while I was pregnant with Emmy. I regret asking my sister if Jamie ever came looking for me. The fact that he never did makes me feel worthless, despite my degrees. It also makes me feel overly protective of Emmy and all around more defensive. Same old shit. In the shorter phone calls that followed, Beth's voice often faltered. Her sadness is palpable. The guilt could swallow me, if I let it. Bethany has Matt. I've reminded myself of that fact often over the years. And now, despite her devastating losses, she still has Matt.

"Maybe I'll call," I say to Emmy.

"*Maybe*? She's your only sister."

Oh, my sister.

I start sleeping in Emmy's bed, regardless of the back pain it gives me. Emmy's mattress is a piece of crap. I purchased it years ago at a Punjabi furniture store that used to be a gas station and is now a sari boutique. Emmy's never complained about her mattress. I'll price new ones. I washed all the bedding in my bedroom because it smelled like Spencer's soap and cologne, also a trace of sawdust. Now it just smells lonely. Spencer and I haven't spoken since our fight. I fear my confession got to him and he's never going to call. I wouldn't blame him. Although I keep myself in shape, he could get far younger women than me, and less fucked up.

The origami mobiles and chains of paper animals and birds hanging in Emmy's room also make me lonely. Worse, they force me to realize, not for the first time but never so poignantly, just how lonesome—safe but lonesome—Emmy's childhood has been. I think of Laura Wingfield and her glass menagerie, which, maybe not so ironically, is one of Emmy's favorite plays. But Emmy isn't crippled like

Laura, at least not physically. Not emotionally either. Maybe a little. Have I oversheltered her? When I left Moses Lake, Beth begged me to keep Emmy close under my wing. At least I buy her cute clothes—too much, in a lame attempt to make up for Beth and me having to wear those hideous dresses as teenagers. Baptists are obsessed with women not wearing "that which pertaineth unto a man." They'd be mortified by *Twelfth Night*, which must be why it's *my* favorite play. Actually it's the melancholy tone and the siblings tragically separated by the sea. "I had a sister," Sebastian laments.

I wish Spencer would call. I miss him. I keep checking my answering machine. I've spent most of my life missing loved ones. Half my childhood I missed my mom. Then Jamie. Then Beth. Now Emmy and Spencer. I feel tired and restless at the same time. The last three nights I've had to force myself to stay put in Emmy's bed—not get up, dress up, and go visit a honky-tonk bar, or maybe drop by one of those sports bars Spencer likes. I need a man for a night who won't hesitate to punish me a bit for having been a hooker, a bitch, a female. No, I don't. *I don't.* Why is Spencer so fucking kind? Sexy *and* kind? He'd be more than willing to buy Emmy a new bed. But I've never let him spend much money on us, other than the two times he put my car in the shop, for which I tried to reimburse him with checks he never cashed. I don't want to feel obliged to a man, as I did with the married professor, or to become financially dependent in the least. Spencer even offered me a job once, as the secretary for his company: health insurance, steady hours. I told him that I love teaching too much to give it up, and I do. By teaching junior college, I help kids and adults who, like me, screwed up but are trying again. A giant stuffed dog, with a name tag "Tangles," keeps watch over Emmy's room. Spencer bought it for her on her thirteenth birthday. Why, why, *why* didn't I accept that man's marriage proposal two years ago? On top of wanting to play hard to get, I was terrified. Like Tess, I knew I couldn't marry a man who didn't know my past, and I wasn't ready yet to divulge it.

I planned to get out of the apartment today, nice and early, take a weekend drive by myself into the Sierras, get away from my silent phone, the city, and the valley heat for a day. But I just don't have the ambition. I'm in my car too much during the week, and I don't mind the heat, even without air conditioning. It melts the memories of my last winter up north. And I like Sacramento—not necessarily downtown with the capitol, windowless government buildings, married lobbyists, and convention centers, but midtown, with its sycamore-lined streets, funky shops, and the diverse restaurants that Emmy and I rarely have the funds to eat in. I walk to Emmy's favorite coffee shop with a stack of student papers. I've never fallen so far behind with grading. I'll hit one of the many farmers' markets on my way home. I've lived in California now for almost as many years as I lived in Washington, but I'm still amazed by the variety of produce available. And by the mixed ethnicities of the people selling them and of my students.

Spencer is waiting on the outside steps that lead up to my apartment—my breath catches—when I return with a dull headache instead of produce and, instead of graded papers, the strong desire to drink a bottle of cheap wine and crawl self-piteously into Emmy's shitty bed for the remainder of the day.

"I'm sorry, Kate," he says right away, "for the comment about your furniture."

"No biggie."

"It *is* a biggie. I had *no* right to insult your stuff. I'm sorry."

"My stuff forgives you." I invite him inside.

He still hasn't hugged me. Maybe he only stopped by to make a formal good-bye.

"Good," he says, sitting down on the couch. I point the floor fan toward him and turn it up to high. He works outside in the heat most days, but inside, he likes to be cool. I offer him a beer, but he shakes his head. I'm heated from my walk. I sit in the wicker chair. "Good," he repeats. "Because I want you to bring it all with you."

"Bring what—where?"

"Your furniture. You can bring it all to the house I'm building us."

I wish I were sitting on something more solid than wicker. What did he just say?

"I've been building it for almost a year. My brother's been helping. I had our entire crew there last month."

"What are you talking about?" He's more wound up than he gets on his rare days off when he accidentally drinks a work morning amount of coffee. He also seems more confident than usual. Which, I have to admit, is incredibly attractive.

"I built us a house, Kate. With a big room for Emmy. And an office for you, so you won't have to keep all your books in the living room." He's talking fast. "And there's air conditioning." He wipes his brow.

"Seriously, Spencer." It takes me a minute. "*What* are you talking about?"

"But you have to marry me first. Or agree to marry me before we move in. We can surprise Emmy when she gets back from Washington."

I want to get up and pace—match his energy, which I usually can—but right now I simply can't budge.

"Oh, and I bought us tickets to Europe. We leave right after your summer session." He just keeps going. "I'd planned to propose marriage to you in Paris. In a museum or someplace romantic." Spencer isn't into museums, plays, or readings. He likes ball games, sports bars, and hardware stores. "But I can't wait. I can't fucking sleep."

I never thought I'd see Europe. Sure, Emmy and I talk about going there. I collect maps. But just getting to California was enough for me.

"You're crazy," I say.

"So are you."

"Well, yes."

"Why did you call twice last night and then hang up?" he asks. "I knew it was you. And the night before and the night—"

"I get the point."

"I don't care about your past, Kate. I only care about *now*."

I've rarely cried in front of Spencer. But last night I dreamed I was back in that truck stop, and when I woke up, my teeth throbbed. I wanted Spencer to rub my back. I thought I was more capable of being alone. I should've made some girlfriends. The few times in college that I invited a fellow female student over to study, Emmy looked sad and left out. I wonder if Beth has girlfriends at the church.

"Let's give Emmy a real home her last year before college," he says.

"Emmy has a *real* home right here." Why can't I stop crying?

"You're right. That came out wrong. I'm sorry." I can tell he's sincere. He talks slower. "I want to be your husband and Emmy's dad. It's *all* I've wanted since I first met you."

He's proved as much, no matter my insecurities and bullshit.

"You've worked hard for years," he says. "You've taken great care of Emmy. Let me take care of you now. Both of you."

"I like my books in the living room."

He laughs, tenderly. "I'll add bookshelves."

"Why me, Spencer?"

"You and Emmy—you're different. Maybe because of where you guys were born. I don't know. There's something—"

"I'm not special. I'm ruined."

"You're *not* ruined. Far from it." He looks a little tired, suddenly. "You're very alive, Kate. And you're special to me."

"The Bible says a nonvirtuous woman is like rottenness in her husband's bones."

He laughs again tenderly. "Since when do you quote the Bible?"

Every day in my head—regrettably.

"Come here, baby," he says.

I used to hate being called that by guys, but never by Spencer. I go to him.

I sit down close beside him on the couch, but he doesn't want to touch. He pulls a small velvet box out of his pocket. "I'm not going to get down on my knee," he says. "Last time you rejected me before even seeing the ring." He says his brother has never stopped giving him hell about that. "I'm going to leave this here on the coffee table." He puts it down. "It's a different ring, by the way." He stands up. "I'll give you a week to think about it. If you don't call me, or if you call and hang up, then this is good-bye for good, Kate." He means it. "But I hope you'll still let me see Emmy—take her to games and stuff." His voice falters for the first time. His love for Emmy has grown deep, or maybe it always has been.

I stand up too, hoping he'll at least hug me. I suddenly want him to hold me very badly—because I'm afraid I won't call him. I'm afraid the part of me that's still stuck back in that truck stop parking lot won't let me call him. And then he won't ever show up again on my steps. And when Emmy goes away to college, I'll be all alone and miserable. Or else I'll become too loose and split open with men. Spencer doesn't hug me, but I can tell he wants to comfort me. I've so rarely let him. He touches the ends of my hair that I tugged at last time. "Know that I'll always love you." He can barely speak. "That I love you *more*." He drops his hands, then squares his shoulders. "But I can't do part time any longer."

He's God about to spew me from his mouth.

The first weeks I started climbing into truckers' cabs for money were by far the most shocking and degrading in my life. Prior to that, Jamie was the only boy I'd kissed, let alone slept with, and sex with him had been romantic, despite being tinged with fear that I was losing him to his father and the land. Jamie whispered his love while inside me and even more passionately afterward. Truckers slobbered on my neck, grunted vile and nasty things that I'd never heard before, and the physical pain was worse than giving birth. I do not exaggerate. I thought I was tough. I thought I'd made myself strong as a young girl so that all the Baptist crap about females being the "weaker vessel" and "in subjection to your own husbands" and "shame-faced" would never apply to me. To Jamie Kagen I submitted willingly and sweetly. In cramped cabs with truck drivers and their road smells, large hands, and male strength, I was utterly defenseless. After my seventh trick, the most holy of numbers, I drove straight home to Beth, instead of trying to calm my nerves first by drinking beside the lake. The truckers gave me alcohol, and so did the kind, pockmarked dishwasher in his BLACK SABBATH T-shirt. I needed my sister that day in a way I can't explain. When I got to the trailer, I didn't rush into her arms. I curled up on the sofa, trying to ignore the pangs between my legs, and watched her fold laundry.

For three weeks she'd been questioning me: Why wasn't I eating? How did I tear a second blouse? How had I gotten so much extra tip money? Was it a man, the same man, leaving me such big tips? Was he a kind man like Boaz had been to Ruth, letting her glean wheat in his fields? When Beth began to question me that particular day, I sat up, trying not to wince, and pulled more twenties from my apron pockets. *Here, sister, are my sheaves of wheat, and the fields I'm gleaning aren't Jamie's.*

"I follow truckers out to their rigs," I said.

"What?" She stopped folding laundry.

"I turn tricks."

"Tricks?"

"Sex, Beth. I have sex with truckers." I pushed up the sleeves on my white waitress blouse to show her the bruises on my upper arms. I didn't show her the ones on my thighs.

"Oh, Kate." She looked horrified. "Kate, *no*." She covered her mouth and shook her head. She kept shaking her head and staring at me. Then, with as much authority as she could muster, she said, "You're *never* going back to that truck stop. Do you hear me? Matt and I can cover the rent."

"I still owe the hospital. I have layaway payments at Kmart."

"The money will show up," she said. "I can cut back on groceries."

"No, you can't." I tried to eat at work to save groceries. The cook would sneak me a chicken fried steak with gravy or a patty melt with the bowl of soup or side of fries I actually paid for. "And *how* will the money show up?"

"Matt can ask his parents."

"They've done enough."

"I can go to work at one of the factories," she offered.

"In your long dress? Who will watch Emmy? And the factories are making layoffs, not hiring. Remember, I tried?"

"I've been praying."

"Don't bother. I found a way to make money."

I waited for her to start sobbing. Or to quote the Bible. She did neither. She picked up the plastic basket of folded laundry and chucked it across the front room and into the kitchen. It was such an unexpected thing for her to do—like Mom, Beth rarely got angry—that I actually started laughing. Just for a second and not cruelly.

"You're *not* going back there," she insisted. "I'm going to tell Matt everything. He'll know what to do."

I jumped up. "You can't tell Matt." I grabbed her arm. "I couldn't bear the shame." She looked determined. "If you do, I'll—I'll leave town."

I didn't mean it.

Her determined look turned back to one of horror. She grabbed my other arm. "You can't leave me."

"Then promise you'll never tell Matt. This is between sisters."

She promised. Then she tried to get me to promise her that I'd never again turn a trick. I told her I'd ask for more shifts at work. But I'd already asked the manager twice for more hours and been shot down on both occasions because I refused to follow him out to his Bronco.

"Go take a hot bath," Beth said. "I'll make us grilled cheese sandwiches."

After Mom died, Beth and I ate grilled cheese sandwiches every day. It was all we knew how to cook until Dad insisted I learn to fry a pound of ground beef and plug in a crockpot.

I took a bath, and then we ate our sandwiches together, sitting close, as if we were still little girls. We savored each bite, as if our white bread, margarine, and American cheese sandwiches were gourmet. As if our problems had been solved and the very next evening I wouldn't climb into another trucker's cab. As if I would never leave her.

And I wouldn't have, sister. You know this. Only you know this.

6

Reuben

As soon as I get out of the shower, I'm heading next door to help Emmy make a birthday cake for her aunt. It'll be the sixth time we've hung out, and yes, I am keeping track: two times the first Sunday we met; then Tuesday morning for a few hours after her aunt left to clean the church; then Wednesday evening, when her aunt and uncle went to prayer meeting and she had me drive her into town for cake supplies; then Friday, the best day, for almost five hours when her aunt left again to help at the church. The hours I'm not with Emmy, I'm thinking about her.

I think about how she's the quietest girl I've ever known. She didn't say more than two words the entire drive into town, but she smiled whenever I looked over at her, which I did a lot. Usually with quieter girls, I try to talk more to compensate and to bring them out of their shells. I don't feel the need with Emmy. She's not in a shell. Well, maybe she just recently crawled from under her mom's shell. I can't tell for sure. But I don't think she's ever hidden herself intentionally from the world.

Emmy does hide her body a bit more than most girls her age who aren't overweight, and even some who are. She probably doesn't dress quite as modestly in California. Don't get me wrong, she doesn't, like her aunt, wear big, baggy dresses that could double as wagon tents. She wears tank tops, for example. Who doesn't love a girl in a tank top, right? And nothing else, Ray would say. But she always has a shirt overtop—unbuttoned at least. I'd like to see her shoulders and maybe a bra strap. I got a peek at her belly button once when I snagged her hippie hat and teasingly made her reach high for it. I turn the water to cool. Some girls, and especially some women, usually the curvy type, have bodies that don't stop speaking, even when hidden under layers. Emmy's body isn't like that. She's thin, and I would say graceful, only she's also kind of clumsy. Guys at her school might walk right past her without a backward glance. But her body definitely speaks to me. I turn the water to cold. I can't tell if she's a virgin. I've never really cared about that with girls, as long as the white ones haven't slept with half the football team and the Indian ones haven't slept with Benji.

My hair is still damp when I knock on the screen door.

Emmy answers in a dress and an apron—like in a sitcom from the 1950s. It works for me.

"All you need now is a strand of pearls," I tease after she invites me inside. She fingers her diamond heart necklace. "Diamonds work too. Nice apron."

"I like my apron," she says, blushing a little.

"I do too." I try not to imagine her naked underneath it.

She offers me an apron, but I tell her I'm wearing an old T-shirt. I usually only get new clothes once a year, in the fall before school, unless we happen to get Indian Money during the year and Mom decides not to give any to my younger sister Lena's white dad, who seems to know exactly when to show up repentant and broke. As a result, most years, by summer, my two pairs of jeans and three T-shirts look like shit. Last summer I bought new clothes with my job money. I'd planned as well to buy my own football gear at the end of last summer, so I didn't have to borrow the school's falling-apart gear and bucket helmet, but I wound up paying the rent for Mom instead. I have to figure out a way to make money again this summer, and quickly, now that I kind of got a girl. Maybe I can mow lawns, like when I was ten—fuck—or something. The summer I was twelve, Ray and I made bank tending horses for some white ranchers.

Maybe Teresa was right about Emmy's aunt. Except for the Bible verses written on index cards and taped on the cabinet doors and the fridge, Beth's kitchen looks like a medicine man's with bundled herbs hanging to dry and small vials and jars. This is the first time I've been inside the aunt's trailer. Emmy hung with me inside Teresa's trailer on Friday. I was a little embarrassed at first—okay, a lot. But at least Teresa's floor and ceiling aren't soft and rotting like trailers on the rez. The kids and I cleaned the place, and I warned them to leave the couch free for Emmy and me. They didn't listen, except Grace, the oldest, who kept too much distance. Kevin, Audrey, and the baby, Emilio, whose name I always pronounce with a cholo accent to piss off Teresa, crowded Emmy on the couch. She didn't seem to mind. I got the floor. We watched a couple reruns of *The Fresh Prince of Bel-Air* and one stupid episode of *Murder, She Wrote*, which unfortunately Teresa has the girls stuck on. Emmy had never seen either show before. She and her mom don't have cable in California, which is odd because she doesn't seem religious or poor.

"I'm glad we chose cherry chip," Emmy says now, referring to the box of cake mix we picked out together in the store. "Are you sure you want to help?"

I assure her I do. I assured her I did on the drive home from the store when she said it might be boring for me. As if.

"Oh, look," she exclaims. "I found this muffin tin way in the back of the cupboard. I thought—" She pauses, maybe a little embarrassed by her enthusiasm over a tin pan. I try not to grin. "I thought I'd make a cupcake for each of the kids." She nods toward Teresa's house. "There should be enough batter."

"Cool." I try to act casual. She says we can dye the frosting with food coloring, a different color for each kid. "That's cool." I nod when she asks if I know their favorite colors, even though I have no idea.

I get the eggs and milk out of the fridge, and she gets the oil from the pantry. She prefers to mix the cake batter by hand, she says, with a wooden spoon. She has to at home in California because her mom refuses to have an electric mixer in the house.

"Is the professor afraid of electronics?" There's old people on the rez who are. There's also people on the reservation without electricity—despite how Coulee Dam is in our backyard.

"We have an electronic pencil sharpener," she says. "I think it's more a feminist thing. Betty Friedan rather than Betty Crocker."

"Who?"

She asks me to mix for a while. Her arms—pathetically, she says—

always get tired. I oblige, flexing my muscles a little more than necessary.

"That was fun," she says after we get the cupcakes and the cake into
the oven and set the timer. "I've never baked with anyone my age before."

"Why not?"

"I don't know." She smiles. "I've organized bake sales for clubs at
school. But I don't really have any friends."

"Get out of here." I think she's joking. She's not. "Why?"

She shrugs her shoulders.

"I think you're great." I didn't mean to say that out loud. I quickly
recover. "You have a boyfriend."

"It's not the same." We start making the frosting.

"It can be."

"I don't think so." She's told me some about her boyfriend when I've
asked. She seems pretty loyal, despite having to try a little too hard to
hide the fact he's a fucking chump. "Here, taste this," she says. "See if
it needs more vanilla."

Jesus. Is she really offering me her finger with frosting on it?

"It's perfect." I hold her wrist loosely. I wonder what she'd do if I
kissed her. Or put her finger back in my mouth. She's looking at me as
if she might not mind.

Stepping back, she says, "You're the best friend I've ever had."

The phone rings—I'm almost relieved—before I can respond.

It's her mom. I gesture toward the front door and mouth, "Should I
go?"

She shakes her head.

I try to act busy with the frosting. Ray's always been my best friend.
We spent hours and hours of our childhoods together: on the trampoline in his mom's front yard in Nespelem, or under the trampoline after trying to summon Big Foot; at our great-aunt's place along the
Sanpoil River; in the back of a rusted-over truck and on our bikes
around Omak, mostly on the rez side; with his dad's ponies. As for
others, I don't have a problem making friends, but something does
feel different with Emmy. I've got a giant crush on her, sure, but I've

had crushes before. I had it pretty bad once for one of Teresa's friends. I finish mixing yellow, which I claimed was Emilio's favorite. I try not to listen to the conversation, but I can't help it. My eyes lock on Emmy's after she tells her mom that she likes it here. Who is this girl? I'm not sure she herself knows—she just asked her mom why she was never told who she was named after. I can't imagine that. Indians might have too many names, but we damn sure know who or what we're named after or for. If not, how can a name hold any power?

Emmy's voice suddenly changes, and she looks away. She turns and lowers her voice. I concentrate, like when I'm hunting with the elders. Emmy says something into the phone about a ceremony and admits to being scared. I should leave. Many ceremonies, by definition, should be kept private. I head for the door. She puts her hand over the receiver and asks me to please stay. I have the feeling I could never say no to this girl. And not because she's white, as Benji would claim. I broke it off with the rodeo queen, not the other way around. I grab the flowered apron off the table and put it on. Emmy laughs, and I curtsy.

"She's your only sister," I hear her say. It sounds like she's trying to convince her mom to call back later and tell her only sister happy birthday.

White people.

I read the Bible verse directly in front of me. I've been trying to ignore them, and not just here and now, but everywhere and always. This index card looks way newer than the others, which have yellowed: "For I have heard a voice as of a woman in travail . . . the voice of the daughter of Zion."

What the fuck?

Emmy's eyes are watery when she hangs up the phone, but she pretends they're not. We get the cupcakes out of the oven and then the cake fifteen minutes later. We leave on the aprons, my suggestion, while the cakes cool and we run next door to check on the kids, who giggle, even Grace, who tries not to. By the time we finally get the cakes frosted, there's only ten minutes to spare before Emmy's aunt and uncle are due to return. We take off the aprons. She looks so sweet in her dress that I want to hug her. I've been wanting to hug her all week. "What ceremony were you talking about on the phone?" I ask.

"Oh, that. Nothing."

"But you're scared." I hold a plate with four cupcakes.

"No."

"I heard you say you were."

"It's embarrassing, Reuben." She blushes.

"I'm Indian. We have ceremonies for ceremonies—for ceremonies."

"Cool ones, probably."

"Not always."

She opens the screen door for me.

"Tell me tonight then," I say. "I mean, if you want to get together." She nods. "And make out," I joke. Not really.

She punches my arm, lightly. Most of the girls on the rez, and the cowgirls in Omak, have brothers and know how to wallop, even in jest. I feel Emmy's punch, though, in my gut.

She brings me a giant slice of cake when we meet that evening by the bench in her aunt's garden. We have only an hour and a half. Would her aunt and uncle really care that she's hanging out with the neighbor kid, even if I am Indian? I don't think she's asked them, and I don't want to seem pushy. But shit, we're both going to be seniors come fall. She told me her mom doesn't know she has a boyfriend, even though they've been going out for six months. When I asked her if her boyfriend in California is white, she nodded, but said her mom would probably like him better if he weren't.

Only in California.

"Let's go for a walk," I suggest now after finishing my cake. Even as hungry as I am—Teresa's cooking sucks compared with Mom's, and we're low on groceries—the frosting tasted better on her finger. She wears the same dress she had on this morning, as I was hoping. "You have different shoes?" I ask. She's worn flip-flops every time we've been together. She goes inside and changes into low-top black Converse. Only the punk or oddball girls at school wear Converse, rather than Sketchers or Adidas. But somehow, Emmy pulls them off with her dress.

We start walking down the road, not toward town, but the other direction. Irrigation sprinklers are clunking full blast in the potato field. Emmy stops to look. The leafy plants are still small on the raised mounds. She says, "The water arching that way is kind of pretty."

"I guess, maybe, in a farmish sort of way."

She laughs. "How cold do you think that water is?"

"Why, do you want to run through the sprinklers?"

"No way." She shakes her head adamantly.

Her uncle's work truck says BASIN IRRIGATION. He's often wet or even covered in mud after work. I think he works on farm pumps.

We start walking again. "It's Columbia water," I tell her.

"What do you mean?"

"The arching water is from the Columbia River."

"How do you get there?"

"You have to drive. It's north, west, and south of here. The river curves to avoid this area. Do you blame it?" She looks around, but I don't think she hates what she sees. "It's a cold river. It used to be colder."

"What happened?"

"I'll take you there sometime." She must want to stall talking about the ceremony.

"Do you promise?"

"I promise." I brush a mosquito from her arm. "They're going to eat you alive with your perfume." She put on a spray of perfume when she ran back into the trailer to change her shoes. It's not heavy or musky. Usually she smells a little like peppermint, shampoo, soap, herbs. But right now she smells like fruit—apples? berries?—and it makes me fucking dizzy. "Hasn't your aunt or uncle taken you for any drives yet?"

"Around town, yes."

"I'm surprised your uncle hasn't taken you fishing." The dude fishes a lot.

"They—that is, Aunt Beth wants to wait until after—"

When she doesn't finish her sentence, I ask, "After what? The ceremony?"

"Yeah." She points. "Look, a stack of hay."

"Now, that's truly amazing," I mock. "Shall we?" She looks confused. "Climb to the top? Come on." I run ahead of her. I have so much energy.

"I can't climb," she admits when she makes it to the stack of staggered hay bales.

"Of course you can climb. You got arms and legs."

"I can't ride a bike."

Is she serious? Isn't her mom a professor? "Listen, if you passed precalculus with an A, then—"

"An A minus."

"You can climb a stack of hay bales." I worked my ass off in algebra II last year and only got a C+, which my counselor said was great. She meant great for a tribal kid. This school year I have to take trigonometry. "Come on, city girl. I'll help you." I go first, since she's wearing a dress. She does just fine. We make it to the top, and she immediately sits down. "I wish there were more of a view," I say. There's views on the rez I'd like to show Emmy—views I haven't wanted to share with anyone before, which must make her my best friend. What do you know?

"How are we going to get back down?" she frets.

"Don't worry, Emmy." I sit beside her on the same hay bale and take her hand. She lets me hold it for a minute until her pulse steadies. "You okay?"

She smiles widely. "That was fun." Damn, I love her teeth. I don't think she's had a lot of fun in her life if cupcakes and hay bales excite her. She's mentioned a few times how she wants to travel when she's older to Europe and India. When white girls in Omak talk about traveling, if they talk about it at all, it's always to Seattle or California. Emmy is like the quote on the back of the novel she lent me: a mix of "appetite and innocence." It's this mixture, not just her perfume, making me dizzy. To use football lingo, she's juking me out of my cleats.

I won't ask Emmy about the ceremony now because I don't want her to quit smiling. She'll tell me when she's ready. We sit mostly in silence. I brush mosquitoes from her arms, her knee. Then we climb down.

"I'm not a virgin," she announces when we're almost to the trailer park.

Where did that come from? "So," I say. "Neither am I."

She stops walking. "Well, Aunt Beth thinks I am."

"Why does she care?"

"The ceremony. I'm supposed to be a virgin."

"They sacrificing you to the gods?" I picture the Aztecs. No, the lighter-skinned Greeks.

"No, but—"

I wait. You got to have a little patience with this girl.

"I'm supposed to lay my hands on Aunt Beth at some Baptist healing ceremony," she finally says. "It's why I'm here. So she won't have another miscarriage. But I'm not a virgin *or* a Christian. I'm just—" She pauses. "I'm a liar."

"Emmy." I grab her arm as she starts to walk away. "Where are you going?"

"They're going to be home in a minute. I need to hurry."

"You're shaking."

"I'm scared. I'm scared of everything. Fucking hay bales even."

"You were brave for coming here."

"No." She shakes her head. "My mom *made* me. She thinks I'm a virgin too."

"It's really none of her business. Or your aunt's."

"You don't believe that, Reuben. You and your sister are close. You don't believe—"

"I do." I hug her to me, and not loosely. When I let go, she doesn't, not for a few more seconds anyway. I keep standing there after she has walked away. I want to follow her, but my dad has placed his hand on my shoulder, gently but firmly, like an elder. Which he never was. Even if he'd lived long enough. He couldn't feed his own fucking family, let alone worry about the tribe. Coyote brought salmon to the people, but in some tales he refused to hunt for his own hungry kids.

Those tales used to give me a stomachache, despite the fact I knew, even as a toddler, that Coyote teaches us *not* how to act as much as how *to* act. Has Dad come to warn me about Emmy? What happened to "Give the boy some space"? Is his warning a joke? It's hard to tell with him. If it's not, he can go fuck himself. He's good at that. Coyote bravely killed monsters for his people and in preparation for human-kind, but then he'd go and get himself severely wounded being proud and foolish. My dad's no longer my protector. He quit slaying mon-sters for me long ago and, in some ways, turned into one instead. I'd tell him as much if his hand didn't feel so comforting suddenly on my shoulder.

"It's not like that, Teresa," I protest. "Come on. I'm here, aren't I?"

We've been arguing at the table, ever since I mentioned wanting to find a part-time summer job. She's in one of her moods this morning, which, thankfully, she doesn't get in that often: once a month on her period or if she happens to weigh herself at the hospital—and she'd kill me for saying so. Emilio has another ear infection and won't quit fussing. Kevin and Audrey are fighting over who gets to wear the stethoscope Teresa brings home occasionally so the kids can play doc-tor. Grace, in a surgical mask, stands calmly behind her mom, braid-ing her hair, despite my telling her twice to go hold her brother, go check his diaper, go do beadwork. Something. She doesn't need to hear this.

"All I'm saying is she'll break your heart like any other white girl."

"I've dated plenty of white girls. Not one—let me assure you, again, sis—has broken my heart. Not even close. And, she's not my girl-friend."

"Yet," Grace mumbles through her paper mask.

"Go," I tell her, and point. "Now."

"If she's not your girlfriend," Teresa says, "why do you need a job to buy her things?"

"I'm not going to buy her things. She has enough things." I think of her necklace. It must be from her Sacramento boyfriend because she touches it whenever I ask a question about him.

"Then what?"

"Gas money, for starters. A new shirt for me so I don't look like a slob. Cold pops on occasion. You know what I mean."

"You're too handsome, brother, to ever look like a slob." She reaches for her purse. "I can spot you a ten."

"I'm too old to be taking money from your purse or Mom's."

"You're not a man yet. Slow down."

"Just start asking around tomorrow at work. I'll do anything. Lawn work. Take care of horses. Construction." I point toward the farm fields. "Even fertilize fucking potatoes." She doesn't respond. "I'll check the want ads. I can still watch your kids." I squeeze her hand. "We'll figure out a schedule." I'd never leave her high and dry.

"Damn white girl—wanting to ride bareback."

"Don't, Teresa." That pisses me off. "Not okay." I stand up. "I don't need this shit from you or from Dad."

"Did you just say *from Dad*?"

Oh, fuck. Her face lights up. I've never told Teresa or Mom about seeing Dad. They think he's just been showing himself randomly to other wayward sorts and to elders, as he did in life.

"Mom's been waiting years—"

I stop her. "I said—what do you need at the store besides bread, Top Ramen, and more medicine for Emilio?" I lay on the accent good and thick.

The only girl, until now, who ever came close to my heart was Teresa's younger friend Audrey, whom my niece is named after. I was as much in love with her as any junior high boy could be. Audrey was traditional, or tried to be. She spoke the Salish language fluently and would try to teach it to anyone she could. It was amazing listening to her—not just watching her mouth and tongue, which, in and of itself, was a rush, but feeling the words, knowing what they meant even when I couldn't quite form them. Audrey went to the longhouse to sing and dance. She wove baskets and bags, dug bulbs and roots. But she also had a thing for white rodeo guys with names like Cody and Bubba. I hated all her boyfriends, even the occasional Indian ones. At the annual Omak Stampede and Suicide Race—the largest event of the year, both on and off the rez—the white guys rope and wrestle bulls and the Indians ride horses down a sheer cliff and across the Okanogan River. I wouldn't miss it. The last time I ever saw Audrey was at the Indian Encampment at the Omak Stampede. Teresa already had Grace and Kevin by then. Audrey, nineteen that summer, competed in the Indian dance competition. She held a feathered fan, and I swear she kept staring straight at me. She moved so slowly. The truck that hit her car later that night did not. She was killed instantly, and by an Indian, not a white guy. Her death made the front page of the *Omak Chronicle*. But so does every weekly wreck that kills another cowboy or Indian: teenage parents with their babies, in-the-middle-of-messy-divorces-so-driving-drunk millworkers, tired-looking moms, relatives visiting from Spokane, drunk rodeo folk, elders, schoolteachers, sober-but-in-debt millworkers, stoned women, hunters, yuppies from Seattle who cross the mountains for a change of scenery, an Indian father who lost his way, an Indian fancy dancer who stared at a boy.

I worried there might be awkwardness between me and Emmy after our Sunday evening hug. But first thing Tuesday she puts her arms around my neck. This time I hold on.

"Can I show you something?" she asks. On second thought, she does seem a little upset.

"Anything."

"You have to promise not to laugh." I do. "Come inside."

She escorts me into the bedroom where she sleeps. My pulse starts racing as Emmy's had after she climbed the hay bales. Her night-light, which sets on the dresser by the window, is a pair of ceramic hands held together in prayer. That's the faint glow I've seen from outside.

She points to the bed. "Look."

I don't notice anything unusual at first. Probably because I'm picturing Emmy stretched out there in just a T-shirt, or little pajama shorts and a tank top with no shirt overtop. I have to focus to see what exactly she's pointing at. Draped on the bed is a dress like those her aunt wears.

"Beth made that for me," Emmy says. "For the healing. She was so excited."

I go over to the bed and touch the dress. It's hokey as hell, no doubt. I pick it up. "You'd look good in anything." I mean it. She's stylish, even if I'm not sure what style it is. I try to hold the dress up to her.

"Oh, don't," she says. "I'd rather die."

That seems a bit dramatic. "Than wear this dress?"

"No—than have *you* see me in it."

Is that a compliment? Or a serious lack of trust?

"I'd go anywhere with you in this," I say.

"No, you wouldn't."

"I would." She moves closer to me, or it's my imagination. "I'm not saying the dress isn't awful. It is." So awful, in fact, I put it back on the bed. "But I'd go to the store with you in it. Or to the movies."

"What about to school?"

"Sure."

She is moving closer.

"The reservation?" she asks.

She's testing me.

"In a heartbeat." I grin.

"You're lying."

"I don't lie. Put it on right now. We'll go somewhere." I'd love to help her change.

"I can't wear that dress." Her tears spill. It's the first time I've seen her cry.

"You can. It's just for one day."

"I can't." Gray is now my favorite eye color for white girls.

"I've worn fringed buckskin and feathered headpieces," I tell her. But never at Omak High, like the real traditional kids do in the cafeteria for one period each day. "We have healing ceremonies. Small ones. Ones that last for days. You can do it."

"I can?"

I don't wipe her tears before I kiss her on the cheek because I want to taste the salt.

She kisses me back on my cheek, as if we were in Czechoslovakia or something.

I kiss her back on her other cheek. She laughs. I need to sit down before I pass out.

"Let's go back outside," I suggest. I have yet to light up in front of Emmy, but I could use a smoke.

"Why?" She wipes her eyes. "Don't you like it in here?"

I like it too much, except for maybe the crib, which seems strange—her aunt isn't even showing yet—until I realize it was probably Emmy's old crib. "Cute," I say, pointing to the wooden letters on the wall that spell her name.

"Do they creep you out?" she asks. I sit on her bed, but not near the dress.

"Why would they creep me out? You're weird."

She doesn't seem bothered by my sitting on her bed, although she remains standing.

"I have some gifts for your nieces," she announces, and heads for the closet, where she pulls out a small suitcase. "I brought all this stuff with me."

"They don't need anything." I get up. "They got everything they need." I try not to sound pissed, but I am a little.

"Oh. I didn't mean—" She already unrolled a few scarves that were protecting a set of little glass bowls and what looks like fancy chopsticks.

"I have to go check on them," I say.

"Okay." She blushes deep red. "I didn't mean anything. I don't think you're poor."

"We are poor," I say. "But not in need." Or we won't be after I go stand in line tomorrow at a USDA food distribution site. Tribal food commodities sometimes include frozen ground buffalo or canned salmon. No irony there. Off the rez, it'll be oatmeal, rice, maybe cheese, canned vegetables. I need a fucking job.

"It's just I liked these Asian bowls and stuff when I was a little girl." She sounds so nervous. I head for the door. "I don't have any younger sisters or nieces to give them to."

Damn it.

"I'm sorry," she says. "Don't be mad."

I turn back. She doesn't need to apologize. She's on her knees, wrapping the bowls back into the scarves. Her hair is coming loose. It was pulled back in one of those elaborate white chick braids. "Emmy." I go to her.

"I don't know how to act in front of people," she says. "I never have."

I kneel down. "You don't have to *act* in front of me." I pick up one of the bowls. It's decorated on the inside rather than the outside. "Grace would love these."

"Do you think?"

I pick up a pair of the chopsticks. "Can you use these things?"

"When no one's watching, I do pretty well." She smiles.

"Come here," I say. I'd like to finish unbraiding her hair.

"I'm here already." She's seeming a little coy today. She doesn't move any closer.

I have to get up and sit on her bed to put some space between us. After I catch my equilibrium, I tell her, "I've started that book you lent me." I grab the prairie dress. "I was thinking how Sister Carrie Meeber is ashamed of her clothes when she's first in Chicago."

"Do you like the novel?" She's carefully putting the little bowls and chopsticks into a gift bag she pulled from her suitcase. She rearranges them three times. She did the same thing when frosting the cakes— kept trying to make them look better, as if her aunt or the kids would judge.

"I keep seeing you as Carrie," I say. She sits down on the bed. "I mean, as I'm reading the book, Carrie has your face and hair and— figure."

"You know what they say about white people? We all look the same."

"Yeah, maybe—well, but not quite." I can't take it in her room any longer, especially not sitting on the bed with her. "You want to go for a run?"

"Actually"—she touches her necklace—"I have to make a call before they get home."

I stand up. "Phoning your mom?" She's not, of course, and it's none of my business. But I want to see if she'll tell me the truth.

"No. I haven't been able to get ahold of Connor lately."

"Did he give you that necklace?" I've wanted to ask. She nods. I'm not usually an angry guy, or the jealous type, necessarily. "Did you promise to wear it for him all summer?"

She nods again. "But—he didn't ask me to."

"Then he's an idiot." A fucking idiot.

When we go for a run Wednesday evening, Emmy isn't wearing the necklace. I didn't mean to make her self-conscious about it. Or did I mean to? I think girls usually remove jewelry before exercising. Her bare neck is torment. I want to trace her collarbone. We run only as far as the hay bales, which Emmy wants to climb up again. Once on top, sitting close, I ask, "Did you get ahold of him?" I'm not about to say his name, ever.

"I don't want to talk about Connor. Or the healing. Let's just sit here. Do you have a cigarette?"

"Why? You don't smoke. And I certainly don't light up on haystacks, weirdo."

"I wish we could stay up here longer." She leans her head on my shoulder and then says rather contemplatively, "The sky's turning pink."

"Which makes Emmy think."

"The whole world could shrink." She doesn't miss a beat. "And slip down the sink."

"In less than a wink."

"We're on the brink, my friend, and I need a goddamn drink."

I laugh and put my arm around her shoulder. "You're my best friend, Emmy," I say. Emmy and Reuben.

"I've never had a best friend."

"I know." Ten minutes pass. Then ten more. I break the silence. "Up north," I tell her, "it doesn't get dark this time of year until almost eleven."

"Would you ever take me there?"

"To the rez? Sure. Why wouldn't I?" I can think of a dozen reasons. Two dozen.

"There's so much to see around here," she says, and I grin. "Where did you used to go, Reuben, late at night in your truck? I'd hear your tires in the gravel. You don't have to tell me."

"On drives. Mostly to the river." Sometimes to drum, but I'll keep that part to myself for now.

"Why don't you go anymore?"

"I like being near you," I own up. "Even if we aren't hanging out." She snuggles into my chest. I fix her scrunchie, which is slipping off. Then I hug her tightly. This damn girl.

Friday I offer to take her for a short drive while the two youngest kids nap. Last summer I found a place along Crab Creek that probably looks the same as it did when Chief Moses was a pup, before he became a warrior, carrying his rifle in front, then a diplomat, carrying it in back. Crab Creek alone used to drain into Moses Lake. Now every canal in the county dumps its runoff into the lake. No wonder it looks like algae soup. Before Moses was forced north onto the Colville, he won a separate rez for his people, but then he lost it. He's the chief I feel the most alliance with, which used to irritate the fuck out of my dad, given that our last name is Tonasket. And Chief Tonasket rocked, no doubt about it. For a while Tonasket, who became a rancher, thought Moses nothing but a drunk, gambling renegade. But they eventually became bros. They even took sides together against the famous and highly spiritual Sanpoil chief Skolaskin, whom Moses was partially responsible for getting jailed at Alcatraz. Not cool. My dad never forgave Moses for this act, but he still married one of his descendants.

Emmy says she's too nervous to take a drive. She's afraid her aunt or uncle might come home or that we might pass them on the road. I try to assure her not to worry and that Indians use back roads. Moses certainly couldn't have been a diplomat without them.

"After the healing," she promises, "we can start going places."

I'm not sure I've ever known a teenage girl, white and Christian or

Indian and traditional, who obeys her relatives as much as Emmy does. She may not be hiding in a shell, but sometimes it feels like she's on a leash.

We're sitting on the back steps of Teresa's trailer. Emmy's been quieter than usual, if possible. She wears a silky kimono top that's pretty—Emilio kept rubbing it—but it covers her collarbone, and I can't tell if she's wearing the necklace. "You get ahold of that guy?" I ask.

"I talked to his mom." I grab her hand so she'll stop picking her nail polish. She lets me hold it. "She said I'm wasting my time. Her son is just like his father."

I keep quiet so she'll continue talking.

"She informed me that Connor's had lots of girls in his room already this summer, but none as well mannered as me. What does that even mean?" She lets go of my hand. "I barely ever talked to the lady. And what I did with her son—it wasn't mannered."

Fuck if that isn't the last thing I want to hear about.

"Who cares, right?" she says, standing up. She doesn't cry. I almost wish she would. She says she knew this would happen if she left Sacramento. "Connor's the type you have to constantly throw biscuits to."

I bust up. Then I stand and put both my hands on her waist. "I care if he hurt you, Emmy." But I couldn't be happier it's over between them. I pull her close, and not only to hug her. She smells like warm berries. How does she taste? I should show some restraint, but I don't want to. The summer is short, and already I can't bear the thought of her returning south, ever. I reach just my thumb under the hem of her silky shirt to touch her bare skin. I kiss her cheek, then her ear. I whisper something intended for only her to hear. God, I want to taste her mouth. Her breath catches right before my lips find hers, and the sound unhinges me. Scared, I pull back, and a bit too abruptly because Emmy almost loses her footing. The next thing I know I'm climbing into my truck and hauling ass for Virgil's sweat lodge in Omak.

7

Matt

I ran into Jamie Kagen once in a diner in Colfax. I never told Beth. Emmy would have been about ten years old then. Although she and Kate could've been dead for all Beth and I knew or for all Kagen cared. He was sitting at a booth with a woman who looked nothing like Kate. Her hair was blond, for starters, and styled in such a way that I knew she came from money. Jamie and this woman had not one but two small boys eating with them. *How fair is that?* I thought at the time. But that was back when I still hoped against all odds for a son of my own. Everyone in the diner seemed to know Jamie and his family. I was in the area with a sales rep who invited me to have lunch with him and a vendor. There's not a lot of irrigation business in the hilly Palouse region because most of the farmers are dryland wheat farmers. They own some of the richest soil in the West, and they know it. Jamie knew it.

He knew me too, when he glanced in my direction. I'd wanted to hunt him down after his daughter was born, exchange a few words and punches. But after a decade, I had nothing left to say to the man. Neither was I about to eat in the same diner as the bastard. I made excuses and headed out the door. I was almost to my work truck when I heard my name being called. I could've just kept walking, but I owed it to Emmy.

"Kagen," he said, offering me his hand, which I didn't shake. He'd lost a little of his confidence. But not enough. "Jamie Kagen."

"I know who you are."

He put on the cowboy hat he was holding. "How is she?"

Did he mean Kate or Emmy?

"How is Katie?" he asked.

Should I tell him how Kate used to come home late from her waitressing shifts drunk and stinking? Either she was chasing some rough men back then, trying to get over Jamie, or they were chasing her. Both times I tried to act like a brother and talk with Kate about her dating life, she got pissed, and I didn't blame her. Beth would bring Emmy into our bed.

"I wish I knew," I said.

"Listen, Matt." He tried to reason with me. "I'd like to know how they are."

"No one's heard a word from Kate in over nine years." Damn, how Beth used to sob in my arms for her sister and niece. "Thanks to you."

"I heard she took the baby and left town."

"The baby's name—your daughter's name is Emmy."

The name seemed to jolt him, as if he'd never heard it. Surely he'd made inquiries.

The diner door opened, and the older of his small boys came running toward us in cowboy boots. "Daddy." He skidded to a stop and yelled, "Mommy said finish your lunch or no ice cream."

"Back inside, son," Jamie said firmly. The boy listened. We waited. "You don't happen to have a picture of the baby, do you?" he asked

I shook my head.

"You don't have to give it to me. I just want to see her face."

I pulled out my wallet. The snapshot looked twenty years old. "Keep it," I said, and turned to leave.

"Wait." He fumbled trying to hand me his business card. "In case the girl ever comes looking for me."

A business card for his kid?

"Or if she and Katie ever need my help."

I took it, saying, "It's a little late." If I knew Kate, she'd just as soon starve.

"How many children do you and Bethany have by now?" he asked, but he didn't lift his eyes from Emmy's photo.

To this day I don't know why I told him the truth. Maybe because he remembered Bethany's name. "None. We can't have any."

He looked at me. "I'm real sorry to hear that." I think he was. He offered me his hand, but I just couldn't.

———

I love the Lord, but I love my wife tenfold more. If only there was a way to drug her and drag her to the doctor. I've been wanting out of our fundamentalist church for years—maybe clear back to when the old minister condemned Kate from the pulpit and her dad did nothing. He may have even said, "Amen." I told my future father-in-law that I would look after his two girls at camp. I failed with Kate. But not as much as he failed as a father by shunning his pregnant daughter and then his grandbaby.

Sure, I was taken with the church at first, but only because of a soft-spoken girl named Bethany, so unlike the girls at the high school. There was a quietness in her that tamed me. I was more rowdy than wild. My older brother and I had a lot of freedom growing up: fishing, hunting, dirt biking, snowmobiling, having girls in our basement bedrooms, blasting our Zeppelin and AC/DC records, even drinking beer practically under our parents' noses. Something was obviously missing because my brother started snorting coke in motel rooms with naked girls and then older women and then total skanks he'd pick up at parks. I know, cast the first stone. I began attending church with my cousin. For a time I even considered becoming a minister, which pleased my dad about as much as putting his oldest son in rehab. He wasn't all that pleased, either, about my getting hitched at seventeen, but over the years he's let me know how proud he is of me for taking care of Beth. Once when I was over at his place smoking fish, he started to hint that life with Beth couldn't be easy. I stopped him. He backtracked, saying he couldn't fathom our loss.

Emmy is a lot like her aunt: quiet, easily satisfied, timid almost to a fault, wholesome. But she's also smart and, when she relaxes, funny like her mom. She's even occasionally sharp-tongued *about* her mom. And she's a bit strong-willed like both sisters. I have yet to get Emmy to switch lanes when we go out for a driving lesson. We've only been out three times because it makes Beth nervous. Emmy won't do anything to displease her aunt. The love between those two blows me away. It did sixteen years ago, and it does now. They've spent hours upon hours gardening together these last weeks and making oils.

Beth's happier than she's been in a decade. She needs female compan-
ionship. She seems alone even when among the other women at
church, uncovering dishes at potlucks and whatnot. It makes me uncomfortable when Beth starts talking heavily to Emmy about God's
love and divine will. I get so nervous Beth will repel the girl she has
longed for the better part of our marriage that I have to walk away.

Which is what I'd like to do with the church, if only I were certain
Beth would follow me. I tried to switch churches after my father-in-
law died, an event that I admit didn't sadden me. For years I attempted
to understand that man for Beth's sake, figuring if she loved him so
much, there must be something I was overlooking. I used to invite
him fishing and hunting, but he always declined. I told the old coot
more than once that I'd love to hear about his days as a logger. You
don't meet many loggers on this side of the mountains. Most old-
timers around here built the dams. My father-in-law always replied
that there was nothing to tell other than he'd breathed smoke and
eaten sawdust from ages seventeen to twenty-five. I gave up trying.
Beth took his death harder than I expected. At the same time, she
saved very little from her parents' house. Not that there was a lot. "In
my father's house are no mansions," Kate used to say. Still, I thought
Beth would try to keep every scrap. She narrowed her inheritance
down quickly to half a dozen boxes, all but one of which are stored at
my parents' place until we move out of Quail Run Mobile Home Park
into a larger house with acreage.

The kid next door has taken quite a liking to Emmy. She doesn't
think I know. She'd be embarrassed if I dared to tease her. And she'd
be mortified if she thought Beth knew anything about it, which she
doesn't. I've always liked the boy. He seems to have his head on
straighter than a lot of white kids, even though he hangs with a rather
sorry-looking bunch from the reservation.

I have nothing against Indians, unlike my boss and coworkers, who
think Indians are nothing more than drunks on welfare. The other
field technicians, shop welders, dispatchers, and sales reps all gripe
how "no-good Indians," but not "hardworking Americans" like them,
are allowed—by the federal government, not the state—to hunt and

fish anywhere and everywhere without a license and with all kinds of nets. It's not quite that black and white. The Colville Tribe writes its own fish and game regulations. I've read them. And only certain tribes can fish in certain areas off the reservation without licenses. Not every tribe on every waterway in the state. That's a gross exaggeration.

Besides, who really gives a crap? There's plenty of places to land trout, bass, walleye, and kokanee with the largest reservoirs in the state located just north of here. An hour south is the free-flowing Hanford Reach of the Columbia, where chinook spawn in the fall, steelhead run, and sturgeon bite. What more, seriously, could an angler ask for? As far as nets, don't commercial fishermen use them on the lower Columbia, Puget Sound, the East Coast, and around the world? I've been fishing on the lakes and rivers that border the Colville Reservation my whole life. You can't beat the trout fishing between the dams. But the poverty on the reservation is unbelievable. Third world, in fact.

Then again, so is the way Bethany bleeds out our babies onto the sheets and carpet.

It really is unfathomable. If I told people the gory details, they wouldn't believe me, and why the hell would I? I wouldn't humiliate or hurt Beth for all the world.

I miss the days Beth used to fish with me. We were still kids really. When I worked swing shift or graveyard at the factory, she and I would go fishing almost every day after Kate left and before Beth suffered her second miscarriage. Sure, I had to fish from shore, no boat. My wife's terrified of water. But I didn't mind so much. I still go fishing a lot, only without her. Beth never asks me *not* to. And because of that, I don't argue about attending church with her. Fishing, however, is my real church.

I'd like to adopt a baby, but Beth's too afraid the birth mom would change her mind and take the baby away, as Kate did with Emmy. I'd like to move my wife onto a small farm, maybe even in another county. I've picked some perfect spots over the years. I think migrating south to the Walla Walla Valley would suit Beth best of all, although it would distance me a bit from my favorite fishing spots and most of my family. The landscape in Walla Walla isn't quite as rugged as here. Less snow, more trees. Beth could plant a large garden. I could install irrigation and build her a greenhouse. We could get her mother's piano back from the church. Beth wants to wait to move until we have a baby. Her first couple of miscarriages I attributed to the sadness of her losing Kate and Emmy. At times now my wife's frailness scares me. Her hands twitch too often while she sleeps, and her pulse is unsteady. Another miscarriage may kill her. If only she'd let me get a vasectomy. A better man would've stopped having sex with her altogether, and I try, but then she massages my sore neck and back with her oils. Or she slides in naked under the sheets beside me, and the paleness of her skin, which in the daytime might look unhealthy, glows in the moonlight like the inside of a shell.

We leave for the healing ceremony in half an hour. Beth is in the kitchen "anointing" Emmy's hands with oil. We'll meet Bro Mathias and a busful of church members at a lake by Dry Falls at seven. He chose a weekday in hopes there'll be fewer crowds, and he selected evening time for the backdrop the setting sun provides. He's from the South, which some of the deacons hold against him. They think he's trying to put on a show this evening at the O.K. Corral to prove he's been westernized, and maybe he is. But there's more to it than that. Mathias was over yesterday for dinner. He wanted to meet Emmy and say a prayer to start the twenty-four-hour fast that he and I planned to begin after the meal. He asked Emmy to fast also, which wasn't part of the deal, and even Beth, who can't fast in her condition, looked troubled by his request. Emmy quickly agreed. I have to admit, Mathias was good with Emmy. But I still don't like the guy. It's not his accent. It's the way he looks at my wife. I get that they connect on a spiritual level. The whole church can see that. And I know she cleaned and typed for our old pastor, but sometimes now, when I think about her alone with Brother Mathias and all those empty pews, I can barely get through the workday without messing something up. Beth told me she plays hymns for Brother Mathias on her mother's old piano. If that doesn't beat all.

I'll put up with it and more, I've conceded, if he can help heal my wife. I can't convince her to see a doctor, but somehow he has her convinced the Lord has finally heard her prayers. Or maybe she has him convinced: Beth has a certain hushed power.

I step onto the front porch for some fresh air. The smell of herbs has been overwhelming the last few days—years—with all the teas brewing and oils distilling. I nudge my dirty work boots farther into the corner of the porch, where I also store my hunting boots and coveralls. I keep a few poles in the extra bedroom closet in case on a whim Beth ever wants to go fishing. Everything else I store at my parents': not just big stuff like my boat, but my tackle box and power tools. Even my old record collection, which Beth thinks I threw away. I want to move out of this trailer park. A man needs a garage.

Reuben's truck has been gone since Friday. I wonder where the kid took off to. He told me he was here for the entire summer this year to help his sister. Emmy doesn't seem to know where Reuben is, either, or when he'll get back. She's been eyeing the trailer next door more than ever, and Sunday evening Beth and I returned from church to find Emmy sitting on the garden bench, looking almost as bewildered as she did her first couple of days here.

I hope Reuben's not messing with her in any way. I had to smile the time I saw the two of them together. I'd left a service manual at home on accident. I drove right past the trailer park after I spotted them. *Good for Emmy,* I thought. Kate had told Beth on the phone that Emmy didn't have many friends.

I open the screen door now for my wife and niece. "Doesn't she look beautiful, Matt?"

"You both do." And they do, but Beth more so. Emmy looks uncomfortable in their matching long dresses and with her hair pulled back tightly in a bun.

"Go get in the car, Beth," I say, kissing her cheek. "Give me a minute with Emmy."

"Listen, honey," I say to Emmy once Beth's in the car. "I know you're scared."

"I'm okay." But she isn't.

"I'll be right there beside you, I promise." She nods. She looks more like Kate than I realized. It's the dress and her wide-open eyes. It would drain the confidence right out of Kagen to see her. "Thanks for doing this, kid. It means everything to your aunt."

"Thanks for inviting me."

"I wish you'd stop being so polite with me. It's painful." I take her arm to escort her to the car. "You threw up on me more than once as a baby, you know."

"That's embarrassing. And gross."

"Nah. That's just family."

We drive into the scablands mostly in silence. Beth is praying her heart out, I can tell. I say a few prayers as well. The scenery must look strange to Emmy: the fields of boulders, then the towering basalt cliffs that not only shade but dwarf the car. It's desolate coulee country up here, and it would be even more so if not for Grand Coulee Dam and its chain of holding reservoirs. Emmy's eyes remain wide whenever I catch them in the rearview mirror, especially after Dry Falls itself comes into view. A basalt cliff of epic proportion, four miles across, it dwarfs not just our car but Steamboat Rock and Grand Coulee Dam. It's the ledge over which Glacial Lake Missoula spilled with the combined force of all rivers on earth at the end of the last ice age. The catastrophic flood shaped the entire Pacific Northwest. The church of course doesn't believe in the ice age. God sculpted Dry Falls *as is*. The earth existed without man for only five days. I wish I could think of something comforting to say to Emmy. I don't think she's a Christian, which should concern me, but she's young. If Beth were asleep, I'd tell Emmy this is the way to the reservation where Reuben's from. We pass the lake where my relatives gather in late April for the statewide opening of trout season. It's great fun hanging at the campground for the weekend. Lots of fish, food, beer, and campfires. It overwhelms Beth. I go without her—she sends food—but I no longer stay the night. I turn off the highway now onto a gravel road that winds down plateaus of sage to a less popular park and lakeshore.

The white church bus with CALVARY BAPTIST painted in red on the side is already in the parking area. When we get out of the car, Beth, a proud aunt, loops arms with Emmy. My family knows nothing about this healing. Despite what my brother thinks, I'm not drinking any-one's Kool-Aid. I get a little tired of trying to prove this to my family and to me. This ceremony has divided the church. At least two thirds of the congregation think Brother Mathias has devoted too much time to it. The other third thinks Beth is worth it. Actually most of them have seemed disgruntled lately. Like a true shepherd this evening, Mathias has gathered his entire flock around him. The crowd parts as we near. The women smile in varying degrees, and the men dutifully say, "Amen."

"Sister Bethany." Mathias rushes to her as if it's been weeks. He looks so nervous I almost feel sorry for him. He has a feminine air to him that Beth finds endearing and attributes solely to his southern heritage. I'm certain he'll be dismissed if this healing fails to work. I see the way the more rugged and hairy men size him up. If Beth mis-carries, his ministry will be the least of my concerns. "Brother Mat-thew," he says. "And let me introduce to the congregation Sister Emmy." She looks at me for support. I smile. He continues. "An exam-ple of purity for all you young ladies." I move nearer to Emmy and take her arm. "To the water's edge," says the effeminate shepherd as he leads his flock.

I feel out of sorts. Probably just my blood sugar. It's been awhile since I've fasted. But if my teenage niece can do it, so can I. I prom-ised Emmy I wouldn't, but I have to let go of her so she can wade into the water with Beth and Mathias. I wait on the shore with the rest of the congregation. The wind picks up, as it always does in the coulees as sunset nears. Did the preacher think of that? But at least this eve-ning it's a warm wind. I have to strain to hear Mathias, who talks slowly in his southern accent. Giving examples and reciting verses, he claims Jesus was partial to suffering women. If only Jesus were half as partial to my wife as Mathias is. He quotes the very words hanging in our kitchen on a note card: "For I have heard a voice as of a woman in travail." It's all I can do, suddenly, to keep myself from passing out. Maybe I did sip the Kool-Aid. I fall back some in the crowd.

The minister talks next about virtue, and I see Emmy place her hands on Beth's belly. They cup her womb. It's a moving sight. But then Mathias puts one of his hands over Emmy's hands and his other hand on Beth's shoulder. He seems anything but feminine now. The crowd, becoming spirited, inches nearer the water and breaks out in "Amen" and "Praise Jesus." I try to take a step forward as well to yank that man's hand off my wife—and my niece, for that matter—but my foot catches on a reed. Someone grabs my elbow firmly to prevent me from falling into the water, which would've been humiliating. I turn around. It's the kid Reuben. Where the hell did he come from? No one else seems to notice him, even though he's the only one not in dress clothes. He says something to me, but not in English. I turn back to my wife. The minister finishes up. "Thy faith hath made thee whole."

The women quickly spread out a picnic. Most of the younger boys go off to fish. There's less than an hour left of daylight, and the wind intensifies. But everyone's spirits are high. Even the staunchest opposers pat me on the back. I thank them all for giving up their evening. Beth and Emmy have walked off together for a short stroll. I imagine Beth is thanking Emmy and professing her devotion. Trying to, anyway, over the flap of their matching wet dresses.

I'll be damned if Reuben is nowhere to be found.

If Emmy didn't see him, and I'm thinking I'm the only one who did, then I'm not saying a word. He must love Emmy to have shown up here like that. The thought gives me serious pause.

"Brother Matthew." It's the preacher. I've been trying to avoid his now beaming face.

I scan the park once more for Reuben, and then, feeling stupid doing so, I scan the cliffs.

"Brother Mathias." I shake his hand. I want to disrespectfully call him bro, or worse, but I won't wreck this day for Beth. "Thank you for this, sir," I say. "I know there's been resistance."

"All worth it if Jesus turns your and Bethany's house into a home."

I try to swallow my pride. It's not going down. "And when will the parsonage be a home?" I used to tease Mathias about finding a wife— back when he first moved here and Beth and I, being close to his age, considered him our friend as well as our preacher. We used to have him for dinner. But then I began noticing his eyes lingering a little too long on Bethany's face, which in some ways *isn't* better than his eyes lingering on her body.

"The Lord will send me a Rachel of my own, all in good time," he says. "For now the Lord has taken the reproach from your Rachel."

"Reproach?"

"Shame," he explains. "The shame of being a childless woman of God."

I want to punch his jaw, what little he has. "Beth has nothing to be ashamed of."

"I have told her as much," he says. "'For he that hath suffered in the flesh hath ceased from sin.'"

Here comes Beth now, still arm in arm with Emmy. I want to take my family home, not pretend to fellowship with these people on a patch of grass in the scablands. After Beth falls asleep tonight, I too will cup her belly in my hands, as I have so often before, willing the life inside it to stay put, to not be so eager to slip from his mother's womb or to move on to the next world without giving us a chance to know him first. "Linger awhile, kid," I'll whisper. "But if you must go, don't take your mother with you."

8

Emmy

Aunt Beth knocked on the bedroom door. She'd knocked earlier, but I hadn't replied then either. Since waking, I'd been going over the events of the previous evening. The drive through eerie coulees and the way the silence had fitted the landscape and my mood. The minister who seemed to be in love with my aunt, and I didn't want him to be, even if it distracted him from my guilty face. The lake water that was so cold I thought it must've come from Reuben's Columbia. Mostly I kept recalling how when I'd placed my hands on Aunt Beth's belly, I felt not only a lump—a baby, a real baby, my cousin—but a surge. If I'd only imagined the surge, then why did my hands still feel so warm this morning, glowing almost, like the night-light? Was it all the hand massages Beth had given me in preparation for the healing? And how was I to explain the sensation to Mom, who might scoff, or to Aunt Beth, who might be afraid? I needed to tell Reuben. He was supposed to be my best friend, but he'd taken off suddenly in his truck a week ago and not returned.

I missed him, far more than I'd ever missed Connor. Missing Reuben was to become such a large part of my life in the years following that summer. Even if I could have known then, I'm certain I wouldn't have changed a thing.

"Come in," I said when Aunt Beth knocked again twenty minutes later.

"You all right, honey?" She poked her head into the room. "I've been so worried."

I wasn't all right. I was overstimulated. My whole childhood I'd searched that shop below our apartment for things to make me feel even a tenth of the way I felt in that lake with my hands on Aunt

Beth's belly or with Reuben's mouth close to my ear. What he'd whispered, right before he took off, wasn't naughty, as Connor's first note to me had been, but it was intensely personal. A month ago I could've passed Beth Miller or Reuben Tonasket on the street or down a store aisle or heard their names on the news and felt no connection. Actually I wasn't sure I believed that. I was no longer sure what I believed. I was seriously considering becoming a Christian if it would help my aunt not miscarry. If only I'd taken the leap and asked Christ into my heart *before* the healing, but I'd been too scared, too unsure I wanted a god living inside me. Mom thought my presence alone would prevent Aunt Beth from having another miscarriage. All morning I'd been trying to convince myself she was right.

"I feel a little strange," I admitted to Beth.

She hurried to the bedside and handed me the glass of water she was holding. I drank it all. Tap water tasted good in Washington. Reuben had made fun of me for being amazed by the fact. Beth checked my forehead for fever. I was glad she didn't take one of my overly warm hands in hers. Smiling, she said something about how God's love, when manifested to the extent it was last night, could feel overwhelming. Actually it was *her* love that overwhelmed me. I'd never felt more loved than in the last month.

Not one day growing up did I doubt that Mom loved me. She told me she did often. But her expectations for me were always so high. My fear of disappointing her was constant. I still get a stomachache thinking about how many different musical instruments she rented for me in elementary school, how many art supplies and kits (which weren't cheap) she bought for me over the years and with which I mostly made crafts. Luckily I had just enough skill in sketching to get accepted into Valley Art Academy. My scholarship reflected my top grades and Mom's lower-income and single-parent status, *not* my creative talent. Most of the kids at my school were sure of their artistic abilities, even their genius. Some were also sure already of their places in the world. I stammered. Not that I would've done better at a public high school, but maybe.

Aunt Beth thought I was great at everything I did. If I were to fall down in front of her, she'd compliment my landing. Uncle Matt too. He didn't get frustrated at my ineptitude during driving lessons. Maybe I was good with plants, as my aunt said. She gave me a lot of freedom in her garden: to try out different herbs as companion plants, to overharvest the leaves and stems, to underwater or to overwater. I kept expecting Mom to say over the phone, "Well, you can't exactly put *herbs* down on your Berkeley application." But she hadn't yet. Neither had she asked me outright if I'd been studying for my SATs. Or for that matter, if I'd started looking for my dad, which I hadn't. For now, my aunt and uncle were enough family.

"I made you a big breakfast," Aunt Beth said. "I've been keeping it warm in the oven. You'll feel better after you replenish yourself."

And I did. She herself had never looked better. Though Mom and Beth had similar features, they had completely different types of beauty. Neither was gorgeous like models, though Mom at times could look stunning. Her strength and the independence in her eyes made her beautiful. Spencer thought so, I knew, even if those two attributes were the very things that made loving her a challenge. Aunt Beth was pretty in a softer, more feminine, and, at times, airy or dreamy way. Uncle Matt seemed in awe of her, although occasionally it seemed he wanted to shake her awake.

Today there was faint color in Beth's cheeks, which made her seem almost feverish with life. The ceremony had been carefully scheduled to take place during Beth's twelfth week of pregnancy. She'd never before carried a baby into the second trimester. "Every day from here on out is like a miracle," she'd said to me yesterday evening, right after the healing, as we'd walked arm in arm through the small park with looming cliffs.

"What do you want to do today?" Beth asked now.

I suggested we work in the garden for a few hours. I wanted to be outside working in case Reuben came back. Was he coming back? I didn't want to miss seeing him, even if only once more for a few minutes, even if only across the yards.

After Reuben first left, Teresa had to haul her kids somewhere to be watched. I wanted to offer to babysit, free of charge, but I didn't know if Teresa would get offended or what Aunt Beth would think. She was a bit envious of Teresa's four kids, which made me sad. The last two days a very old Indian woman had been at Teresa's. She was too old to be Reuben's mom or even his grandma. One afternoon Teresa caught me sitting on the bench staring at her house and listening to her tinkling chimes. She'd come outside to rotate the sprinkler. She didn't talk to me. I didn't think she liked me. But she shrugged her shoulders and raised her open hands to let me know she didn't know where her little brother was either.

Aunt Beth and I had been outside working for about two hours when Grace, with Emilio on her hip, brought the kids outside to run through the sprinkler. For some reason Grace didn't wave back at me. Had Reuben told her not to? Kevin, in his favorite oversize rodeo shirt, and Audrey, in a swimsuit, came running toward me until Grace called them back. Emilio didn't listen when Grace finally put him down. He beelined it for me. He called me Em. Reuben had tried to get him to call me Auntie Em, like in *The Wizard of Oz*. I gave Emilio a hug and let him smell different plants before sending him back, though I didn't want to. "You made some friends, I see," Aunt Beth said, beaming at me. I wondered if she'd beam if Reuben had stepped over to say hello. "You know, we should do a vacation Bible school here in the park for the kids." I had no idea what that was, but I didn't like the sound of it.

"Actually," I said, "I was thinking I'd go to church on Sunday."

"Oh, Emmy." She put down the egg carton in which she'd been preparing clippings. Her eyes got teary. "I've been praying." She paused. "But Kate said you couldn't."

"I can go to church, just not to yours," I clarified. "Other than for the healing." I didn't really blame Mom for not wanting me in Aunt Beth's church. In fact, how could Beth still go there week after week, year after year, after they'd called her sister a whore? Maybe she *was* a bit brainwashed. Mom thought all Christians were. It made me feel like a bitch to pass even the slightest judgment on Beth.

"That's fair. But we do have Brother Mathias now, not the old minister." She smiled. "He's kind and forgiving." As was Aunt Beth. Too forgiving. That's why she continued to attend that church. "Still, that was gracious of Kate."

"You guys can drop me off at a different church on the way to yours." Did you have to be praying in a church to become a Christian? It might make the experience feel more authentic. I needed to become a Christian without Beth's knowing because she thought I was already a believer, or she wanted to.

"We'll figure it out, sweetie." She was still smiling. "But I don't think your uncle will let you go alone. Oh, I'm overjoyed." She hugged me. "I'm also dusty and beat. Let's go inside."

I was dusty too. The dust worsened as the summer progressed, and the air was getting even drier. The dust felt coarser here than in Sacramento, like sand, and because of the wind, it covered everything, including the furniture, as Mom said. It hadn't once sprinkled. There'd been dark clouds one afternoon, but Reuben—where was he?—said that around here in the summertime, dark clouds usually brought only the smell of rain. As Aunt Beth and I climbed the front steps, I looked behind me once more to the place where Reuben parked his truck. Beth thought I was looking back at the bench. "I sometimes pretend Kate sits there," she said. "Do you think your mom will ever return home for a visit?"

California was Mom's home. My whole life I'd heard her sing the praises of California. But until now I'd had nothing to compare it with. "I'll make her visit here with me next summer. I promise."

"I imagine your mom can't say *no* to you."

Oh, Mom had no problem saying no to me.

In the evenings Aunt Beth and I, and sometimes Uncle Matt, had been going through a box of family photos and mementos. I started to realize that Mom had brought more with her across the California border than I thought. We found a tiny calico dress that Aunt Beth had sewn for me as a newborn. Other than being a different color, it looked identical to my favorite baby doll dress, which Mom used to tell me to be extra careful with when I was little. There was a crocheted bookmark that matched one that Mom used faithfully and claimed to have found in a secondhand book.

By far my favorite snapshots were of Mom and Beth as little girls. They were poor, I could tell from the scarcity of the toys and furniture, but there was something between those two, some childhood bond I couldn't imagine and would never experience. To have slept beside someone all those years. What comfort. And what pain for Beth when Mom left. Of course Beth had Matt by then. And Mom had me. *And now I have Beth, Mom.*

At Aunt Beth's request, I'd brought with me copies of school photos and snapshots from my childhood. I had plenty of leftover school pictures, even though Mom purchased the smallest available package (not to be mean, but to spare me the embarrassment of surplus). Mom had arranged my pictures in a special album for Beth, and I often found my aunt sitting on the couch in the morning, looking through them after seeing Matt off to work.

The night after the healing, I finally found the photo I'd been hoping for. It was stuck to the back of another. Mom and Jamie. My dad looked out of the photograph at me for the first time. The goose bumps all over my body confirmed the boy was Jamie. Aunt Beth was at the stove preparing us tea. I ran the photo to my bedroom and hid it under my pillow. I wanted to study that photo later by myself. From the beginning, I'd suspected that Aunt Beth, but especially Uncle Matt, would tell me anything I wanted to know about my dad but that I had to broach the subject. I had yet to broach with Aunt Beth the subject of Mom's leaving. I had to find the missing link. But I didn't want to risk making Aunt Beth sad by asking her to relive what must've been one of the most sorrowful times in her life.

I excused myself early for bed. Beth asked if I felt well enough for her to go into the church tomorrow morning. Yes. I wanted as many hours as possible alone with that photo.

Jamie was more handsome than I expected, despite the stupid cowboy hat. No wonder Mom hated cowboy hats. The photo wasn't from camp, because my parents stood beside a pickup truck that must've been Jamie's. Was the girl in the photo really my mom? Were her dress pockets full of rocks? Actually her dress was horrible and hid her shape. But her hair was gorgeous, pulled seductively off to one side. Why weren't my parents smiling or touching? Even friends embraced for photographs. Maybe it was from the day Mom met his family. She didn't look sad in the photo, but almost. There was a softness about her that was completely gone now. The look on Jamie's face was of someone who knew things would work out, at least for him, because they always had. Unlike the image I had in my head of my parents meeting by a lake at camp, this real image didn't make me feel warm. Still, I pressed the photo to my chest.

I grabbed Mom's Bible from the desk. I'd been reading it and even memorizing verses, instead of SAT vocabulary, in preparation for the healing. I planned to keep the photo in the Bible. The page I randomly opened to had Mom's handwriting, only bubblier, all over in the margins. We had lots of books at home with her notes in the margins. I read her writing on the Bible page: *Jamie doesn't love me. He did love me. I know he did. He did!* (underlined three times). *He has forsaken me. I must go on without him, but how when I have his baby in me? His baby!!* (underlined four times). *Jamie doesn't want his baby. He doesn't love me anymore. I'll write it here over and over.* And she did, page after page. *Jamie doesn't love me. He doesn't love me. He never loved me!* I got a pen. *I LOVE YOU, MOM,* I wrote over her handwriting. *THE BABY LOVES YOU!!!* The boy in the photo, my smug dad—who'd probably never looked for me—he could go fuck himself.

I woke to the sound of Reuben's truck pulling into the gravel driveway next door. Both Uncle Matt and Aunt Beth were already gone. The sky was clear and bright. Teresa's van was also gone. One car and another truck followed Reuben's truck. Teresa and Reuben had a lot of company, on and off, usually relatives. I moved to the front room blinds to get a better view. A bunch of teenagers piled out: all Indian, except one white guy in a rodeo shirt and sunglasses, who immediately put his arm around a girl's waist. I'd seen the extralarge kid before, but I'd never talked to him. It was Reuben's cousin Ray Tonasket. They all were laughing, even Reuben, but I could see he kept glancing in my direction. He wore a checked button-up shirt, one I hadn't seen him in before, and baggy cargo shorts, though not too baggy. He looked preppy. Usually he wore T-shirts with jeans or basketball shorts. He didn't have a lot of clothes. Neither did Aunt Beth or Teresa. I felt guilty when Reuben complimented my outfits. Back in Sac, at school, I never felt I had enough clothes to keep up. I think Mom bought me all the clothes she possibly could, at the expense of dinners out or the occasional movie, to prevent me from being totally shunned, and it worked. But it was my timidity that kept me from having any real friends. I noticed now that the two girls couldn't take their eyes off Reuben. I could. I turned away.

I decided to water the garden after I showered and got ready. I took a Vicodin pill before my shower and then another one afterward. I was no good around groups of kids, especially in nonacademic settings, but maybe if the edges were blurry, I'd do better. At the last minute I chose to wear the dress Aunt Beth had made me for the healing. She'd already washed it and hung it in the closet. I fastened my hair back in a bun like Beth had, only more loosely. Reuben had said he'd go anywhere with me in the dress. I wanted to see if he'd even acknowledge me in front of his friends. And maybe I also wanted to know how it had felt for Mom with Jamie.

I hoped I didn't trip down the steps. I was seriously high for the first time in my life. More than just the edges were blurry. Reuben's friends instantly got quiet when they saw me. All I could hear was the wind in the tall poplar trees that lined two sides of the trailer park. I loved the sound. Reuben wasn't out there with his friends. He must've run inside for something. They started to snicker, then laugh. Who cared? I filled the watering can. The plants had dust all over them, as if they'd been neglected the whole time Reuben was away. He was back outside when I turned around. Ray pointed. Reuben looked straight at me. He didn't hesitate, even for a second. He almost ran.

"Emmy." He took me in his arms and gave me a bear hug. His friends cheered, mockingly or for real, I couldn't tell. "I missed you, girl."

"You *didn't*." I began to cry. I'd been so afraid that I wouldn't see him again, that he and I would never again climb the hay bales down the road and stare at the sky or watch the horses in a fenced pasture and have Reuben laugh at me when I asked him, a Colville Indian, if he knew how to ride a horse. And now here he was hugging me. His brown eyes looking into mine. Connor also had brown eyes, but Reuben's were darker, like soil deeper in the earth when Aunt Beth and I gardened. I felt dizzy.

He cupped my face in his hands. They smelled like cigarettes. "I flinched, Emmy. That's all. You scared me." He wiped my tears with his thumbs. "I want to kiss you so bad. It's all I've been thinking about. But not in front of them." He nodded in their direction. "Do you want me to kiss you, Emmy?" He knew I'd let him, that any girl in the world would let him. Same with Connor. Same with Jamie Kagen. He let go of my face and took both my hands in his. "Your hands are so warm, Emmy. I can't quit saying your name. Are you okay?" I nodded. "I missed you so much." He hugged me tightly. "Come meet my friends."

"Not in this dress."

"Why not? I'm proud of you for wearing it." He stepped back to get a better look at me in the dress. "So many buttons." He touched the first three, but then stopped as he got near my breasts. "And a bun." He touched my hair. He was in a playful mood. "You didn't convert while I was gone, did you, Sister Emmy?"

"Why? Because I missed you so much?" It was the first mean thing I'd ever said to him.

He paused. "I'm sorry that I hurt you."

"You didn't hurt me—you *couldn't*."

I looked away. Hurting him didn't make me feel better, as it used to with Connor. Mom had claimed eastern Washington was flat, but it wasn't really. It was a broken landscape of basalt cliffs and coulees. Even from where I stood at that moment, I thought I saw a few slopes or outcroppings in the distance. I'd never been good with directions. Were the slopes to the north, as was Reuben's reservation? In which direction were my father's wheat-covered hills?

"Emmy," he called, as if I were farther away, on those slopes, and maybe I was. He called my name again. I looked at him. "Where are you?" he asked.

"Where did *you* go?"

"I'll tell you later. I promise." His friends were shouting for him. "And you can tell me all about the ceremony? Okay?" His clothes looked brand new and too crisp. "Are you okay?" His hair was freshly cut.

"Where did you get that outfit?" I liked him better in his usual clothes.

"I swapped furs for it with a white guy." He grinned.

I didn't dare ask him where he got the money, which was a touchy subject with Reuben, and none of my business.

"I chopped firewood for four days on the rez. My shoulders ache." He rolled them. "I'm trying to pretend they don't. Now, come meet my friends."

"Let me change first."

He drew me close, and I let him. He whispered in my ear, "You're my girl." He'd never called me that before. He made eye contact. "My *only* girl."

Before venturing outside, I'd put an origami bird in my dress pocket. I'd been folding them for my aunt for weeks. The one I gave her at the airport she wanted to hang above the crib in my room. I told her to wait—I'd make her a dozen birds and design a mobile for the baby. I'd made nine birds so far that I was satisfied with. The paper bird I pulled from my pocket now was the best. I handed it to Reuben. He looked at it strangely for a second, then smiled.

Going back inside to change, I undid my bun. I'd noticed outside that both girls had waist-length dark hair that blew around in the wind. My hair fell past my shoulders, but not to my waist, and was light-colored like Beth's (and like my dad's, I now knew). Mom sometimes teased me for being a blonde. I ratted my hair big, like a blond bimbo. "An example of purity," the preacher had called me. What the hell did he know? Or Beth? Or Mom? Or even Reuben? Only Connor knew I was blemished. He'd blemished me, and I'd let him. I put on a pair of my pajama shorts, since they were the shortest ones I owned. One of the girls wore a denim miniskirt. The other one was dressed like a guy. I put on a tank top but no blouse overtop. My pink bra straps hung out. Then I put on my widest belt and heavy eye shadow. For the finishing touch, I dug from my suitcase the only pair of high-heeled shoes I owned. Mom let me buy them at a thrift store—I begged—but only to wear around the house. They were black peep-toe stilettos. She called them my hoochie heels. I'd packed them so she wouldn't toss them.

The irrigation sprinklers across the road had clicked on. They'd run all day and evening. Reuben didn't dart toward me this time. He seemed frozen in place by his pickup truck, which was the reaction I'd hoped for. I let one of my bra straps fall down. There were five boys altogether, counting Reuben, and two girls. I strutted toward them. I'd practiced plenty in the shoes when Mom wasn't home. Reuben and Ray were the only two boys who didn't hoot call. Ray looked scared, in fact, and kept looking from me to Reuben.

"Hi," I said when I made it over to them. "I'm Emmy. From Los Angeles." One boy wore a Tupac T-shirt. He and Ray had long hair. They all were drinking sodas (pops) and beers from a cooler, except Reuben, who wasn't drinking anything. They said hello back. The girl who was with the white boy was beautiful, and I almost faltered, despite having taken two semesters of drama (which I sucked at). "Anyone got a spare cigarette?"

"I'm Benji," the skinniest boy said, coming forward with a pack of smokes. He was dressed like a gangster in superbaggy shorts and a bandanna. "I'll be goddamned," he said. "Better than a rodeo queen." He'd almost lit my cigarette for me when Reuben knocked the lighter from his hand. "Fuck you, dude," Benji said, picking up his lighter from the gravel. Reuben yanked the cigarette from my mouth and threw it on the ground. After pulling up my bra strap, he grabbed my arm. Ray stepped toward us, but Reuben told him to get the fuck back.

"Let's go," Reuben said to me. I had no intention of moving. His face was close to mine. In my heels I was almost as tall as him. I kissed him on the lips. I'd intended to lay a good one on him, but I was too embarrassed. He started to kiss me back, then realized what was happening. "Don't," he said with disgust. He actually wiped off my kiss.

"That's jacked up, Tonasket," said the not-so-pretty girl, glancing at me kindly for a second, then back at Reuben. "You're such an asshole."

His grip remained firm as he walked me back to my aunt's house. I wasn't scared, not for a second. If I'd tried to get free, he would've let me. He didn't dump me at the steps but climbed them with me. He opened the door, still holding my arm, and escorted me inside. "Put on some clothes," he said.

"This is how people dress in California, where I'm from."

"You don't. And you're from here."

"I hate it *here*." I felt a wave of nausea hit as I kicked off my heels. I hadn't eaten. I'd meant to fix some peanut butter toast right after I took the pills. "And I'm not *your* girl." I almost fell taking off my belt, which I'd cinched too tight. Reuben caught me. He helped me into the bedroom. "I hate it here," I said again, just in case he hadn't heard me.

He sat me on the bed. "I'm sorry I hurt you, Emmy." He sat down beside me. "I can make it up. Give me half a chance." He sighed. "Don't get back at me this way."

"Kiss me, Reuben. If you really missed me."

He shook his head. "Not with you dressed like that."

"Like what?"

"You know."

"Like what? Just say it."

He did, but he looked away first. "Like a slut, I guess. Shit. The thought of Benji's seeing your bra straps." He looked back. "Only I know you're not slutty."

I wanted to crawl under the covers. I felt like a fool and like a slut. Had Aunt Beth pulled up and seen my outfit, she would've been mortified and probably had a miscarriage on the spot. But instead of getting under the covers like a bashful girl, I took off my tank top.

"You don't know anything about me," I said.

He stared at my bra for a few seconds. Reaching over with one hand, he traced my collarbone. Then he stood up and went to the dresser and pulled out a T-shirt. It happened to be the BERKELEY T-shirt Mom had recently mailed to me—as a not-so-subtle reminder to study for my SATs. He walked over to me and sat back down and then put the shirt on me. "Come here," he said, taking my face in his hands as he had outside. "I do know you." He kissed me. "I know you," he whispered. I felt each of his next kisses deeper inside me, though they all were gentle. It hadn't felt this way with Connor—this easy or direct—maybe because of his pierced tongue and all the tricks he did with it and all the tricks he tried to teach me to do with my tongue. I wouldn't let Reuben pull away. I leaned back on the bed and took him with me. He tried to keep the weight of his body off me. I wanted to feel it. He slowly slid his hand up the back of my shirt and under my bra strap, but then he just rested it there. His other hand found the pill bottle on my bed, where I'd tossed it earlier. He sat up.

"What are these?" he asked. It was a prescription bottle, but the label had been ripped off.

"Just some pills." I sat up too quickly. The room spun.

"Your pills?" I nodded. "You're on medication?" He sounded pissed. "For what? And why's the label torn off?"

"Someone gave them to me."

"Who?" he demanded. "What are they? Don't lie to me."

"They're just Vicodin." I hesitated. "Connor gave them to me. They're his mom's."

"What?" He stood up. "Why?"

"He thought they'd help me relax while I was here."

"What kind of douche bag gives a girl drugs?" Did he expect me to answer that? "Are you high right now?" Again, I didn't answer. "I don't go out with druggies." He looked at me with disgust for the second time that day. "There are plenty of them in Omak."

"I don't do drugs, Reuben." How ridiculous.

"Except today, right?" He was being too harsh.

I could be harsh too. "Today, and the first day we met. Or I wouldn't have talked to you." I meant I wouldn't have been *able* to talk to him. I would've been too shy.

He made a pained face. "Maybe I don't know you." He threw the pill bottle back onto the bed, careful, though, not to hit me with it. "No, on second thought." He came over and grabbed the bottle. He walked out of the bedroom, and a few seconds later I heard the toilet flush.

"I feel weird," I said when he came back into the room. And I did. "I've never taken two pills before at one time.

"Hold me," I said. "At least until the room quits spinning." I climbed under the covers and motioned for him to join me. He didn't. "Everything is spinning but you. Will you hold me?" Still no response. "My hands are glowing from the healing. Let me touch you with them." I held them out. "And then you'll forgive me." He came to me, said there was nothing to forgive. "I see only you clearly, Reuben. Mom says never to tell a boy you love him first, before he tells you, so I won't." I asked him to take off his shirt. "There," I said, touching his shoulders, which were sore from chopping wood, and then his chest, and then his belly, in the same way I'd touched Aunt Beth's belly in the lake. "Aren't my hands warm?"

I slept in his arms, a fitful sleep. I woke every five minutes or so to ask, "You still here?" and to tell him that I hadn't meant it when I'd said I wasn't his girl. There were tears on his cheeks as he talked to me about drumming, and about an elder named Virgil who had a sweat lodge in his garage, and then finally about his dad. My warm hands seemed to have loosened something in him. He spoke a few words in a language I'd never heard before, even in California. It sounded old and somehow like the land.

"You still here?" I asked.

"Stop. I'm not going to leave you."

He did leave the bedroom, though. He had to before Aunt Beth got home. He thought I was finally asleep when he left, but I got up and watched him through the blinds. He said not a word to his friends, who were still hanging by their vehicles. Ray tried to get into Reuben's truck with him, but Reuben wouldn't let him. Ray gave Reuben the finger, and then so did Benji. He would be back. When he passed by the window—he didn't know I was awake and watching—the look on his face was a grave one. What had I done to him? Just weeks before he'd jumped boldly off the back steps of his sister's trailer to say hi. I didn't mean to freak him out. But I *did* want my hands to be the warmest hands that had ever touched him.

9

Reuben

Emmy. Emmy. Emmy. Emmy.

I say her name to the four directions. I say her name for each week she's been here.

I knew nothing of love before holding Emmy yesterday, as she fell in and out of sleep, so afraid I would leave her again. I knew nothing of the pain Mom and Teresa have been dealt. Now I understand better why Mom wants me to be like my "no-good son of a bitch" dad. Why, despite everything, she misses him. I now understand, at least a little, why she gives her Indian money to a white man, a bona fide son of a bitch. Why Teresa doesn't hate the three men who fathered her four children and then left her. Why so many Indian girls let themselves get pregnant and drop out of high school.

I love Emmy.

I cannot drum her out of me. I cannot sweat her out.

Her warm hands are my council fire.

My dad saw this coming.

Love is complicated, but it doesn't have to be disastrous. *I can handle this, Dad. Thanks for the warning. I'll do better than you did.* Dad with Mom was like Coyote when Buffalo Bull gave him his daughter, telling Coyote he could cut some fat off her every day to feed himself and he would have meat forever, but not to kill her. Hungry for her marrow Coyote of course killed her anyway, and his people were ashamed and left him.

This morning there are rain clouds, and then there is rain. I walk outside. Emmy stands on the small front porch with her aunt and uncle. They look at the sky, watching the rain. They all three see me. I wave. Then I gesture for Emmy to come get wet in the rain with me.

She turns to her family for permission, as if she were ten, as if she'd known them her whole life, and probably she has in some far corner of her mind or heart. It moves me. She walks down the steps, then runs toward me as the rain starts to soak her. I take her into my arms, just for a moment, like a best friend would, and we are best friends.

"Ask them if I can drive you to the lake real quick to see the rain," I say. "It's only five minutes from here. I'll have you back in half an hour."

She does, and they agree.

"Be careful," the aunt yells. I've never heard her raise her voice.

At the lake, we don't stay in the truck. I chase Emmy through the park. I could catch up with her in half a minute, but I don't want to. We sit on a picnic table and watch the rain on the surface of the lake. I look past the algae clumped along the shore to the deep middle of the lake named after my people's chief. Emmy leans her head on my shoulder. It's time to go back. She's cold and shivers. I call her a wimpy Californian. We stand up. The shape of her breasts and her nipples show through her wet shirt. She notices me staring.

She crosses her arms in front. "Oh, my God." She blushes. "How embarrassing."

"No." I pull her arms loose. "How beautiful."

She smiles, then dashes for the truck.

I hand her the plaid flannel shirt I keep behind my seat. She puts it on, and I button it up.

"You're always dressing me. Is that an Indian thing?"

"Smart-ass. Kiss me." I wasn't going to try.

She moves close. "You won't wipe it off?" I shake my head. Her kiss is more breathy than I expect. It leaves me hardly able to drive back to the trailer park.

"See you tomorrow then," I say before she opens the truck door. The rain has stopped. Her uncle still stands on the porch. His wife probably made him stay there.

"Oh, Reuben, I forgot." She turns back toward me. "I'm going to church in the morning. I told Beth I would while you were—away." Damn it. "Only not to their church."

"I'll go with you. I can drive us."

"Really?" she asks. "My uncle was going to take me. But are you sure?"

"I've been to church before, Emmy."

"To a Christian church? *Really?*"

"*Really.*"

"I haven't," she says.

"What?" I've never met a white girl who hasn't been dragged to church at one time or another, or an Indian girl for that matter. "For real?"

"Never. I've been to a Sikh parade." I raise my eyebrows. "Indians from India," she explains. "Punjabis."

"I'll take you tomorrow. We can go to pizza or something afterward." I have money left from chopping wood.

"Are you asking me out on a date?"

"You better get your butt out of this truck, young lady," I say with a hick accent. My dad could imitate the voices of John Wayne, Clint Eastwood, the warden in *Cool Hand Luke*, Marlon Brando in *The Godfather*. His imitation of Pa Ingalls crying on *Little House on the Prairie* would get Mom to laughing so hard. "Your uncle's standing on the porch," I tell Emmy. "He's probably got his rifle."

Her eyes get big. "Do you really think he owns one?"

I nod. "More than one, I'm sure."

"Like a militia member?"

Her uncle goes inside, as if he'd heard her question. No, he's just giving us space. I drop the accent. "No," I say, "like a hunter. A rifle for deer and elk and a shotgun for pheasant."

In reality there's no shortage of Timothy McVeigh types lurking in the woods and small towns around the rez and in lone trailers here in the basin and in Spokane basements and probably even mansions on the sound. Not as many as in Idaho and Montana. But plenty. They're as anti-Indian—even though we've been here thousands of years longer than their white asses—as they are antifeds. It's the federal government, after all, that upholds the treaty rights of Indians: rights that include, among other things, the "privilege" to fish and hunt in areas off the rez where our ancestors did without a state license. These rights, and the audacity of the Colville Nation or the Yakama Nation to consider ourselves a sovereign nation, piss off those camouflaged fucks so badly they shave their heads and carve swastikas into their arms in protest. Even nice white guys get irked that we require them to buy a tribal license to fish on our lakes and from the rez shores of the Columbia. But how is that any different from the state of Oregon requiring Washington anglers to buy a separate license to fish from the southern shores of the lower Columbia?

"I own a gun," I confess.

"You do not."

"Yes, I do." I laugh. "Not here, of course. It's at my mom's. I hunt deer and elk. One day I want to hunt moose."

"You've killed a deer?" Her eyes get even bigger.

"I've skinned and quartered many a muley. Don't people hunt in California?"

"Rednecks."

"Well, I'm a redskin." I don't mean to make her feel stupid. She's hard enough on herself. "We have to eat up north. The snow can get deep. Old people on the rez and even off the rez, they can't hunt for themselves anymore," I explain. "The elders take us older boys hunting to help stock their freezers." She keeps silent. "But even if they didn't, I love to hunt with a bow *and* a rifle. The elders encourage it."

Shit, they practically beg us teenage boys in the tribal newspaper to learn to hunt. Almost as much as they plead with us, and our parents, to stay off drugs and off the bottle, or I should say off the can, six-pack, half rack, full rack.

"I should keep my mouth shut," she says.

"Don't do that." I squeeze her hand. "I love your teeth."

"My what?"

"I love your teeth." I could go on. "I love your collarbone." And now I love her breasts.

"Thanks for the rain, Reuben." She smiles, then widely like a goofball to show me all her teeth. "And thanks for the flannel shirt." She smooths the hem and pretends to fix a button. "I don't plan on giving it back, by the way. It's very grungy. Very Kurt Cobain."

"It's an Indian shirt. And what do you know about Kurt Cobain? You seem more the Lilith Fair type."

She laughs. "I'm both."

Come to think of it, she does occasionally wear a "grungy" green jacket, worn looking, and one day she wore a thermal and that explains her Converse. She looks cute as hell in my shirt. "Call me about tomorrow," I remind her. "I want to take you to pizza."

Even better, she shows up in person at Teresa's a few hours later. I happen to be outside, smoking on the front porch, which is hidden from her view.

"Caught you," she says. I go to put out my cigarette. "Don't, Reuben. I like the smell." She climbs the steps. "I'm going to smoke all through college."

"A girl with plans."

"I find smokers sexy," she says. "Does that make me old-fashioned?"

"You're making me nervous, Miss Emmy." I stub out my cigarette. She really is making me nervous.

"Wait until you hear what I came to ask you." She tells me her aunt and uncle agreed to let me take her to church. But they want to join us for pizza afterward. "It was Matt's idea."

"I'm game."

"It was supposed to be our first date."

"I just want to be around you." I grab her hands. "Chaperoned or not."

"I'm happy, Reuben."

She kisses me sweetly, as if we were twelve and I hadn't yet seen her bra.

"Your hands," I observe. "They're glowing again."

She says she thinks she's having an allergic reaction to the oils her aunt massaged into her hands before the healing. But that's not it.

"I've never been happier," she says.

She can't quit smiling, and I can't speak because of it. The Fourth of

July Pow Wow in Nespelem has already started. It always begins about a week before the Fourth, ever since Chief Joseph's band of Nez Perce settled on the Colville after their exile to Indian Territory. It was Moses who invited Joseph onto the Colville, which outraged Skolaskin, whose land they were occupying. The Not-So-Great White Father was overcrowding the rez, a dozen tribes, while at the same time slicing off strips to give to white miners and cattlemen. It's the descendants of these very same miners and cattlemen whose dicks I like to knock in the dirt during football games. Not that I haven't had my own ass handed to me by them a time or three. This year, for the first time ever, I'm not going to the Pow Wow. I don't want to be away from Emmy. If only I could take her. She could hear my dad's name being called during the first laps of the horse procession when people submit the names of their lost loved ones to be read along with the names of all war veterans, my grandfather's included. The third lap is a celebration. This year Emmy's smile is my celebration.

"I'm being sappy," she says. "Sorry, best chappie."

I laugh. All I can think to say back to her is "Come climb on my lappie," which isn't appropriate given that she hasn't yet. Yet.

"Neither of us has a pappy," she continues, "so let's curl up and take a nappie."

"You're the weirdest girl. I swear." I push her back toward her aunt's house.

Teresa is laughing when I go inside. I forgot the door was open, only the screen shut.

"She's funny," my sister says. "And kind of dorky."

"In a good way?"

"What other way is there?"

"I'm going to take another crack at your washer." My adrenaline pumps. I need to do something to get my mind off taking a nap with Emmy.

"Give it up," Teresa says after half an hour. "I'll call Felix." Felix is Emilio's dad. He's Mexican. "If he doesn't bring me a decent washing machine, I'll take his ass to court for back child support."

"You go, girl," I say jokingly, but I mean it. I look around for the screws Kevin was supposed to be holding for me. "I'm sorry about Felix, sis. Seriously. All the men. Their dads." I point at her kids.

"Be quiet. You got slacks to wear tomorrow to church?"

"Shit, no. I didn't even think."

"Don't get mad," she says, "but in my van are two bags of clothes from a nurse at work. Her son just graduated from high school. He left early for college. She asked what size you wore. I've been toting them around because I knew you'd get pissed."

"You suck, Teresa."

I go outside and smoke two more cigarettes. Then I go get the bags of clothes from her van. At least I didn't go to high school with the guy, right? There's a pair of dress pants, two pairs of Levi's, shorts, T-shirts, a thermal, a track jacket, and a zip-up hoodie with the tag still on. All my size and hardly worn. If Teresa had an extra dime to her name, I'd be suspicious. I'm still suspicious. I'd rather she'd gotten clothes for her kids.

"You don't suck," I say. "Neither do the clothes. Thanks."

"You suck," Emilio says to no one and everyone. "You suck. You suck."

Emmy listens intently during the church service. She brought her mom's old Bible and tries unsuccessfully to find verses when the minister says to flip to a certain passage. She's probably this attentive in all her classes at school. I picture her using lots of sticky pads and highlighters. That's cool. It's better than the girls who twist their face piercings all class period or eyeball me or sleep off their hangovers or stretch ten times to show off their thongs. The chicks at this church wear normal-fitting dresses, but Emmy's the only girl wearing a vest buttoned over her dress. Does Emmy wear thongs? I don't think so because I've seen her underwear lines. Her uncle Matt picked this particular church because some of his coworkers attend it. Emmy said Matt asked one guy to make us feel welcome. He comes up to Emmy as soon as the service is over and introduces himself. He doesn't give me the time of day. Which is fine. Indians already know it. And I know his type. But Emmy is appalled. "That guy was fucking rude," she says once we're in my truck and driving away. "What a fucking asshole."

"Jeez, Emmy. You just came from church." She rarely uses the F word.

"Mom said people were like that here. I didn't believe her."

"Not everyone is." Why am I defending white people? I don't want Emmy to hate it here. I want her to stay for the whole summer. I want her to stay for good. She and I could go to the high school here together, to Moses Lake High School, home of the Chiefs, rather than the Omak Pioneers. She could live with her aunt and uncle, and I could live with Teresa. As if her mom, the professor, would let her. Or Emmy would even want to. I can't think of the alternative.

"Well, I'm sorry," she says. "You definitely don't have to come with me next Sunday."

She wants to go to church again? I was hoping it was a one-shot thing. A whim. I hope she doesn't ask me about the sermon. I paid no attention. Mostly during the sermon, I tried to look comfortable in another boy's pants and I stared at Emmy's legs, which are a bit skinny, and I thought about the way she came strutting out Friday in that outfit and heels, wherever the hell she got them, and how my friends had better not ever bring it up and how I'm going to punch Benji right in the fucking mouth when he does, and he will.

We get to the pizza joint before her aunt and uncle and grab a table. She's all smiles and tells me she's never eaten at a restaurant with a boy before.

"Poor Emmy. So sheltered."

"Butt face." She looks around at the NASCAR decorations on the walls, the checkered pit flags and posters of race cars. "Mom hates places like this."

"Places like what?"

"Homey places. Small town. She likes artisan pizza."

"Art pizza?"

"Yeah," she says. "Van Gogh Veggie, Meaty Monet, Pepperoni Picasso."

"Now who's being the smart-ass? I bet you can't name three more."

"Dali Delight, Garlic Chicken Gauguin, and, this week's special, Combo Kahlo—she was half Mexican, half Jewish."

Never heard of those three. "Little Miss Art School."

"That reminds me. I made you something."

"Another bird?"

"Close your eyes." When I open them, she's scattered a bunch of 3-D paper frogs on the table in front of me. Some are as small as quarters. No shit. And all are made from different patterned paper. "They jump," she says, and shows me how.

"Damn, you need to get out more," I tease. She already told me she learned to do origami in after-school programs. Probably while the other kids played together.

"I know." She starts to put the paper frogs away in her purse. I didn't mean to hurt her feelings. "I've been told that before." By whom, I wonder, that dickwad in California? "You'd laugh if you saw my bedroom in Sac. I have chains of paper animals."

"No, I wouldn't." Her aunt and uncle are walking in the door. "I wouldn't. And I want those back after we eat."

Emmy's uncle wants her to pick which type of extralarge pizza to order. She refuses. She's embarrassed to be the one who decides. I suggest Hawaiian to get things moving. Her aunt notices this as a kindness and smiles at me. Up close, Beth doesn't look right. She looks ill. Has Emmy noticed? She's too pale, even for a white lady. For a few minutes the aunt talks to Emmy about the church service we just attended, but not loudly like most Christians would in restaurants. No wonder Emmy paid close attention. She must've known her aunt would ask. Emmy says the sermon was on the difference between grace and mercy. She said mercy was God not giving us what we deserve and grace was God giving us what we don't deserve. Say what?

"I was sort of confused," Emmy confesses.

"*I'm* confused," Matt says, loosening his tie. "So, Reuben, you play basketball at Omak High?"

"Football actually."

We talk sports, local divisions, and the chances of the Seahawks making it into the playoffs. Then we talk about fishing, which gets his blood pumping, I can tell, and mine. He asks about tribal fishing with dip nets, and even gill nets, without the usual white angler mock or extremely biased environmentalism. The nets used by commercial fishermen are a necessary evil, anglers claim, and dams are important for irrigation and vital for the economy of the Pacific Northwest, but then they claim Indian nets are a hazard to fish populations and should be outlawed. After we're almost done eating our pizza, Matt asks if I'm considering college.

"WSU," I say. "If I can get in."

Emmy chokes on her bite. "That's my dad's school."

I didn't even know she had a dad. *Neither of us has a pappy.* I mean, obviously, I knew there was a man at conception. But she's never said a word to me about him. Her aunt and uncle look just as surprised as I do at the casual mention of her dad. Nobody says anything.

Emmy looks nervous but determined. "Mom said he went there." She takes a drink. "But Mom told me a lot of lies. Did he go there, Uncle Matt?"

"Sure, honey," Matt says. "I believe he got his degree in ag science."

Beth takes Emmy's hand across the table. "If he had known you, he would've loved you," she says.

"He knew Mom and didn't love her."

"He loved her," Beth says. "But not enough."

"What does that even mean?"

"Real love involves risks or loss. Look at how God gave up his only son."

"Mom wasn't good enough for him."

"Maybe she was *too* good."

The two of them. I didn't know Emmy had become so close to her aunt.

"Whatever," Emmy says. "Mom didn't need him. She did fine without him. Screw him."

I'm surprised she said that in front of her aunt. I hope Beth doesn't correct her.

"Kate has done a great job with you. I am so proud of her." Emmy is taking a deep breath so she won't cry. "Do you miss your mom?"

"No." She gets control. "I mean, a little." She looks at me, then Matt, then back at her aunt. "But I like it here better." She looks at me. "*Way* better."

She has us all three a bit teary eyed. But I think the "way better" part worries her aunt, who catches my eye briefly.

Matt changes the subject again and gets us laughing. It's time to go. I want Emmy to drive back with me. But when we stand up, she goes to her aunt. They hug.

"You kids, take a drive or something," Matt says, shaking my hand in the parking lot. "We'll see you after a while."

"You could've ridden with her," I say to Emmy after we get into my truck. "You really love her, don't you?"

"Does it seem strange to love someone so quickly?"

"No, Emmy." No way, Emmy. I start my truck. Does she love me? She told me her mom warned her not to say it to a guy first, but that's not necessarily a confession of love, and she was high. I drive through town, past irrigation supply yards, the bowling alley, the Salvation Army, the feed store, taverns, churches, a tackle shop, fast food.

"Aunt Beth doesn't really know me, though," Emmy says. "She thinks I'm pure."

"You are."

"I wish I was." She sighs. "For her, and for the baby, and maybe even for God. If he exists." I feel her eyes on me. "Do you think he exists?"

Does she mean just the Christian God? Shit. Or all higher powers? "I'm no atheist."

"I'd planned to become a Christian today at church." She laughs. "Isn't that crazy?"

"No."

"I don't mean it's crazy to be a Christian." She pauses. "But maybe it's more innate—not really a choice. Like being left-handed or even gay. What do you think, Reuben?"

"I couldn't say." I keep my eyes on the road.

"But—" She's struggling. "Aren't notions of purity in all faiths? In yours?"

I'm a sweat lodge junkie, as was my dad. She's obviously confused. Why else would she have dressed up like a Baptist and then like a hooker in the same day, same hour. Who wouldn't be confused, I guess, in her position? I can't give her spiritual answers, but I can give her some space. "Listen, Emmy. We don't have to touch." I hate the sound of that, as if it were a dirty thing.

"Can I still hold your hand?"

"You don't have to ask."

When she takes my hand, there's a tiny paper frog in hers. I put it on the dashboard, and she names it Darwin.

We go a week this way, barely touching. We don't kiss or even hug. We hold hands or she leans her head on my shoulder. That's it. On the Fourth of July, she goes fishing with her aunt and uncle in the morning, but in the evening they let me take her to the lake to watch the city fireworks. Even then we don't kiss. She keeps squeezing my hand as we sit close together on a blanket. She's hot and rolls up her shorts. Her bare thighs and her painted toenails drive me nuts. Not to mention the way she relishes the Rainier cherries I brought her and even feeds me a few. We study together for our SATs, now that she's persuaded me to retake them in the fall. She has flash cards, for Christ sake, and Christ, she's really smart. Probably the most academically smart person I've ever known. I'd like to see her bra again—the whole thing, like before, not just peeks when we play doctor with the kids. She paints with my nieces and nephews, colors, and does origami. It's Japanese, I learn, and way complex. She praises everything they do but dislikes her own stuff. Grace hesitates to share her native crafts, beads, and feathers with Emmy, but Emmy doesn't get offended. I do. Also, when Emmy braids Audrey's hair like a white girl's, Grace tries to undo it after Emmy leaves, which makes Audrey cry. Emmy helps me make Hamburger Helper, claiming she's never had it but digs it. She likes the smoked salmon some Klickitat dude who fishes way down by The Dalles—and who *isn't* Grace's dad—leaves on the porch for Teresa. She tries to like the venison her aunt makes but cares only for the summer sausage and pepper sticks. Health care workers on the rez push native kids to eat deer and elk burgers rather than fast-food burgers, gas station nachos, and casino burritos. Emmy does a tarot card reading on my nieces and nephews from a deck called *Healing with the Fairies*. Grace and Audrey are equally ecstatic. Emmy attempts to do a reading on me, but I can't stop grinning about getting advice from the fairy kingdom. Plus she smells so damn sweet. She switches to a deck called *Zen*. I'm advised that unless I drop my personality, I won't be able to find my individuality.

"Indians don't believe in individuality," I say with true Hollywood-style Indian stoicism. "Only tribal personality." She quickly apologizes. "I'm joking. Relax."

We take Grace and Kevin to the park to shoot hoops. Grace is good, really good actually, great ball control, but Emmy in her BERKELEY T-shirt sucks. She decides just to watch and to cheer the loudest for Grace. Emmy and I take drives almost daily, short ones because she feels guilty—about what?—and I'm running out of gas money. We drive past endless potato fields. The plants are flowering, and she likes the purple and yellow flowers: same colors, ironically, as the camas my people used to dig here. We drive along canals and spillways until finally I can't stand it any longer and drive her to the Columbia by Vantage and Wanapum. There's no real shore for us to stand on, thanks to the fucking dams that have widened and deepened the river, making it less accessible. It leaves her speechless nonetheless. The wind this near the river whips her hair. She lets me take her into my arms to block some of the force. When I warn her to watch out for rattlers in the sage, she cuddles closer. On the drive home, I tell her the story of how Rattlesnake killed Salmon, who used to live in the cliffs, because he envied Salmon's beautiful wife. She was made a slave. When Salmon was brought back to life by Mouse, he slew Rattlesnake and freed his wife. He then took his wife to a new home under the great falls where they'd both be safe from the Land People.

I go to church with Emmy the next Sunday. On Tuesday, when her aunt leaves to clean the church, Emmy comes over to watch TV with me and the kids. I expect her to sit next to me on the couch, but not too close, and to take my hand. Instead she sits on my lap. She doesn't straddle me. She sits on my lap as a kid might, sidesaddle. She leans her head on my chest and drapes one arm around my neck. Something is wrong. She seems languid: her mood and her body. She's usually a bit tense. The letting go is incredibly sexy. We watch TV, or I do, with the kids, though fuck if I know which program: *Barney? Murder, She Wrote? Can You Believe This Price* on HSN? Emmy begins kissing my neck, so softly at first that I'm not sure. Then I'm absolutely certain. "I can't be good," she whispers in my ear. I don't even respond. I hate that Christian bullshit. She sleeps or I think she does because she feels so slack. I could sit here all day this way. "Touch me," she whispers next. I am touching her. I have an arm around her waist and a hand rubbing her bare knee. "Touch me, Reuben." I tell her I am. "In places you haven't before. I can't stop thinking about you touching me."

"Outside, kids." I gently push Emmy off me to get the kids out the door. "Don't argue. Two bucks each, and five for you, Grace." Then I'm broke. "Give me an hour. Drink from the hose. You won't die. Two bucks each on candy at the store in one hour."

I return to Emmy, stretched on the couch. I don't even know where to begin. With a kiss, always, and then another. I'm on top of her, she's on top of me. I can't get enough of her mouth on mine, her breath, her smell, her taste. "Emmy." I reach up her shirt and unhook her bra. Her back arches and I slide my hand lower to her ass. Finally I touch her between her legs. I've touched other girls there before, but never one that I love. The intensity is not comparable to anything. When her body trembles, so does my being. "Emmy." She touches me too, but even it's not the same. We don't have sex. We don't need to, yet. I want to tell her I love her. But I don't want her to think it's just because she's let me touch her in places I haven't before. In places I could spend the rest of my life trying to get back to.

Her aunt is taking her on the first of three short trips. They're leaving on Monday for a few days. "Beth's so excited," Emmy tells me. Her aunt and uncle are gone, and it's just us. We sit on the garden bench for old times' sake. She's even wearing her floppy hat. She says her aunt never goes on trips, but she's been feeling so well since the healing and has all this energy. "We've been studying the map with Uncle Matt. My eyes keep going up north to your reservation."

"Don't go there." It's not a tourist attraction. "I mean without me. I'll take you."

"I don't want to leave you. Will you wait for me?"

"Do you really have to ask that? Hold on, what do you even mean?"

"I mean," she says, taking off her hat, "will you see other girls while I'm gone?"

"Fuck, Emmy. Really?" I stand up. After the way we touched the other day on the couch? Did she not feel anything? "You don't trust me very much."

"I wish you were taking me instead of—"

I don't let her finish. I bend down and kiss her to silence her. She may regret what she was about to say. Her aunt doesn't look well. Having never been around her before, Emmy wouldn't know this. I know the look because I see it on the rez with Indians who refuse to go to the doctor, like Emmy's aunt, or who refuse meds for their diabetes, or who can't get to the doctor or pay the co-pays when Indian Health can't fix them. "Please go with your aunt," I say. "Have fun." I sit back down on the bench. I tell her I plan on going to Omak and the rez for a few days or a week to chop some more wood and to check on my mom. I also plan to hunt as often as I can, but I don't tell her that. Buck season on the rez has already begun. I assure her I'll be back and I'll be faithful. "I've been wanting to tell you something," I say. "I've never said this to a girl before." I'm nervous as hell. "After I say it, you have to trust me."

Because it is just for her to hear, I whisper it into her ear.

"I love you more," she says, but out loud, into the wind. I shake my head.

She stands up, dropping her hat, and starts pacing.

"Hey," I say. "What's the matter?"

"What if my aunt and uncle had never found Mom's number? What if I'd spent this summer alone in mine and Mom's apartment? Or in

Connor's bedroom, where he likes me to do weird things to him and he makes fun of me for not wearing thongs?"

I stand up at that one. What weird things? But I can't get mad. I've had sex with other girls—not kinky sex, but sex. And why would he give a fuck what type of underwear she wears? I loved Emmy's underwear the other day. In fact, I haven't stopped thinking about them.

"What if I'd never met Aunt Beth, like I've never met my dad?" Snot starts to pour from her nose. She wipes it. "What if you hadn't come over to say hi to me? I would've never been brave enough to go over and talk to you. Do you know that?" She's freaking out. "Do you ever think about that? What if you would've stayed in Omak this summer? It's practically in Canada. Do you think about that? Do you, Reuben?"

I grab her. "I would've found you."

"You would have? How? How do you know? You don't know."

"I would have found you."

Was I lost before Emmy? I don't think so. I avoid drugs and alcohol and stay on the path. What path? The peace path? The war path? The in-between path, like Chief Moses? He wore out many ponies traveling between cavalry camps and tribal councils. The I'm-forced-to-give-all-my-land-away-despite-riding-the-iron-horse-all-the-way-to-D.C.-twice-to-beg-for-my-people path? The any-path-but-my-dad's path? The I-want-to-leave-the-reservation-and-go-to-college path? The I-learn-just-enough-from-the-elders path? The I-play-football-like-a-white-boy path? The-I-won't-put-on-a-feathered-headpiece-and-dance-in-the-cafeteria-one-period-a-day path? The paved path? The fucking BIA's bullshit fill-out-another-form-and-then-wait-in-another-line path? The path between the white man's ways and the native way. The Okanogan River divides the Indian side of Omak from the nonrez side. On one side of this river, white boys wrestle bulls. On the other, Indian boys ride horses down a cliff. I safely watch from my stadium seat. As kids Ray and I used to run down Suicide Hill barefoot, but that doesn't count. On the phone this morning Mom said we need to talk. She wants me to come back for the rest of the summer. I didn't tell Emmy. It can mean only one thing: she's drinking heavily because her latest man is threatening to dump her. The some-fucking-loser-fucks-over-my-mom-again-and-I-have-to-fucking-clean-up-the-mess-because-my-dad-is-a-sorry-example-of-Coyote path?

I didn't just find Emmy. She also found me. I'd been hunting for days in the woods, feeling strong and agile, despite the jumble of paths, and trying to ignore the way my legs and shoulders had begun to ache a little in the cold and my belly had begun to feel empty. I was trying to fill the freezers of the old people, not realizing my own hunger until Emmy stepped into the clearing.

10

Bethany

I defer to Matt's judgment about Emmy and the neighbor boy. I trust Matt completely. I trust Emmy also. I feel such a calm when I am with her, and I marvel at her every move as if she were still an infant. But I worry because she *is* so young, and both Kate and I fell hard for our first boyfriends. Before Emmy arrived, I feared she'd be all grown up, but she's not, and she's not hardened or edgy like a city kid. Kate has kept her close under her wing, as I made my sister promise to do when she left here. A few nights before the healing, Emmy asked me to sing to her when I tucked her into bed. She seemed sad. I usually go to sleep hours before she does, but I like to get her settled first with a book and a cup of chamomile tea. Singing to Emmy erased years of sorrow from my heart.

I trust Reuben also, or I am trying to. Matt swears he's a good kid. And he's right that we've seen the boy grow up over the last five years or so that Teresa has lived next door. It used to endear me to Reuben— not that he and I ever talked—to think how he was the same age as Emmy. And it shouldn't matter at all that he's Indian. Matt's adamant about that. As far as Reuben's not being a Christian, Matt says he himself didn't convert until he was the boy's age. Matt reminds me that I've never been on the Colville Reservation. He claims the poverty is indescribable, and half the tribe walks around in an alcoholic stupor. But that has to be an exaggeration.

I remember a few summers back Reuben appeared at his sister's place with his arm in a cast, eye black and blue, and lip cracked and swollen. I took over herbs for his cuts and bruises. Unlike the ladies at church, Teresa took them without smirking. She wasn't as willing the year before when I brought her a Bible and tracts. Matt said then that

Reuben probably just fell or maybe he got into a fight with another boy. Matt and his brother and cousins used to brawl and get busted up on dirt bikes. He said it was good if the boy had a little fight in him. Regardless, I added Reuben's name to the church prayer chain that week and the following.

Watching Emmy run to Reuben the other day in the rain was tender but left me restless that night. Should I call Kate? Matt told me to wait, to let Emmy have a summertime friend. He said it might be just a crush and no point in provoking Kate. It was the first time I'd seen Emmy and Reuben together. Matt didn't seem surprised. Nor should I have been. I've seen their waves and smiles go from awkward to familiar to playful. When Reuben and Emmy hugged, I knew it was already far more than a crush. In fact, I got the strange feeling Emmy had just run into the arms of her future husband. I've felt more intuitive than ever since the healing. Emmy must also because my garden has thrived lately in her hands. Only how can it ever work for Emmy and the boy? Kate and Jamie lived only two hours away from each other, not two states away, and the distance tore them apart and eventually left my sister selling her body to truckers. All these years I've labored to keep Kate's secret from Matt. I've longed, desperately at times, to deliver myself of the burdensome memories from Kate's last months here: her bruises, ripped blouses, bladder infections, the sound of her throwing up or sobbing in the shower.

There's another secret I've had to keep from Matt all these years—so intertwined it is with the first. *I told Kate to leave town.* I begged her to leave, in fact, and I insisted she take Emmy. Kate had threatened to leave town once, and maybe that planted the seed. *I sent my sister and her baby away on a bus.*

Shortly after a trucker cut off Kate's hair, I went to our father behind her back and pleaded with him for any money he could spare. My faith in God had begun to wane for the first time in my life. Where was God's mercy? Why wouldn't Jesus help my sister as he had Mary Magdalene? I began to doubt the Lord's benevolence outside the pages of the Bible. Then, shamefully, I even began to doubt the Bible. It turned out, unbeknownst to Kate or me, that our mother's family had left us some money in a Seattle bank. Praise be. I promised the Lord my faith in him would never again waver, and it hasn't.

When I secured the money, I brought it to Kate and said, "You can stop now."

She shook her head. Emmy was asleep.

"If you don't stop, there will be nothing left of you."

She stared out the window. It was an ugly, overcast day. "I don't want the money," she said flatly. "You and Matt keep it. Keep Emmy too. She's better off—"

I didn't let her finish. "You don't mean that. Look at me." I barely recognized her with her choppy hair, smeared eye makeup, distant gaze. "*Your* little girl needs you," I said. "She needs you more than she needs me."

I *had* to make that true: *Emmy had to need Kate more than she did me.* It was the key to my sister's survival.

My voice trembled as I continued. "She needs you more than I need you." Kate had no idea where I was headed with my reasoning, and maybe I really didn't either until that exact moment. "Leave town, Kate," I said, taking a couple of deep breaths. "Take the money and leave town with Emmy." I told her to go make a new start somewhere far away from all the bad memories of Mother's death, Father, the church, Jamie, and especially the truckers, who I hoped with all my heart burned in hell. I'd never had such thoughts.

"I can't leave you," she protested. And she never would have—I firmly believe this—if I hadn't begged her to. I told her I'd rather lose her on a Greyhound bus, lose Emmy also, both of them for a while, than have her climb into one more trucker's cab.

I was fighting for her soul, and maybe for mine as well.

I miss Kate more with Emmy here, if possible. I had no idea the day I told my sister to leave that she'd never return or ever be in touch. Sometimes I fear, had I known, I would've given up eternity to keep her and Emmy by me on earth. Kate looks better than I expected in the photos, certainly better than when she left here: too thin, slouchy shoulders, globs of lipstick. Perhaps Kate holds her shoulders back a little too stiffly now. Since the healing I've felt healthier than I have in years, but I still don't think Kate would say I look better than she expected. Maybe I've missed her too much. Because I don't remember Mother, Kate fills all my memories of childhood. The warmth of her hair, her daring, and her love. It didn't spill out of her. But it was there, like an ember, and if she let you move in close—and she let me—the heat was intense.

How Jamie could turn away, it still astounds me.

For years after Mother died, I wouldn't leave Kate's side in town, at school, or even at home. If I did, a coldness crept over me as if I'd stepped into water. I'd get the same feeling when she'd talk about leaving America to be a missionary overseas. My clinginess never irritated Kate. It irritated her classmates at school, so Kate quit hanging around them, even after the girls apologized. My sister doesn't do things halfway. Why didn't I take Kate's determined nature into consideration when I told her to leave? Kate hasn't called again since my birthday, when she nearly broke down on the phone. I'm afraid to bother her. Emmy says her mom puts in twice the teaching hours over the summer to make ends meet the rest of the year. I want to tell Kate about the mobile Emmy recently finished and hung above the baby's crib. I've never seen anything quite like it: a flock of delicate paper birds suspended by threads.

Matt loves the idea of my taking Emmy on a trip. He hasn't seemed this proud of me in years. I was hoping he'd come with us. I've never driven far without him. I married Matt when I was sixteen. He taught me to drive, as he's been trying to teach Emmy. Kate was fond of looking at maps, but they make me dizzy. Studying one with Matt, I decide on three short excursions rather than one long trek. The idea of coming home between destinations—to rest up, water my garden, and see Matt—sets my mind more at ease. First, Emmy and I will go to Leavenworth, a Bavarian village in the Cascades foothills. Next, to the Columbia Gorge, which divides Washington from Oregon. Third, we'll go to Walla Walla and the Whitman Mission. I want to take Emmy there most of all.

I treasure the pioneer story of Narcissa and Marcus Whitman. Narcissa, in 1836, was one of the first two white women to cross the Rocky Mountains. Her daughter was the first pioneer child born in the West, although she drowned tragically at age two. Narcissa's letters were published in a book, a copy of which is in our church's small lending library. Missionaries to the Cayuse Indians for eleven years, the Whitmans were eventually killed in a massacre. But their spirit lives on. Emmy had no idea her mom ever wanted to be a missionary. I tell her that not only does Kate's bravery remind me of Narcissa's but that Narcissa was separated from a sister she deeply loved and never saw again. "You'll see Mom again," Emmy says, and I want to believe her. Narcissa used to ride out to meet the wagon trains when they started coming over the mountains, looking for her sister, whom she never found.

The night before Emmy and I leave, Matt holds me particularly close. He's never slept alone in our bed. I do occasionally when he goes on extended hunting and fishing trips with his brother. Lately it seems he's been trying to hunt closer to home. I've never complained or hinted at how alone I feel when he's gone.

"Sorry, I've been so nervous," I say to Emmy once we're on the road. I hesitated to leave behind any of my oils and teas. I had Matt go over the directions with me so many times that he almost came with us. "This is nice, Emmy."

"We're adventurers now."

We chat in a more relaxed manner than we ever did in the trailer. It's the open road, I suppose. I don't get sleepy. I feel wide awake.

"Oh, Aunt Beth, look!" It's the Columbia River. We have to cross it at Vantage. It sits far down in a canyon, and there are no shores. It looks magnificent and deep. I forgot what a mighty river it is. The wind gusts as we cross the bridge, and I have to grip the steering wheel. "I could look at it all day," she says. I just want to get across.

In Leavenworth, we walk around the village, listen to yodelers, watch men in shorts, suspenders, and knee socks play the accordion. We visit a nutcracker museum. I buy Emmy a music box. We eat German food, then sit on a bench surrounded by pots of geraniums and watch the other tourists. The mountains surround us, but not too closely. I'm almost giddy. Emmy too seems exuberant.

"I love you," she says to me once we're back in the hotel room and nibbling on chocolates. "I can't wait to have a cousin." We are sitting in huge German chairs that we pushed right up to our third-story hotel room window, to watch the sun set on the mountains and the pines and the fairy tale–looking buildings of the village. "Do you want a boy or a girl?"

"Either would be a blessing." Emmy and I haven't talked much at all about the baby. I think she feels awkward with my history of miscarriages. She doesn't know the extent, and I hope never will. Kate either. Only Matt knows. And now Brother Mathias. Should I have been so open? "Well, maybe a boy for Matt. After all, I have you."

She smiles. Where did my niece get that smile? It's not Kate's. Or Jamie's, from what I remember. Or even a combination. It's entirely her own.

"You can have more babies," she says. "You can have both."

"No, Emmy. This is it." Narcissa Whitman had no more children after her firstborn drowned. "I'm getting older."

"No, you're not." She sounds worried. "You and Mom are still young."

She looks tiny in the big chair, like Goldilocks. Does Emmy think if I miscarry this time, it will be her fault? I hadn't thought about it until now. How foolish of me.

"If this healing doesn't work," I say, "it won't be your fault in *any* way."

She gazes out the window a long time. I shouldn't have said anything. "God wouldn't do that to you," she says. "Would he?"

The way Emmy struggles day to day with faith reminds me of her mom, except that Emmy, bless her heart, tries to pretend otherwise, at least around me.

"Oh, honey." I don't want her sad.

"I would never forgive him."

I've never blamed God for my miscarriages. "The Lord is nigh unto me," I tell her. "Unto us."

I suggest we eat the whole box of chocolates instead of saving any for tomorrow.

"I'm going to be the best cousin. Just wait."

I sleep beside her for two nights. I keep having to tell myself I'm not dreaming.

For our second trip, we head south to the Columbia Gorge, which is the only sea level route through the Cascades. We follow the river on the Oregon side because the highway is lower. As we travel west, I can see pines beginning on the cliffs farther down the highway, and snow-covered Mount Hood looms. The wind in the gorge nearly rips off the car doors when we stop at The Dalles Dam. We spend an hour in the attached museum. Emmy loves all the old photographs of Indians fishing on wooden piers built out precariously into the raging Columbia before it was dammed. I'd had no idea the river *ever* looked like that. The place used to be called Celilo Falls, and it was a major native fishery. Now the falls are silent and below water. A tiny dilapidated Indian village still remains, but the interstate separates it from the river. We cross back over the Columbia to the more rugged Washington side to find the heritage marker for Celilo. I've lived in Washington my whole life and never heard the story of Celilo Falls or felt wind as fierce as the wind by that marker. Actually I feel more than wind. The sense of loss is enormous and foreboding, especially in an already barren landscape.

How did Narcissa, born and raised in New York State, handle the bleakness of the land out west, especially after her only baby drowned? She adopted eleven children, mostly orphans from the Oregon Trail, trying to fill the emptiness.

"I can almost hear the falls in the wind," Emmy says. "Can't you, Aunt Beth?"

I get back in the car, but she stands there a long time by that marker, looking down at the river. Emmy belongs here, more even than I do, more than Kate. The Columbia scares me. It always has, and the wind close to the river is too harsh. Kate wanted to love the rivers and lakes of eastern Washington, even the rocks she used to collect, but Dad kept her back, and then the land for her became symbolic of Jamie. Emmy accepts the wind and the barren cliffs for what they are, and she finds beauty. She accepts me also. What more can a person ask from a niece, or even from a daughter?

On the drive home from the gorge the next day, I start to feel weary and heavy in my bones. I don't say anything to Emmy, but I wish she knew how to drive. We stop for lunch at a café in Umatilla. Emmy likes the Russian olive trees that grow in dense strands here. To me they appear ancient and biblical. I sip coffee. The cook is Indian and looks more like Reuben the longer I stare at him. He brings out our plates because the waitress, who has Kate's hair color and suddenly looks like Kate, is too busy flirting with a couple of cowboys in the corner booth. *Sister, is that you?*

"Are you okay?" Emmy asks.

I nod, sipping more coffee. I try to eat as much as I can so Emmy won't worry and the baby will be nourished. The waitress touches my arm, inquiring a little too late how everything is and if I want her to box up my leftovers. I don't remember my reply. Only her touch. *Kate?*

Emmy smiles wide when we pull into Quail Run and see not only Matt's truck but Reuben's. She thought Reuben would still be in Omak with his mom or on the reservation chopping wood for the elderly. Matt and Reuben stand in the driveway talking about fishing, obviously, because Matt is pretending to cast. I missed him incredibly. Emmy notices Reuben's black eye and busted lip before I do. Her eyes widen. But thank the Lord, no broken arm this time. He quickly comes to Emmy's side of the car as Matt comes to mine. The kids hug. Emmy is worried. They walk to his truck, for privacy, I assume.

Matt hugs me tightly. "You look tired, darling. A long drive?"

"The wind got to me." He helps me inside. "I just need a nap." I get a drink of water and then head for the bedroom. Matt tucks me in. "Did Reuben say what happened to him?" I ask. I'll prepare some herbs for him. Emmy has been telling me since she first got here that in California I could make money off my oils and herbs. But I can't imagine I could. Only the missionary wives in service overseas, who occasionally visit our church to raise funds, show the least interest in my tonics.

"The kid assured me he isn't in trouble," Matt says. I think my husband is feeling a little fatherly toward Reuben. He's fatherly with Emmy, but that makes more sense. Matt has blood nephews: his brother has a son, and his sister has two boys. Matt loves them dearly, but he thinks they've been given too much. They don't need him. Maybe he thinks Reuben does.

The bed feels so nice. "Will you sit beside me, Matt, until I fall asleep?" I tell him to let me rest only a few hours. I sleep until the next morning. I dreamed all night of the river. Emmy made me eggs and potatoes and kept them warm in the oven. I've been teaching her to cook. She already knows how to bake all kinds of cakes, cookies, and muffins. She does charity bake sales at her school, which makes me so proud. I feel much better. By Friday I feel well enough to go into the church and help.

Brother Mathias is excited to see me. He tells me how much the congregation missed me. "It doesn't feel the same without you, Sister." He almost hugs me, but then gives me a lengthy handshake instead. "How are you feeling? And your lovely niece?" He invites me into his office, even shuts the door. But once inside, he seems to have forgotten what he was going to say to me.

I thank him again for the healing. He put everything on the line for me.

"It was the best evening of my life," he says. "I should be thanking you for your belief in me."

We sit in silence a few moments. He stares intently at me. I feel uncomfortable and levitated at the same time. He's an attractive man, in a different way from my husband. I never believed Matt until after the healing that Brother Mathias has feelings for me. Which, in truth, is a tiny part of why I wanted to take the trips with Emmy: to get away from Mathias's eyes. But are the feelings mutual at all? I don't think so. I never intended.

"Eastern Washington is a desert," he says. "All great men in the Bible did time in the desert." I nod. He sometimes has a roundabout way of speaking. "I'm not a great man, but you have been like a balm to me in this desert."

Does he mean my faith has been like a balm?

"I should get started on the bulletin," I say.

"Stay five more minutes. You are a dear friend." He puts his hand up to his heart. "And a deeply loved sister."

His confession of love shakes me like a gust of wind from the river, but it doesn't scare me. It saddens me, and I begin to weep. Have I in any way led him on? Led him astray? If so, I have wronged two men. "And you, Mathias, a dear brother." I wish he were my real brother, my handsome younger brother that I could watch fondly and loop arms with occasionally and encourage to find a wife to soothe his loneliness. Wiping my eyes, I say, "I should go."

"Stay, Bethany. Please. I'll never ask again."

I give him five minutes, or maybe ten. We don't talk. He just looks at me, and I look at him, and then he bows his head in prayer. I pray too, and silently like him, with him.

The bleeding begins the following night. I wake to it.

I am sixteen weeks pregnant, further along than I've ever been, so the bleeding should feel heavier, but not this heavy. Matt's hand slipped off my belly in sleep. In fact, he has his back to me, which is better, or he'd be sticky. The pain isn't sharp. It's a deep, dull ache. It presses me to the bed, and I feel it even in my teeth. I remember Kate's teeth hurting while she was pregnant. My heart races, then slows. Races. My pulse has been unsteady for years, but nothing like this. I sit up and pull back my side of the covers. In the moonlight I can see the swath of blood. *When thou passest through the waters, I will be with thee.* If I can just make it to the bathroom before Matt wakes up. *And through the rivers.* I find myself in the kitchen. *They shall not overflow thee.* I leave a trail, despite keeping my legs together to hold what remains of my baby inside me. I make a phone call to my minister, Brother Mathias. I whisper frantically into the receiver for him to pray for me because I have no prayers left. I hang up before he can reply. I need clary sage oil to calm me. I accidentally drop the first bottle. The moans start deep inside me, like the pain, and I can't stop them. The second bottle I smash. I tear open my precious bags of different tea leaves and scatter them, but there is no wind in here, no breeze, no air at all.

Then I smash another jar and another and another.

How long has Matt been standing there? At first, his look is one of love and sorrow, then a shadow passes over his face. Fear? Terror? I cannot bear it. I will my vision to blur, but then I see Emmy to my left. Her eyes are wide, and she covers her mouth with both hands. Matt yells at her to stay back. He yells again. "Emmy, damn it, I said stay back!" Why would he tell her to stay away from me? He keeps trying to approach me, but I moan louder and won't let him. He begs me to calm down and not to move or I'll cut my feet. I feel so weak. Hours seem to pass, but of course it's only minutes. My pulse slows. Years and years in this kitchen making oils and teas.

Finally I give up. I am done making a spectacle. Matt catches me.

I hear a siren, and men I don't know strap me to a gurney. My heart races. They fit a mask tightly over my mouth and nose, and they carry me outside. I see Emmy with Reuben. She again tries to reach me, but he holds her close. May he always. Is that the minister? My brother? Did I summon him? I'm cold. Where is Kate? Bright lights temporarily blind me, and the siren deafens. I am all alone. No, Matt is here. Matthew is right beside me in the ambulance and talking to me, but I can't hear him. *Speak up.* He holds my hand. *Don't let go. Don't let me go.* He brings my hand to his mouth and kisses it. That is how he first kissed me. *Do you remember, my love?* My sister wasn't the only one to get her first kiss at camp that summer. Jamie talked Matt into taking my hand, even though it was against church policy. But the kiss was all Matt's idea. And it wasn't a shy peck on the back of my hand. He waited until we were alone before he opened my palm and pressed it to his lips for what seemed a full minute, and for what has lasted all these years. *I am sorry, Matt. You are more to me than seven sons.* I have one last prayer left in me, and it is not for a baby. I want to live for Matt.

For you alone, my only love.

Part Two

11

Reuben

I wake on the couch to the sound of a siren. It gets louder. Too loud. I sit up. Too close. Fuck, not next door. Please, no. I look out the blinds. Sure enough. *Fuck.* Emmy loves Beth so much. I get dressed as fast as I can. Twice I bump my busted lip. Fucking Benji. I'm not through with him yet. He slammed Emmy, so I punched his face. Then he got two hits on me. The bastard's quick, like his brother, who used to cage fight before he killed himself. Benji's last words to me were to tell my white bitch she could suck his cock again anytime. I'm going to bust more than his nose, but I have to wait until Ray's not around to step between us. Teresa and the kids are in the front room. I'm trying to put on my shoes, but Emilio clings to my legs. Teresa pulls him off, tells me to hurry. I run outside, but then I don't go into the aunt's trailer. The door is open, the screen propped. I pace by the steps. The blood on Beth's nightgown says it all when the EMTs carry her outside on the stretcher. Emmy rushes to me in hysterics, then tries returning to her aunt. I don't let her. Matt asks the EMT for one second. "Take Emmy," he tells me. "Don't let her back in there." He turns to Emmy. "Leave the mess." I hold her close so she can't get loose. "Don't follow. You've seen enough."

"Go home," I say to the other neighbors, who have gathered around like fuckheads.

I put Emmy in the cab of my truck to wait, while I grab blankets from Teresa's and some of my warmer clothes for Emmy to put on over her pajamas. We can take a drive and maybe even sleep some-where in my truck. Anything to get her away from the scene. As I start to drive off, I realize the door to the Millers' place is still wide open. I stop and get out. I run up the steps. I avoid looking inside as I reach for the knob. The smell of herbs is strong as in a shaman's shack. As I walk down the steps, I notice a man standing in Beth's garden. Why do trailer parks always have freaks? "Dude," I say. "Show's over." When he turns around, he looks vaguely familiar. It's the minister from the healing. He wears jeans instead of a suit. He mumbles something about Bethany, but I can't make it out. He keeps studying his hands, then staggers off toward his car.

I drive fast toward the Columbia. It's the first place I thought to take Emmy. She won't move close or take the warm clothes I offer. She hugs the passenger door, leaning her head on the window. After a while she sits up abruptly, as if just remembering something, and tells me she's been reading her mom's old Bible at night. She says there are lots of verses about harlots underlined in her mom's Bible. "As if just for me." I don't respond. "'For a whore is a deep ditch,'" she says, barely taking in air before quoting another. "Thou hast polluted the land with thy whoredoms.'"

"Stop it, Emmy." When did she leap from being a nonvirgin to a whore? I drive faster. No one is on the road. No white person knows the spot along the river where I'm taking Emmy, or at least none knows the legend associated with it, which is the same thing.

She quotes another verse about a girl playing the whore in her father's house and how the men in the city stoned her.

"Quit saying stupid shit." I raise my voice. "You're smarter than that."

"Smarter than to believe in the Bible?"

I can't answer that.

We make it to the river. I park my truck. The moon is bright. "I'm sorry I yelled. Come here." She doesn't budge. She's shivering. "It's not your fault, you know." She opens the truck door. "Wait." But she doesn't. She gets out and walks nearer the water. I follow right behind. She could easily fall down the bank. She's wearing fucking flip-flops. Is that all people wear in California? "Be careful." She's in a daze, like the minister in the garden. I wonder what all she saw before the paramedics showed up. "Be careful," I repeat. I shouldn't have brought her here. The Columbia may not be as swift or cold as it once was, but it's still dangerous. Even Coyote, who created the Columbia, was often rendered powerless by it. I can't yell or she might slip. I can't try to grab her for the same reason. She freezes when I warn her sternly in my native language. She looks at the river, then at her foot so close to the edge of the bank, then at me.

"None of this shit is your fault." I cup her face. "It's *not* your fault." I tell her how pure she is, how good. I tell it to her over and over, but she just shakes her head. Frustrated, I say, "Fuck the word of God." I know, not cool. And it only further upsets her. "Take *my* word instead, Emmy." Then I whisper into her ear that she already took my heart.

She reaches up and kisses me so hard that it hurts my busted lip, but I'm glad of the pain. She kisses me again with urgency. Everything is about to change, and she's terrified. What she needs from me at this moment I can't give to her by just holding her like this. I spread the blankets in the bed of my truck. We lay facing each other for a few moments before touching. The wind blows all around us, through us. It smells like the river, and when she reaches for me, so does her skin. Her touch is painful, though not physically so. I almost pull back, but I won't flinch again. As I move inside Emmy, it's not just my body responding at a level it never has before. I slow and hold perfectly still for half a minute, and she does too. Part of my spirit settles into hers. Then again my body and my blood take over, and I make love to the only girl I ever will. I promise this to myself and to Emmy and to the river.

We return to Teresa's at first light. Emmy is frantic for news about her aunt. Teresa left a note for me to wake her up as soon as we get back. She must have news. I leave Emmy on the couch and go into her bedroom. Teresa tells me Beth was airlifted from the Moses Lake hospital to a larger one in Spokane. Just as my dad—fuck, *fuck*—was transported to Spokane from the local hospital in Omak. Matt will call back around three to give an update.

"I'll take Emmy to Spokane right now," I say.

"No." My sister sits up. "Matt doesn't want Emmy seeing Beth until she stabilizes."

"And if she doesn't?"

"He specifically asked that you *not* bring Emmy to the hospital just yet."

"I don't fucking agree."

"He doesn't think Emmy can handle it. We have to respect his wishes."

"Says who?"

"Just wait a day or two, brother." For now she tells me to bring Emmy into her room. We can have her bed, and she'll sleep on the couch for a while.

Hours later Teresa sticks her head in the bedroom door. Emmy finally fell asleep. She was distraught, begging me to take her to Spokane, swearing if she knew how to drive, she'd take herself. I almost caved a dozen times. Teresa gestures for me to come into the kitchen. Her new washing machine is spinning. I like the sound.

"Hey, kid. We have to go clean that place." She nods toward the Millers' trailer. "I used a sick day at work and took the kids to Rosa's." Rosa is Emilio's Mexican *tia*. She'll watch Emilio for free but charges a fortune to keep the others. My sister points to a tub of cleaning supplies by the front door. She says an orderly from the hospital who has a crush on her brought them by. "They're industrial strength."

"Matt said not to go back in there," I say. "I thought we *had* to respect his wishes."

"Reuben Tonasket." I rarely backtalk her for real. "How much blood was there? Did you see? We *can't* leave blood."

"There was a lot of blood." It's Emmy. She's in the kitchen. "I'll go clean it," she says. She looks small in my sweatshirt, which completely covers her pajama shorts. Fuck, my heart.

"We'll help," Teresa says before I can. Emmy tries to protest, but my sister insists. "You both need to eat something small first. Sit down." She makes us toast and strong coffee. Then we head next door. What a mess of blood and oils and herbs. The stench is sickening. Nurse Teresa takes charge. We open all the windows. I find garbage bags. Emmy looks faint, but she won't let us clean without her. Neither will Teresa let Emmy go into the master bedroom. She and I go in there. I throw up twice in the back bathroom. We get the sheets off the bed. I make a run to the park Dumpster. The mattress is ruined. Matt will have to take it to the dump. In the meantime, we pour solvent on it. Matt will also need to pull up the bedroom carpet. We spend about three hours altogether. Emmy thanks Teresa numerous times, and then she hugs her. Surprisingly, or maybe not, my sister hugs her back.

"She-who-hugs-white-girls" will be my new name for her.

Emmy wants me to wait in the bathroom at her aunt's while she takes a shower. After she starts the water, she asks me to close my eyes so she can get undressed and step behind the curtain. "Come in with me," she says a minute later. "I'm scared." The hot water feels so nice after scrubbing all that blood. I can't quit staring at Emmy's body, entirely naked as I've never seen it. Her breasts look fuller, but not her hips. We wash each other's hair, though not playfully. The hot water runs out. We move to her bed.

I feel a little guilty afterward. Her uncle told me to take Emmy away from here, not to bring her back and have sex with her. He trusts me with Emmy. He has family in the area, but he chose me. I tell her to pack some things because she's staying with me at Teresa's. Before we leave the bedroom with her name in pink letters on the wall and a dozen paper birds floating above an empty crib, I suggest she shut off the praying hands night-light for safety.

She panics. "Beth leaves it on day and night. I can't. Don't make me."

"I'm not going to make you."

"Okay, Uncle Matt, but I *want* to see her. . . . Yes. I love you too. Can't I *please* come today? *Please?* Reuben says he'll bring me. . . . Okay. I understand. Tell her I love her. . . . No. I'll try calling Mom too. . . . I just love you guys so much." Emmy crumples on the kitchen floor after hanging up. Teresa is asleep in the kids' room. She was going to organize it while they were away and she was still in the cleaning mood, but then she fell asleep on Grace and Audrey's bed.

I sit on the floor beside Emmy and rub her back until she gets control.

"Aunt Beth's in a coma from hemorrhaging," she finally says. *Fuck.*

"Uncle Matt said the coma, for now, is her body's defense. Do you believe him?" I nod. "I miss her."

I take Emmy back into Teresa's room. She sobs in my arms. I feel undone, already, and things are only going to get worse. I need Virgil's sweat lodge. I need to drum. I need to see certain views on the reservation. I need to show them to Emmy. What if I never get the chance?

"I don't want to call my mom," Emmy says. Her mom is in Europe with her boyfriend. Emmy likes her mom's boyfriend, a lot. I try not to be jealous of her fondness for him or to be annoyed by how many times she's told me she wants her mom to marry him. "I don't want Mom to come here," she says now, "but I'll hate her if she doesn't. I already hate her."

I can't picture Emmy's mom in this trailer park, or by the lake, or anywhere in eastern Washington. I can't picture her period.

"You'll hate her too after you meet her. She's so different from her sister. And she did this to Aunt Beth. She broke her sister's heart when she left here with me."

Damn. I am going to hate Emmy's mom because she's going to leave here again with Emmy. I know it. I have to think of a way to keep her.

"Will you take me to Spokane the day after tomorrow?" she asks. I nod. "Matt wants me to wait until then, which I think is kind of bull. But he sounded so sad."

It's total bull the way adults don't want kids to see their relatives— all fucked up or not—in the hospital. I argued to stay every minute with my dad, but my bossy aunts and even bossier sister claimed it was better for me to remember my dad the way he was before the accident. Bullshit. Then why did I hold Emmy back from her aunt all bloody on the stretcher?

"I have plenty of money for gas," she adds.

"I have money, Emmy." Though not much. Not enough.

She falls silent. I think she sleeps, so I close my eyes.

When I wake up, she isn't beside me. I linger in Teresa's bed for just a minute before getting up to find Emmy. I slept with Teresa for weeks after Dad died. I had such a hard time keeping it together. Finally a medicine man was called.

Neither Teresa nor Emmy is in the trailer. Teresa's van is gone. Is Emmy next door? I go over. I knock, but no one answers. I enter and call her name. I hear a sound from the master bedroom. "Emmy?" She doesn't answer, so I go in there, even though I really don't want to. Emmy is standing in the middle of the room, staring wide-eyed at the stained mattress and floor.

"Help me," she chokes. "I can't look away."

I grab her arm. "We're leaving here. I'm taking you to Omak." She needs to get away from this trailer park. And Omak isn't that much farther from Spokane than here.

Teresa talks me into waiting until the morning to leave for Omak. Emmy tries to call her mom's hotel in Paris, but the room line just rings. The second time she calls, she speaks to the manager—in French, for fuck's sake. I had no idea she spoke French.

"Why did you go over there without me?" I ask later when we lie together in Teresa's bed. "And why didn't you tell me you speak French?"

"I don't."

"What language was that then?"

"I mean, yes, I've had three years of French. But I suck. The concierge snickered."

"The what?"

"I went to Beth's to get my money and calling cards. Spencer gave me lots of money before I left Sacramento. We don't have to worry."

"We don't need his money."

"You sound like my mom."

"What do you mean?" How could I possibly sound like a professor?

"Mom has problems with her wisdom teeth. The pain keeps her awake at night. Spencer loves her and wants to pay for a dentist, but she won't let him. I don't understand."

"Be glad you don't." I respect Emmy's mom for not taking the dude's money.

"We're using Spencer's money for gas tomorrow," Emmy says. "And for food."

"No, we're fucking not." I pull away from her.

"Yes, we *fucking* are. You don't have much money. I looked in your wallet."

"Shit." I sit up. "Not very cool."

"You don't have a dad to give you money."

What's her fucking point? "Neither do you, remember?"

"I know." She sits up. "But I have Spencer."

"Do you have a thing for him?"

"What?" She looks confused.

"Do you and Spencer have a thing? Don't be shy. You know what I mean."

She's shocked. I am too. She jumps out of bed. "So, you *do* think I'm a slut?"

God, I'm an asshole. What a thing for me to imply, especially when she blames her "impurity" for the healing ceremony's not working, and with our just having had sex together twice in the last twenty-four hours.

"I don't fuck my mom's boyfriend," she says. "That's disgusting, Reuben. How could you think that? He's the closest thing I've ever had to a dad. He loves me."

She has this way of sounding so young.

"He even told me so at the airport."

She heads for the door, but I stop her. "I'm sorry. I was being a prick. I'm sorry."

"If I had anywhere to go," she says, "know that I'd be gone."

I actually kneel. "Forgive me, Emmy."

"We're using Spencer's money." I shake my head. "You're so stubborn. You drive me crazy." She punches the tops of my shoulders, but lightly. Then she reaches under my arms and tries to pull me up. As if. I fall back on the floor, laughing. "Screw you," she says. "I need a cigarette."

"Come on then." I stand up. "Have you ever smoked before?" She says no. We go out the back door. Her aunt's trailer is dark. We stare at it a long time before I light her a cigarette. She's a natural, doesn't choke, inhales just right and exhales with ease. It's damn sexy. She's making it more so on purpose by being breathy, as she gets sometimes when we kiss.

"Jesus," I say when she's done with her cig, "you better not smoke that way in college."

We both become silent. College seems irrelevant suddenly, which is scary. It's all I've thought about for years. But I don't want to go to college, or anywhere, without Emmy.

She gets up, says she has to get something out of her bag in Teresa's room. "Look," she says when she returns. It's the diamond necklace she wore the first weeks she was here. Why show it to me? "We can hock it for gas money." I'm not sure. "Come on, Reuben." When I don't respond, she sings, "R-E-V-E-N-G-E," instead of R-E-S-P-E-C-T. I grin, but I still don't want anything to do with the necklace.

"Did you know Connor has his tongue pierced?"

"Really? What a fag."

"You shouldn't use that word."

"Sorry. What a cocksucker. Does he really?"

"Yeah, and sometimes he'd cover my eyes when we had sex."

"What the hell?"

"So let me hock the necklace. It'll make me feel better"

"Let me throw it in the fucking Dumpster."

"He didn't cover *your* eyes. He covered *mine*."

Good point. I tell her we'll hit the pawnshop on the way out of town.

"Wait in your truck," Emmy says as I pull in front of Basin Gun & Pawn. "This is between Connor and me."

"What? No way." Pawnbrokers are sleazy. She can't talk very well to people she knows, like Teresa, let alone a greasy-haired stranger with a pinkie ring and a sour toothpick dangling from his mouth. "I'm not letting you go in there alone. Forget it."

"Connor always made me strip. *Always*. He'd never undress me. I was like his personal porn star."

"Fine." I cave. "Just don't tell me any more shit about that guy."

She comes back out ten minutes later with three hundred dollars. She probably got only forty bucks for the necklace. I can't picture Emmy bartering. The rest of the cash is Spencer's. I'm not an idiot. But I love her smile and the confidence she tries to fake.

We drive north on highway 17 into the coulees. White people are fishing for trout and bass off the side of the road and in boats on the various reservoirs. These holding lakes, engineered together with pipes, pumps, smaller dams, and canals, make a fake branch of the Columbia— white man's branch—so basin farmers can irrigate their thirsty crops. Just past Coulee City, I get on 155 to the dam. I could head west instead and take 97 north to Omak, but then we'd only skirt the rez. On 155, we have to go right past Grand Coulee Dam and then through a large portion of the rez to get to Omak. Emmy's eyes practically pop out when she first sees the dam. Whose wouldn't? It's only fifty feet short of being a mile across. Whites love to brag about how much concrete Coulee Dam contains: enough to pave a highway from Seattle to Miami; three times more than Hoover Dam. It's the largest concrete structure in the United States. Emmy knows how I feel about the dam, what it's done to the river, the salmon, my people. I already told her. Her great-grandfathers probably helped build it. Fuck, so did mine.

We're on the rez. She's been sitting close but scoots closer. After about ten minutes, we pass the agency headquarters. I point them out to Emmy. Across the highway, I point out the Nespelem Community Center and powwow arena. We pass the state's POINT OF HISTORICAL INTEREST sign for Chief Joseph's grave. I don't point to it—out of respect to Chief Joe and his descendants who live here. Emmy starts to point to the sign but then only looks back at it. As a rule, I don't take white girls driving around the rez. Other Indian boys do, but not me. We pass decent-looking trailer houses, then junky ones, some even with the "skin" torn off, others bandaged with plywood. Emmy says nothing. Every once in a while there's a nice trailer set off with a well-maintained yard and outbuildings. We pass houses and shacks in the town of Nespelem. She must see the rusted cars and appliances, strewn garbage, broken trampolines and swing sets, but she stays silent. "Poverty isn't looked down upon on the rez," I tell her as we pass the Nespelem longhouse. "The elders say we're all in this together."

The scattered pines thicken as we start to climb the pass.

When the trees get dense and shade darkens the cab, Emmy whispers, "I love you, Reuben." I feel the words in my joints. "I love you *more* than I love Beth."

"You don't have to say that."

"I *do* have to say it. I feel so guilty."

"Just breathe," I tell her. It's not safe to pull over here—way too curvy—or I would. "We'll go to Spokane first thing in the morning."

"Are we in the Cascades?" she asks between breaths. "Aunt Beth and I stayed in the foothills."

I explain that the mountains on the rez are part of the Okanogan Highlands, not the Cascades. "But you'll see the Cascades as soon as we head west."

Emmy relaxes when the land opens back up. Right here is one of my favorite parts of the rez. I point to the snow-covered Cascades in front of us. At least whites can't flatten them as they've slowed and backed up the flow of the Columbia with their, what, fourteen dams on the main stem alone. When Coyote returns—and the elders promise he will—he certainly has his work cut out for him.

Emmy is doing much better. She points to horses and ponies that she finds pretty, which is damn near all of them, and there are a lot.

We're back in sage as we make it to Omak by two in the afternoon. I drive Emmy around town, show her the stampede grounds, Suicide Hill, the high school. I want her to meet my mom while she's at work, in hopes she'll be somewhat sober. I try to find parking in front of the bar or the Laundromat next door. Shit. A church youth group is singing on the corner. I park across the street. We get out. Emmy seems mesmerized by the group of teenagers, holding signs and crosses and singing about victory in Jesus. "Can we watch for a minute?" she asks when I grab her hand to start walking.

"Sure." I'd love nothing more. Not.

"Her voice is beautiful," Emmy says about the girl holding a megaphone. "Like Beth's."

"That's Jenny. She goes to my school."

"She's kind of pretty."

I've never really thought so before. "Her dad's a rodeo drunk." I explain how the bar where Mom works caters to whites and Indians. Hence the Christians singing on the corner. Jenny's dad drinks in the white cowboy bar a few streets over.

"I'm sorry I made you go to church with me," Emmy says.

"You didn't make me."

We cross the street. Jenny, who is between songs, smiles at me. I think her dad hits her. She and I partnered on a school project last year and she had suspicious bruises. The project, proposed by a new-to-the-area teacher, was to incorporate some Colville Coyote tales into the literature curriculum. The Christian kids, white and Mexican, had a hard time grasping the "slipperiness" of Coyote. Was he considered a god or not? We Indian kids, for the most part, kept our mouths shut. The teacher finally concluded that Coyote, like Jesus, had been sent by the Creator to do work for humans. One kid decided Coyote was the Antichrist. Even Jenny struggled, though in a far less obnoxious way, with Coyote being both a good and a bad example. The teacher pointed out that the Greek gods were also "complex"— pursuing fleeing maidens, deceiving, losing their tempers, but also helping with wisdom and kindness. She stated that perhaps striving to mirror the perfection of Jesus Christ was self-defeating. Wrong thing to say. Flustered, she moved the class on to Edgar Allan Poe's tales of madness, which practically sent the Gothic kids into orgasm.

"Hello, Reuben," Jenny says now.

"Hi, Jenny," I reply, squeezing Emmy's hand. Emmy smiles at her. Of course she does.

Emmy looks different from the Christian girls singing on the corner. She looks different from the most popular girls at Omak High, who have ten times Emmy's confidence and just as many clothes. I didn't fully realize the difference until now. It's not just Emmy's mix of styles but the way she wears each piece. I sound gay as hell. The popular girls here wear a lot of pink. Emmy doesn't. Neither does she have long fake nails with white tips. She paints her nails but keeps them short. It's also the way Emmy holds herself and walks: not with certainty, like the wealthy white girls, or attitude, like the tougher Indian girls, but something. Maybe grace. Femininity. But she's not docile or even dainty. I can't figure it out. Certainly I don't think it's a California thing. Every once in a while Emmy loses it in a big way and slouches or becomes awkward or even stumbles. The girl sure can move during sex, though, especially for someone who can't ride a bike, shoot hoops, or supposedly dance.

Before Emmy and I left Moses Lake, Teresa said she'd call Mom for me and explain the situation. Mom was mad at me the last time we saw each other, and drunk. If Mom listened to Teresa, as she does on occasion, she'll be a saint today. If not, she'll be drunk off her ass in spite. Where Emmy and I stay the night depends on which it is.

We walk into the dark bar. I hear Mom calling my name before I see her.

She yells again over the honky-tonk music. She sits in one of the back booths, next to the white guy who's been giving her so much hell lately. He wears a cowboy hat but sells cars, and I guarantee he's never ridden a horse down Suicide Hill like Dad. Mom's boyfriend has a wife, but he likes to screw Indian women on the side. Fuck him. I make it a point to never stick around when Mom has a new guy, Indian or white. I stay with one of my aunts or with Ray or wherever. Her relationships never last long. Dad was by far the longest. Until recently, my little sister, Lena, has been keeping Mom sober. Better than I ever could. Mom's got two empty shot glasses in front of her. "Hey, baby boy." She gets up to hug me. No wobbling. That's good. I introduce her to Emmy. "You're a doll," she says to Emmy. "Isn't she a doll, Harold?"

"Mom," I whisper. "Can we get a different booth?" I grip Emmy's hand. "Away from Gerald?"

"Sure, baby. It's *Harold*. Go grab a table up front. Let me refill some drinks and I'll be over. You kids want a couple burgers?"

I, for one, am starving. "Definitely."

We grab a table. There's only about six other people in the bar. Emmy looks around at all the cowboy and Indian decor on the walls: dream catchers, horseshoes, oil paintings, neon signs, a beaded Indian vest. "You doing okay?" I ask her.

"I'm fine, *baby.*"

I grin. She's being cool. I thought she might get instantly uptight in a joint like this. I wouldn't blame her. And especially considering her aunt's in a coma. We'll leave extra early in the morning for Spokane. Luckily Beth isn't in the same hospital where my dad never recovered. I can tell Emmy's trying hard not to think about her aunt, but worry clouds her gray eyes. "You want a cigarette?" I offer.

She nods. "I've never been in a bar."

"It's a great atmosphere. Don't you think?" I light us both a cigarette. "Desperation."

"Assimilation." Here comes the wordplay—and a smile.

"Proclamation," I say. "As in the Emancipation Proclamation."

"Confederation. As in twelve tribes on one reservation."

"As in group masturbation."

"As in taking your own ass to the station."

I high-five Emmy.

Mom is standing beside the table, holding two Cokes and looking confused. She puts down the Cokes. I invite her to sit with us. She looks back at the booth where Harold is. "Okay. For a minute." I can see now that she's pretty drunk. She and Emmy talk a little. Mom's going to think Emmy is stuck up, but she's just shy and has a lot on her mind. Twice Emmy brings up Teresa's kids and Grace's beadwork. Mom's not trying at all. She keeps looking just at me and calling me baby. She starts talking in our native language. I don't know it very well. Just enough. But even if I did, I'd reply in English, which I do. The cook calls her. She gets up and comes back with our burgers and fries. "On Harold," she says, serving us, but not sitting back down.

"No, thanks." I hand my plate back to her. Emmy kicks me under the table.

"Tell him we said thanks, Marie," Emmy says.

"You're a doll," Mom says to her. "You go tell him. He speaks English."

"Mom, fuck."

Emmy gets up to go tell Harold thanks.

"Sit down," I tell Emmy. She doesn't listen.

"Sorry, baby," Mom says.

I watch Emmy. I watch the cowboys at the bar who turn to watch Emmy. My dad suddenly joins them. I should tell Mom, but I don't. He's watching Emmy, but not in a lusty way. There's almost a protective look on his face. I'm not sure I've ever loved him more. He gets up and two-steps for a minute to the honky-tonk music. I try not to grin. Then he does a few native dance moves to a far older rhythm—a rhythm he's always heard better than I can. "Listen," the elders say. To the earth, they mean, to the fish, to the wind, to the silence of rocks, to your fathers. But what if your father is a drunk? Your uncles? My dad stops dancing. He gives me the same warning gesture he did on Teresa's couch. "Listen," he's insisting. He was never pushy with me while he was alive. Then he disappears.

"She doesn't listen to you very well," Mom says.

"I'm not her boss." Why is Dad so adamant with his warning? Doesn't he understand that I hear things in Emmy's quietness? In her breath? I hear the blood in her veins same as he could hear fish in the rivers. I wonder if he hangs at this bar often. According to Teresa, Mom's never seen his ghost. He wasn't easy on Mom. He used to call her Mama Marie. It can't be too long before Dad moves completely into the spirit world. He should've already. I'm his only son, but I never thought his unwillingness to move on had anything to do with me. In life, Dad had his own reasons for things, and they didn't include me.

"She must be *your* boss," Mom says. "You're wearing white boy clothes."

I'm wearing the cargo shorts and checked shirt I bought myself. I look at my mom. I don't hate her. I never could. But I don't always like her. "I hope you don't let Gerald boss you."

She takes my chin in her hand. "Eat. You look thin. Teresa never feeds you enough."

I pull my face free. "Don't start on Teresa." What's taking Emmy so long? She's too damn polite to walk away when a drunk is rambling.

"I'm praying for the white girl's aunt."

"Her name is Emmy." Here she comes.

"See you and Emmy later at the apartment," Mom says. "I'll make dinner for you guys. And Harold. And Lena."

Not hardly.

I pick up Lena from my aunt Lori's house to take her to my great-aunt Shirley's house on the Sanpoil River, where Emmy and I are staying the night. Shirley is my great-aunt on my dad's side. She's also Ray's great-aunt. She was raised in a boarding school and is afraid of white people. She won't mind Emmy, though. Lena, who is seven, insists on sitting between Emmy and me in my truck on the forty-minute drive, but then she leans her head on Emmy, not me. Emmy puts her arm around Lena. "You're pretty," my sister says, taking Emmy's hand. "And your hands are *so* warm."

"Not as pretty as you," Emmy says.

"I like your sunglasses."

"Here, you can have them." Emmy takes off her Hollywood sunglasses and gives them to Lena without looking at me. My sister puts them on immediately.

"I'm a dancer," Lena brags. She is. Mom takes her all over for competitions and powwows and rodeos. Or my aunts do.

"Will you show me a dance later?" Emmy asks.

"Only if Reuben will dance with me."

"No way, little sister."

"Then will you drum while I dance?" Lena asks.

"Be quiet, pipsqueak, or I'll take you back to Aunt Lori's."

"Emmy won't let you." She snuggles in closer to Emmy.

Emmy's been smiling the whole time with Lena. But when I look over at Emmy next, she's crying. I reach over and squeeze her shoulder.

"What's wrong, Emmy?" Lena asks with real concern.

I answer. "Emmy's only aunt is sick. She's in the hospital."

Lena asks Emmy, "You only have *one* aunt?" Shit. Emmy nods. "Then I'll dance for her tonight." Lena turns to me. "Hurry and drive, Mr. Slowpoke."

Ray shows up at dinnertime, as usual. But I'm glad. He can drum for Lena, who is anxious to dance. Aunt Shirley insists we all eat first. The meat is venison. I transfer Emmy's portion to Ray's plate when Aunt Shirley glances at the television that's turned down but never off. Mostly she watches HSN. She never orders anything but has been considering a new set of pots and pans for years. I'm glad my aunt doesn't mention the venison is from me. A small fork horn that I nearly lost last week. I quartered it out and gave half to Aunt Shirley and half to Mom. Aunt Shirley's two sons have been dead for almost thirty years, killed in a single vehicle accident, and her husband for twenty. It's not that I don't want to drum for Beth. I have already. But I can't drum in front of Emmy. Not yet. Ray introduces himself to Emmy in his usual fashion, explaining his name. "I'm Ray," he says. "Short for Rainier. The beer, not the mountain."

Before I build a fire in the pit in the backyard, I sneak Emmy away for a quick walk alone in the pines and along the river. The Sanpoil's current will give her strength. It's nine o'clock and still not dark. I build the fire. Aunt will need more wood chopped before September. Ray drums in his Seattle Mariners cap, and Lena dances in a buckskin dress and Emmy's funky sunglasses. Emmy and I sit side by side in camp chairs that have seen better days. My aunt's house has seen better days. My people have seen better days. Though not for a long, long time. Emmy watches Lena. Ray drums and sings. I sing too because I can't help it. I pray because I can't help it.

Lena begs to sleep between Emmy and me on the sofa bed. Lena is half white and half Indian. I wish she were our child. I wish Emmy and I were older and married. I'd marry her tomorrow. I don't want to be young if I can't have Emmy. There's got to be a way to keep her close. I lie on my side and watch Emmy brushing Lena's bangs back from her forehead as my little sister sleeps. *Really, Dad, this is what you're trying to warn me against? This girl? Look at her, Dad.* Maybe Dad is jealous. Coyote wanted every beautiful maiden for himself, like that Zeus fellow. But Coyote was vain and proud about more than just women. My dad wasn't necessarily a proud man. In that regard, his power was of a different sort. In fact, he could've used a bit of Coyote's pride. Maybe it would've kept him alive. It's like he sought only absolute losers to befriend and make deals with. I'm not talking about relatives, but strangers on every rez west of the Rockies and white slobs. I hear Ray snoring in the bedroom where Aunt Shirley's boys once slept. Emmy's eyes close, her hand on Lena. *Look, Dad.*

I love because I can't help it.

12

Emmy

Reuben and I left his aunt Shirley's house early in the morning. I was sad to leave Lena, who was still asleep. Would I ever see her again? I folded a paper crane and left it by her pillow. Reuben promised we'd come back. But I may never see his reservation again either. Uncle Matt might not let me stay with Reuben any longer. And I wanted to remain at Aunt Beth's bedside. Matt hadn't left it. His parents had brought him clothes. I felt so guilty for having blatantly lied and misrepresented myself to Aunt Beth. I'd known her only eight weeks, but she filled my heart. She and Reuben. She had to recover. I was trying not to blame myself for the miscarriage, not when, as Reuben kept pointing out, she'd had others in the past. But I *was* responsible for giving her false hope.

I wished the trip to Spokane took longer than two hours. I suddenly wasn't ready to see my aunt unable to talk or move. Though I wanted to rid from my head the image of her smashing jars in the kitchen in her faded flowered nightgown that had suddenly bloomed red. And her moans, so guttural. Her hair as wild as her eyes. She'd been like Rochester's first wife locked in the attic in *Jane Eyre*. How ironic that Mom had such sympathy for the "madwoman in the attic." I kept telling Reuben to drive slower as we followed the Sanpoil River south and then took a ferry across the Columbia and off the reservation. We headed east to Spokane on highway 2. I loved riding in Reuben's truck with him, yesterday and now this morning. I treasured the long miles between tiny towns when it was just Reuben and me and the land. I tried to pretend, at least for brief intervals, that we weren't headed to a hospital where my aunt lay unconscious. But small talk was impossible. From the beginning of our friendship, Reuben let me be silent. He knew it didn't mean I wasn't present. Last night, at his aunt Shirley's house, the light in the northern sky took until after ten to completely fade. Reuben sang, his cousin drummed, and his sister danced until it did.

I had to find a way to stay in Washington. If Beth recovered, I didn't want to abandon her, as Mom had. If she didn't, an unfathomable thought, it would be much harder to convince Mom to let me stay for Reuben. The solution came to me as we were driving past an enormous tractor dealership in the middle of nowhere. Excitedly, I said, "My dad wasn't killed by a tractor."

"What?"

"Mom told me when I was little that my dad was killed by a tractor. But he wasn't. He's a farmer. *He* can give me permission to stay. He has legal say when it comes to me, right?"

"Slow down," Reuben said. "*What* are you talking about?"

"I don't want to go back to California. Mom will try to force me." I still hadn't spoken with Mom since Beth's miscarriage, which was fine with me. I'd finally talked with an English-speaking (or willing to speak English) hotel manager who said Mom and Spencer had left on a short Mediterranean cruise. The American gentleman, he said, had completely surprised the beautiful lady with this part of the journey, and there was no phone service. Matt was going to call the Paris hotel today and explain the emergency." My dad can give me permission to stay here."

"I'm confused," Reuben said. "I thought you've never met your dad."

"I haven't. But I bet Matt knows how to find him."

"Hold up."

"I'll have to act fast."

"Hold up, Emmy. Meeting your dad for the first time is huge." He didn't sound excited. "Let alone asking him to fight your mom for you."

"It's all worth it if I can stay in Washington." Clearing my throat, I said out loud what I knew we'd both been thinking for weeks. "I want to finish high school in Moses Lake. Both of us." His grip tightened on the steering wheel. "Don't you want me to stay?"

He pulled his truck off the road. Then he took both my hands in his and looked me in the eyes. "I hurt when I'm with you." He still had bruises from a fight with Benji. "I can't imagine the pain if you were to leave."

"I'm *not* leaving. I *won't*." I was going to stand up to Mom for once in my life. I'd never had enough of a reason to before.

"I'll do everything I can to keep you," Reuben said. "I promise."

After a few more farming towns, the traffic started to increase, as did the pine trees, though the farmhouses remained just as far apart. As soon as we saw a sign for Fairchild Air Force Base, we began passing businesses like credit unions, fast food, Walmart, ministorages, and check cashing. In all the parking lots were soldiers in camouflage. The exit sign for the Spokane airport made me sad. The city came into view: brick buildings, old churches, skyscrapers, two enormous smokestacks, and hospitals. My stomach fell. We exited the highway.

"Bethany Miller," the hospital receptionist said. "ICU. Top floor." She gave us special name tags. When the elevator doors opened on the top floor, there was Uncle Matt. He looked diminished in that setting. I'd been girding myself for the sight of Aunt Beth, not Matt. He was walking toward us, but he didn't recognize us for a second. He stopped. Reuben and I stopped too. My uncle and I stared at each other, as if there were suddenly a river between us that neither of us could cross. Reuben nudged me forward, then hung back. "Uncle Matt," I said, going to him. He took me into his arms. His chest heaved, just once, and then he was okay. "Can I see her, alone?" I asked.

He pointed and told me the room number, but then he called me back. "Emmy, sweetie, they cut her hair. They had to the first night in Moses Lake because it got in the way." I couldn't process what he just said. "You sure you want to go in alone?" I nodded. I didn't tell him I had stuff I had to say to Aunt Beth right away.

Nothing in the world could have prepared me for the sight of my aunt in that hospital bed: shorn hair, a million tubes, a breathing machine, beeping monitors, charts, ugly curtains, dingy gown, gauze wrapped here and there on her arms. Her eyes were not only closed but sunken. Had she always been *so* pale? Her body remained still, yet she didn't look peaceful. That was not the woman who brought me tea before bed and sang to me and thought of me every day of my childhood, any more than that moaning woman in the kitchen had been. I felt dizzy, the sterile but scuffed tile floor coming up to greet me. I needed air.

I rushed out and past Matt and Reuben in the small waiting room. They both stood when they saw me pass by. I put up my hand to warn them off. I pushed the elevator button ten times. Down in the lobby, I almost tripped in my flip-flops, trying to get out the hospital's sliding glass doors. I started walking. Where was I? This wasn't Sacramento. What city was this? How far north? Here there were pines, not sycamores, and the air was crisper. I crossed streets, walked past buildings, crossed more streets, walked under the highway, past homeless people, taller buildings, hotels, military men, businesswomen, a long-haired Indian sleeping on a knoll of grass in front of a Chevron. I was completely lost, but I didn't care. Suddenly I was by a river. What river? Did it flow into the Columbia? Reuben said all rivers in eastern Washington did. I found a bench. I liked city benches. I liked to people-watch from benches. I always begged Mom for ten more minutes. Then ten more. *Where are you, Mom? Your only sister is dying. I am in a strange city and you in a strange country. I am trying hard not to miss you. No matter, I am never coming back to you. Do you hear me, Mom? Never.*

I leaned my elbows on my knees and put my head in my hands. I plugged my ears to block out the rumble of the city where my aunt might die. When I sat back up, my eyes went right to Reuben, standing a little ways off. He didn't wave. In fact, his hands were in his pockets. He didn't smile. He just watched me. I wished he hadn't followed me. I didn't need to be rescued. I could rescue myself, whether lost on the moors or in a city. I put my head back in my hands. A week ago my cup had never been fuller.

We returned to the hospital, and I sat alone beside my aunt's bed for half an hour. I tried to tell her how sorry I was and to beg her to please hang on, but I simply couldn't. My hands kept getting warmer the longer I sat there, but a stronger force—my instinct to survive, a shrink later claimed—repelled me away from her listless body. Uncle Matt invited us to go to the cafeteria with him and get lunch. Reuben said he'd stay with Beth. He seemed agitated with me, probably for taking off like I had and then getting annoyed that he'd followed me. It was a long elevator ride to the basement with Uncle Matt. We found a table but just picked at our food with plastic forks.

"I think she's waiting for your mom," Matt said. "I almost hope Kate never comes." I did too. After a moment of silence he told me, "I booked you and Reuben a room at the hotel down the street. Walking distance. I got a room with two beds. Humor me."

I'd already given him the Paris hotel information. He said he would demand a message be sent to my mom. I wondered if he'd been outside at all for fresh air.

I took a deep breath. "I need to ask you something."

"Shoot, kid." He tried to sound up to it, but he was clearly exhausted.

"Do you happen to know my dad's address or phone number?"

He looked taken aback. "Are you sure?"

"I just want to see him once."

"I understand. I mean, I couldn't possibly. Are you sure this is the right time?"

"I have to see him *before* Mom gets here," I explained. "Growing up, I thought he was dead. Does he live very far from here?"

"No, actually. About an hour south is all."

I was only an hour from my father. "Do you have his phone number?"

Uncle Matt pulled his wallet from his back pocket. "I've been carrying around his card for years." He handed it to me. "For just such an occasion." My hand trembled. He put his hand over mine for a moment. "I'd go with you, Emmy, under *any* other circumstance."

"I know. Do you think my dad will want to see me?"

"Absolutely. But he doesn't deserve you."

"Is he mean?"

Matt shook his head.

"Was Mom and Beth's dad mean?"

He hesitated before replying. "With Beth, he was too stern. With your mom, an absolute tyrant. And he never liked me."

"I like you. I wish *you* were my dad." He choked up. I'd almost said the same thing to Spencer when he drove me to the airport—only two months ago, though it seemed years. I waited. "Reuben will take me to see Jamie."

"He's a good kid."

"I love him."

"Be careful, sweetheart. You're awfully young."

I offered to stay the rest of the day with Aunt Beth so he could go somewhere and get sleep. "I can't leave her," he said. "And hospitals are no place for kids." He tried to hand me some cash, but I refused. "Take the money," he insisted. "It'll make *me* feel better. You two get out of here, now. Go to Riverfront Park. There's a carousel there. Or take a ride over the falls." He started to choke up again. "Come back this evening or in the morning. I'll call the hotel if anything changes."

Reuben and I checked into our fifth-floor hotel room, which had two beds, just like Uncle Matt said. Reuben went to the window and stared at the city without saying anything or calling me over to look. He was edgy. Only later did he tell me that his dad had died in a Spokane hospital. "Thanks for bringing me here," I said.

"You know you don't have to thank me." He kept his back to me at the window.

I undressed. "Thanks for finding me today."

When he turned around, I was completely naked. He didn't come toward me. Maybe it wasn't appropriate given the circumstances. But I wanted to be naked with him in this room, even if it meant I was "playing the whore." He stared but didn't come nearer. Embarrassed, I reached for my shirt on the bed.

"Don't get dressed. You look beautiful."

"What's the matter, Reuben?" His face was extremely tense.

"You really scared me today," he said. "You don't know what you're doing sometimes."

What did he mean?

"I'm afraid you're going to lose yourself in a big way someday."

"Don't say that." Now I was scared. "You won't let me."

"Emmy, I—"

"You won't let me."

I stretched out on one of the beds so he'd come to me, which he did. We had sex, and I felt the furthest thing from a biblical harlot or even an adulteress. I felt so safe and clean and loved. I'd never be lost as long as Reuben and I were together. I told him so.

When he dozed off, I slipped out of bed and went to my bag for my sketchbook. I hadn't sketched much this summer. I'd sketched Aunt Beth's hands one day and then her face another time. *Oh, Aunt Beth.* I'd sketched her plants—the various stems and leaves. Now I wanted to sketch Reuben. I grabbed his T-shirt off the floor and put it on. Then I quietly moved a chair close to the bed. The light from the window was perfect. The light in the north seemed clearer. Still, I wasn't sure I could get the angle of his cheekbones quite right. He had incredible cheekbones, as did his youngest niece, Audrey. Reuben woke up before I finished. "Hey," he said. "Nice shirt. What are you doing?"

"Nothing." I tried to hide the sketchbook and pencil behind my back.

"Were you sketching me?" He grinned.

"No," I lied.

He sat up. "It's like that scene from *Titanic* with your lover boy, Leo D. Wait. Isn't the chick supposed to be the naked one?"

"This *chick* can get naked," I said, hoping he'd forget about the sketch.

"Why didn't you tell me you were an artist?"

"I go to art school. I can't sing, dance, act, or play the piano."

"Let me see the sketch."

"No way." I stood up and headed for my bag. He beat me to it. "No, Reuben."

"Please. There's so much I still don't know about you."

"I'm not very good."

"Why do you always say that? No good at frosting cakes, no good at climbing, at math. Jesus Christ. No good at speaking French, at sketching. Tell me one thing you're good at." I shook my head. "Just one, Emmy, and I'll leave you alone."

I handed him my sketch pad. There were sketches in there he'd wish he hadn't seen, but I found myself wanting to share that part of me with him. He climbed back into bed with my pad. "Come on," he said. We both sat up, leaning against the headboard. "These are better than I expected. Seriously. Way better."

"Thanks, but—"

"No buts. I mean it. Are these buildings in Sacramento?" I told him yes. "And this bridge?" I nodded. "Is this your mom? Wow. Nice to meet you, Professor Kate." I laughed. "Whose male arms are these?" He knew whose they were. "Don't say his name." I had numerous sketches of Connor. Reuben flipped through the first set of them quickly. But there were more sets. He came to Connor's sketches of me. Connor had a different style from mine, looser, more freehanded. He also had the best perception at school. It was as if you could reach right into his sketches and paintings. "The dude didn't get your eyes right." Reuben flipped the page. "Fuck, I can't." He closed the book. "I want to know you better than he did."

"You do," I said. "You have from the very beginning."

"I hate that fag." He got out of bed and put on his jeans. He went to the window. "He fucking nailed your smile. Dead on. I hate him."

"He's far away. And he rarely made me smile."

Reuben turned. "You can't go back to him. Promise me."

"I'm *not* going back period." But he still looked upset. "My favorite animal is a sea otter," I said. "Connor didn't know that." Reuben came back to the bed. "I saw them in the aquarium in San Francisco. When I was little, I had a book about a baby sea otter named Otis." Reuben laughed. "He slept in a kelp bed. The book came with a matching stuffed animal. I told Otis all my secrets and talked to him when I was scared."

"What were you most scared of as a kid?"

"That's easy," I said. "My mom dying and leaving me all alone. Otis lost his mom, and he couldn't pry the abalone without her." He kissed me. "And you? What were you afraid of?"

"My dad dying."

His worse fear had come true. "I'm sorry. I can't imagine."

I went to hug him, but he stiffened and said, "I'm fine." He hated pity. I knew that. But even sympathy?

"Well, I can't imagine, never having a dad to begin with." He was trying to deflect. "Or having no relatives other than my mom—and then being afraid she'd die. That's fucked up."

"I'm fine. You're fine, I'm fine. I don't need you to feel sorry for me either."

"You feel sorry for me?" he asked with sudden attitude.

"You're a fucking hypocrite."

"What? How?"

"You want to know all about me. Yet there are parts of you that you'll never open to me."

I got out of bed.

"That's bull," he said. "You have no idea."

"Why? Because I'm white? A spoiled white girl from California?"

"I don't think you're spoiled. And you're from here. I mean you have no idea how open I've been with you. I feel almost—gutted."

What a thing to say. It made me incredibly sad. I felt the fight go out of me. I sat back down on the bed with my back toward him.

"I don't want to argue," he said, pulling me to him. "Let's be careful with our time together." He kissed my forehead.

His stomach growled for a second time. "You feel gutted because you're hungry."

"I've been hungrier. And you're the skinny one."

"I'm not skinny. I have a little belly pooch." Connor had pointed that out once.

"What the fuck? Where?" He lifted up his shirt that I was wearing. "Where?"

"Reuben, stop."

He laid his hand flat on my lower belly. Maybe I would carry his baby one day. Was that what he was thinking too? He said something to me in his native language. The words sounded like a prayer. He repeated them.

———

An hour later, when I dialed Jamie Kagen's number, a woman answered. "Hello," I said back to her. "I'm calling to speak to Mr. Jamie Kagen." I put my hand over the receiver and whispered to Reuben, "She wants to know who's calling."

"Tell her," Reuben said.

"This is Emmy Nolan, his daughter."

The woman didn't sound as shocked as I'd expected. Though certainly rattled. She asked me to hold on. Then she got back on the phone and asked if I'd please call back in half an hour. Jamie was in the field. She'd go get him right away.

"Do you think she'll disconnect the phone line?" I asked Reuben.

"Don't call back, Emmy."

"I have to." I was panicky now. I held Reuben's hand, and we waited.

A man answered when I called back. "Hello," he said. I couldn't reply. He sounded younger. What did I expect—a fifty-year-old? He was Matt's and Spencer's age. About thirty-five. His voice was deeper, though, than either of theirs. "Hello, Emmy?"

My dad just said my name.

"Hi," I said, so he wouldn't hang up.

"Is it you, Emmy?"

"Yes, it's me," I said. "Emmy Nolan." I took a deep breath. "My uncle Matt—Matthew Miller—gave me your card. I hope you don't mind."

Reuben shook his head. He'd already told me not to apologize for calling.

"How are you?" he asked.

Did he really care? "I'm in Washington. In Spokane."

"With your mom? Is Katie there?"

I had never heard anyone call my mom that before. It made my knees weak. So did his deep voice. He could've taken good care of us.

"No," I told him. "I'm here with my aunt and uncle. Aunt Beth's in the hospital."

"I'm so sorry to hear that." He sounded sincere.

"And my boyfriend," I added. "I'm here with my boyfriend, Reuben Tonasket."

Reuben grinned.

"Where is Katie?"

"In Europe," I was proud to reply. "With her boyfriend." I wished I could've said "husband" or at least "fiancé."

Jamie didn't respond right away. "We should meet, Emmy. You're close by."

"That's why I called. I'd like to meet you, if that's okay?"

Reuben shook his head again.

"Of course." He cleared his throat. "There's nothing in the world I want more." If he really meant that, why had he never searched for me? Maybe I'd ask him *why* in person, but not until *after* I asked for his help persuading Mom to let me stay in Washington. We made the arrangements for our meeting. Noon, tomorrow. I wrote down the directions to his farm on the small hotel tablet. "Until then," he said. "Give Matt and Beth my best."

"I will."

"Emmy?"

"Yes?"

"Please come."

I hung up the phone.

"His voice was so deep," I said to Reuben.

"All kids think their dad's voice is deep." He kissed me. "You're a brave girl. Don't ever think otherwise."

"His voice *was* deep."

Reuben and I walked to a restaurant to have dinner, but then we decided to get the food to go instead so we could eat with Uncle Matt in the hospital courtyard. I told Matt that I'd called Jamie and was meeting him tomorrow. He said he'd gotten through to the hotel in Paris, and a message was being sent to the cruise ship. After we ate, Uncle Matt took me upstairs to say good night to Aunt Beth. With him beside me, I actually touched her hand and told her I loved her. But I couldn't confess what I still needed to, not with Matt in the room. Not in the morning either because Matt's brother was at the hospital with his wife. That was my excuse anyway. After all, his family waited in the lobby, as did Reuben, while Matt took me upstairs. For Aunt Beth, time had completely stopped. Her body was in the exact same position as the night before. Her blankets had no wrinkles. She was suspended between life and death. As Uncle Matt walked me to the elevator, he said he had booked Reuben and me another night at the hotel. "If your mom calls here," he said, "I'm going to say you've been staying with my family. I'll tell her the truth later. Let me worry about that." As if he hadn't had enough to worry about. "Tell Reuben to drive safe. The Palouse is hilly."

He wasn't kidding. Rolling wheat fields, mile after mile, on both sides of Reuben's truck, behind, in front. I'd never seen anything like it. It was the most peaceful place. California was beautiful: the valley, the Sierras, San Francisco, farther up and down the coast. I also admired what I'd seen of the Cascades with Aunt Beth. And the starkness of the scablands and Reuben's reservation was haunting. But this was different. This place felt familiar. These hills and the wheat swaying in the wind and the clouds casting shadows, I'd dreamed. No, this wasn't dream territory. It was memory. I'd physically been here before. I felt it in my bones. The continuous contours of the land and the endless wheat comforted me. Red barns appeared every once in a while, and I sighed each time.

"You okay over there?" Reuben asked. I was on the edge of my seat.

"I've been here before."

"When?"

"I don't know." He smiled. "Will you pull over a second?" He did. I got out of his truck and walked right into a wheat field. Rueben got out of his truck also, but he wouldn't follow me, not even when I yelled for him to come on. I was in the land of my father. How many generations back? I didn't know. The land pulled on the bones of my feet. I kept my hands in the dry, rustling wheat and just breathed. A warm, earthy scent rose from the soil. But the breeze smelled of morning: bread toasting and a newly opened box of cereal.

Returning to Reuben, I said, "I love it here." He was smoking a cig-arette, leaning against his truck. He kept his eye on the road. "You're watchful."

"I'm Indian. No farmer wants me on the edge of his field."

"I'm sorry." I felt stupid, though still euphoric.

"For what?" He pushed up the sleeves on his thermal shirt. It was getting warm outside.

"I don't know." But I did know. "I'm sorry for what white people did to your people, for the dam. I'm sorry for the way they still treat you now, for—"

"Holy shit." He put his hand up. "Enough."

We got back in his truck. He took off his thermal. He had on a T-shirt underneath.

We drove awhile in silence.

"What mountains are those?" I pointed to the east.

"The Rockies. That's Idaho over there." More silence. "This area suits you, Emmy."

"You're making fun."

"I wouldn't. And I'm talking about the land, not the crops."

I loved both.

"Washington State University is only fifteen minutes from here," he said. "I've been on school field trips."

"Are you applying there in the fall?"

"I am." He shifted in his seat. "I was." We avoided the subject of college. "I am."

Maybe I could apply there too. But Mom didn't have a dime to send me to college. She had fifteen more years to pay on her own school loans. She was counting on my receiving state grants, doing work-study, and writing essays for private scholarships. Mom swore that not only did California give more student aid to kids than any other state, but tuition rates in California were some of the lowest in the nation. At WSU, I'd have to pay out-of-state tuition.

"Here we are," Reuben said. "Colfax."

The town was set among steep hills with scattered pine trees on them. Old brick buildings lined the main street. It was a small town, but far more charming than the ones we'd passed through yesterday on our way to Spokane. My dad had walked these sidewalks his whole life. Mom too had been here. Maybe they'd eaten together at that café.

Jamie's farm was south of town on Shawnee Road. We followed the directions I'd written on the hotel tablet. Suddenly I could see the roof of his two-story farmhouse, nestled in more gently sloping hills than the town. He had a red barn (gasp this time, not a sigh) and shop buildings and large farm equipment and a tractor like the one that had supposedly killed him. The horses in his pasture were almost as pretty as the horses on the reservation, but not quite. The place was like something out of a magazine: the hills of wheat, a long gravel driveway, shade trees on the lawn, pots of flowers on the porch. "Don't pull in yet," I said. "Let's park along the road for a moment."

We sat in silence, just looking down at the place. Before long, a boy about eleven years old drove past the truck on a four-wheeler and turned into the driveway. He stopped and looked back at us. He had the same color hair as I did. My stomach fell. "What if that's my brother?" I asked Reuben. Before he could respond, another four-wheeler whizzed past with a younger blond-haired boy driving. He took the corner too sharply, and the four-wheeler went up on two wheels. I grabbed the door handle to jump out if he fell, but the boy was fine. He laughed. He stared back at us. Shit. He looked like me. He must've realized it too because he kept staring. Finally he waved. Then they both sped up the driveway. "Why didn't Jamie tell me on the phone that I have two brothers?"

"You don't know for sure."

"But I do."

All those years alone in Sacramento, and I had two little brothers.

Nauseated and hot, I climbed out of the truck. The wheat on the hills around my dad's house started swaying too fast, and suddenly it was too much. I doubled over and threw up. My throat burned. I couldn't tear apart this family. I was my dad's secret, his sin. Mom was the madwoman in the attic of his past. What would Mom say—

how would she tear at herself—if she knew that Jamie had gone right on living without her? He didn't skip a beat. I hated him for that, or I wanted to. Mom had never recovered. Her teeth hurt. She wouldn't let Spencer get close to her. I wished my hair were the color of Mom's hair to remind my dad, to reprimand him. Instead my hair was the color of the wheat fields that surrounded his house. I threw up again.

Reuben was beside me with a water bottle. "You don't have to do this," he said, rubbing my back. "You're making yourself sick. We'll find a different way."

There was no other way. I needed Jamie's help if I wanted to stay.

Obviously my dad was ready to face his sin and make amends. He'd already told his wife—that was clear in the way she hadn't screamed or been rendered speechless on the phone when I said I was Jamie's daughter—but what about his sons? Would they forgive him? If I were to interrupt their lives, they might not forgive *me*.

"Oh, shit," Reuben said. "Here he comes."

I looked up the driveway. A man was walking from the house. My dad. *My dad.* Yes, he had the stride of a man for whom life had worked out. I couldn't let him see me all sweaty and with barf in my hair. Why was he coming out here? Couldn't he wait? I almost threw up a third time, but there was no food left.

"Get in the truck," Reuben said. "This is fucking bullshit." He started the engine. My dad walked faster. "Emmy, do you still want to do this? If you do, I'll pull into the driveway. I'll hold your hand the whole time."

I shook my head. I didn't need Jamie. I never had. And I'd make damn sure I never did. I could fight my own battles. Reuben drove me away. I didn't need a dad to love me when I had Uncle Matt and Spencer.

Then why did I look back?

I shouldn't have looked back. My dad ran to the end of his driveway. Then the cocky boy from camp, who had chosen this land—this wondrous land—over my mom and me, went down on his knees. I forgave the man instantly for all the loneliness and longing he'd caused me, but not for what he'd done to Mom. That would have to come later, if ever. I didn't ask Reuben to turn his truck around. I curled up on the seat, rested my head on Reuben's leg like a pillow, and kept my eyes closed tight until we were out of the Palouse, away from my father's hills—and the land my brothers called home.

13

Jamie

I saw her, Katie, our daughter.

I've been told over the years by uncles, brothers-in-law, and neighbors that a daughter can bring a man to his knees. Now I know this is true. My sons have kept me awake at night with their fevers, fears, even broken bones. But they are sturdy again come morning. Our daughter—*my* daughter threw up at the edge of my driveway, so nervous was she to meet me, her own dad. My child. My baby girl I never held. That I never once assured things would be okay. I can't stop thinking about her. About the three of us. All I should've done but didn't. What type of man does what I did? Not a respectable sort. That's for sure. What type of man tucks his stout boys into their beds, night after night, making sure their bellies are full and their worries calmed, while his baby girl may be hungry somewhere, anywhere?

I thought I heard an echo of your courage, Katie, in our daughter's voice. Your courage used to astound me. I was cocky and sure. But I faltered in the face of the first challenge that presented itself to me. That says a lot about a man. A boy. I pray my sons grow up to be better men. I thought when Emmy called, how brave she must be. I understand now she's not as brave as all that. She's fragile, and I made her that way. Emmy is as fragile as this land, which I am trying to be a good steward of. I try harder than my father ever has anyway. He might be a better businessman than I am, but I try harder.

An Indian boy brought Emmy here in his truck. At first I thought that meant our daughter was troubled, to be hanging with an Indian. But I don't think so. After all, he, not I, was rubbing her back as she threw up. And I've promised myself not to do to my kids what my parents did to me, no matter. Let them love whom they love. That is one of the greatest gifts a parent can give to a child.

And speaking of gifts, I realize now that you didn't hold back any part of yourself, Katie. You gave it all to me: your mind, body, heart, soul, spirit. And what spirit you had. I was too young and stupid to see how rare it is for one person to give herself so completely to another.

I pressured you a bit the first time we had sex to meet me at a motel and make it "official" between us. Up until then we'd been meeting every Saturday, or every other, mostly by the Snake River. We'd spend three or four hours together at a park or, once it started getting cold, in the cab of my truck: talking, touching, and listening to songs on the radio. One afternoon together could sustain you for weeks, you said, because you'd relive every moment, every touch, word, and song. You had so little, then, that it was enough for you. But I needed more. You were naturally nervous when we met at the Appaloosa Inn. You'd never been in a motel room. You looked in all the drawers, peeked in the shower, held the little soaps, rearranged the chairs—as if it were a fancy hotel in Spokane or a quaint B and B instead of a cheap motel paid for with a farm boy's allowance. You made us coffee and turned on the fuzzy TV. I was dumbfounded again that your family didn't own one. You had no idea who Farah Fawcett was. Nor had you seen a single image of the hostages in Iran or heard the newly elected Reagan speak. My body had been aching to be inside yours for months. When the ache became palpable in the motel room, you stood, shut off the TV, and started to unbutton your dress. I held my breath. One bare shoulder, another, and then the dress slipped off you. To this day I've still never seen anything more provocative. You reached behind and unhooked your bra and then took off your underwear. I was speechless, and I couldn't move from the chair. I couldn't even reach for you when you stepped directly in front of me—as if I were the inexperienced one. You took my hands and placed them on your body. "I'm yours, Jamie." For a moment I just rested my forehead on your beautiful belly, the soft weight and lure of your breasts hovering above me.

"Do whatever you want with me," you said. "But be gentle."

Your offer scared and deeply aroused me. I cupped your ass. When you bent forward to kiss me, your hair enshrouded us both.

You didn't cry afterward, like other church girls. You didn't feel dirty or the least guilty. I made sure as I held you between the sheets. You seemed more alive than ever. Full of joy. Your body lit somehow from within.

"My faith is in you, Jamie," you said with enough conviction that I should've felt invincible. After we slept awhile, you again offered yourself to me. I'd brought only one condom. I thought I could pull out in time, but our bodies had such cadence.

Only after putting your dress back on did you become sad. I shouldn't have let you leave. And you almost couldn't because your piece-of-crap car wouldn't start. I had to clean the points and retime the ignition. I should've pretended I couldn't fix the problem. I should've stranded us there together until I got the guts to ask you to marry me.

I've put up one hell of a front all these years. I finished high school after caving to my dad and turning my back on you. I drank a lot. My freshman year of college is a blur of alcohol and girls whose names I didn't need to know. My only moments of clarity were when I allowed myself to think of you as I walked the Pullman campus in the chilly and then frigid early-morning hours. I was an eighteen-year-old college student with a baby I didn't acknowledge. I heard you were working at the truck stop café at the intersection of I-90 and state highway 17. My cousin claimed to have seen you climbing out of a trucker's cab. He recognized your hair. But I told him he was mistaken. I told myself you'd find some other way—*any* other way—to survive.

I drank so heavily my third semester that my dad threatened to quit paying my tuition. He strongly suggested the army to help get my head out of my ass. And what, back up his? When I got into one too many scrapes, the university suspended me for a semester. I returned to the farm. When I got back to college, I threw myself into my agricultural classes. My study emphasis was soil erosion, which I thought was the reason my dad had sent me to school. But he didn't want to hear how the land he farmed, and supposedly loved, was formed. He especially didn't want to know how agriculture has altered it—no more than he wanted to know how I was changed by what I'd done to you, Katie. My dad didn't find it fascinating that the Palouse hills contain little or no bedrock. The light, fertile soil goes all the way down to the hard lava surface. The soil is so rich, I learned, because of enormous floods from Montana that ripped through eastern Washington. The floods actually missed the Palouse region, leaving it far less scathed than the scablands surrounding it. But years of westerly winds blew rich flood sediment back eastward, along with volcanic ash from the Cascades, to form dunes. Upon these dunes, wheat grows at a higher yield per acre than anywhere else in the United States: the only fact of interest to my dad.

He certainly didn't want to know that the lightness of the soil is what makes it so susceptible to continued erosion. Some movement is natural, but intensive agriculture in the Palouse is washing away the land and clogging the rivers. Annually the Palouse loses an average of fourteen tons of topsoil per acre. Storms can double the loss. My old man already knew these statistics, he claimed, but he didn't find them staggering.

Did it ever stagger him that he had a grandchild out there somewhere who might be hungry or lonely? Did all the blood ever rush to his head at the thought? Walking proudly through his fields, did he ever have to stop short for a moment as I did occasionally on campus? The time I saw a young dad carrying textbooks in his arms and a baby in a pack on his back, I followed him clear to the Children's Center. I thought my head was going to explode. Then I went and got drunk. It was the last time I ever did.

I should've known my dad wouldn't implement any of the conservation methods I was learning in my ag classes and in fieldwork at WSU research stations. My whole childhood, he and neighboring farmers were pissed off at the USDA for trying to tell them how to farm. "I'd like to tell Uncle Sam what I tell my boy," I heard my dad say more than once when I was young. "Keep your doggone hand in your own pants."

I finally realized my dad had sent me to college to learn chemicals and ag business in order to keep his yields high *despite* the erosion.

I had one "radical" professor at WSU who claimed land-grant universities, farmers, chemical and farm machinery manufacturers all had lobbyists working triple time to stymie even the mildest conservation legislation. According to this professor, the USDA had yet to grow a full set of balls. Government agents let farmers bitch slap them into turning regulations into recommendations and thus never actually withholding subsidies as punishment for lack of land stewardship. This professor wasn't against farming. He thought it was the central relationship in any settled society. But he also wanted his students to realize agriculture hadn't been around that long in "big history" and might even be transient. I had to rein in my fascination, which could've propelled me into graduate school and away from the farm and who I am at the core: I am a farmer, as I made painfully obvious to you, Katie.

I was in college to learn how to save the Palouse. But I was also trying to save myself.

I met my wife at the end of my junior year. She was a business major at the University of Idaho, only eight miles from WSU. She comes from a large potato farming family on the Snake River Plain in lower Idaho. Her extended family owns two tractor dealerships, and she'd hoped to manage one after college, before I proposed. Her dad had never wanted his only daughter's help on the farm. My parents more than approved of our engagement, as did hers. Everything fell into place. We got married as soon as I was graduated. She never finished her program at UI. With financial investments from her parents and mine, we acquired our own wheat farm, a foreclosure from earlier in the decade, almost adjacent to my father's. But *not* my father's. Before long our son was born. Then we acquired more acreage as the overseas markets began to recover, another combine as the markets steadied, more debt to my father and the bank, another healthy son, another harvest, then a bumper year and another. Something was missing, but I tried never to let it show in my step. I thought I could redeem myself by being the best husband and dad. By working the land as faithfully as my father, grandfather, his father, but with smart soil-conserving methods. From the beginning, I've let USDA field agents and WSU researchers and extension workers give me all the help and advice they can to save this place for my boys. I don't care if it means I have to labor longer hours turning over stubborn stubble, instead of burning it, or growing peas and beans so as not to leave any of my acres fallow and more susceptible to erosion. I don't care if my dad thinks I'm nuts, a tree hugger, a Communist, an overeducated plowboy, a traitor for advocating conservation to local legislators, an embarrassment for always talking stewardship to fellow farmers at county ag meetings and picnic days.

For the first five years of my marriage, questions about Emmy consumed my thoughts on large family holidays, especially if both families were gathered: my parents, in-laws, cousins, uncles, nieces. I'd have to leave. "Let him go," my mom would say. She knew. My dad knew too, but I'll be damned if he still didn't shake his head. I had long ago quit blaming him for my lack of character when it came to you. And as far as what I did with my portion of the Palouse—I told my dad, as well as my father-in-law, when they helped me secure my first acreage, that it was either my land to manage how I learned to in college or I was walking away from it all.

If only I'd had half the courage when it came to you, Katie.

At first my wife thought I split during holidays because I was rebellious and restless. She claimed to like a man with an edge. Probably because her brothers are bores and have their potato heads so far up their old man's ass. She also didn't harp that I never attended church with her and our boys. What right did I have to sit in a church?

Then, Katie, I ran into your brother-in-law, Matt, in a café right here in Colfax, the café where we ate together right before you found out you were pregnant. We sat close on the same side of the booth. You seemed so open at camp and in that motel room, so eager for life and hungry for knowledge about anything: farming, places I'd visited with my family, subjects I took at school, news stories. But in that café, when kids from my high school came in, you shrank behind my shoulder. It still breaks my heart. You were embarrassed by your old-fashioned dress. I was too. What was wrong with me? Especially after I'd seen what was underneath it. I followed Matt out to his truck that day. He told me you'd left the state with our baby before she was a year old and hadn't been heard from since. You hadn't even been in touch with your little sister, whom you loved and protected so fiercely that I used to be jealous. I am to blame for separating you from your sister. You wanted to give me everything, Katie, and goddamn if I didn't take it from you, despite turning my back, and without realizing. It's mind-boggling what a boy can take from a young girl.

The photo Matt gave me of little Emmy unhinged me. I am so ashamed to admit that I hadn't heard our daughter's name, had purposely *not* found it out, until that day. *Emmy.* You named her after Emmylou Harris, whom you heard sing for the first time in my truck, in my damn arms. I confessed to my wife. She was shocked. A little too much edge. And she'd desperately wanted a daughter, having had only brothers growing up. She gathered "her sons" and left the house, went back to her family's farm in southern Idaho. I didn't care. My apathy must have terrified her. She'd given up her dream of being a businesswoman to marry me. And she'd been a good wife. She'd loved me as much as possible. Not with all of herself, as you had, Katie, but she tried. Maybe she held back simply because she sensed a portion of me was already gone. The week she was away, I drove to Moses Lake and ate in the truck stop café where you had once worked. I drove past your dad's house. It looked more run-down than ever, and another family was living in it. I'd forgotten over the years how poor your family was. Maybe that's why your dad was such a mean son of a bitch. I'd promised you at camp, and afterward, that I'd get you away from him. That you wouldn't have to have his last name any longer. Now my daughter has it.

"Is it you, Emmy?" I asked when she called.

"Yes, it's me," she said. "Emmy Nolan."

Her name should've been "Emmy Kagen."

If I'd known my little girl wouldn't make it to my front door the next day, as she and I had arranged, I would've kept her on the phone longer. I would've asked her questions. I would've told her things.

"I'm pregnant," you told me over the phone. "I can leave here." In other words, "Come and get me." The snow kept us apart, but my truck could've made it. I knew that even then.

"Don't tell anyone just yet." That was my initial response, and it got worse from there. "How do I know it's even *my* baby?"

Katie, I'm sorry.

Our daughter showed up here in the quiet before harvest. My mechanic, two of my brothers-in-law, an uncle, a few WSU and UI students, my dad, his hired crew, and I had been working on the combines and equipment for weeks. My back was bracing for the long hours of labor ahead, the danger of plowing on steep hills with hulking machines. My adrenaline was pumping. The wheat in the fields was bountiful, the stalks heavy with grain. I'm glad Emmy saw my fields before they were plowed.

They are her fields too. My older boy will inherit my dad's place. Emmy has equal rights to my fields with her younger brother. I told myself this during harvest, told myself I was harvesting for her. My wife told me to put Emmy out of my mind until after harvest. She said for now I had my boys to consider. For the first time I lost control of a combine. I've been driving large farm equipment since I was twelve years old. I came out less scathed than the combine, but harvest was slowed on my land and my dad's. He just shook his head. As did my wife's brothers. From the beginning they've thought I was a cocky bastard, that all dryland farmers are because we don't have to constantly move irrigation pipe. And maybe I am cocky. I try not to be when I go to southern Idaho every year for two weeks to help my in-laws with their harvest. I've never felt more humbled than when Emmy drove away in that truck.

She told me you're in Europe. I hope you get to see the world, Katie. I hope the man you are with loves you. I hope he takes better care of you than I did.

I found you by a lake, stuffing rocks into your pockets, like a girl of seven, rather than seventeen. Over the years I have put many a rock in my pocket. My wife finds it endearing and then irritating when she finds them in her washing machine. She has no idea.

I was never afraid for you. I should've been. I'm afraid for our baby. Why was she so far from you? Does that boy love her? I keep watching the road for that truck to return.

If I could go back, I'd start by rubbing your back the time you threw up in front of me, sick from pregnancy, instead of looking away in disgust and in fear. That was the last time I ever saw you, Katie. I was terrified that day of far more than losing my birthright. I was afraid of your love. I was afraid of the life inside you, which was there even before I got you pregnant. My greatest fear now is never seeing our daughter again. "She'll come back when she's ready, James," my wife says. She's trying hard to be understanding, but she's terrified again and wants to try once more for a girl. She wants a daughter to quilt and can and ride her horses with. Our boys prefer to ride dirt bikes and quads, fish with my dad, shoot their rifles. I tell my wife no more children for me. I don't think Emmy is in Washington anymore. It's been months, and I feel her absence heavily in the plowed fields. I don't even want to replant them.

I start attending church with my wife and boys. She begs me to make peace with God. But this has nothing to do with the old man upstairs. It never did. Nor does it have anything to do with my old man down the road.

I stand now looking down at Palouse Falls. Remember I took you here, Katie, but for the wrong reasons? I wanted you to understand why I was about to choose the land over you. You looked so stunned, your hair and dress blowing in the wind. For the briefest moment I thought you'd jump. Many nights I've reached out my arm to stop you.

The Palouse River starts in the Rockies, flows across the Idaho state line into Washington, through my hometown and into the scablands, where it plunges hundreds of feet off the edge of a basalt canyon before it reaches the Snake River. The Snake carries my wheat to the

Columbia and then to the sea and to Asia. The falls are still muddy with rich topsoil. Soil from my land. Soil that has settled, after thirty-five years, into the crevasses of my skin. I'm sorry, Katie. Send Emmy back to me. I will make it up to her. I will make good. I will find a way to deserve our daughter.

I speak to the wind. The sound of my voice is muted by the roar of the falls.

14

Emmy

Uncle Matt insisted I leave Spokane the morning after I almost met my dad. I tried to argue. I pleaded. But I was a mess and only adding to his worry. I couldn't quit thinking about Jamie on his knees, my two brothers, the lack of wrinkles in Aunt Beth's hospital bed, and if I'd have to leave Reuben soon and for good. The doctor said that in addition to Aunt Beth's miscarriages, her heart had been weakened over the years by severe anemia, and she'd suffered other undiagnosed health issues since childhood. Uncle Matt said I could return to Spokane in a few days. He assured me Beth would hold out for Mom, with whom we still hadn't made contact. Saying good-bye to my aunt in that hospital room was one of the hardest things I've ever had to do. I made my confession and begged her to squeeze my hand if she could hear me, if she forgave me. I told her that I used to look for her during the night when I was younger. "I'll look for you always," I whispered into her ear.

Matt gave me permission to go back to the reservation with Reuben for one more day. Reuben drove me all around, crisscrossing the reservation. There was an urgency, as if he too were fearing it would be his only chance to show me his world. In a clearing in the pines, we saw elk. He showed me a particular mountain where clouds hovered—in response, Reuben told me, to whites' wanting to mine its minerals. For miles, we were the only people on the reservation roads. We unrolled the truck windows. I didn't ask him to slow down.

He showed me the various towns on the reservation, which were depressing and far apart. The poverty was severe. The east side of Omak seemed the worst, given that the west side (the white side) wasn't. Nearly every house in east Omak was run-down with broken vehicles parked haphazardly around it. The only businesses in east Omak, besides the closed-down rail yard and mill, were a few dilapidated firework stands and cigarette shops. Reuben told me about gangs and drugs on the rez, about high unemployment, suicide, diabetes, teen pregnancy. He said drugs used to come just from Canada by floatplanes landing on secluded lakes or cars sneaking across the international border. Now drugs also came from Mexico. In fact, Mexicans snuck onto the Colville to grow pot in the woods, big operations, and there weren't enough tribal cops to monitor. He told me he'd got his arm broken a few years back when he and Benji stumbled across some mean Mexican dealers in the woods. His arm still ached sometimes, he said, and during football he had to wrap it with rolls of athletic tape. Benji knew the dealers were there, no matter what he claimed. This alarmed me. I wanted to tell Reuben to be more careful, but he was one of the most careful people I knew. He drove me past all four longhouses, the tribal jail, a couple of shabby health clinics, and, I swear, forty different relatives' houses. He pulled over so I could read the graffiti on a wall in Nespelem: WHY CHOOSE A GANG? YOU ARE A TRIBAL NATION. WHY SPEAK STREET LANGUAGE? YOU HAVE A NATIVE TONGUE.

He took me to Chief Joseph Dam, where like at Grand Coulee, there were no fish ladders. He explained about hatchery fish versus native stock and how the hatchery stock was further destroying the native salmon runs by interbreeding. Prone to disease and pumped with chemicals, hatchery salmon left native fish unable to find their birth streams. But without hatcheries, no one, Indian or white, could fish.

Reuben wanted to save the best place for last. We went slightly off the reservation, north to a place called Kettle Falls, where Reuben's people used to fish for thousands of years before Grand Coulee Dam drowned the falls in backwater. Every Memorial Day, Reuben told me, there's a Ceremony of Tears. I'd already told him I'd seen the marker for Celilo Falls on the lower Columbia with my aunt. So much loss. We took another ferry across the Columbia. It looked more like a narrow lake than a river, and it was even called Lake Roosevelt. But the river was still in the lake, Reuben insisted. He pulled off the road, and we climbed through a few scattered pines and down an embankment to a sandy strip of beach. There he tried to teach me how to see the river in the lake, how to use the memory of those who had already crossed into the spirit world, but I couldn't. We walked up and down the beach, studying the currents, and I tried to see the ancient shorelines far below the surface as Reuben could. Finally he held my hand in the water—the first time I'd touched the Columbia. He told me to close my eyes so I could feel the river's pulse. It was faint under all that backwater, but it was definitely there. It was the most spiritual experience I'd ever had.

Once we were back in his truck, Reuben didn't start the ignition. He just sat there. He didn't talk. He didn't look at the river or at me. He was waiting to be sure I'd absorbed all he'd shown me that day so deeply inside that it could never seep out.

We returned to Omak for dinner. Reuben said Dairy Queen was the local hangout, but hardly anyone was there. There weren't a lot of people anywhere in eastern Washington. I was glad the restaurant wasn't busy. We sat on the same side of a window booth. I let myself feel happy, despite everything. Reuben fed me fries dipped in tartar sauce (a northern thing). An SUV pulled into the parking lot. "Shit," Reuben said. "Here comes trouble." I thought maybe Benji, except Reuben was smiling. Three white boys hopped out of the SUV. They ran over to Reuben's truck. One boy jumped in the bed and howled out Reuben's last name like a wolf.

"TO-NA-SKET!"

"Do you know those guys?" I asked.

"I'm on the football team with them." I hid behind his shoulder as they approached the restaurant doors. "Don't be scared, Emmy."

"I'm not." But I was. Jocks intimidated me. I never really thought of Reuben as a jock, although I knew he played football and liked to shoot hoops or do pull-ups on the monkey bars at the park.

"Rube," the biggest boy yelled after strutting in the door. "How's it hanging?"

They all three came over to our booth. They had a lot of energy and a lot of muscle among them.

"What the fuck, Tonasket?" asked the boy in the Seattle Seahawks T-shirt. "*Where* do you always disappear to in the summer?" Before Reuben could reply, the boy said, "And *who* is this?"

"This is Emmy," Reuben said. He'd taken my hand under the table, and now he squeezed it. "Emmy, this is Kimble, Anderson, and C.J."

"Dude, you get the lookers," the same boy said, sitting down across from us in the booth. "Last summer it was Danielle Lawton. *Dude.*"

"Rube and Rodeo Queen Danielle."

Benji had brought up a rodeo queen also. I'd thought he was joking. Why would Reuben date a cowgirl? I let go of his hand. I'd rather date a boy with a pierced tongue, any day of the week, than a cowboy.

"So, where you from?" the third boy, C.J., asked me. He and the biggest boy remained standing. "I haven't seen you around."

"And we'd remember."

I couldn't respond. My face was burning.

"I met Emmy in Moses Lake," Reuben said.

"No fucking way," the big boy said. "Moses Hole. Home of the Chiefs."

"Dude, if I'd known girls were looking that fine in Moses Lake—"

"Shut the fuck up," Reuben said. But he kept it cool. "What are you d-bags up to?"

"Looking for Danielle." They laughed. "Or your cousin Yvonne."

"Keep away from her, Anderson, you asshole," Reuben said to the boy in the Seahawks T-shirt. "Her dad will scalp you."

"He'd have to sober up and get off his couch first."

They all three laughed, but not Reuben.

"Practice starts in two weeks," C.J. reminded Reuben. "You keeping yourself in shape?"

"Always."

Suddenly they all started flexing. Even Reuben. Maybe I *wouldn't* do so well in public school.

"Does she speak?" Anderson asked, pretending to do sign language.

I felt Reuben's body tense.

"Look at her," the big guy said. "Does it matter?"

"Back the fuck off," Reuben said. "Seriously."

I had to say something. I was being a freak. What was wrong with me?

"Hello," I managed.

"What grade are you in?" the calmest boy, C.J., asked me. "I know a guy who goes to high school in Moses Lake."

"I bet you *know* a guy," the big boy said. "The way your eyes wander in the locker room."

"Fuck you, Kimble. You fat ass."

"You wish. Keep your eyes on your own shit."

Even Reuben laughed at that.

"What grade?"

"Actually," Reuben said, answering for me, "Emmy goes—went to high school in California."

"Fucking A," Kimble said. "A California girl." He tried to high-five Reuben, who ignored him, so he high-fived Anderson instead. "I *knew* she wasn't from here."

"How long are you staying?" C.J. asked me.

I shrugged my shoulders.

"Reuben treating you okay?" he asked.

I smiled and nodded.

"I bet he's treating you *real* nice," the big boy said, thrusting his groin repulsively. "*Real* nice and—"

C.J. shoved him. "Will you shut the fuck up?" he said.

"He doesn't know how to shut his mouth," Reuben said. "That's why he's so fat. Maybe I should shut it for him."

"Go tribal on his white ass, Tonasket," Anderson said, grabbing Rueben's pop and finishing it in one gulp. When he reached for mine next, Reuben stopped him.

"Where do you live in California?" C.J. asked me. When I didn't respond, Reuben nudged me under the table. "Do you know any movie stars?" Another nudge. I definitely liked C.J. the best, and if it had been just he and Reuben, I would've been able to hold a conversation. Giving up on me and addressing Reuben, C.J. said, "Hey, man, she all right?"

I almost spilled my drink trying to get out of the booth. I stayed in the ladies' restroom a long time, though it didn't smell so good. I was humiliated, and I'd definitely embarrassed Reuben in front of his friends *again*.

When I came back out, Reuben and his friends were gone and our table was cleared off. I looked through the windows. He was out in the parking lot with the boys, who were showing off football moves. Reuben fitted in with those jocks. Or he was trying to. No, they liked him. The boys got back into their SUV and left, hanging out the windows and shouting back at Reuben. He walked over to his truck and leaned his elbows on the side, and for a brief moment he put his head in his hands.

I moved closer to the window. When he looked up, he waved for me to come on.

I started to cry as soon as I got into his truck. I hadn't cried in the stinky restroom. For the first time all summer, I wanted my mom more than anyone else. My shyness and awkwardness irritated Mom—her dream daughter, I knew, would be a go-getter—but she could also be incredibly understanding. She was always assuring me I'd outgrow my bashfulness. Aunt Beth was oblivious to it. I wanted to sit between them on the couch. No males around. I wanted to smell Mom's musky perfume mixed with Aunt Beth's lavender lotion.

"I'm sorry," I said. "You see why I don't have friends in Sacramento?"

He looked at me. "Jesus, Emmy, just be yourself. It's not that hard."

"Is that what you were doing? Just being yourself out here in the parking lot practicing football moves with white boys? Dating a cowgirl?"

"Would you rather have me join a gang on the rez?" He was pissed.

I shook my head. "I'm sorry."

"Quit fucking apologizing. You're too polite and too damn scared." He grabbed one of my hands, but not to hold it. He looked at the nail polish I'd peeled and scraped partway off in the restroom. "Fuck, Emmy." He let go. "How are you ever going to make it?"

Hadn't he just called me brave the day before yesterday for calling my dad?

"I'm going for a walk." I grabbed the door handle. I'd seen a park. "Don't follow me."

"No problem."

I got out of his truck and slammed the door, but not very impressively. The sun was starting to set. I made it to the edge of the parking lot before hearing the driver's door open. I wasn't athletic like Reuben, but Mom and I were brisk city walkers. I hurried my pace. He grabbed my arm.

"Slow down, girl," he said. "You break my heart."

I tried to lighten things up. "Breaking hearts in Omak."

He smiled apologetically. "With a killer smile and not a bad rack."

"Not a rodeo queen," I said, "just a fucked-up teen."

"Not an Indian guide, but I'll stay by your side."

He took me into his arms.

"I wish I made you happy, Reuben."

"You do. Those boneheads don't mean anything to me." But I also made him sad. I wasn't making his life any easier. He had enough to deal with. I certainly saw that today on the reservation. His obstacle course included drug dealers, extreme poverty, high school jocks, and the mammoth Coulee Dam.

"Let's go to the movies," I said, smiling wide for him. "We can pretend everything is okay and we're just bored kids in a small town."

When we returned to Moses Lake the next day, Aunt Beth's garden was partly dried up. Teresa had watered it once, and Uncle Matt's sister had swung by. But the potted plants hadn't been rotated. Also, someone had shut off the night-light in my bedroom. I freaked out when I saw the ceramic hands not glowing as they had been since I first arrived in Washington. "Why would Matt's family do that?" I asked Reuben. "Don't they love Beth?"

He turned the night-light back on. "I'm sure they do."

"Do *you* love Beth?"

He looked tired. "I barely knew—know her."

"Lena barely knows me, and she told me three times that she loves me."

He grinned.

After lunch, Reuben drove me to the library to look through herb gardening books. I wanted to save Aunt Beth's garden. Mom was on her way from Europe. I still hadn't talked to her. Uncle Matt said Spencer was bringing her. They'd be here the day after tomorrow, which was as soon as they could get connecting flights. Once I was seated at a library table with gardening books, Reuben walked off to check out the enlarged photo of Chief Moses hanging on the wall. I saw one of the librarians hurry over to him. He'd told me just yesterday that most people liked Indians in theory—in libraries, in history books—but not in practice. Mom said the same thing about educated people and communism: they liked it in theory but couldn't fathom it in practice. I'd grown up watching the triumphant collapse of communism on the news, but it seemed to go hand in hand with cities being gutted in Eastern Europe and kids dodging snipers— completely confusing to me. Parts of Reuben's reservation looked as poor as Sarajevo.

He came back with a book. Sitting down, he whispered, "Librarian Deb recommended I check this out." He handed it to me. It was a book of Northwest Indian tales, but it had a picture of Raven, not Coyote, on the front. "Recently compiled," he said. "White people, I swear."

"You don't mean me, of course."

"Of course I mean you," he joked.

"What do you want to study in college?" I was tired of avoiding the subject.

"Fish biology. I want to help bring salmon back to the rivers on the rez."

"That's awesome. Seriously, Reuben. And I believe in you with all my heart." I had to get that out in case we went mum again on the subject of college.

He looked away for a moment. I probably embarrassed him. "What about you?" He turned back. "What do you want to study?"

"I just want to be a teacher."

"Why do you say *just*?"

"Mom's already talking PhD. She thinks I should be a college professor. But I mean teach little kids."

"I like that." He smiled. "Miss Emmy."

I told him he should go see if the library had any books on fish or ecology. "We can study, like we're in college."

"You're kind of a nerd." He stood up. "It's kind of a turn-on."

While he was gone, I came across a warning list of herbs that shouldn't be used during pregnancy, especially not brewed as teas, which "concentrated the chemicals." Many herbs used by nonpregnant women to regulate periods actually stimulated the uterus and caused miscarriage. What the fuck? Even rosemary, not as a spice, but as a tea. Blue cohosh could induce labor. Black cohosh ripened the cervix. The list went on. I returned to the gardening section and found a book on medicinal herbs. Same warnings. I had to sit down on the step stool. *Oh, Aunt Beth. Even the chamomile we drank together before bed.* She didn't know. She was hurting herself, and she didn't know.

Fuck the church. Fuck God. Mom was right: this place sucked. If Aunt Beth could've just come here and checked out even one book. How could a library be off-limits? That seemed like communism. Knowledge? The Tree of Knowledge? Beth was naive and trusting. And ignorant. Not stupid. My English teacher mom had explained the difference to me many times. How could a doctor be off-limits? How could a book be evil that warned you not to stimulate your uterus if you wanted a baby more than anything in the world?

I stood up, too pissed off for tears. I wanted to call the hospital right away and tell Uncle Matt. I found Reuben back at our table with ecology books. My hands shook with anger.

"Jesus, Emmy, what is it?" he whispered.

"Beth's been misusing herbs." I sat down beside him. The next sentence was almost too painful to say out loud. "She's been causing or, at least, abetting her own miscarriages." I explained in more detail, showing him the warnings in the books.

"Jesus. I'm sorry, Emmy." His eyes looked watery. Not mine.

"Let's go." I shoved the books away from us. "I need to call Matt at the hospital."

During the drive back to the trailer park, I sat stewing. "People here—white people—are so ignorant. Not in California."

"That's not really fair," he said.

I knew it wasn't. I was just so pissed. "Why do you defend them?"

"I don't. I think there's ignorance everywhere."

"Yeah, but it abounds here."

"It abounds in that church." He was right. "Do you hate it here? Not enough intellectual stimulation?"

"It's been the most stimulating summer of my life."

We pulled into Quail Run Mobile Home Park. We both stared at Aunt Beth's garden.

"Hey," he said, then hesitated. "Don't tell Matt about the herbs, not yet."

"What? I *have* to."

"If—when Beth recovers, then you can tell Matt so he can make sure his wife doesn't take the wrong herbs again. For now, though, don't say anything."

"Why?"

"I'm sure your uncle is already feeling a lot of guilt. At the healing, he—"

"What do you mean *at the healing*? Were you there?"

"It doesn't matter."

"It certainly does." I got goose bumps. "Were you there?"

"I saw that preacher put his hands on your aunt. Matt wanted to kick his ass."

I couldn't believe Reuben had been at the park that day. He'd been so watchful of me all summer. "Fine," I said. "You're right. I'll wait to tell Matt."

We sat quietly for a few minutes in his truck. Then I moved close to him, needing to feel the weight of his body beside me. How could he have been at the healing without my noticing? It reminded me again how just three months ago I could've passed right by him on the street and possibly felt no connection. I scooted even closer. Still not enough. I needed to feel him *in* me. Teresa was gone. I reached up my skirt and carefully took off my underwear. He didn't protest, even though a neighbor was out a few trailers down. Then I took his hand and slid it slowly up my skirt as I parted my legs just enough. "Hold your hand still," I told him. "I'll move."

We migrated inside—to the couch, where Reuben tasted me, the bedroom, where he undressed me and I took him into my mouth, to the couch again, where he tried to just hold me until I reminded him that I'd left my underwear in his truck. He took me back to bed one more time before Teresa and the kids got home. We were young. Our bodies told us we were, no matter how heavy our thoughts.

Aunt Beth died the next day while I was outside working in her garden. The heat was oppressive. For the first time since I'd been in eastern Washington, no breeze lifted my bangs. Teresa's chimes were silent. I'd already pulled up a few dried plants and trimmed back the leaves and stems on others. I'd left the door and windows open (and the air conditioning off) so I could hear the phone. Reuben was at the med clinic with Kevin. The other kids were at some babysitter's house. Uncle Matt sounded so far away that I knew he wasn't just calling to give an update. "She fought hard, sweetie," he said. "But she passed peacefully."

How had she fought hard? Just lying there? And fuck Matt for making me leave Spokane. *Fuck you, Mom, for not making it on time.* Mom's voice and touch might have snapped Aunt Beth out of her coma, at least briefly. If I'd had a sister, I would've never left her.

I went into my bedroom and shut off the night-light. I cut the threads holding up the origami birds. They fell without a sound or a flutter into the crib, just as Aunt Beth had slid silently into death in that hospital room. I went back outside. I felt totally removed from myself. I watched my hands prune. I accidentally pulled up a plant. The roots came right out. I pulled up another and another. I tugged. I got the spade and dug. I'd dug up more than half of Aunt Beth's garden before I realized what I'd done. Ashamed and drenched with sweat, I saw myself lie flat down on my belly in the grass, in a patch of shade. I wouldn't get up for Reuben when he returned, no matter how tender, frustrated, mad he got. Finally he went inside and called Teresa, though I didn't know until I heard her clunky van pull into the driveway.

"Take Kevin and leave," Teresa said to Reuben. "I called Roxanne to bring Nelly." Reuben tried to protest, but she held firm. "No men."

"Let me help you get her into the house, at least."

"Leave her alone, brother. She's in shock." He asked her if the ritual would work on white people. "It's not going to work," Teresa said, "if *you* keep staying here."

Teresa waited until Reuben's truck pulled away. Then she said something to me in the same language Reuben had spoken to me. I saw her help me off the grass. We went inside her trailer, where it was cool. Another Indian woman, about Teresa's age, showed up and that old, old lady who'd been at Teresa's before. She was older than Reuben's great-aunt Shirley. They didn't speak English as they washed me, then performed the ritual or the prayer or whatever it was. I smelled herbs, and there was smoke. They slowly circled me until I had memories of things I didn't remember: my grandmother in a lake, my mother standing by a muddy waterfall, Aunt Beth holding me as a baby. Suddenly I was with Beth by the Columbia. The wind was fierce, but I could hear her voice because it was inside me. I don't remember what she said.

I woke up in Teresa's bed. The house was still. It was half past eight in the evening. I needed to find Reuben so he could tell Teresa to come home with her kids. I couldn't take over their house and lives. Teresa had now done two unforgettable things for me, though I still didn't think she liked me. She'd really done them for Reuben. I opened the front door. He was right there. He'd probably been waiting on the porch since Teresa and those other women left. Of course he had. *Reuben.* I looked at him through the ripped screen. It was almost dark. The wind had returned. Aunt Beth was gone from this earth. Mom would be here tomorrow. I went to him. His chest heaved, as Matt's had in the hospital, only more than once as I sobbed against him.

We walked around to the back steps to sit. The wind was warm, like on the evening of the healing. Reuben said Teresa and the kids had left for the night. He kept rubbing my back, touching my face. I assured him I was doing better.

"I feel your mom getting close," he said.

"She can't make me leave."

"She can, Emmy, especially now."

"You don't let your mom boss you around."

"I do more during the school year."

I lit a cigarette, or tried to in the wind. "If she called you right now and told you to come home tonight, would you?"

"Yes, if she really needed me." He lit the cigarette for me. "Or if Lena did. Sure."

"If she said you *had* to live in the apartment with her and Harold, would you?"

"Fuck, no," Reuben said. "But I have lots of relatives I could live with. You don't."

"I have Uncle Matt. I can live with him. He'd let me. I can replant Aunt Beth's garden. You can move in with Teresa. We can go to high school together." I smiled, hugging his arm. "Every morning in your truck."

"I'd love nothing more." But when I looked up at his face, he wasn't smiling. "Matt may not want to stick around," Reuben said. "He may take off. I sure as hell would."

"He'd stay for me."

"He would." Reuben squeezed my knee. "And so would I."

"Mom can't make me leave," I insisted, though legally I knew she probably could, especially without my dad to intercede. Then it came to me. Why hadn't I thought of it before? Probably because it was kind of preposterous. More preposterous, even, than asking Jamie for help. But I was desperate. "Come inside." I took Reuben into Teresa's bedroom.

"I'm not in the mood," he said as politely as possible.

"Lie beside me, is all." I hesitated, trying to muster the courage and to not sound trashy. "Get me pregnant, Reuben. We've been so careful all summer." He looked instantly pained. "Hear me out. Mom can't make me leave—or she can't make me stay away if I'm pregnant with your baby."

He rolled onto his back, putting his arm on his forehead to block his face. He lay there like that so long, I thought maybe he'd fallen asleep.

He jumped when I touched him lightly and said his name. He got out of bed. "Can you give me a little time? I need to take a drive— alone." He looked frightened. "I'll be back." He absolutely wouldn't make eye contact. "Will you be okay? I'm really sorry about your aunt." I tried to go to him, but he backed away. I tried to speak. "Don't say anything more, Emmy. Not yet. Will you be okay? Don't leave."

Where exactly was I going to go?

He walked past me without giving me a hug good-bye. I heard his truck start. It wasn't quite ten. I knew he was going to the reservation, and it would be hours. I pictured him driving through the scablands, past Coulee Dam, or maybe he knew another way or a back way. He liked to brag that Indians knew pathways that whites didn't. If only I'd had my license, then at least I could've driven Beth's car to the lake. Instead I cleaned the kitchen, even inside the fridge. I scrubbed both bathrooms. I did tons of laundry. I liked washing Reuben's and my clothes together. We'd find a way to make it with a baby—through high school, even college. We'd manage. Mom had.

Reuben looked exhausted when he finally returned at 4:00 A.M. But he also seemed sure of something. I was sitting on the couch, sleepily folding laundry and thinking about how if I had a baby girl, I'd name her Beth. "Don't get up," he said. He came to me. He put all the laundry back into the basket, the folded and the unfolded, and moved it out of the way. He sat beside me. "Listen, Emmy. I love you more than I love anyone—my dad, Teresa." I started to speak. "Wait. And because of that, I can't—I *won't* get you pregnant at sixteen."

"I'll be seventeen in a few weeks. Please, Reuben. You promised to do everything you could to keep me."

"I won't do this. No way. My mom. Your mom. Teresa. We can do better for ourselves. We're smarter."

"What does smart have to do with it?"

"Everything. I want more for you, for myself, for my kids. You saw the towns on the rez. Do you know how many Indian girls drop out of high school pregnant?"

"But you'd never leave me like the men left your sister. Or like Jamie left my mom."

"You're right. I wouldn't."

"Then?"

"Where would we live?" he asked. "Shit, Emmy. Grow up." I looked at my hands. That hurt. He didn't backtrack.

"Mom will make me leave." I started to cry. "Wait and see. You'll be sorry."

"I won't be sorry. I'd rather break every promise than ruin your life."

"*Ruin* my life?" My voice pitched. "My life is *over* when I leave here!"

He grabbed my arms. "Don't say that."

"Don't you see? My mother is going to rip me away from you!" And I knew, though I didn't say, that losing Aunt Beth *and* Reuben might destroy me.

"She can't." He tightened his grip. "You're part of me." He said something in his native language. "You're part of this land."

"You don't know her, Reuben. She's a force. Look what she did to her sister."

"I'm going to talk to her. I'm not scared."

But he held me the rest of the night as if he were terrified.

15

Spencer

I wish to God I'd been walking by the Sacramento Greyhound station the day Kate stepped off the bus with Emmy on her hip. I like to think I could've saved them both a lot of heartache. I know I would've fallen as hard for Kate then, at only twenty years old, as I did the day we bumped into each other at a gas station by the coffee counter. Actually I bumped into her and her paper cup tipped. I apologized. A splash of coffee burned her hand. "Sorry," I said again when I realized. She barely glanced at me. Most women give me one good look, if not two.

"No biggie," she said, cleaning up the mess on the counter.

"Can I see your hand?" I set down my stainless steel travel mug.

"Oh, I'm fine. I used to waitress. I've been burned worse than this before."

"Let me make it up to you." I'd already noticed her sexy legs.

She finally looked at me. Christ, her eyes. "What, over coffee?"

I laughed. "How about dinner?"

We moved to the cash register. She wasn't a lingerer. "It would have to be lunch. I have a kid." I tried to pay. It was the least I could do. She refused, stubbornly putting her quarters on the counter.

"Dinner," I said, "and bring your kid." We were outside. She said she was running late for work. Her brown hair blazed in the sunlight. Normally I didn't find redheads attractive, but her red looked as if it would be warm to the touch. "But first I need your number."

"First, *I* need your name."

"Spencer Hensley."

"Nice to meet you, *Spencer Hensley.*" Why did she say it like that? She offered me her hand and a slight smile. "I'm Kate." She was kind of a smart-ass. "You have a pen?" she asked.

"I'll remember your number, *Kate*."

She gave it to me rather quickly

"I'm sorry," I said. "I didn't catch your last name."

"If you actually call my number, I'll give you my last name."

Fair enough.

She got into a junky Honda, probably still from her waitressing days, and drove away.

I called the number on four different occasions before someone finally picked up: a girl, real quiet, who said her mom was in the shower. I asked her to write down my number and have her mom call me back. Kate never did. I returned to the same gas station on the same day of the week and at the same time. She didn't appear. Then I remembered she'd said she was late. I showed up extra early the following week. I did paperwork in my truck. She pulled up and went inside. I gave her a minute, then followed. She was getting coffee. "Kate," I said.

She jumped, but luckily no spills. "Damn," she said. "You scared me, Mr. Hensley. I didn't think anyone around here knew my name."

"I called your number."

"Can we talk outside?" Again she refused to let me pay for her coffee, and somehow she managed to pay for mine.

"The teacher lady already took care of it," the Punjabi cashier said with a smirk.

"I'm a thirty-year-old single mom who works a lot," Kate said.

"What's your point? I'm thirty-one and *I* work a lot."

"I just thought we should cut through the bullshit."

"Are you free right now, Miss—? I'm sorry, I still didn't catch your last name."

"Ms. Nolan." She presented me her hand again and the same slight smile. "I teach class until twelve. Sorry, Mr. Hensley."

"Spencer."

"And then I have another class at three."

I gave her my business card. The fact that I own a custom home-building company impresses most women. She stuck the card in her pocket as if I'd given her my number scribbled on a matchbook. I named a Mexican restaurant by the college where she taught and asked her to meet me there at twelve-thirty. I'm pretty sure she nodded. But she sure as hell didn't show.

I found her junky Honda—with the faded CLINTON 92 bumper sticker—in the staff parking lot the next week at noon and waited with two coffees. "You stood me up," I said. "I guess there's more bullshit to cut through."

"Isn't there always?" Her arms were too full of books to take the coffee. "I didn't *exactly* agree to meet you."

"Do you agree to lunch right now?"

We wound up at my place in bed. I'm not *exactly* sure how that happened. Who cares? And I missed an appointment with a county inspector. Same thing the next week and twice the next. The sex was fantastic, but I felt bad that I still hadn't bought her lunch. Single at thirty-one, I'd had a lot of women. Kate hadn't had a lot of men, or at least not a lot who knew how to touch her. She didn't have to tell me this. Her body was supersensitive, which was a major turn-on and contrasted nicely with her stubbornness. I couldn't keep my hands out of her hair. I found her vulnerability in bed incredibly sexy, but it left me unguarded. It wasn't the vulnerability of a young girl. No, thanks. But of someone who desperately wanted to open herself up. She had this way of putting her arms above her head—not just when we fucked in my bed but in my kitchen or elsewhere—as if totally surrendering. It drove me nuts. I'd think about her body all day at work. But as soon as she got her clothes back on, she was all about her job and picking up her daughter from school and telling me "no, no, no" about hooking up over the weekend, maybe taking in a movie with her kid.

Months later, when I finally met her twelve-year-old kid, I fell just as hard, but obviously in a completely different way. I had the same strong urge to take care of Emmy as Kate. We had dinner in a restaurant in Old Sacramento with a view of the river. Kate and Emmy sat on one side of the table, and I sat across from them. Emmy looked like her mom, but not as much as I'd anticipated. She had lighter hair and a better smile than Kate. But Kate's eyes were larger and more intense. Emmy kept whispering things to her mom. Kate would mouth to me,

"I'm sorry," but it didn't bother me. Emmy wasn't being rude or snotty. Painfully shy, she blushed easily. A curious girl, though. When she thought I wouldn't notice, she'd glance at me. She watched all the families around us with interest. She watched the river. So did Kate. I watched the two of them watching the river.

I tried to act relaxed so Emmy would relax. It was easy, actually. I asked her a few questions about school. She answered politely. When Kate went to use the restroom, I could tell Emmy wanted desperately to follow her. But she didn't. She shrank down in her seat, as if hoping I wouldn't notice she was still there. It was cute. I asked about her best friend.

She twisted her cloth napkin. "I don't really have one, *yet*."

"Your mom maybe?" I suggested.

She smiled. "Yeah."

"I was close to my dad at your age," I told her. Silence. One more question, and then I'd leave her alone. Poor girl was beet red. "If you had a puppy, what would you name it?" I realize now this was more a question for a four-year-old than a twelve-year-old. "I know you can't have pets at your apartment. But if you could?"

She didn't even have to think. "Tangles."

I wanted to take them walking down on the docks. When I mentioned it, Emmy seemed excited, but Kate insisted they had to get home. They both had homework.

"Bye, girls," I said at their apartment, more to tease Kate than anything. She objected to grown women being referred to as girls. Kate had yet to invite me inside to her apartment. I wanted in.

Four years and two marriage proposals later, the lady is finally wearing my ring.

"Shit, Spencer, you finally got the balls to propose to her again," my little brother said when he took me for a beer to celebrate. "Did she let you show her the ring this time?"

"Not exactly." I shifted on the barstool. "I left it on her coffee table."

"Never mind, then, bro, about your balls."

Our parents built the company from scratch. Dad taught my brother and me how to take pride in the trade and, maybe more important, how not to be afraid of hard work. He also warned us never to marry a woman who was afraid of hard work or she could negate everything. What Dad didn't make clear is how difficult it can be to love a hard-working woman. In the beginning Kate Nolan's lack of interest in my money was refreshing. And I greatly admired her self-reliance. In the beginning. But Jesus Christ, that woman. The first time I saw her cry was because her teeth, her wisdom teeth, were hurting. She had nice teeth in front. But her wisdom teeth were impacted. In fact, it was the first time I spent the night at her apartment. She called me late at night. I hurried over there. She quietly escorted me into her bedroom so as not to wake Emmy. There were books everywhere in her apartment. The place was a bit of a dive—it was clean but run down.

"Will you rub my back?" she asked.

"Of course, baby." She was in serious pain. "Let me take you to the emergency room." She told me she didn't have medical or dental insurance as a part-time teacher. She worked part time at three different colleges, rather than full time at just one. According to my calculations, that meant she worked time and a half. "I'll pay," I offered, and I meant it. She refused. "I can't handle seeing you in this much pain." She told me I could leave. I stayed.

The next time her wisdom teeth hurt, I asked her how long they'd been trying to emerge. She said on and off since she was pregnant. So for thirteen fucking years? Mine were extracted in eighth grade. I insisted she take one of the painkillers I got for her from my doctor. When the throbbing subsided and she relaxed a bit, I asked, "What happened to Emmy's dad?"

"You can't ask me about him." She moved away from me in her bed.

"Where's your family?" I inched closer. She and Emmy were all alone. Too alone. It was beginning to worry me.

"Please don't, Spencer." She put her hand out, as if to block me. "I like you."

I took her hand and held it. "I *love* you, Kate."

"You haven't known me long enough to love me." She pulled her hand away.

"I've known you seven months—you exclusively. No other women."

"Big sacrifice, I realize."

"I didn't mean—"

"Have you ever been in love before?" she asked.

"I'm not answering any question that you won't."

"Well, of course *I* have." Her speech was beginning to slur. "I had his baby."

Ouch. "Emmy told me her dad is dead."

"You asked her about her dad?" She sat up.

"No, Kate. Calm down. I mentioned to Emmy that my old man wasn't alive. She said her dad wasn't alive either."

"Yes. That's correct." She lay back down, thanking me again for the pill.

I rubbed her back. Her face was turned. I put my hand in her hair and whispered, "Do you love me, Kate?" I almost hoped she didn't hear.

She turned and looked at me. Even on pain meds, her gaze was unflinching. "If I could ever love a man again, it would definitely be you, Spencer Hensley."

"I'm not sure that's enough."

"It's all I got."

She turned back around. I felt her back tremble as she tried to sob quietly.

She did love me, though. I felt it most when we had sex—made love. When I was inside her, I felt really *inside* her, inside her fears and worries, and her tiredness, inside her joy and calm. She had a great capacity for both. Inside her goodness and strength. But fuck, *not* her past. I preferred to think of it as her "mystery." Guys like women with a little mystery. Kate had a whole sea of it inside her. I was standing on the shore.

There was something else inside Kate. After a while the way she put her arms above her head began to feel, at times, more than a gesture of surrender. She was pretending to be tied up, I realized, and tried not to be turned on by it. I figured maybe she was just being theatrical. But then Kate's body began reacting strangely during sex, not every time, by any means, but once in a while. Sometimes it seemed she was detached from her own body and it hovered between us like something beautiful but sharp. I know it sounds crazy. Other times it was like she wanted to hurt her body: to make it ache for more by not allowing herself to orgasm or to ache from too much fucking even for a guy. And then at other times she'd suddenly cower. "I'm here, Kate." I'd have to remind her. "It's Spencer." She'd come back from somewhere—where?—and kiss me so softly, whispering my name and sweet nothings until I'd melt. I don't know how else to describe it. It wasn't sadomasochism. I'll never be into that shit, and I've had opportunities. No whips or leather for me, thanks. But it was definitely disquieting and, I almost hate to admit, curiously arousing, especially given her willfulness out of the sack.

In truth, out of the sack, Kate could be a bitch. I don't just mean the way she kept me at a safe distance, as if she feared I would not only hurt but destroy her. I don't just mean the way she seemed to slightly mock me and everyone else at times. She had a biting wit that left me shaking my head. No, she was downright cold occasionally. Even to her daughter. The poor girl lived and breathed for her mom. Kate lived for Emmy too, as far as Emmy was her number one priority. But Kate Nolan, in many ways, was a solitary soul. For a while I liked that about her. She was anything but needy or clingy, which I foolishly assumed at first had to do with her being a feminist. She also had no parents or siblings I had to meet right away and try to impress. She didn't ramble about old boyfriends or cry after sex about childhood woes. What did she have? She had her books. I'd never been out with a woman who read so much. I figured it was because she didn't have cable television. She watched the news more faithfully than I ever had, which checked me. She claimed she had to keep up with current events to teach rhetoric. But she also had a genuine interest in all politics, world events, geography. Kate also read a lot, I realized, because she didn't socialize: no girlfriends, old college pals, favorite coworkers. Again, at first, it was a kind of plus—not to sound like a jerk—that I didn't have to hang with her BFFs. But it was more than that even. She had a deep, almost religious love for literature. Emmy loved books also. Christ, the two of them could spend hours in a bookstore. But

Emmy needed friends and the real attention and affection they provide. She was constantly doing homework. Her only social activities were academic competitions and service club work: bake sales, car washes, charity dinners, blood drives. I hinted once to Kate that I would be more than happy to pay for Emmy to go in for some counseling for her shyness. Big mistake. Huge mistake. She made me sorry. I didn't see her or Emmy for weeks. Kate didn't have a clue how much that pained me.

I haven't always been a complete gentleman with women, so probably I deserve grief from Kate. Women have been in love with me before. Usually I called it off when I realized it or, worse, when they confessed. I had the perfect excuse: too busy with work, which I was, and still am, only Kate doesn't seem to mind. There were a few women before Kate whom I kept sleeping with even after they confessed their unrequited love, kept letting them make me dinner or even take me to family get-togethers. I know for a fact I broke one heart in high school and one just a year before Kate. How many in between, I couldn't say. For the most part I dated or simply fucked the kind of women who hang around bars. Nice bars. But bars nonetheless. I've definitely had feelings for women before, just nothing like what I feel for Kate. I dated a nurse. She was hardworking, ample-breasted, but she drank like a fish. I dated a real estate agent who, before she became too clingy, kept wanting me to invest. I dated a lady who worked PR for the Sacramento Kings. She had a great ass and got me great seats, a running joke between my brother and me, until I found out she was working OT in the bedroom with one of the bench players. I dated some good women, but none held a candle to Kate and her girl. End of story.

When Kate got that phone call from her sister, her past started to emerge. We'd been dating four years, but I didn't even know she had a sister. Emmy didn't know she had an aunt, for God's sake. But that was nothing compared with the fact that Emmy's dad *wasn't* dead. He was alive in Washington, where suddenly Kate was sending Emmy—not to her dad but to her aunt. Not for a week or two but for the whole summer. Not just for a visit but to participate in some backwoods faith healing ceremony that could emotionally scar Emmy. The girl was terrified. "I don't understand," I told Kate.

"You don't have to, Spencer." She was grading papers in my bed, naked, which normally I loved. We still met at my place between her classes, and the sex was still fantastic. She had the key. She'd stop by even when I couldn't: to take naps, use my gym equipment, catch up on grading. I always knew when she'd been there because of her perfume. Sometimes she'd leave a piece of fruit for me on the kitchen table or in my bed.

"I seriously *don't* understand you, Kate. What the hell? You can't make Emmy go."

She looked at me with her defiant eyes. "Are you going to stop me?"

"She's not prepared for this type of change."

"She agreed to go." She'd wrapped a sheet around herself, but it was slipping. Or she was letting it. "I'm not forcing her."

"You're bulldozing her, Kate, and you *know* it." Just fifteen minutes ago, her breasts were all over me, so why was I so desperate now for a peek? Was this what love did to a man? "I've never disagreed with you more."

"This doesn't really have to do with you."

I should've been immune to that comment by then, but it was like a knife. "How could you let Emmy think her dad was dead?"

"I was protecting her. And this conversation is over."

Emmy called me the night before she left for Washington to ask me to come over and help her get her mom out of the bathtub. It was a disturbing sight, to say the least: Emmy sitting on the bathroom floor, crying, and Kate in an empty bathtub, naked and shivering and staring off. Jesus fucking Christ. Life didn't have to be this way.

Kate had had a similar breakdown once, but Emmy, thank God, hadn't witnessed it. She thought her mom just had the flu. And I tried to never think about it. Two years ago, when I first proposed to Kate, she shot me down so quickly I thought maybe she really didn't love me, even though by then she was telling me she did. I broke it off officially and stayed completely away. What else could I do? If Kate still wanted me in her life, she'd have to come to me. And boy, did she. I hadn't asked for my key back. I found her at my place in my bed, na-ked, and sound asleep. We hadn't spoken in a full month. I didn't un-dress, but I climbed under the covers beside her. Of course I peeked at her body, which I'd missed terribly. She had two large bruises on her back. My first thought was to find the motherfucker who had done this to her, and I had to give myself a few minutes to calm down be-fore I gently shook her awake. She jumped, then clung to me so tightly I almost couldn't breathe. Crying, she begged me to forgive her and to never leave her. She didn't backtrack and accept my marriage pro-posal, though. Emmy slept on my couch the next few nights, thinking her mom had the flu in my bedroom. Kate not only had bruises on her back but also had one on the front of her hip—the memory of which still makes me cringe—and on the insides of both her upper arms. Fi-nally she confessed to sleeping with not just one man, but a few of the worst kind. She refused to give me names or addresses. She took the blame for the bruises, not going so far as to say she deserved them, but that she'd *allowed* them. Whatever the hell that meant. I felt utterly helpless for the first time in my life. And so fucking, fucking frus-trated. All I could do was refuse to make love with her, and she kept trying, until the bruises went completely away.

Kate and I will be flying north to Washington in a few hours, at dawn. Emmy has been there for two months now. Kate's sister died yesterday while we were still en route from Europe to New York to Chicago to Sacramento. Kate kept calling frantically at every airport, but didn't make it in time. I watch Kate sleep. She wears my ring. She fell asleep reading a book, as usual, only this time she just pre-tended to read so I wouldn't see her crying. Both utterly exhausted, we fought before going to bed. She decided at the last minute that she'd rather fly to Washington alone. But I knew if she did, she'd never re-turn to me. She'd return to Sacramento with Emmy, but not to me. "We're a family now, Kate." She started to pull off the ring. "Don't do that, baby. I worked too fucking hard to get that ring there." We both had jet lag, and she had to be feeling a lot of guilt, not just sadness, about her sister. Not that she, the most stubborn woman on earth, talked to me about either. "I won't let you go alone," I said. "No way in hell."

She'd confessed to me—during a previous argument, right after Emmy left—about being a truck stop hooker in Washington. The confession almost killed me, and it got me to thinking, instead of sleeping or eating. What had that time done to her? It made me sick. Her sexual complexity had intrigued me for four years. The dark side of it should've turned me off instead. A week after her confession, I asked her a second time to marry me. I told her about the house I was building us and the tickets to London.

We had a good time in Europe, after Kate quit being obstinate about money. She was like a kid at Disneyland seeing all the art, monuments, and writers' houses. I was more thrilled by the continued sight of my ring on her finger. Put together, all those women before Kate weren't as cultured—if that's the right word—as she is. We made love a lot, during which she remained present, never detached, and still playful, even coy, and sexy as hell in the French lingerie she asked me to buy for her in Paris. It was the first thing she'd *ever* asked me to buy. I would've bought her the whole boutique if she had let me. I wondered if confessing her "dirty secret" to me had released her from it. I hoped so. She read me poems. She sometimes did this in Sac, but it felt more fitting in Europe. Every night I wanted to ask her if she would consider having my baby someday soon, after she let me pay to get her wisdom teeth extracted. I'm glad now, given her sister's death, I waited. I didn't even realize women in developed countries still died from having miscarriages. I haven't slept all night. At first light we fly north into Kate's past. I'm ready.

The Spokane airport is smaller than I expected. We rent a car. After a tussle with Kate, who wanted to pick an economy car with tiny tires, we end up with a Land Cruiser. She studies the complimentary map before we venture from the rental car parking lot. She doesn't want to take I-90, the obvious route to her hometown. She shows me an alternative path. She says there's a lake she wants to drive past. We're briefly in pines, then in wheat fields for a while, until suddenly the landscape gets pretty damn desolate. Then even more so. "This area is called the scablands," she says.

"No shit."

There are cliffs and columns. Sagebrush and boulders. And an occasional lake. That's it. No trees. Kate said eastern Washington looked different from western Washington—the Seattle of movies—but I didn't picture this. Who would? We make it to her lake. She asks me to pull over. It's a mineral lake, with suds and black mud. Ugly as hell. We get out of the car. It's windy as hell and dusty as hell.

"My mom's spirit departed from her body in this lake," she says. "I saw it. I was nine."

"What?" Is this the same woman who teaches rhetoric? She believes in visible spirits?

"My dad dragged her body home. I never forgave him."

"Jesus, Kate. *What?*" I'm more than confused. Bewildered. She explains, or tries to, about the cultlike church of her childhood and her mom's untreated cancer. I can't even process it all. She says that Indians used to cure their wounded here. They believe the black mud is Coyote's poop, which is the source of his power. When she was pregnant, she came here alone and smeared the mud on her belly to protect Emmy. I can't picture Kate doing that.

We're an hour late arriving in her hometown, which isn't much of a town. The entire way she stared out the window and wiped her eyes. She directs me to the trailer park where Emmy has spent the summer. Kate's been jealous of how close Emmy seemed to be getting with her aunt and uncle. I thought it was fantastic. Now I'm not so sure. How devastating for Emmy. I've never actually been *in* a trailer park before. We pull in front of her sister's singlewide. What a long journey from the Mediterranean to here. Kate is shaken by the sight. And no wonder she argued that we didn't need a high-class SUV. I should've listened. With Kate, unlike with most women I've dated, I have to worry about *not* impressing her with such things. The trailer has been well maintained structurally for what amounts to basically a plywood box, but it's in no way attractive. Kate puts her head in her hands.

"I can't do this," she says. She looks back up at the trailer. "Oh, Beth." Then she puts her head down in her lap.

I move her hair away from her neck and rest my hand there. She sits up. "I can't do this, Spencer." She looks at me. "Do you love me? I mean, *truly* love me?"

Insecurity is not a normal Kate emotion, or at least it's not normal for Kate in California. It makes her seem years younger. "More than anything," I say. "You know that."

"No, I don't." Is she serious? Her eyes are huge with fear or maybe doubt. "You *shouldn't* love me."

"Why not? And too late."

"I feel sick." She holds her stomach. "I'm going to be sick. I can't do this."

She's coming undone. I think of her in my bed with bruises. Or in the empty bathtub the night before Emmy left. She doesn't break down in small ways or with much forewarning. If she breaks down here, she might not recover. It doesn't take a degree in psychology to see how quickly this place is throwing Kate into turmoil.

"You can do this, baby." I'm trying to assure myself as much as her. "We have to get Emmy."

Her strength seems to return at the mention of her daughter. After taking a couple of deep breaths, she opens the vanity mirror on the visor and starts to fix her makeup.

Before she finishes, Emmy comes out of the not-so-well-maintained trailer next door. Kate doesn't see her daughter. Emmy looks all grown up. Wow. And she holds the hand of a boy. Double wow. I point. Kate looks over. We both get out quickly to greet them. "Hey, kiddo," I say, long before they make it to us. She lets go of the boy's hand and runs toward me. Huge hug. Oh, Kate isn't going to forgive her daughter for hugging me first.

"Mom," Emmy says. She walks slowly toward her mom. I want to nudge her forward. She pulls away from her mom before Kate is ready to let her go. As Kate eyeballs the boy, her strength doubles. I wouldn't want to be him. "Mom and Spencer," Emmy says, "I want you to meet my best friend." She motions for the boy to come closer. He looks scared, but he's trying not to show it. He's a good-looking kid. Mexican, maybe. Emmy takes his arm and brings him forward. "This is Reuben," she says proudly. "My best friend *and* my boyfriend."

To quote the youngest guy on our steady crew, "Oh, snap."

I want to say, "Good for you, Emmy," but I wouldn't dare in front of Kate. When I saw Emmy off at the Sac airport, I told her to have an adventure this summer.

"Nice to meet you, Reuben." I take the boy's hand. He has a firm handshake, makes eye contact. It's been my experience that Mexican kids, in general, not the gangbangers, are more respectful than white ones.

"And you, Spencer," he says. "Kate." He holds out his hand to her. She takes it.

"Mom, what is that?" Emmy points at my ring on Kate's finger. But she doesn't give her mom time to answer. "Oh, Spencer. *Really?* When? Why didn't you call? Congratulations."

Why is she not looking at her mom?

"I guess we've both been keeping secrets," Kate says.

When it comes to Kate, that's the understatement of the century.

Kate stares at that poor boy so hard it makes me nervous for him.

Emmy takes Reuben's hand, and then she says rather flatly to her mom, "Uncle Matt is at the funeral home. They moved Aunt Beth's body from Spokane early this morning."

Oh, Emmy. She's blaming her mom for this one.

"Would you like to come inside?" she asks us, as if—as if a hundred things. She's been through a lot this summer. Too much. She's bracing for more. Reuben holds the door for us, but he doesn't come inside. Emmy goes to him. They whisper. He excuses himself to us and leaves. Kate looks around cautiously, as if afraid to take it all in at once. The trailer is even more ugly on the inside, but tidy, except for some stains on the carpet. "Just don't go into the master bedroom," Emmy says, voice shaking. Her new braveness seems to have walked out the door with Reuben. "It's a wreck." She swallows hard. "Uncle Matt's brother tore up the carpet."

I go to her. "I'm sorry about your aunt, kid." I take her into my arms. I've missed her. She cries, but not for long. Kate stares at us, and then, almost in a daze, she walks into the bedroom right by the front door. There is a strained silence between Emmy and Kate.

Emmy glances out the window behind her, toward the trailer that she came from with Reuben. "I'll be right back," she says, and goes out the front door.

I go in to see Kate. She's sitting on a small bed, staring at a crib. On the wall above the crib are faded pink letters that spell EMMY.

"This was my room," Kate says with pride.

"Growing up?" Jesus.

"Oh, no," she says. "I *wish*. I moved in here when I got far enough along with Emmy that my dad couldn't stand the sight of me." She explains how Matt and Beth got married and Matt's parents bought them this trailer so they all three, soon to be four, could have a place to live. "Pretty amazing," she says.

"And Emmy's dad?" I was going for broke. "Where the hell was he?"

"A cocky farm boy, off at college. I waitressed." She gets embarrassed, obviously forgetting for a minute that she has already told me she did far more than waitress. I sit down beside her on the small bed. "I can't believe Beth kept Emmy's crib up all these years," she says. "Hoping to fill it, I guess."

I can't believe Kate came from here. No wonder she loves her apartment in Sac. And I am so relieved there are no lies or secrets left. Given Kate's past, which I didn't know about at the time of my first marriage proposal and, to be honest, would not have been ready for, I'll never judge her, no matter what. If she ever comes home with bruises again, however, I'll hunt the fuckers down, as I should have last time. I haven't touched another woman since Kate and I first had sex, not even the month we were officially broken up.

I tell her the crib and letters are sweet, but they're fucking sad. This whole place. It's completely depressing. I feel a pang again for having mocked her secondhand furniture.

"I wish you could've met Beth," she says. "She would've liked you, Spencer Hensley." She takes my wrist, feeling with her fingertips for my pulse. This is something she's always done, usually in bed when she thinks I'm asleep. "Emmy's different now," she says. "You were so right about that." She lets go of my wrist and starts to cry. "I was a monster never calling Beth all those years. She must've thought I didn't love her or that I forgot about her. I thought about her every day. Even this summer when I didn't call, I thought about her. Do you believe me?" I do. I nod. "Emmy's different, like you said."

"Slow down, baby." I put my arm around her shoulder. "Let's take things one at a time."

"I've never *really* understood why you love me, Spencer. How can you? *Why* do you?"

She's never asked me that before. It catches me off guard. Has she actually been afraid *all* these years that I didn't *really* love her, that I couldn't possibly because Emmy's dad didn't or because of the way she left her sister? I've never loved her more than right now in this sad room. The fact that she had the strength to get herself and Emmy away from here. It moves me deeply and, frankly, impresses the hell out of me.

"You don't have to answer," she says. "But I'm tired of being afraid that you'll stop wanting me if I love you too much."

I had no fucking idea she was so afraid of *that*. Afraid of needing me, yes. Afraid of appearing weak or dependent, yes. Afraid of another rejection, I kind of figured. But I had no idea she was afraid of losing me if she slowed, let alone turned and gave up the chase.

"I'm not going anywhere." I kiss her forehead. "And as for *why* I love you, just know that I always will." I hear a truck in the gravel driveway. The windows are thin. "I think your brother-in-law just pulled up."

We make it into the living room before he opens the screen door.

"Kate, my God," Matt says. They stare at each other for what seems minutes. He's holding paperwork—on his wife's body, no doubt. Finally Kate speaks. "Matt." She goes to him. He hesitates but then takes Kate into his arms. They both sob. It's gut-wrenching. He drops some of the paperwork. I pick it up. Kate has never sobbed quite like that in my arms.

After Kate gains composure, she introduces me. Matt squares his shoulders and shakes my hand. I give him back the papers he dropped.

"Emmy says nothing but good things about you," he says to me. "Where is she?"

"Next door," I say.

"Did you meet Reuben?" Matt asks. "He's a great kid."

"Emmy introduced him to us as her *boyfriend*," Kate says, getting back in defense mode.

"Yeah, I think so," Matt says, grinning a bit.

"We can discuss that later, Kate," I say. She looks at me. Then back at Matt. He offers us seats at the kitchen table. I try not to notice how the cabinets look like paneling—Christ, are they?—and how the laminated countertops look like crap and how faded the linoleum flooring is. Kitchens were my dad's specialty. Matt gets us glasses of water straight from the tap, and it tastes great. Kate asks a few questions about the funeral. I'm just about to suggest I go get some cold beers at the gas station when Kate brings up Beth's health over the years. Shit. She needs to slow down.

"What do you want me to say, Kate?" Matt asks. "She suffered a lot of miscarriages. She was a scarred mess inside. She wouldn't go to the doctor."

"How many, Matt?"

"It's painful. Let's just say a lot."

This is unbelievable. More than backwoods.

"But I don't understand," Kate says. "Why'd she keep getting pregnant then?"

"Your sister wanted a baby more than anything." Kate needs to back the hell down. "Do you want me to say she begged?"

Christ. Fuck.

"No," Kate says. "Sorry. I just—I don't understand."

"What don't you understand, Mom?" It's Emmy. She let the door slap shut behind her. "Aunt Beth missed you and me. You broke her heart when you abandoned her. She *never* recovered. Don't blame Uncle Matt. He loved her. He *always* loved her."

"Emmy," Matt says. "It's okay, honey."

"It's *not* okay," Emmy says. "It's never going to be okay. Mom needs to know what she did to her only sister."

"Emmy," Matt says again, a little more firmly.

"I just came to say I'm going for a drive with Reuben."

Kate starts to get up from the table, but I hold her arm.

"Be back in an hour," Matt says.

"Okay, Uncle Matt. I love you."

"Sure, sweetie," Matt says. "I love you too." He doesn't mean to hurt Kate, but he has to say it back to his niece. Emmy, on the other hand, means to hurt her mom. This is something new. This is something bigger than Emmy finally having a boyfriend and Kate having to let go a little. I expected this to happen sometime soon in Sacramento. I planned all along to be on Emmy's side, to get her some slack from her mom to be a normal teenager, to do more than just read books and study. This is different, though. Emmy is biting to the bone.

I fear the real heartache of this family is just beginning. I wasn't there to meet Kate and Emmy when they got off that bus in Sacramento sixteen years ago. But I am damn sure here now.

16

Kate

Thank you for finding me, Beth. I wanted to be found. Who doesn't? When I picked up the phone that day in my office and it was your voice on the other end, my beloved sister's voice, I can't tell you how deeply I was shaken.

"It's me, sister," you said.

All our long years apart dissipated for a moment and we were young again and I was standing behind you, brushing the tangles from your hair with Mom's brush and asking, "If you could travel to any country in the world, Beth, where would you go?"

"I like it here," you said. It always freaked you out when I talked about traveling as a missionary to Africa or Bangladesh. Maybe you knew my real intent to disappear with the natives.

"Bor-ing. If you could wish for only one thing, what would it be?"

"A baby."

"That's a stupid answer. Pick something else. Anyone can have a baby."

I was walking back into the trailer the morning after I let a trucker cut off my hair. You and Matt were eating breakfast at the table as if you'd been doing it for years, as if you weren't a young teenage couple just beginning. Emmy was in the high chair between you, as if. And Matt was feeding her, though she was barely old enough.

"No, Kate. Oh, no, Kate." You jumped up. You ran to me. "Who did this to you?"

"I did it," I replied, but not very convincingly.

Matt got to his feet. "Who fucking did it?"

Emmy started wailing.

"I didn't get his name." I was hung over, sore between my legs, and desperate to take off my waitress uniform. I backed away from Matt so he wouldn't smell the sex on me.

"Well, my brother and I will get the bastard's name." Matt grabbed his jacket.

Emmy kept wailing.

"Please, Matt, get Emmy," you said.

You ran me a bath and washed what was left of my hair. You got scissors and tried to even the jagged edges.

I was at that Greyhound bus station. We were walking through crunchy gravel toward the waiting bus and its stinking fumes and rumbling engine. I was carrying a suitcase, and you were holding Emmy. We were just kids.

"I'm off to Africa to save souls." My voice shook like my hands with fear.

"Your soul and Emmy's," you said. "That's all you have to worry about. That's all that matters, Kate. That's your job. Your *only* job."

Emmy wouldn't come to me. She'd been leery of my short hair for weeks. She wouldn't let go of you. We had to pry her little fingers, untangle them from your hair. I took a final glance backward, first at the parking lot for Jamie's truck and then at you, my sister.

Every mile marker, every highway sign, every river, every town and city the bus rumbled through. Until that day we had spent our lives only an arm's reach apart.

I remember back before boys, before Matt and Jamie, before Emmy, when it was just you and me. Remember, Beth?

You claimed you didn't know I'd never return or ever be in touch. But I tried telling you as much before I left. You didn't believe me. There was just no way for you to fathom how absolute would be my abandonment of you. Had I known how you suffered. Your loss. Had I known you had no children of your own, I would've come back. Please believe me. If only you had gone to a doctor. If I'd been here, I would've dragged you. Matt should've forced his hand. But he loved you too much to be a heavy like Dad. He held you closer, I am sure, after each loss.

I'm in a hotel room in our hometown, but I can't sleep. I've been to

Europe, sister. Who would have thought—a girl from Moses Lake, from the scablands? Had I not gone, I could've been at your bedside when you left this world. Why is life like that? I wish I could've had you *and* California. I didn't know how to do both. Like the hymn says, "The world behind me, the cross before me. No turning back." Jamie wasn't the reason I didn't return. Maybe at first. But it became larger than him. California is a large place. I am still trying to take it all in.

"You're beautiful, Kate," you kept telling me as you trimmed my uneven hair. "You'll find love again."

And I have, sister. I didn't realize how deeply I loved him until bringing him here. He sleeps beside me now in this hotel room.

I didn't realize how much Emmy loved you until seeing her in your house today, and especially in your garden, which was dying but must've been beautiful. She was trying to save it. I had no right to keep you two apart. No right. It was my life's mistake. Forgive me, Beth.

I know you already have.

There is so much I want to tell you about now that I am back here: things I learned in college, the different fruits I tasted in California, the art and ancient ruins I saw in Europe. It doesn't seem to amount to much now that I can never tell you. If it could just be you in bed beside me, just one more time. I want to hear you say the names of each of the babies you lost. I want to say the names and cry over each one with you.

Sister, remember when it was just us—just us in all the world?

17

Reuben

🖋 *Okay, Dad. Okay. I'm beginning to understand your warning.* Last night Emmy asked me to get her pregnant, so we can stay together. The thought of my child in her belly, of her and me starting a family—there is nothing I want more. But not yet. Not yet. *Right, Dad?* I want to do right. *You didn't do right by Mom, not often enough.* I am going to try harder than my old man to do right by those I love, and I love this girl the most.

Before Emmy's mom arrives this afternoon, she and I make a plan to talk with Kate and Matt together and see if we can persuade them to let Emmy stay here in Moses Lake and finish high school. But we'll wait until after the funeral.

Her mom and Spencer pull up in the smoothest ride I've seen in this trailer park. Emmy says the metallic beige Land Cruiser is just a rental and that her mom would never drive an SUV. But still. She holds my hand as we walk toward them. I try to notice Spencer first, but my eyes are drawn to Kate's hair like fire. Emmy didn't mention her mom isn't a blonde. Both Kate and Spencer are stylish. They don't look like country clubbers: no sun visors or polo shirts. Neither do they look like outdoorsy tourists from Seattle in expensive fleece. She looks artsy. He wears jeans but not tennis shoes. They're both in shape. They look so different from Beth and Matt. Emmy's uncle is in decent shape, but thin and shorter than Spencer, and he always wears a faded ball cap, except to church. I shake Spencer's hand firmly. Surprisingly, it's as calloused as Matt's. Emmy hugged him first—she ran to him—and the longest. Her mom's eyes are too much. It's obvious she's been crying. She's about to enter her dead sister's house for the first time. I excuse myself.

I sleep without Emmy. I try to sleep without Emmy. Fuck, I slept without her for seventeen years. Now suddenly I can't. It's Matt's first night in that trailer without Beth. I can't imagine. Emmy stays with her mom and Spencer at a hotel in town by the lake. She wasn't happy with the arrangement. I told her not to make a scene because it might hurt our chances later. I keep peeking through the blinds during the night. I want to go next door and say something to Matt, but what? The master bedroom light never goes off.

Teresa finds me sitting on the couch at 6:00 a.m. She wears Scooby-Doo scrubs—well, just the shirt, thank God. No one needs images of that dipshit dog and his always-stoned-and-raiding-the-refrigerator owner on their ass. "Leave the kids here today, sis."

"I think you got your hands full enough."

"Emmy doesn't mean to be so much work."

After starting the coffee, Teresa sits close beside me in the early light. It's a chilly morning—hinting of change, and moons to come without Emmy. I used to lean my head on Teresa's shoulder as a kid. I'm too tall now. We keep sitting there even after the coffee's done brewing. "Don't lose your way," she finally says. "Chasing after a girl who's lost."

I'm glad she didn't say "white girl." But Emmy's not lost, not yet. She's just confused. She's not homeless or on drugs or being abused. Shit, Teresa.

"I just want to help her," I say.

"She needs to find her own way *first*. Take it from me."

"Yeah, but—" I choke. Teresa always thinks she knows everything.

"I know." She squeezes my hand. "I know." Case in point. "But you may have to let her go."

I almost tell her how Emmy asked me to get her pregnant and how I refused. I'm not as naive as she thinks.

"Remember Audrey?" she asks.

"Of course." But I don't want to think about her right now.

"She told me once that you loved her—my twelve-year-old brother. I laughed at her because it scared me. She watched you while she danced."

I always wondered if I'd just imagined it.

"Be careful, baby brother."

She gets up and brings us both a cup of coffee. I know she means well. "I'm sorry I haven't been much help this summer," I say as she sits back down.

"Oh, bull. My kids love their uncle Reuben." She reaches back and peeks through the blinds at Matt's trailer. "The nurses in ER keep asking me about Matt." She takes a sip. "They were so touched by the way he broke down when they had to cut off Beth's hair."

"That's too much, Teresa. Don't tell me shit like that."

"Sorry, kid. You want to help me get my litter up and into the van?"

I'm still sitting on the couch at nine, with the TV off, when Emmy comes to the screen door. I already showered and got dressed, thankful to have those clothes from Teresa so I don't look like a chump in front of Kate and Spencer. Someday I'm going to quit wearing other people's clothes. It's still chilly and overcast, and my arm aches more than it has in months. I wear a sweatshirt with the hood up. I heard Spencer's SUV pull in an hour ago. Emmy looks through the ripped screen. I tell her to come in, but I don't get up. She's all smiles. What the hell? Did her mom agree to let her stay for the school year? If not, why does she smile? And didn't her aunt just die? "Hey, Reuben." She comes to me on the couch. She wears a dainty sweater I haven't seen on her before. I hope the sweater is a gift from her mom and not from her soon-to-be stepdad. I can't help being a jealous asshole when it comes to Emmy's affection for Spencer, no matter how innocent. She also wears jeans for the first time all summer. Usually she wears shorts, skirts, or dresses. She looks hot in jeans. I want to see her from the back. "I have good news," she says. I pull her onto my lap. She smells like shampoo and fruit. Her sweater's so soft. I kiss her neck. "Don't you want to hear my news?"

I keep kissing her neck, then her ear. I whisper how much I missed her body last night. I'm afraid to hear her news. I'm afraid I won't ever be able to touch her body again.

"Nice sweater," I say.

"This old thing? Cashmere from Paris."

"Your sweater's from fucking Paris?"

She answers me in French.

I grin, despite my grouchy mood. "My girl speaks French in a trailer park."

"My guy to me will not hark." She pushes my hood back. "Listen," she says. "This is going to sound crazy, but Uncle Matt asked Mom if I could go to the Whitman Mission today in Walla Walla—with just you."

I don't say anything. That *is* crazy. Why would I want to go there?

"Matt told Mom how Aunt Beth—" The name trips her up. "How Aunt Beth had planned to take me there. They'll be busy all day with funeral arrangements." Again she has to pause. "The mission is only two hours away."

Who am I kidding? I'd go anywhere to spend time with Emmy. "Your mom agreed?"

"Not at first. Spencer convinced her." She puts my hood back up. "You look a little gangster," she teases.

"Since when is Spencer your boss?" That came out wrong.

She studies me for a second. "Since I'm not really talking to Mom. Who cares? I get to hang out with you." She hugs me. "Mom's not thrilled. She wants to talk to you first."

"What?" I throw off my hood.

"We don't have to go. I didn't even ask if you *wanted* to. Sorry." She looks at me coyly. "If you do take me, I'll make up for last night." She reaches under my sweatshirt and T-shirt.

I grab her arm. "Don't, Emmy." I'm not sure why it pisses me off. She's my girlfriend. I've reached up her shirt when it's just the two of us. I guess I don't want her thinking she has to ever bribe me in that way.

"Sorry, Reuben."

I hate how much she apologizes. It's my least favorite thing about her.

Her smile is gone. I feel bad. She's trying to make the best of things. I think she's going to cry, but then she says, "I slept in your flannel shirt last night. *Nothing* else." She had a separate but adjacent hotel room from her mom and Spencer's room. She whispers something in my ear. Jesus Christ. She can be so fucking sexy, and usually when I least expect it. The way she took off her underwear that day in my truck after we'd been to the library.

After she gives me a few minutes to stop thinking of her alone in that hotel bed in just my shirt, I follow her next door. I'm unable to take my eyes off her ass in those jeans. I wish we could get a room in Walla Walla instead of go to the mission. With what—all my money?

"Hey, Reuben," Matt says. I shake his hand twice as long as I do Spencer's. The professor gets right to business, asking me if I know the way to Walla Walla and if I think it's going to storm and if my truck will make it.

"You two better get on the road," Spencer says, getting out some cash from his wallet that he better not fucking hand to me.

"Put that away, Spencer," Kate says. "I gave Emmy money this morning."

"She doesn't need money," I say. "I have cash." I have like a whole fourteen bucks of my own, and we still have money from hocking Emmy's necklace.

"And Reuben's got cash," Kate says. Is she mocking me? Or defending me?

"Well, then, in case of an emergency." He hands a wad to Emmy.

"I don't need it," she says, looking timidly at me as if I'll get pissed right here in front of her family. Kate notices this. I can tell, she notices everything.

"Just take it, honey," Kate says. "Spencer's right. *In case.*" She turns to me. "Have her home by dark—please."

Matt puts his hand on my shoulder like an elder. "Thanks, Reuben. Beth would appreciate it."

Emmy gives hugs around, the shortest by far to her mom, who looks offended and goes into the bedroom where Emmy and I made love the second time.

"Hey, Emmy," Spencer says quietly. "You want to go say good-bye to your mom again?"

"No. I'm good."

Her lack of timidity at times is refreshing. Even, in retrospect, how she got mad at me for following her in Spokane. But mostly I worry for her.

Once we're on the road, well out of Moses Lake, I ask her, "Are you pretty pissed off at your mom for not being here when Beth died?" She nods. It may rain after all, the sky's darkening. I tell her to scoot closer, and she does.

"And for only letting me know Aunt Beth for two months," she says. "For telling me my dad was dead." She takes off the sweater and wads it. "For the way she looks at you. For everything. I can't imagine *why* Spencer wants to marry her."

"She's pretty intense. Some guys dig that."

"Are you crushing on my mom?"

"No." I laugh. "No way."

"I don't want to talk about my mom."

Does she realize we're going to the site of a massacre? Or at least that's what whites call it. I've actually never been to the Whitman Mission. Why the fuck would I? I studied the Whitmans in school, of course. They're hailed as heroes, even martyrs, for being the first white missionary couple—the first white family period—to settle west of the Rockies. Emmy says her aunt talked to her a lot about Narcissa Whitman. I know that after the Whitmans were killed by the Cayuse, who had lost three fourths of their tribe to disease even though Mr. Whitman was a doctor, all the Indians in eastern Washington were rounded up and put on reservations, including, of course, the twelve Colville tribes. I don't like the feel of the place from the get-go.

We go into the museum before walking the grounds. The rather psycho-looking park ranger stares at me a minute too long as he collects our fees. I almost tell him I'm Punjabi, not Cayuse, just to fuck with him. It takes Emmy only about half a minute to realize the place is the site of a bloody conflict between, essentially, her people and mine. She looks at me with wide eyes. "Shit," she whispers. "Let's leave."

"We're here. But thanks." I know she'd leave for real if I wanted to. She apologizes. "Chill out. It was a long time ago." Though not really. Not in Indian time. I definitely sense some lingering spirits.

In the center of the museum are life-size mannequins of the Whit-mans and five Cayuse. Narcissa is on her knees, extending her stiff arms out to a small native girl, which makes me want to puke. "Those are just creepy," Emmy says, taking my hand briefly. I totally agree.

She spends a long time reading the plaques and studying the dis-plays. It reminds me of how she paid careful attention in church for her aunt. She pulls a little tablet from her purse and copies down quotes. The displays tell the story of the Whitmans' eleven years (1836–1847) as missionaries. They didn't have a single Christian con-vert, which is my favorite fact.

"Aunt Beth said my mom wanted to be a missionary when she was a little girl. Mom never told me this, of course. She never told me crap."

"I wanted to be Smokey the Bear."

She laughs, hard.

"Not like the real bear," I explain.

"The *real* bear?"

"Stop laughing. I mean I wanted to be the dude who dressed up and went around to schools. I was like seven."

"Teen."

There's a section devoted to the story of the Cayuse. Emmy stares at the arrowheads and feathered headpiece as long as she did Dr. Whitman's compass and Bible and Narcissa's dishes. There's a large sign with the following quote, which Emmy copies into her tablet: "The Cayuse sprang from the beaver's heart, and for this reason they are more energetic, daring, and successful than their neighbors."

"Bring it on," I say about the sign. She laughs. I look behind me.

We go out the back door of the museum, which leads to the large mission grounds. The unsettledness I felt at first intensifies outside. The wind has picked up, and I hear more noises than I care to. No wonder the ranger looks deranged (a de-ranger). We see the actual wagon grooves in the earth from the Oregon Trail. Emmy kneels down and touches them with both her palms and even closes her eyes. What does she hear? The "pioneer spirit" that led her people west? She doesn't say and I don't ask. There's a paved trail around the old mission homestead. Emmy's pretty quiet and trying to hurry for my sake. I think she actually likes it here. "Slow down," I tell her. But really, I hope she doesn't.

We find ourselves by the gravestone of the Whitmans' only child, a girl who was born here, but then drowned at two years old. Emmy asks me if I read inside about how the toddler's body was found. I shake my head. "Marcus and the other white men," she says, "searched the river for Alice's body after they saw her tin cup floating on the surface." She pauses to catch her breath. "They couldn't find her. Then a Cayuse man jumped into the river and immediately located the girl. Her hair had snagged in the reeds. How did he know where she was?"

"I don't know." I try not to sound irritated. How would I know? She seems spooked and waits for an answer. "I suppose he knew the river."

"Is your arm okay, Reuben? You keep rubbing it. Is that the arm you broke?"

"It's fine." She offers me an Advil from her purse. I shake my head. She offers to rub my arm for me, but the ache is too deep for that. I'd like to leave. I hate it here. But I know Emmy wants to visit the large slab grave that holds the bones of all fourteen pioneers killed.

"Narcissa was the only woman killed," Emmy says, reading the faded names. I walk away for a few, unable to feel the slightest sympathy. For the drowned girl, yes, but not the missionary woman. When I return to Emmy, she stands on the edge of a small unmarked pioneer graveyard—from years later, the sign says. There's no signs saying how many Indians were buried around here, dead from white man's diseases and the Indian wars that accompanied the reservation roundup. "It's so peaceful," Emmy says. Not really. Not at all. "I wish Aunt Beth could be buried here."

Right before Beth died, Emmy asked me if I loved her aunt. I couldn't lie and say that I did, but now I understand the connection I've always felt, and tried to deny, with Teresa's strange neighbor lady: she and I would one day love the same girl. I hug Emmy tightly. She's been brave all day. She loves only a handful of people in this world, one of whom is now gone. She's cold, even shivering a little. Why didn't she say? Her dainty sweater offers no protection. I help her put on my sweatshirt. Though, regrettably, it covers her ass. Pulling up the hood, I say, "Who's the wannabe gangsta now?"

A family passes us, and the kid points at me. "Look, Daddy, a Cayuse Indian."

Emmy and I laugh, a little awkwardly, as we walk back to the lawn area where the Whitmans' second house was built. Emmy wants to have one more look. I want to break camp. The footsteps I hear—only Indians know how to walk that softly, and maybe the Whitman baby. A sign explains that the Whitmans' first house kept getting flooded by the Walla Walla River, so they had to rebuild. "The river was trying to get the baby from the get-go," Emmy says. I disagree and shake my head. Emmy pulls me onto the grass, where there are cement outlines showing the exact locations of the different houses and sheds. We walk, one foot in front of the other, like grade schoolers, on the cement outline of the second house, but I keep glancing over my shoulder. Emmy falls, purposely, or because of her damn flip-flops. When I reach to help her stand up, she yanks me down onto the grass beside her. My first reaction is to jump the fuck up. The Whitmans were killed right here at this spot. I've been taught that the dead, whether Indian or white, are to be respected—out of fear, if nothing else. But I remain beside Emmy for a minute, both of us flat on our backs in the grass, holding hands and looking at the overcast sky.

I go to Beth's funeral service, but alone in my own truck. It's held at a funeral home, not the church. The preacher from the healing leads it, which surprises me. The dude fucked up, pretending he could heal. The Cayuse killed Dr. Whitman as they often killed their own shamans back then for not healing the sick. It's not a power to take lightly. I sure as hell wouldn't want it. All of the women and girls at the funeral, other than Matt's relatives, wear long prairie dresses. Emmy says Matt chose not to hold Beth's service at the church in deference to Kate, who was condemned from the pulpit there when it was first discovered she was pregnant with Emmy. Christian love. I don't think her uncle will keep attending that church or any other, at least for a while. After the minister finishes speaking with his southern accent—he broke down a lot, so it took forever—Kate reads a poem called "Dover Beach." It doesn't seem like a funeral poem, except maybe the first line: "The sea is calm tonight." The poem is typed into the funeral flyer, so as Professor Kate said before beginning, we can read along. Her voice is powerful. The poem seems to be about the loss of faith—"Its melancholy, long, withdrawing roar"— rather than the loss of a loved one. Beth had a lot of faith. Emmy sobs harder than at any other time. I sit right beside her in the front row reserved for family. Her sobs knock the wind out of me. Kate falters only on the final stanza:

> *Ah, love, let us be true*
> *To one another! for the world, which seems*
> *To lie before us like a land of dreams,*
> *So various, so beautiful, so new,*
> *Hath really neither joy, nor love, nor light,*
> *Nor certitude, nor peace, nor help for pain;*
> *And we are here as on a darkling plain*
> *Swept with confused alarms of struggle and flight,*
> *Where ignorant armies clash by night.*

The poem gets to me. I didn't want it to. But for an hour in the hospital I was the only one in the room with Beth. *Nor help for pain.* There should be drumming. *Darkling plain.* Matt and Emmy, who had both prepared little speeches on paper, are too upset to speak at the podium. *Struggle and flight.* I too feel heavy in my seat. *Clash by night.* A small reception follows, during which Emmy stays glued to Matt's side—for her protection or his, I can't tell. *Seems. Dreams.* It's touching. *Pain. Plain.* I cut out early. Emmy says she understands. At tribal funerals, even the Christian ones, we have drumming. *Light. Flight. Night.* There should've been drumming for Beth.

Ray and a few lowlifes, but not Benji, are at Teresa's place when I get there. Fuck. I'm usually happy to see Ray, but if he's hanging with Sergio, it can only mean trouble. Sergio is almost Teresa's age and just got paroled. I'll have to tell them all to clear out.

"Cuz," Ray says. They stand around Ray's truck and Sergio's slammed Honda. Sergio is half Yakama and half Mexican. One of the other guys is full Yakama. I met him once. And then there's a white boy in a backward cap. There's been tension lately between the Yakama and Colville over fishing rights on the Wenatchee. All of them but Ray, who's too fat, wear wife beaters. If Teresa were home, she would've already told them to scram, except Ray. I'll smoke one cigarette with them before I tell them to leave. They offer more than tobacco, but I pass.

"Ray says you got a *sweet* piece of ass next door, bro," Sergio says.

I look at Ray, who stutters, "I didn't say 'piece of ass,' cousin. I just—"

"Shut the hell up, Ray," I say. I'd tell Sergio off also, but he packs.

"He said you're real touchy *about* her," Sergio says. "I think he meant touchy *with* her." He makes some gesture with his hands. "I'd like a turn tapping her sweet ass. Maybe you can introduce us, cuz. What do you say?"

Confirming he's Sergio's bitch, the white guy laughs the loudest.

"Do I know you?" I ask him. He shuts up.

I stare hard at Sergio. I'm not his "bro" or his "cuz." And I sure as hell ain't his bitch. One more word about Emmy.

"You look like you could use a cold one," Ray says. I've only had three beers in my whole life. But I remember all three. I'm more tempted than usual.

I ask Ray if I can talk to him a second. I tell him about the funeral and how Emmy's mom is in town. I ask him to leave and come back next week. "No prob, cousin," he says. I hang back while he goes to his friends. They all three get into the Honda and leave. I meant Ray too.

I light another cigarette. "Great group of friends, Ray."

"You haven't exactly been around." That's true. "You missed the fucking Pow Wow. They called your dad's name, and Mom's."

His mom died of diabetes—an infection in her foot. White man's diseases are still killing off the natives: not smallpox and measles, but diabetes and alcoholism. "Ray. Sorry, man."

He shrugs. "I didn't really feel nothing this year when I heard her name."

Ray not feeling anything at all is worse than his wailing with the women, which he did the first year after his mom passed, but I don't say so. "Where's Benji?"

"Took off." I ask him where to. "Canada." I ask him for what. "Ecstasy."

"To sell on the rez?" Ray doesn't respond. "That's completely fucked," I say.

"Dad hooked him up."

My uncle. Dad's brother. The army vet who flies an enormous American flag outside his rez house to piss off the real traditionals. He used to travel around helping other vets on different reservations. "You want to stay here tonight, Ray?" I feel bad having asked him to leave.

"I'm meeting Sergio in an hour."

"Just stay here, bro. Teresa will be home." I try to entice him. "In her scrubs."

"Next week, cuz. Like you said." I've never asked Ray to leave before, no matter who I'm hanging with. I offended him. Shit.

"Come on, Ray, brother. Please." I speak to him in our native tongue. He answers in English, then leaves.

I leave too, before Emmy and her family return. I drive to the Columbia. Chief Moses lost both his heirs—nephews, because he had no sons of his own—in the Columbia. They both drowned, drunk. Both times Moses remained by the shore, waiting for the river to release their bodies, and both times it did.

Teresa loved to tease Dad, when she got older, that he married *into* the Moses band, not rescued her and Mom *from* it. Dad claimed to have stolen Mom and Teresa in a horse raid. They were hiding under a blanket and he just scooped them right up.

My dad's favorite leader wasn't Tonasket, the Okanogan leader and respected rancher. Nor was it Skolaskin, whom Moses got jailed, though Moses was also shackled twice in Yakima. It was another Sanpoil leader, Chief Jim James. He was the chief who witnessed firsthand the inundation of Kettle Falls in 1939. But not before he oversaw

("with sad dignity," whites claim—fuck them) the removal of generations of Indian bones in the wooden boxes the government so gener-
ously provided. Losing the falls ruined my people. We deeply offended
the Great Spirit. The Sky Chief. We still dance and pray for forgive-
ness, for healing.

I wait by the silent river. I'm hungry. I had cereal for breakfast, but
no lunch or dinner. I could use a burger. I wait. The sun starts to set.
Moses was called Half Sun. I smoke my last cigarette. My hunger
deepens and brings with it fear, instead of clarity. *Dad?* He never
shows up when I need him most. What am I waiting for the river to
release? Dad's waywardness? His drunkenness? Moses's drunkenness?
Half Sun's people? My people? Our pain? My life before Emmy? My
life after she leaves? My hunger? My thirst?

I drum. I keep my hand drum in my truck. I have yet to show it to
Emmy.

Coyote's thirst was so great that he created the Columbia, but then
he tried to drink so much of the river water that he lost consciousness.
He woke up in the swift river and was afraid. Moses's beloved nephews never woke up. My dad—*come on, I need you*—regained full consciousness in the hospital many times before he died, which baffled
the doctors. It was like Fox was there, stepping over him three times,
which is the only way Coyote survived to finish his job of readying
earth for the coming humans. I'm still baffled to this day as to why the
fuck my dad was riding around with a drunk white woodcutter. Hell,
Dad probably got the guy drunk. My dad needed cash, no doubt. My
old man, who sometimes worked cutting trees for the tribal mill and
for the tribal fire department, was as good with a chain saw as he was
with a fishing pole, a dip net, a bow, a rifle, a horse. I miss him so
much. He had this way of making me feel things were going to be all
right, even when I knew they weren't—like now—even when I knew
he was leaving again or about to get busted. He never got arrested by
the feds, just the tribal cops, who didn't like locking him up. One
tribal court advocate told Mom, who rolled her eyes, that Dad's spirit
was just too big to lock up. They tried to "make him whole" through
other means. He was even sent to pick berries one time like a chick

and another time to build a sweat lodge. Maybe he's made his peace, though not with me, and crossed over at last.

I miss you, Dad. I've missed you my whole life.

Spencer's SUV isn't in front of the Millers' trailer when I return, but Matt's truck is there. I go over. "Emmy left already," Matt says. "She didn't want to."

"I'm really sorry about your wife." It's way too soon to speak the name of the dead.

He nods. I turn to go. "Reuben?" I turn back. "Emmy says you kids want to have a talk with me and Kate in the morning. She won't let Emmy stay."

"I have to try."

"I respect that."

"I love your niece, very much."

"I know." He looks like he wants to say more, maybe give me some advice. I'd take it. But he doesn't. He buried the love of his life today.

Emmy calls me around midnight from the hotel. She sounds young and so far away, already. If she does leave, I'll never be able to talk on the phone with her. She asks me to sing to her like I did that night at my great-aunt's house when Ray drummed. But I can't. She asks me to tell her a story in my native language. It comes out mostly in English. I tell her how Coyote traveled up the rivers with the salmon, a new food source. Whenever he proposed to a beautiful maiden and was refused by the maiden's parents or by the maiden's tribe, he created natural dams or barricades in the river to keep the salmon from going up any farther. Coyote would swear that tribe would tip many canoes and wear out their moccasins to get enough salmon to survive.

Kate and Spencer bring maple bars and juice. We sit at the table in Matt's kitchen, each of us with a glass of OJ and a maple bar on a plate. Emmy and I scoot close. Spencer makes a quick phone call after his beeper goes off, something about an engineer and a permit. All the hanging bundles of herbs have been removed, but I can still smell them. The note cards with Bible verses have also been taken down. The kitchen and living room blinds are wide open, giving a rather stark look to the place. Kate's tenser than Spencer and Matt, who make small talk for a few minutes. No one eats or drinks. Kate asks Spencer to shut off his beeper. He says he already did. "Mom." Emmy finally begins. "I want to stay in Moses Lake for my senior year. If Matt will let me live here with him. Will you, Uncle Matt?"

"Are you joking, Emmy?" It's Kate. She looks at me. "Did you put her up to this?"

"I want Emmy to stay," I say. We hold hands under the table.

"It was *my* idea, Mom. He never asked me to." That's true, even though I wanted to a hundred times. "Can I, Uncle Matt?"

Matt takes off his ball cap.

"Your uncle has no say in the matter," Kate says. "And the answer is no."

"I'm not going back to California." Emmy lets go of my hand, so she can use both to argue. "And you *can't* make me."

"I damn well *can*."

Spencer moves his arm off the back of Kate's chair—as if to separate himself from her abrupt harshness.

"I'm not leaving Reuben. We love each other. Tell her, Uncle Matt."

"They're in love, Kate." He puts his cap back on. "I know that much."

"And you condone this?" Kate asks him.

"I condone love." He slides the plate away. "Your sister and I married at their age."

"But we want more for Emmy, right?"

"More than love?" Matt says.

"Neither Beth nor I finished high school. You, Matt, had to go to work full time sorting potatoes at seventeen." Spencer looks uncomfortable. Maybe he should go wait in his fancy SUV. She turns on me. "Where do you work, Reuben?"

"He chops wood," Emmy replies before I can. Fuck. I wince. "For the elders on the reservation. And he hunts for them. And last summer he worked road construction, and this summer he's babysitting for his sister, who is a single mom like you. And I've never had a real job, Mom, just volunteer work for school clubs. We're the exact same age."

Emmy needs a drink after all that and takes a swallow of her juice.

"Reuben's a great kid," Matt says. "I've seen him grow up. If I'd had a son—" He takes a second. "I would've wanted him to be just like this boy."

That's quite a compliment. I wish Matt would look at me, so I could nod.

Kate tears her maple bar in half, but then doesn't take a bite from either side. "As touching as that is, Matt," she says, "and it *is*—"

"Kate," Spencer says. "Let's give the kids a chance to finish talking."

"—they'd be wasting their breath." She pushes her chair back suddenly and stands up. "There's no way Emmy is staying here. Sorry, but I've worked too hard."

"I saw my dad," Emmy says.

Oh, shit.

"What did you just say?" Kate asks, gripping the edge of the table for obvious support. Spencer leans forward.

"I said I saw my dad. Guess what? He's not dead. I saw his farm. I saw his boys."

"Emmy," Kate says. She tries to sit back down but almost falls. Spencer helps her. "What, Emmy?" Tears start pouring from her eyes. She doesn't try to restrain them. "His *boys*?"

"That's right." Emmy pauses to down her OJ. Everyone watches her. I take a drink of mine to distract them. "Two boys," she says, after almost slamming down the empty glass. "It turns out I have two younger brothers. He went right on living without you."

"Emmy," I say. Christ. I didn't know she had a cruel bone in her body. She looks at me. I shake my head.

"You saw Jamie?" Kate asks, finally wiping her eyes.

"I did, and he looked happy."

"Enough, Emmy." It's Matt, and his tone is firm. "That man caused your mom more grief than you'll ever realize."

"Did he ask about me?" Kate says. She touches her hair.

"He called you *Katie*."

"Come on, Emmy," Spencer says. He's irked. He takes Kate's hand away from her hair. My body gets tenser, if possible.

"Aren't you going to tell Spencer to stay out of it, *Katie*, like in Sac?" She takes a big bite of her maple bar.

This is definitely a side of Emmy I haven't seen before, and neither has her mom, judging from the look on Kate's face.

"I need some air," Spencer says. He gets up and goes to the front door, but then he turns around and comes back, hesitating before sitting down.

Everyone but Emmy, including me, has by now pushed away the food and drink.

"Not to worry, Mom. Your shy little girl just threw up in his driveway, then left."

"Oh, Emmy." Kate covers her mouth as if she herself were about to throw up. If it wasn't for Spencer's bling on her finger, I'd feel sorry for her. No, I still do. It would've killed Mama Marie had Dad gone off and made a new family. "I'm sorry, honey," Kate says. "I'm truly sorry—for everything. For my lies, my—"

"Then let me stay here. I loved Aunt Beth so much."

"I know you did."

"I can replant her garden, which I tore up. Let me stay."

Kate starts shaking her head.

"I love Uncle Matt and Reuben. I can go to high school *here* every day with Reuben."

"I'm sorry, no."

"He'll protect me, Mom."

"How?" Her abruptness is back. *"How,* Emmy?"

"He's my best friend," Emmy says. I take her hand, on top of the table this time. It's a bit sticky from the maple bar. "He'd never let anyone hurt me."

"Are the two of you using protection?" Kate asks.

Damn. I let go of Emmy's hand.

"Yes, Mom. As a matter of fact." Emmy picks up her maple bar as if to take another big bite but drops it back down instead and pushes the plate hard toward her mom. Matt puts out his hand and intercedes.

"And by the way, Mom, I *wasn't* a virgin when you sent me here. I had a boyfriend at school. We had sex every week in his bedroom." Spencer and Matt cringe. I cringe. "So, you see, I'm a big liar, just like you. Aunt Beth thought I was a Christian and a virgin. I'm neither. I thought my dad was dead, killed by a monster tractor. I used to have nightmares. Reuben is different from Connor. He—"

"Connor?" Kate interrupts. "A smug boy by that name called the apartment three times last month for you."

"Why didn't you tell me?"

"Does it matter, Emmy?" I ask, and she quickly shakes her head. She's not derailed. "Reuben is kind, Mom. He wants to protect me."

"Jamie said he'd protect me also, honey," Kate says. "I wound up working at a truck stop café." She looks briefly at Matt, then takes a deep breath. "And not just waiting tables."

"What do you mean?" Emmy asks.

"Kate," Spencer says. "She's *way* too young to hear this."

"Apparently not," Kate argues.

"Hear what?" Matt says, sitting up extremely straight.

Spencer again tries to intervene.

"I apologize, Matt," Kate says, "for what I'm about to confess."
She pauses.

"What, Mom? Did you also wash dishes or something?"

"I slept with truckers for money. In the parking lot."

Fuck. I did *not* see that one coming.

"What?" Matt stands up. "Did Beth know?" Kate doesn't reply. "Did my wife know?" he demands. Kate slowly nods. "But she never told me."

"Oh, Matt, trust me. Beth wanted to. I made her promise to *never* tell you."

"You were a prostitute, Mom?"

Spencer shifts in his chair. Matt sits back down, looking defeated.

"Yes, Emmy, when I was only a year or two older than you."

That's pretty shocking. Emmy starts crying. "Is that why you underlined all those verses about harlots in your old Bible?"

Kate nods. "The point is, honey, your dad said he'd take care of me, but he *didn't*. I needed money."

"I could've borrowed money," Matt says.

"Your parents had done enough."

I have to butt in. "I would never let that happen to Emmy," I say. "Never." Or my mom—who sleeps with assholes, but never for money.

"Jesus Christ, Kate," Matt says. He's completely stunned. "I should've known."

I hadn't meant to imply Matt *let* it happen.

"The signs were there," Matt says, as if thinking out loud. He's in a fog, or a fog just cleared. "The extra cash, the bruises."

"Bruises?" Emmy asks. "What bruises?"

"I'm sorry," Matt says.

"No," Kate replies with as much emotion in her voice as when she read that beach poem. "You were great to me, Matt. Don't you under-stand, without you—" She can't finish.

"If I was so great, why didn't you tell me?"

"There was *nothing* you could've done."

"What?" He snaps. "You think I could've done *nothing*?" He hits the table but not hard enough to make anyone jump. "Why the hell didn't Beth tell me?"

He'd be heartbroken if he weren't already.

"I asked Reuben to get me pregnant," Emmy interrupts again. "So we could stay together." All eyes shift to her. "He refused. He's not like Jamie, Mom. He's not an asshole. He's the complete opposite. I'm sorry my dad did that to you. Fuck Jamie Kagen and his wheat." She falters. She loved her dad's wheat fields. So much she couldn't look as I drove her away from them. "But it's not *my* fault. Reuben and I just want to go to high school together."

Kate looks directly at me, and only me, but not in a threatening way. She sees further into me than I'm comfortable with. I don't look away or flinch. I try not to see Emmy in her, even though of course there's a resemblance, never more apparent. There's a similar curiosity and loneliness in Kate's and Emmy's eyes. But Kate is a brute.

"Can I talk to you alone, Reuben?" she asks.

"No way," Emmy says. She grabs my hand.

"Sure," I say.

"Is this necessary, Kate?" Matt asks, but she doesn't reply. "Spencer?" he tries.

Spencer's been rendered speechless for a while. He probably won't be visiting another trailer park anytime soon. I don't know, though, if I could date an ex-hooker, let alone ask her to marry me. I give him credit for sticking around. It's got to be a bit humbling.

"No, it's *not* necessary," Emmy replies. "It's absurd. Anything you have to say to Reuben, Mom, you can say in front of me."

"It's okay, Emmy," I say. "I'm a big boy." And scared shitless.

"Let's take a walk, Reuben." Kate stands up.

"No," Emmy says. I let go of her hand and stand up. She stands up. "No." She pulls my arm. She whispers into my ear, "She'll persuade you not to love me."

"She can't." I kiss her on the cheek.

"Mom. Don't do this." She turns to Matt. "He's my only friend, Uncle Matt. My best friend. Spencer, please. *Spencer.*"

He finds his voice. "Kiddo, I—"

Something about the way Emmy asked Spencer for help puts me into action. "Give me a minute," I say to Kate. I take Emmy into the bedroom without asking permission. "Emmy," I say, holding her face. Her breath smells like maple. "You have to trust me." She looks so scared. Her hair is a wreck, falling loose in chunks from the fancy braid she must've tried to weave herself this morning. She could braid Audrey's hair, but she still needed her aunt's help with her own. "We've been through a lot," I say. "We can get through this." I put my hand on her lower belly. "Someday." She knows what I mean.

Kate and I walk down the road, the same direction Emmy and I used to, toward the hay bales. Kate finds a good place to stop, where she can lean on the fence. Irrigation sprinklers are clicking away in the potato field. How fitting. The flowers are gone, and the plants are now about knee high.

"First, Reuben, let me say thanks."

Why is she thanking me? For not knocking up her daughter? "For?"

"For being Emmy's friend."

"Don't thank me for that." I refuse to lean on some farm fence with her.

"And for helping Matt."

"Again, don't." I put up my hand. I'm going to try to be as frank with Kate as she is with everyone. "I didn't do either of those for you."

"I have a *lot* of respect for what you've accomplished so far in your life," she says. She stops leaning on the fence so she can face me. "Matt has filled me in. But I'm sure as a white man he doesn't know the half."

"I haven't had it that bad." And isn't she white?

"Or that easy."

A car is coming down the road toward us. I stand with my back to the road, my heels on the pavement to put as much space between Kate and me as possible. Kate actually reaches for my arm and pulls me from the edge of the road. I almost stiffen and refuse to budge, but I decide to choose my battles.

"I don't pity you," she says after the car passes. "You have too much pride for that."

"You don't know anything about my pride. What do you want, Kate?"

"I want you to let Emmy go." Her eyes are relentless.

"I'm not holding her."

"You've been holding her all summer, it seems."

"Don't make it sound dirty. I love Emmy. She doesn't have any friends in California. Why should she go back?"

"To finish high school."

"She can finish it here."

"With you?"

"I do great in school, Professor. Believe it or not—even an Indian."

"Oh, I believe it. Some of my smartest and hardest-working students are ethnic kids."

"Emmy and I can get through high school together."

"She needs to be in California," Kate says. "I'm sorry. But that's her home."

"No, this is her home."

As if on cue, a truck with a ridiculous six-inch lift kit passes by with country music blaring. The asshole driver has on a sleeveless camo shirt and an enormous wad of chew in his lower lip. He revs his engine as he passes by us, but he also nods—probably at Kate, who'd be easy on the eyes if she wasn't such a bitch.

"You're wrong, Reuben. Emmy was born here, but she doesn't remember it."

She turns back to the fence and leans on it with both arms, studying the field.

"She does." I join her on the fence in case it will help my argument. "She's part of this land. You should see her by the Columbia."

"I worked hard to get Emmy and me out of here," she says. "Away from poverty and the church and rednecks."

"That's not all there is here."

"No. There's you."

"Yes, I'm here. My people have been here a long time."

"Your people are suffering."

Damn. I step away from the fence for good. "Yes, but we've survived." And when Coyote returns, he'll set things right again. He'll break down Grand Coulee Dam.

"I want more for Emmy than survival." Kate also turns from the fence. "In California she can thrive."

"She wasn't thriving. She was lonely as hell. That's why she let her fuckhead ex-boyfriend do things to her—well, you don't even want to know."

That shuts her up for a moment. "Spencer and I are getting married." She twists her engagement ring. "He built a house—a *home* for Emmy and me. It's beautiful. We're going to be a family. Emmy has always wanted a dad. Spencer loves her like a daughter. He always has."

"I love her more."

She looks at me. "You just might." She pauses, and I think *maybe.*

"But you can't provide for her." I should've known. She's just getting started.

A car passes by, slowing down to gawk. Kate waves it on before I can. That's probably more traffic than there's been on this road all summer.

"You're only a kid," she continues. "You need to finish high school yourself. You need to take care of yourself *first*."

"She's part of me."

"Emmy has a chance to go to U.C. Berkeley, one of the best colleges in the country. She's been on track since sixth grade. She's worked her butt off. She's the vice president of three different clubs at her high school—not an easy task when she goes to school with state politicians' kids. If you know what I mean." I don't. "She's been on the academic decathlon team for years and won medals. Did she tell you *any* of this?"

I shake my head. Kate should know her daughter better than to think she'd ever brag about anything. Academic decathlon? What the hell is that?

"She's in the top five percent of her high school," Kate continues. "That practically guarantees her a place in the University of California system. A top system by world standards. Do you want to take that opportunity away from her?"

"That's an unfair question."

"I came from here. I don't know what it's like to be a Native American youth, but I know what it's like to come from nothing."

"I don't come from nothing." How dare she. I take back my thoughts about her attractiveness. That redneck would've nodded at a female skunk.

Hell, Indians nod at our animal ancestors.

"I didn't mean it that way," she says. "I'm very sorry." Again she pauses. "I'm sorry." She regroups. "For sixteen years I've worked to give Emmy more than Beth or I ever had. More than we could have imagined: education, art, culture, travel." She counts on her fingers. "They have travel abroad programs at Berkeley, and not just to Europe, but Asia, India. And Spencer has money."

"Money isn't everything."

"It certainly isn't. But education *is.*"

I wish another car would pass by.

"Are you marrying Spencer for his money?"

She doesn't get mad. "I could've married that man years ago for his money." She twists her bling ring again. "I love him. I'm tired of my pride, and I'm tired of being afraid."

Kate afraid? I seriously doubt it.

"Spencer's a good man. He works hard. Emmy can have the world at Berkeley. She just has to reach out and take it. She won't, though, if you don't let her go."

I hate Kate. "You say that as if it were a choice. As if love were a choice."

"You can choose to let her go. *That's* a choice."

"And you think she'll be happy back in California?"

"Not at first, no. She'll be miserable for a time. We are going to get her into counseling for her shyness and to help her with grief over Beth."

"A shrink? Emmy doesn't need a fucking shrink. She needs *me.*"

"And if something happens to you? She needs to learn to stand on her own two feet."

That sounds like Teresa.

"You are one to talk," I say. "Emmy grew up terrified you might die and leave her all alone. It practically paralyzed her."

"I've definitely made mistakes with Emmy. Big mistakes." She sighs. "I'm going to do better. She has to come home to California."

"This is her home." I start to cry. I can't help it. "Her home is with me."

"Not yet, Reuben."

She's right. She's fucking right. Damn. She is so right. Fuck. Fuck me. There's no fucking way I am going to hold Emmy back from college in California. Maybe I knew this all summer. I start to walk off, farther up the road toward the hay bales. I'm losing Emmy. I lost.

"Reuben." Is she actually following me?

"Leave me alone."

"Where are you going?"

"As if you give a shit."

"I do."

"I'll make you a deal, Kate." I turn back. "I'll let Emmy go. You quit acting like you care about me. Like I'm one of your fucking ethnic students." I take a deep breath, or I try to. It's suddenly hard. "And you leave me the fuck alone."

Emmy finds me, not on top of the hay bales but behind them. I don't want the view from the top. I sit with my back against the hay and my knees up. My head is in my hands. It's never been so difficult to breathe. The lack of oxygen gives me a headache, and my body is cramping. When I first heard Emmy's footsteps, I thought maybe it was my dad. But why would he show up now, when I need him the very most of all? He warned me about today. I guess he feels that was enough.

"Reuben." She kneels in front of me. "I'm *not* leaving."

"Yes, you are," I say. "Don't touch me." I'll have to be a total asshole to Emmy to get her to leave. I can't let her touch me, or I may falter.

"What did Mom say? She's a liar, remember?"

"Don't touch me. I hurt all over." My head. My arm. Both arms. My whole body. The pain is intense.

"She can't make me leave."

"I want you to leave, Emmy." I can't look her in the eyes. "You have to go back to California. It's your home."

"That's a lie. She's a liar. *This* is my home. You know that." She's crying. "You are the only one who *ever* knew that. How can you say otherwise?"

"Because it's true." I force myself to look at her. "You don't belong here."

"You don't mean that, Reuben." The panic in her eyes and the way she doesn't know what to do with her hands—my body can't take any more. *Help me, Dad.* She smiles. Why does she smile? I love her fucking smile, and she knows it. Jesus, I hurt. "Look what I made you," she says, pulling an origami fish from her pocket, as if we were just hanging out. How did she not crush it? "It's a salmon. See?"

It's beautiful—like all her paper creations, only more so. She tries to hand it to me, but I won't take it. "It's a retarded salmon," I say, "from a hatchery." I have to be brutal. "It'll never find its way."

That did the trick. She's too shocked to speak. If only she'd get up and walk away, find the strength to tell me to fuck off. Instead she starts unfolding the paper salmon, carefully, slowly, which is far worse than her just wadding it up in a ball.

I need to make this quick. But time seems to be unfolding with that paper fish. We're back in her aunt's garden, the first day we met, only my head pounds.

"I was born here," she had said.

"No shit."

"That's the first swearword I've heard all week."

"My apologies."

"No. It's refreshing."

Wait. I close my eyes. Wait. I press my temples with my palms. I groan in pain. "I wish you'd never come." And maybe at that very moment, I really did wish that. "You don't belong here." No white people do. This is *our* land. It was the Whitmans who brought the whites. Emmy touched the wagon grooves with her palms.

"I was born here," she says. Like the Whitman child. The Cayuse loved the Whitman child because she was born here. They called her "Cayuse Girl." She spoke their language as naturally as she did English. "I was born here."

"Stop, Emmy." I look at her.

"If I don't belong *here*," she says, remaining oddly calm, "I don't belong *anywhere*. I can't live without you, Reuben. I need you. You are my very best friend, remember?" She sounds so young. She tries to take my hand, to give me the unfolded fish. "Remember?" She smiles again. I'm powerless for a second and let her touch me.

But then I jump up. *Dad, please.*

"No, don't," she says, the panic returning. "Don't get up. I won't touch you again. Here, I'll wad up the stupid fish." She does and throws the ball of paper. "We don't have to be boyfriend and girlfriend." She stumbles trying to get to her feet. I don't help her. "But be my friend. Just be my friend."

"It's over, Emmy. Go home."

"I *am* home." A flash of anger. I wish she had more.

"If you won't leave, then I will. Good-bye, Emmy."

"No, Reuben." She tries to hug me. I push her away. *Dad.* "You need me," she says. "You need me to love you." I shake my head. "Take me with you to the reservation," she begs between sobs. Her braid is completely undone. "Let's run away." Her voice pitches. "We can hide there."

"Whites can't hide there." I try to look disgusted as I push her away more firmly. "And I *don't* need you."

She crumples to the ground.

But she'll get back up. I tell myself this as I turn and start to walk away. Then run. She'll get back up and return to California. She'll go to Berkeley and to India. Emmy may have stepped into my clearing. I may be hungry, even starving, but I won't shoot.

18

Matt

Emmy flies off the front porch to find Reuben when her mom comes walking back without him. Kate tries to stop her, but Emmy won't hear of it. I miss Beth like crazy, but I'm glad she's not here today to witness this fighting. What did Kate say to that boy?

"Kate," I say as she climbs the steps. I'm still trying to digest what she revealed about her past an hour ago. I can't help feeling responsible. It's like a rock in my gut.

"I'm mad at you," she says, never one to hold back. "How could you let those kids get *that* close?" She appears shaken and sits down on the stool where I plop twice a day to put on and take off my work boots. "You knew Emmy had to come home at the end of summer." She rubs her forehead.

"Kate, not even *you* could've stopped Emmy from falling for that boy."

Spencer opens the door before she can respond. He's been pacing inside, giving Emmy and me the porch. "Come in here, Kate," he says. "We need to talk." She goes inside.

I wanted to be mad at her when she showed up here too late to see her sister. Kate and Beth are as different as two sisters can be. But Christ, I saw Beth in Kate when I walked into the house three days ago. My anger disappeared.

Before Kate gave birth, the three of us had some nice evenings, despite her being heartbroken. I felt proud going to work for both sisters, even if it was just to sort potatoes. Kate can be lively and funny. She called me spud stud back then. She felt bad that I supported her. I called her front-end loader. But I was only joking. She got the waitressing job as soon as she was physically able. Emotionally she wasn't prepared to be out in the world. The church likes to keep girls and women that way. It's not *my* church anymore. Kate must've been mortified the first time a trucker propositioned her. I remember hoping Kate's new waitressing job would help her get over Kagen. I was an idiot. What a secret for someone like Beth to have borne all those years. *You should've told me, darling.*

Oh, no, here comes Reuben without Emmy. Something isn't right. He wouldn't leave her on the side of the road. I meet him at his truck. "Stay back, Matt." He's clearly upset.

"Where's Emmy?"

"I didn't mean anything I just said to her." He's so tense that he's rigid. "You believe me, right? I didn't mean a word of it. I had to say it."

"*Where* is Emmy?"

"At the hay bales. Let me leave before you go get her. Please. She has to think I meant it. Please."

"You can't leave her this way, Reuben. We'll figure something out."

"It's over." He breaks down.

I don't know what to do. So I do what I'd do if he were my nephew or my son. I hug him.

He lets me for a second longer than I expected, and then he pulls away abruptly. "I have to go. Let me run inside and get my keys. Give me one second." He does. He grabs nothing else. Then he drives away. Does he even have any money?

I find Emmy behind the hay bales. She's in a ball. I squat down beside her. "Emmy, sweetie, come back to the house." I touch her back. "Emmy?"

"I don't want to go back to California." She looks at me. "Why can't I live with you?"

"If it were up to me, you could."

"Reuben dumped me."

"He didn't." I sit down.

She nods. "He did." She looks terrible. There's straw in her hair and dirt on her face, and her eyes are red and swollen.

"He didn't want to."

"But he did." She smiles, which seems odd. She seems odd right now. "I didn't want to call you and Beth aunt and uncle when I first heard about you guys. I'm sorry about that. I love you both." She smiles again. "I'm sorry, Uncle Matt."

"Stop apologizing." She's worrying me. "Are you okay?"

"I'm sorry I wasn't a virgin for that ceremony."

"Oh, Emmy. It doesn't matter."

"I gave Beth false hope."

"You gave her real love. You made her happy." Happier than I could.

"I want her. I used to pretend I had relatives." She laughs strangely. "I'd tell kids at school that I was at my grandma's house all weekend in San Francisco or that my new shoes were from my aunt in Fresno. Especially after holidays, I'd lie. Isn't that stupid? I'm such a liar."

"No, you're not." I could kill Kagen, I swear.

"Why would God take Beth away from me when I barely had her? Why?"

If God, with his "infinite wisdom and mercy," didn't see fit to give Beth what she wanted most in this world, and what she was slowly killing herself trying to get, maybe I should be thankful he finally "called her home." Now she can rest. No more herbs. No more blood. Emmy told me about the warnings in the library books. In some ways Beth was never of this world.

"I don't know why, sweetheart."

"I want my aunt. She loved me the most." She sounds about seven years old.

"We *all* love you, Emmy."

"I thought Reuben loved me the most. But he doesn't love me at all."

"Yes, he does."

She shakes her head.

"Did he tell you he didn't?" I ask.

She thinks for a second. "No, but he said he didn't need me, which is the same thing." It kind of is. "I want to go to bed." She tries to get up but can't. Her legs must be asleep. I get up and help her stand. "I want to go to bed at your house, in the room with my old crib. I want to go to sleep there. *Not* at the hotel."

That room—Emmy's bedroom by every definition—has always been too painful for Beth and me to use. Which is why Beth kept her sewing machine and I store my fly-tying station in the master bedroom. Beth used to keep the night-light glowing in Emmy's room during her short pregnancies. But that stopped, I guess, when she stopped wanting me to know.

"Come on then, sweetie."

"Don't make me talk to Mom." She grabs my arm. "I hate her. Just let me lie down."

I try, but Kate ambushes us. We're all four in the living room. Kate insists Emmy talk to her right now. Spencer is beyond frustrated, standing with his hands on his hips. His beeper sounds, and he actually throws it out the front door. He and I both tell Kate to let the girl rest awhile first before talking.

"Look at her, Kate," I say. "You've done enough to her and Reuben for one day."

Spencer takes Emmy's arm out of her mom's grip. "You're crossing the line," he says to Kate. He safely escorts Emmy into the bedroom and closes the door.

Kate turns on me. "You men. What the fuck do you know?"

"Shut up, Kate."

She looks at me. "I think I will." She sits on the couch. "I don't know what comes over me."

I sit in my recliner. "Don't fuck it up with Spencer."

"You mean like I fucked it up with Jamie?"

"You know I don't think that. Can't you hear yourself? I'm not the bad guy. You should've told me."

"Told you what?" She implores me with her eyes not to bring up what I'm about to.

"About the truckers. I could've borrowed money or gotten a second job."

"You were lucky to get the job you had."

She's right. Full-time factory jobs around here can be tough to secure, especially at seventeen. I put my head in my hands.

"Please don't blame yourself, Matt. It wasn't just the money. I'd been called a whore. I was shunned by the very people who watched me grow up. I was too young to handle it all. Too young to know that I really *wasn't* what they said I was. I wanted to destroy myself. I wanted to forget Jamie."

We sit for a moment in silence. Quietly I ask, "How did Beth handle knowing what you were doing?"

"It hurt her terribly, as you can imagine. That's why—" She pauses, which, when it comes to Kate, can't be good. "That's why she finally told me to go make a new life somewhere with Emmy."

"She didn't."

"She did, Matt. My leaving here was *her* idea."

"That makes no sense." But of course it makes perfect sense. All along I'd thought Kate left of her own accord. *Beth.*

"Don't tell Emmy," Kate says. She wipes her eyes, which are filled with tears, as are mine. "It would crush her, especially now, to learn Beth had *anything* to do with the two of them being separated."

What I wouldn't give to be out in my boat right now, to find a secluded cove on Lake Roosevelt to camp for a day or two with my tent, cooler, and barbecue. I always wanted to take Beth to a cove for a weekend, or even just one night, to zip our sleeping bags together and hold my wife under the stars.

Kate speaks. "Do you ever regret the day you came walking into that crazy church—was it with your pudgy cousin Randy or Ralphy? Reggie?" She's trying to lighten the mood a bit.

"Only when I'm around you. Never around Beth. Or Emmy."

"Nice."

"What did you say to Reuben?"

"What any parent would, I suppose."

"Help me out here, Kate."

"That my daughter has to finish high school."

"Why not here?"

"The requirements and standards are different in each state." She sounds like a teacher. "Emmy's on track for college in California. U.C. Berkeley."

"Berkeley? Don't the students there hang out in trees protesting all day?" Kate laughs. "That seems a bit much for Emmy." She doesn't respond. "Well, doesn't it?"

"Academically, no. She's in the top of her class."

No wonder the kid needed a desk in the bedroom. I never studied over summer break—seems against nature.

"Emmy's smarter than I am already," Kate says. "And I have a master's degree."

"I'm proud of you for that, by the way." She thanks me. I tell her, "I tried to get Beth to get her GED in case something happened to me." Kate looks at me in a way that tells me she never thought about that scenario. But I certainly did. I took out extra life insurance policies on myself without Beth's knowing. I worked out plans with my parents and siblings.

Before Kate can respond, Spencer comes out of the bedroom. "Let's go for a beer, Matt," he says.

"Matt doesn't drink," Kate says. "And it's only noon."

"It's never too early to start with you around," he says. I think he's joking, but I can't be sure. And a beer sounds excellent. I've had beers over the years with my family. My sister gets a kick out of my having a margarita with her every year on her birthday. Just one. Beth never asked, so I never lied. I never asked her if Kate was hooking, so Beth never lied. I get up.

"Don't go into that bedroom," Spencer says to Kate. "Emmy's sleeping." Kate starts to protest. "I mean it. Leave *our* daughter alone."

I like that. Spencer really loves Emmy. I'm jealous of the four years he's had with her.

"Ready, Matt?"

"What am I supposed to do," Kate asks, but I think she's also joking, "while you asshole men are off drinking?"

"Start peeling potatoes for dinner," Spencer says. He grins at me but not at her.

We spend a few hours in a restaurant bar. One thing about beer, it's never overrated. We talk about my job, his job, the 1979 NBA championship, which the Sonics won. Has it been almost twenty years? We talk about my family, Beth, Kate. Spencer is smooth with the female bartender without flirting. Three different ladies approach him. He lets them down easy, but again without flirting. I'm impressed and *way* out of my league. I get uneasy when he leaves to make a call after his beeper goes off. It had taken us a few minutes to find it in the yard. Spencer offers me his condolences several times and also a job in Sacramento. He says if I don't want to work for him, he knows businesses hiring. The housing market is booming, and labor unions are looking for guys. I thank him but tell him it's too soon. He makes sure to tell me more than once that it's a standing offer.

Surprisingly, when we get back to the house, Kate is making food. "Don't worry, Matt," Spencer says when I tell Kate it smells good. "I've never had her cooking before either."

He goes to Kate and ruffles her hair with both his hands. They're a sexy couple. I don't know how else to describe it. Maybe it's the multiple beers talking.

Kate bought more beer at the store. She pops one open for me and one for her. I'm already light-headed. If only Beth could be here, minus the beer. How happy she'd be to cook in the kitchen with her sister. I try to not see Beth, gown bloody, smashing those bottles. I've never been more terrified in my life. And poor Emmy had to witness it.

The girl sleeps on. Kate has peeked in on her half a dozen times. Finally I take her some water and a small plate of her mom's stir-fry. "It's just me," I say. She sits up. "Drink this." She takes a few swallows. "Can you eat some?"

"I'm not hungry. Did Reuben call?"

"No, sweetie."

"I'm still tired." I leave the plate of food on the dresser. I ask Emmy if she wants me to turn on the night-light so the room's not so dark, but she says no.

"Leave Emmy here for the night," I tell Kate.

"So Reuben can come over?"

"Stop it. He's not coming over. He went back to the reservation."

"Not even to tell her good-bye?"

I shake my head. "It would hurt too bad."

"We'll be back in the morning," Spencer says. "Good night."

"Tell her she can call me, no matter how late," Kate says.

They leave. I take a few moments to regroup. Kate wasn't always such a bully, and she doesn't hold a candle to her dad. I think Kate not only armored but armed herself too heavily when she left here on that bus for California. Maybe she had to. If only Beth had inherited some of Kate's courage and kick, and Kate some of her sister's gentleness. I go in to Emmy. I make her sit up and drink a swallow of water. "Your aunt would want you to eat."

"She's not here. She left me. She left us. I wish Mom had died instead."

"You don't mean that."

"Maybe."

I grab the desk chair and place it close to the bed. I sit down in case she wants to talk some more. I can't look at the crib.

"Reuben knows how to be hungry," she says. "He said hunger is part of being Indian. I miss him." She still seems about seven. "But not as much as you miss Aunt Beth."

"I'll be okay."

"You *won't* be okay after I leave. You'll be all alone."

"I'll be okay if I know *you* are."

That's not what she wanted to hear. "I want to go to sleep."

I grab a beer from the fridge and head out front to drink it on the steps. I hear Reuben's nieces and nephews in the trailer next door. I see Teresa pass by the kitchen window. She doesn't see me because I turned off the porch light. Beth has been in the ground—unbelievable—for more than twenty-four hours. It seems longer. It seems shorter. *Beth.* I put my head down. *My journey without you has begun. Rest, my darling.*

Kate and Spencer arrive early. I have to admit that Emmy wouldn't eat last night. All morning she's been curled up under the covers, even her head. Spencer tries tempting Emmy with her favorite flavor of Ben & Jerry's. By noon we are all three exasperated. Emmy may be shy, but she's also stubborn. Kate goes in alone to be the heavy. At this point, whatever it takes to get Emmy to eat. It's been more than twenty-four hours.

"Enough, Emmy," we hear. "You have to get up. If you don't eat, you're going to get sick. We have to pack. We're leaving in the morning. I know you're hurting terribly, honey. Things will be better in California. Come on now and get up."

Spencer and I pace in the living room. Suddenly we hear movements and thuds. Would Kate actually drag Emmy out of bed?

"Spencer! Matt!" Kate calls. We both dash in there. Emmy sits in the corner, by the crib. On the bed and around the floor beside it are the paper birds from the mobile. Was Emmy sleeping with them? She wears the dress Beth made for her. She must've changed during the night, but she forgot to button the front. Her bra shows. Kate tries to reach and button the dress, but Emmy pushes her mom's hands away. Emmy looks up but makes no eye contact with anyone. She coughs. Her throat sounds parched. Then she gags. Spencer passes Kate the water glass so she can hand it to Emmy, but Emmy pushes it away abruptly, and it spills. "Damn it, Emmy," Kate says. "I'm your mother. We *have* to leave here." She sounds panicked.

This is the bedroom in which Kate slept off her hangovers and the bruises from truckers. No wonder she wants to leave. I always thought, back then, I was providing Kate a place of reprieve, and in some ways I guess I still was.

Emmy covers her ears and begins to rock back and forth.

"Give me a minute alone with Emmy," I say. "Shut the door." I kneel down beside her. "Do you want me to go get Reuben?" She makes eye contact with me. "Will you drink if I get him?" She nods. I gather up the paper birds and put them, for some reason, in the crib. Then I go into the living room. "Kate, I want you and Spencer to leave. And I don't just mean leave this house. I think you guys should leave Moses Lake."

"Without Emmy?" Kate asks. "No way. And where did she get that awful dress? Has she been wearing it all summer?"

"No, Kate, just for the healing. Beth made them matching dresses."

Spencer interrupts. "What were you saying about our leaving?"

I take a deep breath. "I think you should leave Emmy with me for one week. I'll get her on a plane back to California. She needs more time here."

"You mean with Reuben?"

"Yes, Kate, *with* Reuben. Is that so bad? She needs a proper good-bye. She needs to be around Beth's garden and her things for a little while longer."

"No," Kate says. "The sooner she gets back to California, the better."

"She can stay," Spencer says.

"No," Kate insists. "She is coming with us right now. Go get her, Spencer."

"Hell, no. I'm not dragging our daughter—"

"*Our* daughter?"

"You ever question that again," Spencer says, "and we're over." He means it.

"You owe me one, Kate," I say. "I'm not one for calling in favors. But you owe me."

Kate takes a minute.

"You saved my life, Matt. I've never forgotten. You took care of Emmy and me when nobody else would—not Dad or Jamie." She breaks and starts to cry. "I love you like a brother. But Emmy is *my* baby." She puts her hands on her belly. I remember how swollen it was. How miraculous Beth found it, and it absolutely was. "She's coming with me."

"I swear on your sister's grave—" I hate the sound of that. "I'll have Emmy on an airplane in one week. Reuben will make her go back. He already told her to leave and that he didn't need her. He did what *you* asked. She has to hear him say that was a lie."

"He'll ask her to stay." She looks desperate. She's met her match in Reuben, as far as sway with Emmy.

"He never did," I remind her. "He loves her enough to let her go. That's been proven. I beg you. Let me do this for Beth. Emmy's the only baby she and I ever held between us."

Kate's shoulders slump.

I pull out my last card, one I will never use again. "You didn't see what Emmy did that night, Kate. Her aunt smashing jars, gown bloody, hair all—"

Kate puts her hand up. "Stop." She puts both hands over her face.

"Nor did you see her in that hospital room, all the tubes and gauze. Emmy *did*. She can't leave here with those images still so fresh in her head."

"Okay," Kate murmurs. "Okay. She can stay for another week."

"You guys need to clear out of here right now. Reuben won't come back into town unless you're gone. Emmy won't drink until she sees Reuben."

Kate uncovers her face. For the first time I see her age, the wear. Life hasn't been any easier for Kate than it was for Beth.

"Our plane tickets aren't until tomorrow," she tries.

"We can stay in Spokane tonight," Spencer says. He told me over beers that it's been challenging from day one with Kate. "Matt, thanks." He shakes my hand. "There's no one in the world we trust more with Emmy than you. I'm really sorry about your wife. She sounded like a wonderful woman. The offer stands for work in California. Let's go, Kate."

Kate hugs me for a long time. "I'm sorry I didn't make it back in time." She kisses me on the mouth. Her breath is warm. "Take care of my little girl," she whispers. "Just like you used to. Just like you *always* took care of my little sister." She lets go of me and looks around the place. She closes her eyes. She's either praying or speaking to Beth. Her lips move.

Spencer puts his arm around her shoulder. If he can still be tender after this week, he's in it for the long haul. "Let's go, baby," Spencer says to Kate, nodding once more at me.

Teresa isn't home, so I go to the hospital where she works. I inquire at the front desk, then wait in the lobby. It's not in my nature to interrupt a person at her place of employment, but I don't know what else to do. "Matt?" Teresa looks surprised when she walks into the lobby.

"Hello, Teresa. I'm really sorry to bother you."

"What's the matter?" She takes off her nursing cap and points to a more private corner.

"Do you know where I can find Reuben?"

"I don't." She looks away.

"Please, Teresa. Emmy's messed up. She won't eat or drink."

"I'm sure he's not doing any better."

"He's stronger than she is."

"That's what people think," she says. "I happen to know otherwise."

"I'm going to the reservation to look for him."

"Don't go up there."

"I am."

She stares at me so hard I get even more uncomfortable. "Wait here," she says. "Let me make a phone call." She leaves. I'll be happy not to see the inside of a hospital for a while. How does Teresa do it every day? To feed her kids, I guess. Why doesn't she have a steady man? I've seen men of all colors hanging around her trailer over the years, but never for long. A man brought her a washer not that long ago. I've seen Indian men bring her fish. It's none of my business. She comes back with a slip of paper. "If my brother knew Emmy was suffering and I didn't help."

She hands me the paper. I almost hug her to show my appreciation, but her breasts are too large. Not that I've ever noticed, or I've always tried not to.

"He's never loved anyone like he loves that girl," she says. "It could ruin him."

She's absolutely right. It could. I'm overwhelmed for a minute. "I'll do what I can to help Reuben too," I say. She looks doubtful and puts her cap back on. "I promise you, Teresa."

"Try those two places first." She pulls a pair of plastic gloves from her pocket and puts them on. "There's no guarantee."

I head north, passing the lakes where Beth and I used to fish together when we were young. I pass Steamboat Rock. If I could go back to that last picnic there with Beth, I wouldn't leave her alone on that blanket. Goddamn it. I pass the park where the healing ceremony took place. Screw Brother Mathias. That bastard was so in love with my wife from the very beginning. He showed up at the hospital in Spokane. I didn't let him see Beth. What was it he said about her in the small waiting room when I thought I smelled alcohol on his breath? That she was "as the apple tree among the trees of wood." I more or less told him to fuck off. He said that had I come to him even once and asked him to counsel Beth to see a doctor, he would have. He said he left the South to get away from rituals like faith healings. He found them—what was the word? *Carnivalesque.* Would Beth have listened to him if he'd told her to see a doctor? My jealous pride. I let him perform the funeral service—out of guilt but also because he risked his ministry, which he's losing, for Beth. I don't blame Mathias for Beth's death. She was *my* responsibility. I take full blame. I couldn't save my wife, but I can help Emmy. And Reuben. I make it to Coulee Dam, and then I'm on the reservation.

I pass the tribal headquarters, with its BIA sign. The tiny town of Nespelem makes Quail Run Mobile Home Park look middle class. It's a long stretch to Omak, and I have to fight to keep my grief in check. I think about fishing—the sturgeon I fought once for two hours and over two miles of river. Suddenly the snow-covered Cascades are directly in front of me. For the first time their immensity humbles me. Christianity teaches there's a larger peace waiting for us above, and for Beth's sake, I hope so. But here on earth there are also things profound. Reuben's not at the old man's house where I check for him first. I decline the old man's invitation to "take a sweat" with him in his lodge, although I'm tempted. He says Reuben was there yesterday but was too upset. I return to Nespelem, then take a road over to highway 21, which follows the Sanpoil River. The valley here is pretty, but not necessarily the individual lots. I pull up to a trailer set back in pines and practically on the river. No other trailers are around for half a mile. There are a couple of rusted trucks, and Reuben's truck is parked off to the side, almost hidden.

An old lady answers the door. She looks frightened. I quickly ask for Reuben. She shakes her head and starts to shut the door. Does she speak English? I tell her Teresa sent me and that it's important. She studies me. "Out back," she finally says, and points for me to go around. "Wait." She calls me back to the doorstep. She disappears into the trailer, where I see the flickering light of her TV, but hear no sound. She returns with a plate of food covered with tinfoil. "He's been out there all night and day. You make him eat." She studies me again. "Wait." She comes back with another plate of food. "For you." I tell her thanks. "He's the best of all my boys. You make him eat."

"Yes, ma'am."

She says something to me in her native language, then slams the door.

I walk around the trailer and into the backyard and then through pines. I can hear the river. There's something haunting about this place. My brother and I have been fly-fishing on the upper Yakima a few times. We had to hire a guide. I got the same feeling in that canyon, but I attributed it to the Indian stories the guide told us about Sasquatch and little "stick people." My brother attributed the rumored noises at dusk and dawn to meth labs. I see a fire in a clearing. Reuben sits in a camp chair staring at the fire. He's not wearing a shirt. Empty beer cans litter the ground. He stands up when I get close. He saw me way back. "Those aren't mine," he says, and starts kicking the beer cans. He kicks them hard.

"It's okay, Reuben."

"No, see, it's not. See, I'm drinking water." There's a large water bottle by his camp chair. He grabs it. "See."

"I see it."

"For all the fucking good it's done me." He throws the water bottle into the trees. It thuds. Then he starts kicking the beer cans again. "These cans are my cousin's. These cans are my uncle's. These cans are my dad's. My grandfather's. My mom's. Her fucking white boyfriend's fucking beer cans. What the fuck was he doing here? What are you doing here?"

I put down the two plates of food on a log that looks like it seconds as a bench.

"You okay, kid?" He has his back to me. I didn't realize how much I care for the boy until seeing him like this.

"I need to clean this place up," he says, kicking more cans. "This whole fucking rez."

"Emmy's not okay either." He wants to keep his back to me. But he turns at her name. "She needs you, Reuben."

He starts laughing. "No fucking white girl on her way to Berkeley needs me."

"*She* does."

He laughs again. "Did you know Emmy speaks French? She's never even been to France, but she speaks it better than I speak my native language—the language of this land." He gestures around us. "The elders are always begging us kids to learn it before it dies with them." He says something in his native language, maybe to the elders. Maybe an apology.

I wait.

"Emmy wants to travel to France," he says. "Did you know?"

"I know she needs you."

"Sit down, Matt, if you want to have a council." I sit down in one of the other camp chairs. "You want a smoke?" He pulls a pack of cigarettes from the pocket of his baggy jeans. He doesn't normally wear his jeans so baggy. Not that it matters. Maybe they're not his.

"Sure, son," I say, "why not?" Did I just call him son? That's not going to go over well.

"*Son*. Let me think about that." He hands me a cigarette and then the lighter. He's acting as strange as Emmy. He adds a log to the fire, stirring the embers. He takes a few minutes. "Okay, Matt." He keeps his back to me. "You are the only fucking white man I will ever let call me that. But I still want to punch your fucking jaw."

"I love you, Reuben."

He turns. "Now why would you say that?" He looks at me. "Here, you know, at my fire? Can't you white people stay off our rez?"

"I'm not here as a white man." I take a deep puff of the cigarette. God, it's good.

"Well, you sure as hell ain't no Indian."

"Reuben, cut this shit out."

"I love you too, dude." He flops back into the chair. He takes a couple of deep breaths. "Why are you here, seriously?"

"I need your help with Emmy."

"I can't be anywhere near Kate."

"I sent her and Spencer away. Emmy is staying with me for one more week."

He shakes his head. "I still feel Kate close by."

"She and Spencer are in Spokane this evening, and then they fly out in the morning."

"Emmy's staying?"

"For one week only."

"I can't see her."

"She won't get off the floor. Or button her dress." He stands up, starts pacing. He kicks another beer can. "She hasn't eaten," I continue. "And she drank only a few swallows of water yesterday. None today. Only you can make her drink."

"I can't. Shit. I mean—" He rolls his shoulders as if they were stiff. "Shit." I noticed a stack of freshly cut firewood by the house. "I can't see her again."

"Either you come with me, Reuben, or I have to take Emmy to the hospital when I get back. I don't want to go to another hospital. She just needs you to tell her it was a lie—all you told her yesterday. What Kate *made* you tell her. She needs a proper good-bye."

"*Proper? Civilized?* If you white people know a civilized way to dump the girl you love—to rip her fucking heart out—please inform me, missionary man." He takes a deep breath. "Sorry, Matt. I'm done."

I wait a minute. "Listen, kid. My hands are tied. If it was up to me, I'd let Emmy live with me and go to high school with you. But Kate is determined."

"I can't even breathe as long as that woman is in this state."

"If you come back with me, you get Emmy for one more week. I'll leave you kids alone. You guys don't have to be apart—even at night."

"And how is that going to make it any easier when she leaves?"

"I don't know." I sigh. "I know what I'm asking isn't fair to you."

"Fuck."

"*Fuck* is right." I look around. It seems we are in the middle of nowhere and it's a hundred years ago. Two hundred. I'm a white man asking this Indian kid for more than I should.

I hear a voice, older than Reuben's, but similar. I look behind Reuben, then behind me at a man standing in the shadows.

Reuben grins. "That's my dad," he says with obvious pride. "He wants me to tell you he's okay with you calling me son."

I should be freaked out, but I'm not.

"And he's sorry about your loss."

I nod at the man, and he steps back into the pines.

The pride on Reuben's face turns to sadness. He wants to follow his dad—into the pines, farther.

I would've followed Beth.

Reuben looks at me as if confused again by my presence here. Then he says, "I'm sorry too about your wife."

We both stare at the fire a long time, too long because I think I hear drumming, or maybe it's just the river. It's flowing strong toward the Columbia. My grief flows as strong in me. I've been trying to keep it back. I begin to cry, hard. Reuben says not a word, but his breathing is heavy and broken.

When I finally get control, I take a deep breath. "Will you come back, Reuben?"

He starts searching for his shirt. "We should hurry," he says.

"I can't take you unless you eat first." I point at the plates of food I left on the log. "Your aunt insisted."

"Aunt Shirley." He smiles.

"I'll eat with you." We eat quickly. The meat is venison.

I follow Reuben's truck off the reservation and back to Moses Lake. I've been gone almost seven hours. I'm afraid to go into the trailer. Reuben smells like campfire when he meets me on the porch. We enter together. Emmy sits on the couch, leaning her head on the arm. All around her are those damn paper birds. She looks like a bag lady with paper pigeons. She still wears the dress Beth made for her, and it's still unbuttoned. Her hair is matted. She's pale, and her lips are dry. I hear Reuben take in breath. Her eyes are open, but she doesn't see us. The loss of Beth and then Reuben clearly sent her into shock.

"Hey, Emmy," Reuben says.

She hears that. She sees him. She jumps up too quickly and looks faint. He goes to her. She wraps her arms tightly around his neck. "It's going to be okay," he tells her. Then he whispers something in her ear. She nods. He keeps whispering, and she nuzzles her face against him. She doesn't loosen her hold around his neck. He helps her back onto the couch and buttons her dress. "Drink," he says, and she does. I pick up the paper birds. More than a few are completely crushed. Then I fix Emmy a new peanut butter sandwich. I'd left one for her, but she didn't touch it. She eats both halves for Reuben. As easy as that.

I am absolutely beat. "I'm going to bed, kids."

"Can he spend the night, Uncle Matt?" Her voice is weak.

"On the couch," Reuben quickly adds.

"You guys figure it out. Good night." I head for my empty bedroom.

My brother pulled up the carpeting and got rid of the mattress. He bought me a new one. And his wife bought new sheets and bedding. I have yet to sleep in the bed without Beth. I've lain in it. *It doesn't smell like you.* But I have yet to sleep. I take a hot shower. I fall into bed on my stomach. Kids are damn exhausting. I can't be sure if those two out there make me feel younger or older. They just make me feel, I guess. When I wake up hours later, my head aches and I'm thirstier than I ever remember being. I put on pants and go into the kitchen. I look into the living room. Emmy sleeps on the couch. Reuben is on the floor with a pillow. They hold hands. I have plenty of alone nights coming. I feel them gathering. For now, though, I turn on the kitchen faucet. I drink and drink.

19

Teresa

❧ Emmy is gone. Reuben is back in Omak attending high school. I miss them both.

During their last week together, before they took off to the reservation for four days and no one heard from them—except for the quick appearance they made in Omak for the final night of the Suicide Race—they threw together a barbecue dinner between the two trailers. They actually bought a plastic lawn table and chairs. Reuben barbecued and Emmy made samosas, an Indian food, from India, pretty good for her first attempt, even though she didn't think so. There were candles, which kept blowing out in the wind, and a vase full of lavender cuttings. Beth's. Matt stared at them a lot. There were gifts. Grace and Audrey each received a deck of tarot cards from Emmy. Kevin and Emilio got feathers from Reuben. Emmy gave me a set of colorful Tibetan prayer flags, which I hung across the inside of my bare kitchen window. Reuben gave Matt his dad's Zippo lighter with the engraved eagle design. It's been out of fluid for years. Reuben and Emmy said the dinner was to show their appreciation for all Matt and I had done for them. I didn't want the evening to end. A newly widowed man, a single mom with four kids from three different dads, a young couple in love who had only days left together—and yet we were happy for a few hours. I'm almost thirty. Some days, after a long or double shift at the hospital, or when one of my kids is sick, I feel forty. I'll take any hours of happiness I can.

Reuben doesn't play football this fall. He says he just doesn't have it in him. He gets an afternoon job instead. He's losing weight, but his grades have never been better. He's always tried hard in school—something Mom doesn't appreciate. My brother's even got Ray studying and back on track for graduation. And as far as I know, Reuben's not drinking or drugging. He's not in jail like his bud Benji. Emmy faithfully mails letters here to Reuben. Sometimes, when he comes to pick up her letters, he and Matt go fishing. Other weekends Matt meets Reuben on the rez to give him letters and to fish and even to take sweats in Virgil's garage. Reuben says he's teaching Matt to fish like an Indian, but he admits Matt already knew how to read the water like a native. Reuben used to get so excited as a little boy when Dad would take him fishing, which wasn't often enough. Dad was like Coyote fishing. All he had to do was wink and the fish would practically leap out of the water for him. Mostly, growing up, Reuben fished and hunted with the elders. Kevin will be old enough soon. In November, Reuben tries out for the school basketball team and makes it. I really encouraged him. But then he wrecks his pickup, way out on the rez, which scares the crap out of all of us, and he abruptly quits the team. He actually lets Matt lend him the money to get his truck fixed. Matthew Miller has more than kept his promise to do what he can for Reuben.

But my brother just isn't the same kid. His step is slower and a bit off, and he's far quieter, even with me. The kids notice it when he visits, which isn't often now that the snows have started and the days are short. Last time he came to pick up Emmy's letters, he stared out the kitchen window for a good twenty minutes, touching the prayer flags. Then he took a walk alone down the road, past the long-harvested and snowy fields, past the dwindling haystack where he and Emmy used to hang out.

I persuade Reuben to bring Lena and stay for a few days over Christmas break. Grace and Lena spend the entire first day making beaded holiday ornaments for our aunts and for a few of my favorite patients at the hospital. The second afternoon, when I send Reuben and Kevin to the store for groceries, Lena reports to me, "Our brother is sad. Emmy took his heart."

"I don't like Emmy," Grace says. "Or any white girls."

Grace has been having problems at Chief Mo Middle School with white girls and with Mexican girls after they find out she's not one of them and has native pride. She never had problems in elementary school, but she's also become more vocal. I need to call the counselor. Grace doesn't understand why I won't move back onto the rez. She sees only the positive sides: a web of relatives, lots of ceremonies, youth classes at the longhouse, dogs, and horses. Not all the drugging, political bickering, people in your business, my old classmates drinking their health away. I volunteer when I can at the once-a-month women's health clinic in Nespelem.

"If Reuben heard you say that you didn't like his girlfriend," Lena warns Grace, "he wouldn't like *you*. And I'm half white."

"You're family," Grace says. They sit together in my new recliner. My other three kids aren't allowed to sit in it until I pay it off.

"So is Emmy," Lena retorts.

"No, she isn't. She isn't even Reuben's girlfriend anymore."

"Oh, yes, she is." Lena gets up swiftly without putting down the footrest. I cringe, forgetting she's as agile as her big brother always was, until recently.

"Where Auntie Em?" Emilio says, running to the window to look for Emmy. Audrey and I were about to make fry bread before Lena brought up Reuben's missing heart.

"You don't have an auntie Em," Grace says to Emilio. "You never did."

"You're mean," Lena says.

Grace replies in Salish—she's been listening to the language tapes the elders made—but Lena doesn't understand. "Need an interpreter?" Grace asks.

"Stop it, girls," I say. "Both of you." I tell them to take Emilio outside and build a snowman with him. If Emilio went to preschool on the rez, he'd already know how to look for animal tracks in the snow.

Grace likes Emmy or she wouldn't still treasure that set of little Asian bowls Emmy gave to her. At first, much to my annoyance, Grace tried to eat all her meals out of them. Even spaghetti. Now she keeps sacred beads in the bowls. When I performed that ceremony on Emmy after Beth died, my oldest aunt, who is also my oldest living relative, insisted Emmy was Reuben's wife. When I tried to explain otherwise, she scolded me for shortsightedness.

Reuben doesn't write Emmy back. Not a single letter. He simply says, "I can't," when I ask him why not. He keeps the letters in a canvas bag in his truck. The kids got into them once. There was also a book in the bag called *Sister Carrie*, which Emmy obviously left here, and a bunch of tiny origami frogs and foxes and other animals that Emmy must tuck into her letters. I wanted to snoop but didn't.

Reuben and I have a heart-to-heart at the end of January. I'm up north with my kids for the winter dances. My brother and I are alone for a few hours—my arrangement—at Mom's Omak apartment. We sit at the kitchen table, drinking coffee.

"Mom tells me you've been hanging out with Jenny Larsen," I say. Jenny's dad is the worst kind of drunken rodeo asshole. And yes, there is more than one kind. I went to school with other Larsen kids: brothers, cousins, whatever. Basically all trash. Except Jenny. She's one of those rare, genuinely sweet church girls who don't give blow jobs to football players behind the bleachers. She sings on Omak street corners with her youth group.

"Yeah, so what?" Reuben says. He wears his senior sweatshirt with OMAK PIONEERS on the front and the names of all his classmates on the back. "Jenny and I have a lot of classes together this year. We're just friends."

"And she knows that?"

"She knows we're friends."

"*Just* friends?"

There's a stack of bills on the kitchen table, as always. Reuben starts looking through them. "I've done nothing for her to think otherwise."

"You spend time with her."

"I spend time with all my friends."

"Not according to Mom."

"Since when do you take Mom's word over mine?" Good point. "Look," he says, trying to change the subject, "Mom hasn't paid the cable bill in two months. I gave her money."

"Does Jenny know about Emmy?"

The name hits him like a punch in the gut. I shouldn't have said it. I know better, as an Indian. He can't speak. He pushes the bills away, then he pulls up the hood of his sweatshirt as if to shield himself.

I get up and freshen our coffee.

"Jenny saw Emmy and me together this summer," he says when I sit back down. "Outside Mom's work. Emmy liked Jenny's voice."

I look hard at him. "Are you trying to save Jenny like you saved—"

"Stop right there, Teresa. Fuck." He's wound tight. "Jenny is my friend. Do I want to help her get away from her bastard of a dad? Hell, yes. I don't love her, though." He laughs. "Not even close."

"Does she know that?"

"I helped her fill out her college applications—for fucking Christian colleges in western Washington. We've never made out. I've never taken her on the rez."

"She reminds you of Emmy, though."

"No." He laughs sarcastically again. I haven't heard Reuben laugh for real since last summer.

"Not even a little?"

"Emmy Nolan is more alive than Jenny Larsen will ever be. If Jenny is like anyone, it's Beth Miller." Now he's the one not being a good Indian, blurting the name of the dead like that. "So maybe, sis, I should be asking you about her."

"What the heck does that mean?" I wish I had a sweatshirt hood to pull up. "Matt Miller is *your* buddy."

"So, you do know what I mean."

"He shovels snow for me, fixed my van. Being a kind neighbor."

"Mr. Miller mowed your lawn so many times this past fall that there's no line anymore between yours and his."

"Oh, Jesus Christ, Reuben. Only *you* would notice that." I reach over and pull down his sweatshirt hood so I can see his whole face.

He's smiling. I am jolted by how much I miss his smile.

"I feel calm when I'm with Jenny," he admits. "A little calm. Especially after I read a batch of letters from Emmy."

"Do you wish she wouldn't write?"

"At first, I did. I told her not to write, that I wouldn't write back. I thought it would be easier, you know. But I live for those letters, Teresa. I get what she's doing. It's been almost six months since I've seen her."

"*What* is she doing?"

He can't answer for a moment. Shit. I didn't mean to make him cry. "She's not letting me go." He stands up. "But she will." He grabs his truck keys off the hook on the kitchen wall. "She'll get sick of my silence."

When snow leaves the mountains, the elders say, it's time to start anew. I pray for my brother. For his renewal. I dance. I even talk to the chaplain at the hospital in Moses Lake where I work. I've talked to him before when my guilt for not living on the rez overwhelms me. We've prayed together for my people. We pray now for Reuben. We pray for Emmy, and for Matt.

Matt comes to Reuben's high school graduation. Class of 1999. My little brother won a full scholarship to Washington State University in Pullman. Matt beams almost more than I do. It's been a bloody four years at American high schools. Reuben's lucky to be alive. There's a party the next day for Reuben and Ray at a park in Omak. There's salmon and elk, cake, fry bread, macaroni salad, egg rolls, and rice. There's drumming. Jenny stops by for a short time. She also won a scholarship to a Christian college in Tacoma. Reuben took her to the prom. She and Reuben don't touch at the picnic, and probably not at the prom either, other than to dance. But I can tell Jenny wishes more than anything that Reuben would touch her. She steps closer whenever he inches away. But so do a couple of pretty Nez Perce girls visiting here from Lapwai, which is probably why Jenny leaves early. All my aunts keep eyeballing Matt and me, though I've never said a word, and maybe that's why. Mom mentions how well Matt seems to know my kids. Except Grace, I think, who keeps her distance. As far as I know, Matt has never talked to Reuben about Emmy since she left. I assumed it was an unspoken rule between them. Matt occasionally asks me about Reuben and Emmy—if Reuben writes her back and that sort of thing. But I don't think he puts any pressure on Reuben. So I'm surprised at the graduation party when I hear Matt mention to Reuben that he's flying to California the following week for Emmy's graduation and that he'd like to buy Reuben a ticket. My brother disappears. For the rest of the party. For weeks.

When Matt gets back from California, he and I start sitting outside together, between our trailers, careful to keep our backs to Beth's empty garden beds. He got rid of Beth's car awhile ago and brought his boat from his parents' house to park in its place. He takes up smoking, and we share "cigarette breaks" together. He takes breaks from the loneliness of his trailer, which is still silent despite his buying a TV and a stereo and getting his old record collection from the basement of his parents' house. And I take breaks from my kids. We talk about our jobs mostly and my kids, but also our childhoods. Two weekends in a row Matt barbecues hamburgers and hot dogs for the kids and I make mac and cheese and Jell-O, and we eat outside at the table Reuben and Emmy bought. He tells me he quit attending church for good, any church, although he's quick to add that he still believes in God and, for Beth's sake, probably always will. I respect that. The only plants of Beth's still alive are the lavender bushes she planted in the strip between our driveways. They continue to thrive with my pruning and watering.

Reuben remains a no-show, and Matt is beside himself for offering that ticket.

"I didn't mean to drive him away, Teresa."

"You didn't. I told you. It's just Reuben." It's just Indian men.

Finally Matt admits that Emmy put him up to it. "She thought, or hoped, all school year that she'd be back here this summer. She told me she kept asking your brother in her letters if he even *wanted* her to come, but he never replied. She pleaded with me to bring Reuben to California."

Matt's love for Emmy is heartwarming, and heartbreaking. On the rez, love between nieces and nephews and their aunts and uncles is more apparent, or at least more a part of daily life, than off the rez.

"Emmy's going to have a baby brother or sister. Her mom is big and pregnant—and glowing." He takes a long puff of his cigarette and looks off for a few. Beth was never given the chance to glow like that. I have four times. He keeps looking off until I pull him back with a question.

"Is Emmy excited about the baby?" I ask.

"Yes, she is." He looks at me and smiles. I think he's catching on to the way I'm not letting his thoughts wander too near any edge. "But she's not excited about Berkeley. She's sad. Her stepdad worries a lot about her. He told me he worries so much about Emmy that he's having a hard time getting revved about the new baby. I worry too. There's a similar broken look in Emmy's and Reuben's eyes."

And a shattered look in Matt's. Only he doesn't realize. I put my hand on top of his, just for a second, or so I had intended, but it feels right. So I leave it there.

Reuben doesn't return the entire summer: not to collect Emmy's letters, not for the Fourth of July Pow Wow, not for the Omak Stampede and Suicide Race, not for the Indian Encampment. Emmy's been gone now one full year.

He doesn't return to attend college in the fall. *Brother.*

"I did this," Matt says.

"You didn't, Matt. If not for you, Reuben would be a mess."

Matt starts coming over early in the mornings for coffee, except on my days off, when I try to get caught up a bit on sleep, or on mornings when he goes fishing. We scoot our chairs closer as the weather gets colder.

"We don't know that Reuben *isn't* a mess somewhere," he says. "I can't believe he missed his scholarship."

I too am starting to really worry. "Let's just trust that he's okay." I don't tell Matt, but Reuben isn't in Washington anymore. No one on either side of the mountains has seen him. My real dad is Puyallup, and I asked his family to check around and keep an eye out.

"Fuck," Matt says. "I can't live with this."

He lets me put my hand on top of his, like friends. Twice he's put his hand on top of mine. But it has never gone further. I've thought about its going further a lot. His wife's been dead now for almost fifteen months.

"Can you live with this?" I kiss him lightly on the lips.

Surprisingly, he says, "I can."

He kisses me back. There's a lot of something in this man. His kiss almost makes me faint. I don't exaggerate. If he wants, I'll let him take me to bed right now before the kids wake up. I simply wouldn't be able to refuse. I am a sucker for a good kisser. If a man knows how to kiss—and sadly, more don't than do—I'll excuse his not-so-good looks or his not-so-steady job. Matt's nice-looking. I usually prefer Indian men, hands down, but Matt has a job, and he isn't torn between having a job and living on the rez. He kisses me once more, but longer. Oh, Jesus. Then he leaves.

I don't see him for a couple days afterward. No morning coffee. No evening cigarette breaks. I meet him at his truck on Saturday. He left early to go salmon fishing on a stretch of the Columbia that whites dubbed the Hanford Reach, but that natives have older names for. He went fishing despite it being the coldest morning in six months and despite the fact that the fall chinook are nearly done spawning there. The leaves on the poplars are falling. I sent my kids away after I got a letter in the mail from Reuben. I know Matt will be ecstatic, and I want the moment with just him.

"Teresa," he says. "How are you?" He's embarrassed.

"I'm good."

"How's Emilio's ear infection?"

"Emilio's all better."

"Did Grace make the team?" he asks.

She tried out for the seventh-grade girls' basketball team. "She did," I say proudly.

"Just like Audrey and the fairy kingdom predicted."

He's referring to the tarot cards Emmy gave the girls. Grace making the team should help her fit in a bit. She hasn't quit asking to move back to the rez.

"Land any kings?" I ask him.

"Only two keepers, back trolling, but I released them. The flow was too fast. I kept flying past the fish. That, and my mind kept wandering." He smiles awkwardly. "About the other morning—"

"Save it," I say. "Look." I hand him the letter from Reuben, which also contains three money orders: one for me, one for Mom, and one for Matt to pay back the truck repairs. The letter also gives a post office box for me to forward Emmy's letters if she's still writing them, which she is.

"He's been fishing in Alaska?" Matt says, smiling widely. "I'll be damned. The kid's a great fisherman. I swear I've never seen anything like it." He tells me to keep the money order intended for him. I argue. He says he'll tear it up before he spends the kid's money. "Oh, this makes my day, Teresa."

He hugs me. I rub his back. "My kids are gone. Get changed and come over so we can celebrate."

He does. I give him a beer. He's so nervous that his hands shake. After we finish our beers, I lead him into my bedroom. I have extra poundage from my four kids. Beth was slim. But I make up for it with my large breasts, or so I've been told. I'm worried he might not know what to do with so much breast, but he does. He's tender. So tender. I don't remember the last time I was brought to orgasm like that. He cries after we're through. But that's to be expected, I suppose, from a recent widower. I give him space.

"I'm sorry," he says, sitting up.

Does he mean for the sex or for the tears? Reuben told me once that Emmy apologized for everything.

"I led you in here, don't forget," I say. "And why apologize? It was nice, Matt. It was fun. It's okay to have fun."

"You enjoyed it?"

"Didn't I make that obvious?"

He smiles. Matt was devastated at first by Beth's death, but now it seems to be releasing him—not just from grief but from a way of life too restrictive. He must sense this release. How terribly painful.

"Don't leave yet," I say when he gets up and starts to dress. "I still have an hour before I have to get the kids."

"I should leave."

"Why should you leave? I'm not going to tell anyone." And I'm not. "No one has to know. It's no one's business," I say. "Not even Reuben's."

He takes his shirt back off.

Emmy doesn't start that big university in Berkeley until January. Something about deferred admission. During the fall semester—the same fall Reuben was supposed to start WSU and Matt and I began our romance—Emmy lived at home and attended junior college in Sacramento and continued to send letters here weekly for Reuben. One week she sent three, and my heart went out to her. After she moves to Berkeley, I get no letters for a month. Has she finally given up? Then I get a padded envelope from Emmy with what feels like a journal inside it—like one of those composition notebooks. I get one a month. The girl hasn't given up. I have to give her credit for that, having, at her age and younger, waited in silence for Indian boys. In fact, she's stronger than I've ever been about love. Reuben calls in April, after three months without my forwarding anything to him. I was hoping that would work.

"If you want the journals," I say, "come and get them."

It's been eleven months since I last saw Reuben at the graduation party. I can't go a year without seeing my baby brother.

Reuben shows up on my doorstep a week after his phone call. I barely recognize him. His hair is shoulder length, which makes him look like his dad, whom I miss. Reuben's dad—I called him Dad— used to swear to Reuben and his sidekick Ray that he stole Mom and me in a horse raid. The version he told me when I was young was far more romantic. He said Mom and I were his to begin with, but we were stolen from him. It took him many lifetimes to steal us back, but he did. I believe him. His devotion in that story got me through hard times: the idea that someone could love me *that* much. He broke Mom's heart, but he loved her too, very deeply. He loved Reuben the most. Why Dad couldn't be there for my brother, I never understood. Reuben's body is that of a man's now—a man who labors hard for a living. He's not a boy any longer. "Oh, Reuben." His hands are rough when I hold them.

"I've missed you, sis, and the kids."

They all hug him for ten minutes or more. He tells them he's been up north fishing at sea, which the two boys start playing immediately. Reuben says the summer salmon run in Bristol Bay is amazing. He felt high for weeks. And then he followed the fish to more remote places. He's had success securing work, he says, with recruiters and skippers who think, for some reason, that he's good luck.

"You're a bit Coyote," I say, "like Dad."

"Not hardly." He says he's also worked processing salmon, and there isn't the least ceremony or prayers. "The bones are discarded in such a way," he says with sadness, "Dad would be ashamed of me."

"Dad would be proud of you. And don't take this the wrong way, but you're more of a man already."

"If I am," he says, "it's because of you."

That brings tears. "Matt's at work. He'll be so excited to see you."

"I'm not staying. I'm going to Omak later this afternoon to see Mom and Lena and then over to Aunt Shirley's."

"What? You'll break Matt's heart. Stay here tonight. I'll make dinner."

"No, sis. I only have two days." He explains that pollock season just ended. He got a processing job until salmon season starts again in June.

"Let me call Matt at work then. He'll come home now."

"I can't see Matt."

That makes me pause. I tell him to come outside for a cigarette. Grace, as usual, is all ears. Once we're on the front porch, I tell him, "That's messed up, brother. Matt blames himself for you leaving. He loves you."

"I know that. I've felt his love—even at sea."

"Then—"

"The last time I saw Dad was that night Matt came to the rez to get me. Matt called me *son*, and Dad, the wily fuck, appeared awfully quick to give his approval." Reuben takes such deep puffs of his cigarette. "I didn't realize it then," he continues, "but it's like Dad was turning me over to Matt." His cig is already gone. "I didn't allow myself to even consider this until after I left here. Then I felt pissed off, you know. Cheated by Dad. Irritated by Matt."

"Forgive your dad, Reuben."

"I have. I have." He makes a gesture of peace. "In fact, I think it was my fault Dad couldn't move completely into the spirit world. I had to release him."

"Accept Matt's love. It's real."

He looks at me. I probably need to respect the fact that he's a man now, not a boy, and quit being so bossy and pushy. He slowly smiles. "The two of you?"

"What? Matt? He helps out, is all." But I can't help smiling. We've been lovers now for six months.

"I bet Mr. Miller helps." He lights another cig.

"Please stay. Just one night. It'll kill Matt if you don't. And don't say anything to him about me. It would embarrass him. He still feels like he's cheating on his dead wife. But he's coming around."

"If anyone can bring him around, it would be you." Deep puff.

"I haven't exactly had luck with bringing men around." He raises his eyebrows. "At least to stay," I clarify. "You shithead."

"Matt's different."

"Where have you been, brother?" I mean his spirit.

"Canning salmon so the USDA can give it back to Indians as charity." He finishes his second cigarette.

"*How* have you been?" I ask.

"Making money."

"For what?"

"College."

"But you had a scholarship."

"I need to make money."

I take his arm. I lean my head on it. "You've got some muscles going on there."

"Fourteen-hour days."

"Are you happy?" I ask.

"Are you happy when your kids are hungry and you can feed them?" he replies. "Isn't that partly why you live off the rez?"

"But you don't have any kids, Reuben."

"I will someday." He lights another cig. Jesus.

Not that it's any of my business, but I ask, "You got any women, keeping you warm in Alaska?"

His body tenses. "If I do, they're not the one I want."

"It's been a long time, baby brother."

"Nineteen months." Two deep puffs. "But if anything, Teresa, I love her more."

I think Emmy's strength has been like an anchor for my brother. "You want her journals?" I ask.

"In the morning."

"You're staying?" He nods, and I jump up and down. "Thanks, Reuben."

Matt is so excited to see Reuben. My brother is larger than Matt now. I think he always was, but more so now. Overjoyed, Matt accidentally kisses me in front of Reuben.

"Hey," Reuben says with a grin, "that's my sister."

"That wasn't supposed to happen," Matt says.

"Yeah, it was," Reuben says. "Definitely."

"You look great, Reuben," Matt says. "It's just so damn good to see you." They both tear up. "How long you staying? Or are you back for good?"

"One night is all." Matt's face falls. What an emotional day. "I came for Emmy's journals," my brother says.

There's silence at that name. I have to break it with an offer to make dinner while they have a council outside.

Reuben returns again for more journals, but not until the end of salmon season in early October. He has a tattoo on his upper arm, a small one of a baby sea otter. He says it's from a drawing by Emmy. When Audrey asks him the otter's name, as she pretends to feed it fish, he says, "Otis," which makes even Grace giggle. Again Reuben stays only a few days. He is working so that he can have that girl. Matt said Reuben was told by Emmy's mom that he couldn't provide for her. He's changing that. A man can make good money in a relatively short amount of time at sea and in the canneries. But it's grueling work. Reuben looked tired the second time he came back. I insisted he stop sending me money orders, but he still does. I fear he's waiting too long for Emmy. She's a young girl, pretty, smart, and, above all, lonely. Reuben is handsome. All his life I've seen how girls and women react to him. His wounded eyes only make him more appealing. I'm sure he's had a couple flings with women in Alaska. It's mighty cold up there.

In and out of bed, Matt drives me bonkers in a good way. We've been sleeping together for more than a year. I don't think he and Beth had a lot of sex, at least not in the years leading up to her death. The woman was just too ill. I still think Beth was a healer, or could've been if not for that church. I sensed it strong in her. I also, oddly enough, sensed it a bit in Emmy, although I doubt she'll ever recognize or trust it in herself. Matt continues to be gentle in bed. I am teaching him that sometimes it's fun not to be so gentle. "Damn," he'll say. "Damn, Teresa."

Does he love me? He wants to. Will he leave me? No. Do I love him? Yes. Do my kids love him? All but Grace, but he goes to her basketball tournaments. Does he go with us to powwows on the rez? Yes. Did he take Kevin hunting and then drive the meat to Nespelem so Kevin could give it to the elders, as is the custom when a boy makes his first kill? Yes. Has he introduced me to his family? Yes. Were they nice? More cordial than his coworkers when Matt took me to his Christmas party. Has he invited me into his trailer—into his bedroom? No. But he talks about buying us all a house this summer. I think he's still paying off Beth's hospital bills. Do I make him happy? I think I really do. Will I leave him if he doesn't say he loves me soon? I could never.

Emmy begins her third semester at Berkeley. She sends her last journal at the end of January. None in February or March. It's been two and a half years since those kids have seen each other. I don't blame her. A letter arrives from Emmy the first week of April. I am so scared about what it might say and by the fact that it feels like there's a feather enclosed in it that I call Reuben. I put in an emergency call for him, that is. He doesn't have a phone. He calls two days later. The static on the phone line is horrible, and I swear I can hear the sea. I tell him there's been no journals for two months and that a letter arrived—like a warm chinook—and it's about to melt everything he's been working for in the bitter cold. "It's time to stop," I tell him. "It's time to go get that girl."

20

Emmy

The first day of my senior year, Connor corners me in the hallway after third period. "What's up, sexy?" he says. I'd been trying to avoid him. He wears a tie and bright green Vans. The last time I saw him, the tips of his hair were dyed that color green. Now they're bleached. "I missed you, Emmy."

"You have no idea what it means to miss someone."

He moves in closer. "So, you want to chill in my room after school?"

"No, thanks." I think about the numerous fluffy pillows on his bed and how Reuben slept all summer on Teresa's couch without a pillow. "There's nothing between us."

He gives me the twice-over. "You look different." He feigns anger. "Did you have an affair on me this summer?"

"Screw you," I say, but I should've known better.

"Anytime." He softens. "I *really* did miss you." He touches my sleeve. "Don't cry." I'm not. He tries to rub my arm.

"Stay away from me."

His best friend already approached me during first period to tell me that Connor wasted the last six weeks of summer "moping like a bitch" over me.

"I can get any chick here," Connor brags, and no doubt he can. He's attractive and talented. Being an asshole only gives him more edge.

"I'm happy for you."

"You don't look happy." He pulls his car keys from his pocket, so I can see he uses the Tibetan key chain I bought for him. "Where's the necklace?" He dares to touch the spot on my neck where his diamond heart pedant had rested for a few short weeks. I shove his hand away.

I should tell him I sold it at a pawnshop for thirty bucks, but he's not worth it.

"Please, Connor, just leave me alone."

He stares at me for a second, and then he smirks. "Did you heal your Bible-thumping aunt?"

Reuben. I close my eyes, remember the wind in the poplars.

"I had the best summer of my life."

I feel Connor's eyes on my ass as I walk away and he calls me a cunt. He's probably thinking, *Let the games begin,* but he'll find out that I'm not playing.

Reuben's last words to me were to be sure I didn't lose myself back in California. He tried to make me strong during our last week together, so I could make it through my senior year. He took me to the reservation. He tried to give me his spirit power. But I refused to accept it. He begged me, then the spirits of the rivers and the mountains and the land. But he needed to keep his own power. I was drummed over and sang to. I was held. And held.

I will be strong, Reuben. I promised you.

I write Reuben once a week. He never writes back. I tell him I sleep with his flannel Kurt Cobain shirt, and I carry the feather he gave me in my backpack just as he instructed. I tell him about my classes, clubs, homework, more homework. Physics. Economics. Calculus. I write out hard integral problems that I solved and mail them to him. Mom wishes she and I still did our schoolwork together at the table, but those days are over. I draw Reuben comic strips of Otis, the Stouthearted Baby Sea Otter, able to crack open abalone with a single pebble. I tell him about books I'm reading. I make him tiny origami frogs, foxes, elephants, and bears, but not salmon. I tell him about the house Spencer built us (every detail with Mom and me in mind). I tell him I don't belong in Spencer's house. I belong in eastern Washington, where the wind rattles the windows and Indians ride horses down a sheer cliff (I tried to cover my eyes, but he made me watch) and across the Okanogan River. I tell him I stare at the little map he drew me, which hangs on the wall next to my bed. I tell him about Mom and

Spencer's small wedding on the coast. I ask him what to do about Connor, who won't leave me alone. Reuben doesn't respond. I tell him that he'll always be my best friend, and my letters will prove it. I tell him I can't give back his heart, not yet, maybe never. I probably should, for his sake, though I assure him no girl will ever love him as much as I do. I ask him about school, football, his aunts, Lena, Ray, Teresa, his nieces and nephews. I ask him if he dressed up as Smokey the Bear for Halloween. I ask him about hunting and if he's helping the elders fill the freezers of the old people before the snows get heavy.

I tell him I know he wants me to make friends, but I can't. I eat lunch with Hedda and Harpreet just like last year, so I don't have to eat alone. I try to act as if my summer were as uneventful as theirs—as if the only time I was embraced by a boy was also in my dreams. They think I've changed. Mom and Spencer send me to a shrink. But then Spencer gives me permission to stop going. Mom is letting him make some of the decisions. I tell Reuben how at night, remembering the times we made love in that tent on the reservation, I touch myself. The sound of the coyotes scared me at first. Then I kept pretending they scared me to hear his laugh as he kissed my neck. He laughed his butt off at how squeamish I was when he took me fishing. I'd already been fishing a few times with my uncle and aunt and even caught a walleye. Reuben laughed even harder at how terrified I was when he tried to teach me how to ride a horse. He thought I cried because his laughter hurt my feelings, but that wasn't it at all. Rather, I was beginning to feel the enormity of his absence.

I was so watched over by Reuben from the very beginning that how can I not feel miserably neglected by him now.

Mom is pregnant, I tell him, and in a fury that Republicans are trying to impeach President Clinton. "Better blow jobs than no jobs" is her favorite new saying. I tell Reuben I got accepted into Berkeley. I tell him I heard he won a scholarship to WSU, my dad's school. I let him know how incredibly proud I am of him, but not in the least surprised. I'll always believe in him. I ask him if he still wants to major in fish biology and help bring the salmon back to the reservation. I call him Coyote, then my coyote.

I tell him that when I saw the images from Columbine, my first thought was of him and how we should be going to high school together. What if he'd been shot and killed at Omak High? Or been a student running for his life or jumping out an upstairs window?

Connor asks me to prom, though he's going out with another girl at Valley Art and two "virgins" at St. Francis. Spencer finds me a date, the son of an engineer, who is cute and polite. We dance close together but barely talk. I describe my dress for Reuben. I tell him my date liked how soft my bare shoulders were. I had two glasses of champagne. One more, I tell Reuben, and I would've let him kiss me. Not really. He doesn't respond. Did he go to prom? Touch a girl's bare shoulders? Worry about me when he saw the images of Columbine?

Does he believe me when I tell him how lonely I am for the river and the wind? Lonely to drive the reservation roads again in his truck, with the windows down and Nirvana cranked on the stereo or with no music at all. But I am used to being lonely. And I can wait. All my childhood I read novels about British heroines who knew how to wait. Years and years. I can wait also. I tell him he has his Coyote and Beaver stories. I have Tess and Anne Elliot and Jane Eyre and Fanny Price. He'll see how long I can wait. I may not have the courage of an old-fashioned heroine, but I have the patience. I am stubborn. Like him. He'll see.

He doesn't respond when I write telling him I'll come back for the summer—and stay. Mom can't stop me because I'll be graduated and almost eighteen. He is all I want. Fuck Berkeley. I can wait a year and apply to WSU. I will stay with him, get a job. I will stay forever this time. We can be like Salmon and his wife. *Remember you told me that story, Reuben?* They took shelter together under the falls, hiding from Rattlesnake and all the Land People who wanted to keep them apart. *But you have to tell me you want me to come back.*

Tell me, Reuben.

Uncle Matt says Reuben disappeared and no one knows where he is.

I hold my breath and write against the panic in my chest. *Where are you? Please be careful.* I write all that summer and all fall. Because I wasn't officially accepted into U.C. Berkeley until the spring semester

("a spring admit"), I go to junior college in Sacramento for the fall semester. I drive myself. I finally got my license, thanks to Spencer's
persistence. Mom has her baby. A boy named Liam. I hold my baby
brother all the time. If it weren't for Liam, and the way Mom and I
marvel over his toes, his every coo, whimper, blink, and yawn, I
would've by now completely shut her out of my life. I've been retreat-
ing from her since returning from Washington, or maybe since the
moment my aunt hugged me at the airport and I remembered her
smell, and even remembered missing it. I've forgiven Mom for lying
to me about my dad's death, and I understand now why she *had* to
leave Moses Lake—but I'll never understand why she turned her
back so completely. And I'll *never* forgive her for not letting me stay.
It's good, though, that Mom is allowing herself to be tempered by
Spencer's generosity and love. He's always thought the world of Mom,
but even more so now that she gave him little Liam. Spencer kindly
includes me in everything, to a fault even, forgetting sometimes that
I'm no longer a child. They let Liam sleep in my room on occasion,
his bassinet pushed up next to my bed. I sing to him: Aunt Beth's
songs.

Reuben doesn't go to college. He stays gone and misses his scholarship to WSU. It weighs on me every day at junior college. *Where are
you, Reuben? I'm so afraid for you.* Maybe he joined the military. I noticed
GO ARMY stickers on cars and trucks on the reservation and multiple
memorials to veterans. Reuben explained that Indians defend the
land, not the government, and that, regardless of politics, warriors are
highly esteemed. But what if he got deployed to the Middle East or
Eastern Europe? He would have gone to college if he'd never met me.
Or if I had let go of his heart when I left. If I would let go of it now,
maybe it could be wrapped in the skin of a buffalo, like the heart of
the Okanogan warrior in a story Reuben told me. The Sioux had tried
to burn the warrior's heart, but the buffalo's spirit brought it back to
life.

Mom begs me to stop crying. Please stop crying. She comes into
my bedroom at night and runs her fingers gently through my hair to

comfort me while I sob, and sometimes her touch does soothe me. Other times I jerk away. She tries to assure me that I'll get through this because she did. Our tales of woe might overlap, but they are not the same, and it took her most of my childhood to recover. Once, after a long, colicky night with my baby brother, she hints that I should be thankful I'm not one of the millions of Albanian refugees wandering around without a home. But for all I know—for all anyone knows— Reuben is currently homeless. There is no way for me to be okay with that.

I know Mom thinks me foolish for still pining away for Reuben (especially when he has never written me back) like a character in the Victorian novels she now worries she allowed me to spend too much time with as a child. In an about-face worthy of a politician, she tries to claim that sentiments were different back when those novels were written. But that is bullshit, and she knows it. Love is love. I call Spencer at work to come get me from junior college when I can't make it through the day, or through one class, or even find my car in the parking lot. *Reuben?* Mom is home for a year with Liam. Spencer always comes. He takes me with him to inspections, job sites, lumberyards, tile stores, instead of taking me home, so Mom won't know I'm missing classes. I start calling him Dad. The first time I do, he tears up. But then he sides with Mom when she suggests I go back to a shrink. So I stop crying in front of them and I stop calling Spencer from college. I don't stop calling him Dad.

I don't stop writing letters to Reuben and mailing them to Teresa's address. Finally Uncle Matt tells me Reuben sent word to Teresa. I'm so utterly relieved that for a whole day I can't get out of bed, my body limp after months of worried tension. I was not only afraid for Reuben but afraid of what I might do to myself if he hadn't surfaced soon: call Connor, who would make me pay in his way; bleed myself to alleviate the ache; hop on a bus to L.A. and get lost "in a big way," as Reuben feared. Uncle Matt says Reuben's been in Alaska working, mostly fishing at sea. Did I drive him that far away from his people and the land he loves? Where had I pictured him all this time? Actually I hadn't been able to picture Reuben outside eastern Washington. He's too much a part of that place. Which is why I'll never return there unless it's to be with him.

Uncle Matt tells me Reuben doesn't have a permanent address in Alaska, but that somehow Teresa gets my letters to him. My favorite Austen heroine, Anne Elliot, waited eight years while the man she loved, but had been persuaded not to marry, sought his fortune at sea (probably at the expense of natives somewhere). Every Jane Austen heroine eventually gets her man, but not before at least one season at Bath with frivolous family members and class humiliations and usually only after years of struggle and solitude. Mom told me a long time ago that in real life Jane Austen *didn't* get her man. I send Reuben a single picture of me in eighteen months: a Polaroid snapshot of me holding my baby brother. I simply write, "Someday," on the bottom. He knows what I mean. I fill an envelope with sparkly confetti. *Happy New Year, Reuben! Happy New Decade, New Century, New Millennium!*

When I move to Berkeley, I quickly realize letters won't work any longer. I buy a composition journal and begin writing in it to Reuben. I also sketch for him in the journal. I try to stay upbeat. I try to convince him that I'm standing on my own two feet. That I am every bit as stouthearted as Otis. But I am lonely as hell, and my hands are cold. *Remember how they glowed, Reuben, like that night-light?* He must be so cold in Alaska. *Remember when I first touched your belly with my warm hands?*

Berkeley overwhelms me academically. No matter how hard I study, I can't get a solid A. It overwhelms me politically. I have ten flyers handed to me every day, and people wear T-shirts that ask, DID YOUR DINNER HAVE A FACE? and HOW DO YOU LIKE MY MARXIST-FEMINIST DISCOURSE? This first semester in the dorms has been the worst time of my life. I could endure anything if only I knew Reuben still loved me and thought of me in Alaska. OPEN DOORS MAKE HAPPY FLOORS is the sign that greets me every time I step off the elevator. I'm a private person, who grew up without siblings or cousins. When my roommate is gone, the door is shut. Sometimes, when I'm alone in my dorm room, I plug in the praying hands night-light I brought from

Aunt Beth's. Usually I keep it hidden under my dorm bed. A guy on the second floor sells Vicodin. I haven't purchased any yet.

Freshmen girls, primping for sorority parties, walk around the dorms practically naked on weekend evenings, searching through closets for "going-out" clothes. I spend Friday nights at the gym, working out extra long, taking fitness classes, yoga. I've toned up. My body has never looked better, but who cares? Saturday and Sunday mornings I watch the male swim team (with CAL in gold on the butts of their Speedos) practice in the pool adjacent to the gym. I watch them just to spite Reuben for never writing. I've been growing out my hair in memory of Aunt Beth.

I spend the rest of my weekends either sketching in campus art studios or studying in the basement of Moffitt Library, with its desk lamps and domed skylight. Doe is the most beautiful and historic library with cathedral rooms, but it intimidates me, seems too Ivy League (I can't help thinking of Reuben in a ship's cramped hull). I've met some really sweet, down-to-earth, wannabe-hippie girls, mostly from Sierra foothill towns. But I'm too shy to call them, or to join their co-ops, or to wear their I HEART MY CO-OP pins. I just can't seem to put myself out there, but if I could, that would be the group. I smoke cigarettes, just like I planned to in college, but I have to hide and do it in corners, not on benches. It's okay to drink until you puke on the weekends here, fuck everyone, bake pot brownies, or even pop Ecstasy, but cigarettes are just plain trashy and stinky. A few weeks ago an intense-looking, beanie-wearing philosophy student asked me if he could watch me smoke my cigarette. He told me he found girls who smoke sexy because it's like they're wielding their signs of exhaustion and imperfection. *Do you believe it, Reuben? Do you wonder if I let him watch me smoke?* I did. *If I let him take me to his room and then watch as I reached up my skirt and touched myself?* I did. *Do you wonder if the next time I got completely naked and let him watch me touch myself again—before falling asleep for hours in his bed, waking to him still watching me?* I did. *Do you wonder if he ever asked my name?* He didn't. *If the next week, after I again touched myself, he read me Nietzsche and I pretended it was you telling me Coyote stories?* I tried.

I buy a bottle of Vicodin. I don't tell Reuben.

For the fall, Spencer finds me a fourth-floor apartment off Telegraph with antique wallpaper and a view of the bay from every window. My roommate was born in Eastern Europe, though she's far from a refugee. She drinks vodka out of shot glasses with Russian leaders' portraits on them. We crank the windows wide open to feel the breeze. She and I aren't friends, but we get along. She likes my old-fashioned cooking and that I grow herbs in our kitchen. She even likes my night-light, though she's an atheist. She calls it vintage. She's multilingual and helps me with my French homework. A typical Berkeley feminist, she believes empowerment comes through noncommittal sex. She claims that even in drunken stupors, fraternity guys at Berkeley can hold conversations (and usually in more than one language) about global economic principles, good literature, and social policies. I like to sit at the window in the velvet Isabel chair I brought from Sacramento. For hours I sit, sometimes high on Vicodin, looking down at the people walking in the streets, or at the fog in the bay. *I am like Sister Carrie. Am I not, Reuben? Only unlike Carrie Meeber, I know damn well for what—for whom—it is I long.*

Finally I force myself to become more adventurous. *For you, Reuben. Do I still have your heart?* And for Mom, who wishes I realized what a great opportunity U.C. Berkeley is for me—how lucky I am to be in college at all, to live in a state where education is so valued. She's right. Mom and Aunt Beth didn't even finish high school.

I write to Reuben about the bums and street performers. And I send sketches. I grew up in downtown Sacramento, so all my life I've seen homeless people, but there are fifty times more in Berkeley, and they're a far livelier and more musically inclined (though also more aggressive) crowd: young accordion players; aged, bearded guitar strummers; Hare Krishnas in robes beating bongos; ancient-looking Asian men playing lutes. The young bums with guitar cases and blond dreadlocks often have creepy comments, but their signs can be witty, like HUNGRY, HUNGRY HOBO. One young homeless girl tells me, when I stop to give her a cigarette and she asks if I might also spare a tampon, that she travels with a group of kids between the bay and Santa Cruz, living mostly off grass and selling her ass. I think of Mom at that truck stop. I go to the ATM and withdraw all the cash I can and take it back to the girl. I also give her my bottle of Midol, my Mace, and my wool peacoat. In the early mornings, students leave hot coffee and breakfast bars by the homeless who sleep in the doorways of the frozen yogurt shops and bookstores.

Leading up to Sather Gate is a tree-lined strip called Sproul Plaza, which is constantly filled with campus clubs tabling, handing out flyers, and selling food to raise money. I want to join a few service clubs—I enjoyed the club work I did in high school—but I get dizzy trying to decide which ones. Sproul is where all major and minor protests are staged. And there are always protests. I saw a pro-life organization display blown-up pictures of bloody fetuses. I was horrified and appalled. *I wanted to talk to you, Reuben. You saw what I saw. You knew Aunt Beth.* Another time, during a large protest against animal cruelty, I saw white and Asian students carrying posters against the Omak Suicide Race. What the hell did they know about what that race meant to the Colville? There were protesters at the actual race when Reuben took me. White people protesting how Indians treat animals. I couldn't believe it. Reuben told me that night just to ignore the protesters, so I do here as well. *You told me the horse and the rider are one. If the horse gets hurt or maimed, so does the Indian rider's spirit, for good. If the horse gets killed, so does a part of the Indian. Just like with the land and rivers, you said. As long as the Columbia is dammed, so too is the spirit of the Indian. Do you miss your rivers, Reuben, so far at sea?*

Students sit under tents on Sproul to hear talks about third world issues, the environment, race, religious tolerance, atheism, veganism. I mail flyers to Reuben in my journals. I mail him bumper stickers for his truck: EAT LEAF, NOT BEEF and JESUS LOVES ME BUT I STILL MAKE HIM WEAR A CONDOM (both as jokes). GORE 2000 (not a joke). Performers break-dance or rap. A black man faithfully preaches the Bible. I like to sketch him. He never shouts. His gentle manner reminds me of Brother Mathias, who Matt told me left Moses Lake and hasn't been heard from. A white man in a tweed jacket carries a clown horn and a briefcase and yells at students. The other day a student yelled back, "Put down the bottle and go home, Professor."

I want to go home, Reuben. To you and to the Columbia.

Spencer sends me money and tells me to go shopping. I walk around different areas of Berkeley. In the poster shop by my apartment on Telegraph, I buy photo postcards that I glue into my journals for Reuben: the Black Panthers, Frida Kahlo, the Indian occupation of Alcatraz, Bill and Hillary reclining together in a hammock, Tupac. I spend the most time and money in shops that sell herbs, oils, and teas. Just the smell of those shops. I look through comic book stores on Shattuck, thinking of my two brothers in Washington I've never met. Uncle Matt says Jamie has called twice for my number, but I'm not ready yet. Finally I buy a stack of comic books and mail them to my dad's farmhouse without a return address. In the stationery shops on Northside, I pick cards I'd mail to Aunt Beth if she were still alive. I used to make Mom cards when I was young. It feels as if I lost both of them when Beth died.

I am so alone, my coyote.

There is every type of food imaginable in Berkeley. It puts Sacramento to shame. Indian is still my favorite. But I've tried Himalayan, Pakistani, and Ethiopian, to name but a few. *Are you satisfied, Reuben? No?* I have street vendors braid hemp into my hair. I have my hands painted at henna stands. *In a single Sunday, Reuben, I go to an early-morning meditation class at a Buddhist center, a Christian church service at noon, an afternoon "herb walk" sponsored by a herbalist college in Oakland, and in the evening, a Japanese tea ceremony.*

Three times I've gone to Bancroft's special collections and held Narcissa Whitman's actual journal, written in her hand. I don't tell Reuben. I was more scared than excited when I first discovered Narcissa's journal was at Berkeley. The viewing room has long, slablike tables, and I have to wear white gloves. But still, holding the journal makes me feel close to Aunt Beth. Narcissa never learned the Cayuse language, or so she stubbornly claimed, but in one of her last letters to her beloved sister, with whom she was never reunited, Narcissa expressed her deepest longing for her sister in the Cayuse language. It's the only such example in all her correspondence. It moves me. If only

I could express my longing to Reuben in his native language, maybe then he'd believe me.

My favorite part about Berkeley is the amazing lectures. Mom would love to hear me say this (and to hear the lectures), but I won't give her the satisfaction. I either try to scribble down every single word or just sit there in awe and bliss. The most memorable lecture, which I don't tell Reuben about, was a cultural anthropology lecture to which the teacher invited a very, very old Native American man to speak to us about how Berkeley holds the bones of his ancestors in filing cabinets below our museum and he isn't allowed to see them. I had dreams about Aunt Beth's bones and Indian bones and Narcissa's bones and Donner Party bones. I even had a dream in which Narcissa, who couldn't stop bleeding through her long prairie dress, made soup with Indian bones and forced me to drink the broth. I begged Reuben to at least come visit me. I told him I was having nightmares, but not what they were about. I see the Pacific beyond the Golden Gate Bridge. *Come to me, Reuben, if you still love me. Please still love me.* I take four Vicodin pills in one day. *I'm sorry, Reuben.* I don't tell him what for. *Please.*

Mom and Spencer drive to Berkeley for the opening reception of the student art show. My exhibited piece is a four-panel sketch that depicts an origami salmon unfolding itself to reveal genetically crossed wires, parasites, nonhealthy eggs. The last panel shows only a piece of unfolded, wrinkled paper stamped HATCHERY MADE. In my short explication I state that I'm a Pacific Northwest native concerned about natural salmon runs being further damaged by genetically weak hatchery stock. Mom stays relatively quiet, though she gets emotional when, unbelievably, I win third place. I don't tell Reuben about the sketch panel or winning an award. Our final week together he apologized numerous times for calling the origami salmon that I made for him retarded. He said even hatchery salmon need prayer.

I like to go to Sacramento almost every other weekend on Amtrak. I like my bedroom in Sacramento better than my apartment in Berkeley with a view of the Golden Gate. What is wrong with me? I liked the Nutcracker Museum in Leavenworth, Washington—with its Yoda,

Minnie Mouse, and Mormon missionary nutcrackers—as much as I like MOMA and the de Young in San Francisco. I love holding my chubby brother and playing with him. I like to eat dinner with Spencer and Mom, although lately Mom's been hinting again about how she hopes I make friends soon in Berkeley. *Where* are her friends? Then one evening she mentions my finding a boyfriend. I laugh in her face, which confuses Liam in his high chair. He grins, then starts to sob, which makes me cry and then Mom cry. Spencer just puts his hands up.

"Sorry, Dad," I say.

"Don't apologize, kiddo." He has tremendous patience with me. He looks hard at Mom. "You either, Kate."

Both Mom and Spencer talk to me about looking into semester abroad programs. I tell them I will, but I don't. I'm not ready yet to be that far away from Reuben. I'm far enough away. Mom wants me to pick a major. Maybe English or history or American studies or gender studies. I enjoy them all. If I were more outgoing, I'd pick anthropology or international relations. Really, I want to major in education—*I have told that to no one but you, Reuben*—and teach young kids like Lena and my two Palouse brothers.

Finally I mail Reuben a list of a few of the classes I've taken at Berkeley and some textbook titles. I've hesitated to do so because I didn't want him to think I should remain here. But it's becoming agonizingly clear that he already does. So I mail the list, almost in spite, though I also include a few made-up titles as jokes: *The World Split Open: How the Modern Women's Movement Changed America, Chicken Soup for the American Indian Lover's Soul, What Social Classes Owe to Each Other, U.S and the Global Forest, Why "Fag" Shouldn't Be Part of Your Vocabulary, Approaches and Paradigms in the History of Rhetoric, How to Speak French in a Trailer Park.*

I begin my third semester. We have a fire in my apartment building one day while I'm away all afternoon in classes. When I return, the outside doors are propped open, and all the tenants, including my roommate, have left. The building looks so abandoned—like one in Bosnia, only it's not gutted. I freak out. Stupidly, I climb the inside stairs. I meet a boy on the second-floor landing. He tells me the fire-fighters already left. He says the fire was on the fourth floor. My floor. He walks up with me. He says he lives on the third floor. All the doors on my floor have been propped open except my neighbor's and my doors, both of which were kicked open and the frames splintered. It was the apartment right next to mine that caught fire, a kitchen fire. The boy gives me his number and tells me to call him if the landlord won't fix my door before dark. He says nobody, especially girls, should sleep in a city apartment with a busted door. He says he's seen me around the building and on campus. I've seen him too, always carry-ing a tuxedo over his shoulder. A lady down the hall tells me the next day that she saw me talking to the boy. He's a noted violinist, she says, from Pakistan. I've been asked out by a few boys in Berkeley, includ-ing one from the swim team. I've told them all but this one that I al-ready have a boyfriend in Washington, where I'm from.

I send my last journal to Reuben in January. It's filled entirely with passages from my favorite novels—none of my own words—and sketches of hands painted with henna, bums' dirty hands, my baby brother's hands, hands being held, hands holding books, empty hands, reaching hands, closed hands. Uncle Matt told me Reuben has returned to Teresa's twice to pick up my journals. So I give him a few months, during which time I send no more journals. The first of April I send Reuben my last letter, in which I enclose his feather.

Since I began Berkeley, I have begged Reuben to come get me. I have told him I wait for him every Tuesday and Thursday morning from nine to eleven on a bench by Sather Gate, which I have sketched for him numerous times. I ask him to meet me there. I tell him Sather Gate is the gateway to California. Prospective students from around the country and the world have pictures of themselves taken in front of Sather Gate. Berkeley was the first U.C., hence the name CAL. It's multicultural, progressive, scientific, intellectual. Mom sobbed when I got my acceptance letter to Berkeley. Her journey, with me on her hip, from an eastern Washington bus station to California was complete.

My life's journey began when I met you, Reuben. When our paths crossed, they became one. You have kept silent all these years. You thought by your doing so, I would learn to live without you. I haven't. I have kept you as my dearest friend. You still know more about me than anyone. I have made sure of that. I have been standing on my own two feet, Reuben. I can pry open the abalone. I live in an apartment in the Bay Area. I attend college. I study all the time. I can speak French fluently now. Berkeley has to be the greatest people-watching city in America. But I'm lonely, Reuben, and I want to go home—to you and to Washington. I belong in the north with you. I don't belong here. I have let no boy or man touch my body. I am saving it for you. But I need to be touched. I can't go on this way. I won't. I need love. I'm a woman now, Reuben, not a girl. I long for a man to gently spread my legs. I need to be touched and tasted. I feel hollow. I am starting to forget what you look like, how you smell. I can still hear your voice, singing while Ray drums. But it's fading, as the light that evening eventually did.

There is a boy, Reuben. He lives on the floor below me. He's handsome and soft-spoken. He noticed me when no one else really has. He's pursuing me. He is kind and worries that I have no friends. I remind him of his favorite cousin. He's a violinist from Pakistan, and he helped me during a fire. I have agreed to get food with him—sometime. I agree to hear him play—sometime. He asks why I wait by Sather Gate twice a week, as if for an unfaithful lover. He wants in, Reuben. He wants into my life. He is caring. He brings me tea and greets me in Punjabi because it makes me smile. We go for walks, mostly around campus, but also farther into the Berkeley hills. I want to hear him play his violin. But I know when I do, I will fall in love with him. He knows it too. Come get me, Reuben. He is passionate and he has seen poverty and he has gone hungry and he has known displacement. Don't let him touch me. My heart belongs to you. My body belongs to you. I don't want to hurt you. But your silence has hurt me deeply. A sea of silence, and I am nearly drowned. Meet me at Sather Gate. I will give you until the end of this month. I am waiting for you. If you do not show, I will still love you. Forever I will love you, my coyote. But I will love another. With him I will walk this earth unless you come for me.

21

Reuben

I see Emmy Nolan before she sees me. She sits on a bench, staring at the university gate where she's asked me in her journals to meet her. She has no idea I've finally come. I watch her, and my body aches for the months we had together and the years we spent apart. Her hair hangs to her waist now and is tousled. She wears a dress and crosses her legs, which are no longer skinny but shapely. I have missed her every day, every minute. I try not to fucking pass out. Breathe. Guys look at her when they pass by—I scan the crowd for the Pakistani fiddler— but she's oblivious. No one stops to talk to her, but she's surrounded by hundreds of students walking in groups or in pairs or alone, as she has been. There's also lots of street people and hippies. A woman in a tie-dyed skirt hopscotches over to Emmy and hands her a flyer. I whisper her name to the four winds. A mumbling Indian draws no attention here. The breeze smells of the bay, spicy foods, and pot. Emmy pulls a book from her bag—probably one of those British novels she loves or an assigned book on gender theory or global policy—and starts to read. I move in. I sit down beside her on the bench. She doesn't look over.

It's the best five minutes of my life.

"Hey, girl," I finally say, even though I can see that she's no longer a girl. "Do you know where to get a decent burger around here?"

She looks at me with wide eyes. "Reuben?" She's in shock and trying to register. Her book falls to the ground. I bend down and grab it for her, but she's too startled to take it. I stuff it in her bag.

"I had a hard time parking my truck between all the bumper sticker–covered Subarus."

She says my name again. "Reuben?" Only this time I hear a dozen sad questions and pleas in her tone.

Her tears start, as do mine.

But instead of throwing her arms around my neck, she puts both her hands on my chest and tries to push me away from her—hard, almost violently. It doesn't budge me physically. I've been fighting the relentless sea for eighteen months. But her shove jolts my being.

Sobs shake her frame. I put my arms around her, pulling her to me. She tries to resist, but I don't let her. "I'm sorry, Emmy." Her sobs intensify. I keep hold. A few people gawk, but most are busy talking or watching other activities. The coiled tension in Emmy's body has been there for a long time. "I'm so sorry," I repeat. She makes another stubborn effort to get away before her body suddenly goes slack. She rests her head briefly on my chest but only to catch her breath. "It's okay," I say into her hair. "I'm going to make everything okay." She shakes her head to let me know I can't. I want her to look at me before I make any promises to the contrary. I scan around again for the Pakistani fiddler. When her sobs slow, I release my grip.

She instantly pulls away. "Why didn't you come for me?" It's been so long since I heard her voice. "Didn't you love me?"

"Every day, Emmy." I try to take her hands, but no way. "You're all I thought about."

"But you never wrote me. I couldn't go a single day without checking my mailbox. Most days more than once. I'd try not to." She pauses to keep composure. "Sometimes I'd make it until right before bed."

My long silence had hurt her far worse than I ever allowed myself to fathom.

"This moment is all I've dreamed of," she says. "But now that it's here." She stops to pull her long hair to one side, giving me a clear view of her face. "Now that *you're* here, I don't feel relief. I'm pissed, Reuben. I'm so pissed." She's more than pissed—she's afraid.

Fuck. I waited too fucking long. I've had moments of panic before at the thought—plenty of them, whole nights of panic, miles of panic on my drive here—but nothing as tangible as this. I can't speak.

"I take pills," she confesses. "Vicodin. For the loneliness. Don't be shocked." I'm not. "I tried to be strong. Don't be ashamed of me."

"I'm not ashamed of you." I could never be ashamed of her. And I did things too that I wish I hadn't—to fight the cold, fill the empti-ness. "I'm so sorry for the pain I caused. Please, don't be afraid." But I'm also afraid: to try to touch this girl again, to sound the depth of her sadness.

I don't blame her if she can't forgive me. But I have to at least ex-plain myself. "Listen, Emmy. I left you alone, at your mom's orders, so you could finish high school and go to Berkeley. I honored that. She and Spencer were capable of giving you a better life than anything I could offer." She shakes her head but doesn't interrupt. "Not answer-ing your letters was hell. It tore me up." It became easier the further I sank into despair, but she doesn't need to know that. "Then it became a matter of pride, Emmy. I had to know I could take care of you. I had to make money—for us, and I have. You'll see."

"Oh, Reuben." She shakes her head again.

Meaning—what? Oh, God.

"My pride." I break down. "My fucking pride." It's destroyed every-thing.

She touches my hand. I remember her touch—the warmth of it, the sincerity. I remember her pulse and the flow beneath her skin. I remember her taste. I have forgotten nothing about this girl.

"You found me just in time, Reuben. That's all that really matters. Right?"

I can't answer that for her, and she knows it, even as she searches my eyes. I can't answer, but I can pray. And fuck, do I ever. I pray so hard I don't realize when she starts smiling. A wide smile. I've been waiting two and a half years to see that fucking smile, those teeth. She's so beautiful.

"You found me again," she says.

"Of course." I've been tracking her since the day I was born.

She puts her arms around my neck. "I love you, my coyote."

I whisper into her ear, first in English. Then, with only a few words of my father's language, I release my time at sea and on faraway shores in cold and ice and rubber boots and rain gear. I return fully to dry land and to her.

She finds my lips. I find the part of my soul that's been missing since I last saw this girl. This woman. I want to make love to her every day for the rest of my days. I long to touch her between her legs—oh, how I've longed—and to be inside her. My silence was brutal. No wonder she was ready to let that Pakistani fill it with his violin and tea. Fill it for good, because I know how Emmy loves. I'll make up for my silence: I'll sing to her and drum and tell her Coyote stories.

"I'm ready," she says, not even giving herself time to catch her breath after our kiss. I'm still reeling. "Let's go."

"Let's smoke first." I pull a pack of cigarettes from my pocket. She gets as excited to have someone to smoke with as she did the day I made that birthday cake with her and she offered me frosting on her finger, good Lord. "Let's wield our exhaustion first," I say with a grin, mocking that asshole philosophy student who watched Emmy smoke, among other things. That part of her journal really got to me. Hell, it all did. Still, I'd like to bust that punk's face. I feel anything but exhausted.

I play with her hair while we smoke, as if no time has passed and we're still kids sitting on top of those hay bales and I'm not glancing around for a Pakistani fiddler.

She reaches behind my neck and tugs my ponytail. "I like it. Though it's going to take me longer to wash in the shower."

I can't even respond to that. I just grin as she blushes.

"Are you sure you want to walk away from all this?" I ask. I point to the gate and the massive nineteenth-century marble buildings I see on the other side. Libraries, no doubt, of knowledge and multicultural awareness and artifacts and maybe even some Indian bones. The buildings, to me, are as solemn as Coulee Dam, which was probably fucking engineered right here in Berkeley's halls.

She drops her cigarette butt, gets up, and starts walking away, not even taking her backpack, which I grab.

A year later we'll walk together on another college campus, but one that gets snow, as study partners and as husband and wife.

"A boy from the rez," I'll say, "and a girl who left Cal."

"All she really ever wanted was a best pal."

We'll live in an apartment—with Emmy's sketches on the walls—in

Pullman by the university. I'll pay the rent. Emmy's dad, the Palouse farmer, will offer to buy us a house. No, thanks. "My wife weaves hemp into her hair," I'll tease, "which makes the farm boys stop and stare." Their stares will actually piss me the fuck off. Emmy won't respond, so I'll continue. "She paints henna on her hands and dreams no more of other lands." Pakistan, for instance.

"Don't say that, Reuben." We'll lie naked in our bed, where some nights I'll tell her Coyote tales and other nights she'll read me French poetry or chapters from British novels, in which all the female characters wandering alone on the moors will have Emmy's face. "I didn't give up anything to be with you."

I'll tease, "Okay, Emmy Nolan-Tonasket. My little feminist."

For the most part we'll be happy, yet sometimes sad in ways too deep for words.

"You miss the reservation," she'll say. "You talk about it in your sleep."

"I'm still close to it," I'll argue, sitting up.

"No, Reuben, you left. It's a million miles away."

I won't be able to speak.

"I don't miss California," she'll continue. "I'll travel to other countries one day, or not. I don't care, as long as I'm with you." She'll pull me close. "I fell for a boy who finds the river in the lake."

"My girl, my love, I'll never forsake."

By then I'll know my years of silence will always be a part of my wife, and her lonely childhood a part of me. She'll be kept awake by my dreams of Kettle Falls before Coulee Dam, when Coyote brought salmon and the people never went hungry.

But for now it's enough that I catch up with Emmy and take her hand as she walks away from Sather Gate. Together we make our way through the lively crowd of hoboes, intellectuals, politicians, and crazy fucks. We climb into my truck, and I drive her back to where we both were born, back to our river, back to the north.

Mountains and establishing the first pioneer home in the Pacific Northwest. To Chief Moses, on whose ancestral land I was born and raised. I'm indebted to the following nonfiction writers whose work taught me about home: Robert H. Ruby, John A. Brown, Blaine Harden, and Andrew P. Duffin. To the Confederated Tribes of the Colville Reservation: may you find in Reuben a tribute to your enduring spirit and continued commitment as caretakers of the land.

Finally, thank you to the California fireman who years ago went back in for a barefoot, frantic writer's computer.

ACKNOWLEDGMENTS

Heartfelt thanks to Erica McLane, for her wisdom, humor, and guidance during the long hours spent reading and revising by the woodstove at her parents' farm on the Sacramento River. Deep gratitude to my wonderful agent, Lisa Grubka, for her early belief and tireless work. Huge thanks to Julie Miesionczek, my terrific editor, for her passion and stamina, and for her ability to add grace and cut bullshit. Thanks also to Amber Qureshi, for her enthusiasm for the book, and to the entire Viking team for taking a chance on me. To my beginning creative writing teacher, Catherine Fraga. And special thanks to my mentor of many years, and now my dear friend, Carole Simmons Oles. I'm sorry I gave up poetry, Carole. Thanks to Sharon May, for a decade of exchanging work and friendship. Much gratitude to the editors who have published my short stories, in particular Tom Jenks and Carol Edgarian at *Narrative Magazine*.

Thanks to my husband, Carl, for all the years stretching back to the day an eighteen-year-old waitress from Washington met a twenty-one-year-old airman from West Virginia. To my daughter, Austin, for coming so early into my life and for teaching me as much as I hope I've taught you. To my son, Luke: I always wanted a brother, but instead I got you. Sorry about the Irish freckles, kid. Thank you to my dad, for everything, but mostly for *not* being like the father in this novel. Mom, I still miss you after all these years. To my older sister, Angie, whose generous spirit keeps me in awe. To Jenny, my younger sister, with whom I have laughed more than with any other person. To my brother-in-law, Tony, for the fish stories. To Paula, my baby sister, for sharing my love of British heroines. To Margo, my sister-in-law from The Netherlands, but really my sister. To my beloved aunts, Mary and Jerri.

To Narcissa Whitman, for riding sidesaddle across the Rocky